Thus Saith Eve

"Short, but definitely entertaining ... and serious between the lines." Lee Harmon, A Dubious Disciple Book Review

" ... a truly wonderful source of feminist fiction. In addition to being an extremely enjoyable and thought-provoking read, the monologues can also be used for audition and performance pieces." Katie M. Deaver, feminismand religion.com

Snow White Gets Her Say

"Why isn't anyone doing this on stage? ... What a great night of theater that would be!" szferris, Librarything

"I loved the sassy voices in these stories, and the humor, even when making hard points." PJ O'Brien, Smashwords

Deare Sister

"You are clearly a writer of considerable talent, and your special ability to give expression to so many different characters, each in a uniquely appropriate style, makes your work fascinating and attractive. ... The pieces are often funny, sometimes sensitive, always creative. But they contain an enormous load of anger, and that is where I have problems. ... I know at least one feminist who would read your manuscript with delight (unfortunately she is not a publisher), who would roar with laughter in her sharing of your anger. ..." rejection letter from Black Moss Press

Particivision and other stories

"... your writing is very accomplished. ... *Particivision and other stories* is authentic, well-written, and certainly publishable. ..." rejection letter from Turnstone Press

"... engaging and clever ..." rejection letter from Lester & Orpen Dennys, Publishers

"As the title indicates, this collection of stories is about getting into the thick of things, taking sides, taking action, and speaking out loud and clear, however unpopular your opinion may be. ... refreshingly out of the ordinary." Joan McGrath, *Canadian Book Review Annual*

dreaming of kaleidoscopes

"… a top pick of poetry and is very much worth considering. …" *Midwest Book Review*

Soliloquies: the lady doth indeed protest

"… not only dynamic, imaginative verse writing, but extremely intelligent and intuitive insight. … I know many actresses who would love to get their hands on this material!" Joanne Zipay, Judith Shakespeare Company, NYC

"'Ophelia' is something of an oddity … I found it curiously attractive." *Dinosaur*

UnMythed

"… A welcome relief from the usual male emphasis in this area. There is anger and truth here, not to mention courage." Eric Folsom, *Next Exit*

"… With considerable skill and much care, chris wind has extrapolated truths from mythical scenarios and reordered them in modern terms. … Wind handles these myths with and intellect. Her voice suggests that the relationship between the consciousness of the myth-makers and modern consciousness is closer than we would think." Linda Manning, *Quarry*

"Personally, I would not publish this stuff. This is not to say it isn't publishable—it's almost flawless stylistically, perfect form and content, etc., etc. It's perverse: satirical, biting, caustic, funny. Also cruel, beyond bitter, single-minded with a terminally limited point of view, and this individual may have read Edith Hamilton's *Mythology* but she/he certainly doesn't perceive the essential meanings of these myths. Or maybe does and deliberately twists the meaning to suit the poem. Likewise, in the etymological sense. Editorial revisions suggested? None, it's perfect. Market potential/readership targets: Everyone—this is actually marketable—you could sell fill Harbourfront reading this probably. General comments: You could actually make money on this stuff." anonymous reader report for a press that rejected the ms

Paintings and Sculptures

"You know that feeling—when you read the first page and you know you're going to like the book? That happened when I read the first poem. … I loved 'Mona' and I could picture the scene; it might have happened that way, we'll never know …." Mesca Elin, barnesandnoble.com

Satellites Out of Orbit

"*Satellites Out of Orbit* is an excellent and much recommended pick for unique fiction collections." Michael Dunford, *Midwest Book Review*

"... I also love the idea of telling the story from the woman's perspective, especially when the woman is only mentioned in passing in the official story, or not mentioned at all. ..." Shana, Tales of Minor Interest

"Our editorial board loved it. Our readers said it was the most feminist thing they've read in a long time." rejection letter from publisher

As I the Shards Examine / Not Such Stuff

"*Not Such Stuff* challenges us to rethink some of our responses to Shakespeare's plays and opens up new ways of experiencing them. ... " Jeff, secondat. blogspot.com

"This world premiere collection of monologs derive from eight female Shakespearian characters speaking from their hearts, describing aspects of their lives with a modern feminist sensibility. Deconstructing the traditional interpretations of some of the most fiercely fascinating female characters of all time, the playwright is able to "have at it" and the characters finally have their say. And oh, what tales they have to weave. ..." Debbie Jackson, dctheatrescene.com

Let Me Entertain You

"I found this to be very powerful and visually theatrical." Ines Buchli

"I will never forget 'Let Me Entertain You.' It was brilliant." Kate Hurman

ProVocative

"Timely, thought-provoking, dark, and funny!" Kevin Holm-Hudson, WEFT

"... a great job making a point while being entertaining and interesting. ... Overall this is a fine work, and worth listening to." Kevin Slick, *gajoob*

The Art of Juxtaposition

"A cross between poetry, performance art, and gripping, theatrical sound collages. ... One of the most powerful pieces on the tape is 'Let Me Entertain You.' I sat stunned while listening to this composition." Myke Dyer, *Nerve*

"We found [this to be] unique, brilliant, and definitely not 'Canadian'. ... We were more than impressed with the material. *The Art of Juxtaposition* is filling one of the emptier spaces in the music world with creative and intelligent music-art." rejection letter from a record company

"Controversial feminist content. You will not be unmoved." Bret Hart, *Option*

"I've just had a disturbing experience: I listened to *The Art of Juxtaposition*. Now wait a minute; Canadian musicians are not supposed to be politically aware or delve into questions regarding sexual relationships, religion, and/or sex, racism, rape. They are supposed to write nice songs that people can tap their feet to and mindlessly inebriate themselves to. You expect me to play this on my show?" Travis B., CITR

"Wind mixes biting commentary, poignant insight and dark humor while unflinchingly tackling themes such as rape, marriage (as slavery), christianity, censorship, homosexuality, the state of native Americans, and other themes, leaving no doubt about her own strong convictions upon each of these subjects. Her technique is often one in which two or more sides to each theme are juxtaposed against one another (hence, the tape's title). This is much like her *Christmas Album* with a voice just as direct and pointed. Highly recommended." Bryan Baker *gajoob*

"Thanks for *The Art of Juxtaposition* … it really is quite a gem! Last Xmas season, after we aired 'Ave Maria' a listener stopped driving his car and phoned us from a pay phone to inquire and express delight." John Aho, CJAM

"Liked *The Art of Juxtaposition* a lot, especially the feminist critiques of the bible. I had calls from listeners both times I played 'Ave Maria.'" Bill Hsu, WEFT

"Every time I play *The Art of Juxtaposition* (several times by this point), someone calls to ask about it/you." Mars Bell, WCSB

"The work is stimulating, well-constructed, and politically apt with regard to sexual politics. (I was particularly impressed by 'I am Eve.')" Andreas Brecht Ua'Siaghail, CKCU

"We have found *The Art of Juxtaposition* to be quite imaginative and effective. When I first played it, I did not have time to listen to it before I had to be on air. When I aired it, I was transfixed by the power of it. When I had to go on mike afterward, I found I could hardly speak! To say the least, I found your work quite a refreshing change from all the fluff of commercial musicians who whine about lost love etc. Your work is intuitive, sensitive, and significant!" Erika Schengili, CFRC

"Interesting stuff here! Actually this has very little music, but it has sound bits and spoken work. Self-declared 'collage pieces of social commentary'. ...very thought-provoking and inspiring." *No Sanctuary*

more at
chriswind.net and chriswind.com

Writing as Peg Tittle

Gender Fraud: a fiction

"A gripping read ...." Katya, Goodreads

Impact

"Edgy, insightful, terrific writing, propelled by rage against rape. Tittle writes in a fast-paced, dialogue-driven style that hurtles the reader from one confrontation to the next. Chock full of painful social observations ...." Hank Pellissier, Director of Humanist Global Charity

" ... The idea of pinning down the inflictors of this terror is quite appealing ...." Alison Lashinsky

It Wasn't Enough

"Unlike far too many novels, this one will make you think, make you uncomfortable, and then make you reread it ...." C. Osborne, moonspeaker.ca

"... a powerful and introspective dystopia .... It is a book I truly recommend for a book club as the discussions could be endless ...." Mesca Elin, Psycho-chromatic Redemption

"Tittle's book hits you hard ...." D. Sohi, Goodreads

Exile

"Thought-provoking stuff, as usual from Peg Tittle." James M. Fisher, Goodreads

What Happened to Tom

"This powerful book plays with the gender gap to throw into high relief the infuriating havoc unwanted pregnancy can wreak on a woman's life. Once you've read *What Happened to Tom*, you'll never forget it." Elizabeth Greene, *Understories* and *Moving*

"I read this in one sitting, less than two hours, couldn't put it down. Fantastic allegorical examination of the gendered aspects of unwanted pregnancy. A must-read for everyone, IMO." Jessica, Goodreads

"Peg Tittle's *What Happened to Tom* takes a four-decades-old thought experiment and develops it into a philosophical novella of extraordinary depth and imagination .... Part allegory, part suspense (perhaps horror) novel, part defense of bodily autonomy rights (especially women's), Tittle's book will give philosophers and the philosophically minded much to discuss." Ron Cooper, *Hume's Fork*

Sexist Shit that Pisses Me Off

"Woh. This book is freaking awesome and I demand a sequel." Anonymous, barnesandnoble.com

"I recommend this book to both women and men. It will open your eyes to a lot of sexist—and archaic—behaviors." Seregon, Goodreads

"Honestly, selling this in today's climate is a daunting challenge—older women have grown weary, younger women don't seem to care, or at least don't really identify as feminists, men—forget that. All in all a sad state of affairs—sorry." rejection letter from agent

Shit that Pisses Me Off

"I find Peg Tittle to be a passionate, stylistically-engaging writer with a sharp eye for the hypocritical aspects of our society." George, Amazon

"Peg raises provocative questions: should people need some kind of license to have children? Should the court system use professional jurors? Many of her essays address the imbalance of power between men and women; some tackle business, sports, war, and the weather. She even explains why you're not likely to see Peg Tittle at Canada's version of an Occupy Wall Street demonstration. It's all thought-provoking, and whether or not you'll end up agreeing with her conclusions, her essays make for fascinating reading." Erin O'Riordan

"This was funny and almost painfully accurate, pointing out so many things that most of us try NOT to notice, or wish we didn't. Well written and amusing, I enjoyed this book immensely." Melody Hewson

" ... a pissed off kindred spirit who writes radioactive prose with a hint of sardonic wit .... Peg sets her sights on a subject with laser sharp accuracy then hurls words like missiles in her collection of 25 cogent essays on the foibles and hypocrisies of life .... Whether you agree or disagree with Peg's position on the issues, *Shit that Pisses Me Off* will stick to your brain long after you've ingested every word—no thought evacuations here. Her writing is adept and titillating ... her razor sharp words will slice and dice the cerebral jugular. If you enjoy reading smart, witty essays that challenge the intellect, download a copy ...." Laura Salkin, thinkspin.com

"Not very long, but a really good read. The author is intelligent, and points out some great inconsistencies in common thinking and action .... may have been channeling some George Carlin in a few areas." Briana Blair, Goodreads

" ... thought-provoking, and at times, hilarious. I particularly loved 'Bambi's cousin is going to tear you apart.' Definitely worth a read!" Nichole, Goodreads

"What she said!!! Pisses me off also! Funny, enjoyable and so right on!!!! Highly recommended." Vic, indigo.ca

Critical Thinking: An Appeal to Reason

"This book is worth its weight in gold." Daniel Millsap

"One of the books everyone should read. A lot of practical examples, clear and detailed sections, and tons of all kinds of logical fallacies analyzed under microscope that will give you a completely different way of looking to the everyday manipulations and will help you to avoid falling into the common traps. Highly recommended!" Alexander Antukh

"One of the best CT books I've read." G. Baruch, Goodreads

"This is an excellent critical thinking text written by a clever and creative critical thinker. Her anthology *What If* is excellent too: the short readings are perfect for engaging philosophical issues in and out of the classroom." Ernst Borgnorg

"Peg Tittle's *Critical Thinking* is a welcome addition to a crowded field. Her presentations of the material are engaging, often presented in a conversational discussion with the reader or student. The text's coverage of the material is wide-ranging. Newspaper items, snippets from *The Far Side*, personal anecdotes, emerging social and political debates, as well as LSAT sample questions are among the many tools Tittle employs to educate students on the elemental aspects of logic and critical thinking." Alexander E. Hooke, Professor of Philosophy, Stevenson University

What If?... Collected Thought Experiments in Philosophy

"Of all the collections of philosophical thought experiments I've read, this is by far the best. It is accessible, uses text from primary sources, and is very well edited. The final entry in the book— which I won't spoil for you—was an instant favorite of mine." Dominick Cancilla

"This is a really neat little book. It would be great to use in discussion-based philosophy courses, since the readings would be nice and short and to the point. This would probably work much better than the standard anthology of readings that are, for most students, incomprehensible." Nathan Nobis, Morehouse College

Should Parents be Licensed? Debating the Issues

"This book has some provocative articles and asks some very uncomfortable questions ...." Jasmine Guha, Amazon

"This book was a great collection of essays from several viewpoints on the topic and gave me a lot of profound over-the-(TV-)dinner-(tray-)table conversations with my husband." Lauren Cocilova, Goodreads

"You need a licence to drive a car, own a gun, or fish for trout. You don't need a licence to raise a child. But maybe you should ... [This book] contains about two dozen essays by various experts, including psychologists, lawyers and sociologists ...." Ian Gillespie, *London Free Press*

"... But the reformers are right. Completely. Ethically. I agree with Joseph Fletcher, who notes, "It is depressing ... to realize that most people are accidents," and with George Schedler, who states, "Society has a duty to ensure that infants are born free of avoidable defects. ... Traditionalists regard pregnancy and parenting as a natural right that should never be curtailed. But what's the result of this laissez-faire attitude? Catastrophic suffering. Millions of children born disadvantaged, crippled in childhood, destroyed in adolescence. Procreation cannot be classified as a self-indulgent privilege—it needs to be viewed as a life-and-death responsibility ...." Abhimanyu Singh Rajput, Social Tikka

Ethical Issues in Business: Inquiries, Cases, and Readings

"*Ethical Issues in Business* is clear and user-friendly yet still rigorous throughout. It offers excellent coverage of basic ethical theory, critical thinking, and many contemporary issues such as whistleblowing, corporate social responsibility, and climate change. Tittle's approach is not to tell students what to think but rather to get them to think—and to give them the tools to do so. This is the text I would pick for a business ethics course." Kent Peacock, University of Lethbridge

"This text breathes fresh air into the study of business ethics; Tittle's breezy, use-friendly style puts the lie to the impression that a business ethics text has to be boring." Paul Viminitz, University of Lethbridge

"A superb introduction to ethics in business." Steve Deery, *The Philosophers' Magazine*

"Peg Tittle wants to make business students think about ethics. So she has published an extraordinarily useful book that teaches people to question and analyze key concepts .... Take profit, for example .... She also analyzes whistleblowing, advertising, product safety, employee rights, discrimination, management and union matters, business and the environment, the medical business, and ethical investing ...." Ellen Roseman, *The Toronto Star*

more at
pegtittle.com

Writing as Jass Richards

The ReGender App

"This book is brilliant. ... The scene at the airport had me laughing out loud. ..." Katya, Goodreads

"Recommended to any book club and to people who are interested in gender differences and gender discrimination." Mesca Elin, Psychromatic Redemption

License to Do That

"I'm very much intrigued by the issues raised in this narrative. I also enjoy the author's voice, which is unapologetically combative but also funny and engaging." A.S.

"I love Froot Loup! You make me laugh out loud all the time!" Celeste M.

"A thought-provoking premise and a wonderful cast of characters." rejection letter from publisher

The Blasphemy Tour

"With plenty of humor and things to think about throughout, *The Blasphemy Tour* is a choice pick …." *Midwest Book Review*

"Jass Richards has done it again. As I tell anyone who wants to listen, Jass is a comedy genius, she writes the funniest books and always writes the most believable unbelievable characters and scenes …. I knew this book was a winner when … a K9 unit dog kind of eats their special brownies … and dances Thriller. … Rev and Dylan are not your ordinary guy and girl protagonists with sexual tension and a romantic interest, at all. They both defy gender roles, and they are so smart and opinionated, it's both funny and made me think at the same time. … They tour around the USA, in their lime green bus that says 'There are no gods. Deal with it.' Overall, I highly recommend anything by Jass, especially this one book, which is full of comedy gold and food for thought." May Arend, Brazilian Book Worm

"If I were Siskel and Ebert I would give this book Two Thumbs Way Up. … Yes, it is blasphemy toward organized religion but it gives you tons of Bible verses to back up its premises. And besides, it's pure entertainment. There's a prequel which I recommend you read first. *The Road Trip Dialogues*. … I only hope there will be a third book." L.K. Killian

The Road Trip Dialogues

"I am impressed by the range from stoned silliness to philosophical perspicuity, and I love your comic rhythm." L. S.

"This is engaging, warm, funny work, and I enjoyed what I read. …" rejection letter from publisher

"Just thought I'd let you know I'm on the Fish'n'Chips scene and laughing my ass off." Ellie Burmeister

"These two need stable jobs. Oh wait, no. Then we wouldn't get any more road trips. Fantastic book which expands the mind in a laid back sort of way. Highly recommended." lindainalabama

Dogs Just Wanna Have Fun

"Funny and entertaining! I looked forward to picking up this book at the end of a long day." Mary Baluta

"… terrifically funny and ingeniously acerbic …." Dr. Patricia Bloom, My Magic Dog

"… laugh-out-loud funny." M.W., Librarything

This Will Not Look Good on My Resume

"Ya made me snort root beer out my nose!" Moriah Jovan, *The Proviso*

"Darkly humorous." Jennifer Colt, *The Hellraiser of the Hollywood Hills*

"HYSTERICAL! … There are really no words to describe how funny this book is. … Really excellent book." Alison, Goodreads

"This book is like a roller coaster ride on a stream of consciousness. … Altogether, a funny, quirky read …." Grace Krispy, Motherlode; Book Reviews and Original Photography

"Brett has trouble holding down a job. Mainly because she's an outspoken misanthrope who is prone to turn a dead-end job into a social engineering experiment. Sometimes with comically disastrous results, sometimes with comically successful results. (Like pairing up a compulsive shopper with a kleptomaniac for an outing at the mall.) I don't agree with everything she says, but I will defend her right to say it — because she's hilarious!

"My favorite part was when she taught a high school girls' sex ed class that 70% of boys will lie to get sex, 80% won't use a condom, yet 90% are pro-life. She was reprimanded, of course. I think she should have gotten a medal.

"You will likely be offended at one point or another, but if you are secure enough to laugh at your own sacred cows instead of just everyone else's, this is a must read." weikelm, Librarything

"Wonderful read, funny, sarcastic. Loved it!" Charlie, Smashwords

"I just loved this book. It was a quick read, and left me in stitches. …" Robin McCoy-Ramirez

"First, let me just say I was glad I was not drinking anything while reading this. I refrained from that. My husband said he never heard me laugh so much from reading a book. At one point, I was literally in tears. Jass Richards is brilliant with the snappy comebacks and the unending fountain of information she can spout forth. … The quick wit, the sharp tongue, the acid words and sarcasm that literally oozes from her pores … beautiful." M. Snow, My Chaotic Ramblings

A Philosopher, a Psychologist, and an Extraterrestrial Walk into a Chocolate Bar

"Jass Richards is back with another great book that entertains and informs as she mixes feminism, critical thinking, and current social issues with humour …. The wedding intervention was hilarious. …." James M. Fisher, *The Miramichi Reader*

"I found myself caught between wanting to sit and read [*A Philosopher, a Psychologist, and an Extraterrestrial Walk into a Chocolate Bar*] all in one go and wanting to spread it out. I haven't laughed that hard and gotten to spend time with such unflinchingly tough ideas at the same time. … [And] the brilliance of the Alices! … I can now pull out your book every time somebody tries to claim that novels can't have meaningful footnotes and references. [Thanks too] for pointing me to the brilliant essay series 'Dudes are Doomed.' I am eagerly watching for *The ReGender App* …." C. Osborne

TurboJetslams: Proof #29 of the Non-Existence of God

"Extraordinarily well written with wit, wisdom, and laugh-out-loud ironic recognition, *TurboJetslams: Proof #29 of the Non-Existence of God* is a highly entertaining and a riveting read that will linger on in the mind and memory long after the little book itself has been finished and set back upon the shelf (or shoved into the hands of friends with an insistence that they drop everything else and read it!). Highly recommended for community library collections, it should be noted for personal reading lists." *Midwest Book Review*

"We all very much enjoyed it—it's funny and angry and heartfelt and told truly …." McSweeney's

"If you're looking for a reading snack that has zero saccharine but is loaded with just the right combination of snark, sarcasm, and humor, you've found it." Ricki Wilson, Amazon

"What Richards has done is brilliant. At first, I began getting irritated as I read about a familiar character, or a familiar scenario from our time living on the lake. Then, as the main character amps up her game, I see the thrill in the planning and the retribution she undertakes for pay back." mymuskoka.blog spot.ca/2016/07/book-review-turbojetslams.html

Substitute Teacher from Hell

"I enjoyed reading "Supply Teacher from Hell" immensely and found myself bursting out laughing many, many times. It is extremely well-written, clever, and very intelligent in its observations." Iris Turcott, dramaturge

more at
jassrichards.com

Also by chris wind

prose

Thus Saith Eve
Snow White Gets Her Say
Deare Sister
Particivision and other stories

poetry

dreaming of kaleidoscopes
Soliloquies: the lady doth indeed protest
UnMythed
Paintings and Sculptures

mixed genre

Satellites Out of Orbit
Excerpts

stageplays

As I the Shards Examine / Not Such Stuff
The Ladies' Auxiliary
Snow White Gets Her Say
The Dialogue
Amelia's Nocturne

performance pieces

I am Eve
Let Me Entertain You

audio work

ProVocative
The Art of Juxtaposition

Writing as Peg Tittle

fiction

Fighting Words (forthcoming)
Jess (forthcoming)
Gender Fraud: a fiction
Impact
It Wasn't Enough
Exile
What Happened to Tom

screenplays

Exile
What Happened to Tom
Foreseeable
Aiding the Enemy
Bang Bang

stageplays

Impact
What Happened to Tom
Foreseeable
Aiding the Enemy
Bang Bang

audioplays

Impact

nonfiction

Just Think About It
Sexist Shit that Pisses Me Off
No End to the Shit that Pisses Me Off
Still More Shit that Pisses Me Off
More Shit that Pisses Me Off
Shit that Pisses Me Off

Critical Thinking: An Appeal to Reason
What If? Collected Thought Experiments in Philosophy
Should Parents be Licensed? (editor)
Ethical Issues in Business: Inquiries, Cases, and Readings
Philosophy: Questions and Theories (contributing author)

Writing as Jass Richards

fiction

(the Rev and Dylan series)
The ReGender App
License to Do That
The Blasphemy Tour
The Road Trip Dialogues

(the Brett series)
Dogs Just Wanna Have Fun
This Will Not Look Good on My Resume

*A Philosopher, a Psychologist, and an Extraterrestrial
Walk into a Chocolate Bar*

CottageEscape.com: Satan Takes Over (forthcoming)
TurboJetslams: Proof #29 of the Non-Existence of God

stageplays

Substitute Teacher from Hell

screenplays

Two Women, Road Trip, Extraterrestrial

performance pieces

Balls

nonfiction

Jane Smith's Translation Dictionary
Too Stupid to Visit

This
is
what
happens

chris wind

Magenta

Cover design by chris wind

Formatting and interior book design by Elizabeth Beeton

Library and Archives Canada Cataloguing in Publication

Title: This is what happens / chris wind.
Names: wind, chris, author.
Identifiers: Canadiana (print) 2020018637X | Canadiana (ebook) 20200186388 | ISBN 9781926891743
    (softcover) | ISBN 9781926891750 (PDF) | ISBN 9781926891767 (EPUB)
Classification: LCC PS8595.I592 T55 2020 | DDC C813/.54—dc23

Feminist theorist Dale Spender wrote, in *Women of Ideas and What Men Have Done to Them*, "We need to know how women disappear ...." Although Spender spoke of women who disappear from the historical record, all too many women seem to disappear from any sort of public life as soon as they leave high school: so many shine there, but once they graduate, they become invisible. What happens?

1

As soon as she opened the back door of the cabin—the cottage, she corrected herself—she looked right through it, through the wall-sized windows, to the lake. To the bright sun sparkling on the dark water, circled by a wilderness of trees. Yes. *Yes.* Her whole body, her whole mind, responded as if the most wonderful drug in the world were coursing through it. She stood there, letting it happen, welcoming it with every … with everything she had left.

She set her bags down then, and crossed the open-concept room. She opened the sliding glass door to the left of the windows, and stepped out onto the small deck. A slight breeze caressed her face, and she paused at the simple joy of it. Then she followed the short, steep path to the dock and— It was almost too much. Her eyes started to tear up as she gazed at the glittering cove, at the nothing-but-forest along the curving shoreline that ended in the pretty peninsula on the other side—   *Yes.*

She stood there for a long while, a very long while, just staring out at the water, at the sparkles, as they were whispered by the breeze into a gleaming sheet, then as they separated again into discrete points of brilliance …

There must be a lounge chair in the shed—the garage, she corrected. She'd bring it down.

It was September, so it would be another couple hours before the sun disappeared below the tree tops. She had time.

First she'd unpack and get set up.

It took only two more trips out to her old Saturn, parked in the dirt driveway. She hadn't brought much. She didn't have much to bring.

The fireplace between the two large windows had an insert, she noticed, with a sort of bay window door. You could probably see the fire from the couch, she thought. Nice. She'd bring in some wood later.

The couch, a fold-away, was in front of the window on the right, but it was turned to face a large-screen television mounted on the wall dividing the main space from the rest of the cottage. She shook her head with disgust, and turned it to face the window instead, to face the lake. When she had it angled just so, she lowered herself into it. And sighed with contentment. It wasn't quite right, but still. The view was quietly stunning.

There was a dining table with four chairs in front of the other window. She moved the entire ensemble away from the window, to the kitchen area.

The remaining corner had been walled off into what she presumed was the master bedroom.

God, how did people use that term without embarrassment?

She struggled to get the mattress off the bed and through the door, then dragged it to where the dining set had been. She opened the window. Now she would hear the loons at night. Unless they'd already left …

When she unpacked, she saw that they'd put up a wall in the adjoining room, to make two small bedrooms, and had managed to squeeze into each of them a set of bunk beds and a cot.

Right. That way they could say 'Sleeps 10'.

She went back out then, not to her car, but to the shed. The garage, she corrected herself again. And there it was, at the back. A Pamlico 100. Not the fastest kayak around, but virtually untippable. While in it, you could give yourself over to the beauty. Completely.

She carefully extracted it from the clutter, the water toys and yard tools too numerous to mention, let alone need, then carried it out and gently lay it onto the grass. It hadn't been used in a long while. She smiled. She gave it a thorough cleaning, then hoisted it onto her shoulder and carried it down to the water. Once on the dock, she eased it into the lake, then secured it. She went back up to get the paddle, a life jacket, and a seat cushion, cleaned them as well, then carried them down.

She glanced behind her at the sun. Soon it would be time.

She went back up, plugged in the kettle, then found the lounge chair. While her cup of tea steeped, she cleaned it, then took it down to the dock as well. She positioned it just so, facing the end of the little cove.

She followed with her a cup of tea and settled herself onto the chair. Perfect. She took a long sip of her very good tea. She'd splurged on half-and-half.

Then, exactly as anticipated, the sun, at just the right angle, started to light up the cove, bit by bit, as it slowly panned from left to right, filling it with the most incredible emerald luminescence—   It was magical.

An hour later, during which she hardly moved, hardly breathed, she got into the kayak and paddled out. She wouldn't be able to see the sunset from the dock.

She glided past the unoccupied cottages, past the other docks, many already pulled onto shore for the winter. Then she turned slightly and headed straight for the gleaming path of the setting sun, a dancing golden brick road. She glanced up every now and then, and as soon as it no longer blinded, she stopped paddling. And just sat there, in the middle of the lake, watching as the colours became visible, dusty rose, soft lavender … The sun edged the clouds with a bright jagged line of lightning … The colours crescendoed, slowly, imperceptibly, into fuchsia and purple … Then she watched them fade, dissipate, dissolve.

She should go back, she thought.

Or she could go on. Tomorrow would be soon enough to start.

So she continued, past the stream that flowed into the lake. The current would have been too strong in spring, but now, tomorrow perhaps … She passed the marshy part, where there would surely be duck nests, then paddled along the stretch of crown land that led to the next populated cove.

She looked for the slink of otters, listened for the slap of beavers. Around the next curve, the lake was no longer accessible by road, so there was just forest. Beautiful forest. She took her time, relishing every stroke. She made her way past the little island, all the way to the end. And then she settled back, rested her paddle across her lap, and just drifted. It all— It took her breath away. And then she didn't need to breathe. The beauty was pure oxygen to her.

A loon called. And her heart—   surged.

It called again. And received an answer.

Their haunting voices in the otherwise silence, the dark of the night wrapped around her, the moon glimmering shimmering silver on the water, her hand resting in cool of it— She felt such a complete peace.

She had a month. Just one month. But one whole month.

It was well past midnight when she got back, but she had no trouble finding her way. She retied the kayak to the dock, then carefully went back up the steep path to the cabin.

She set a fire and simply gazed at it, listening to one of the CDs she'd brought. It had taken a while to choose her top thirty, and on this first night, she played her favourite arrangement of Pachelbel's *Canon*. Over and over.

2

Next morning, she carried another good cup of tea and the first journal down to the water. She'd given herself one month. One month to figure it out, to understand—

Eventually, she opened the journal. September 1972. The very first entry was a carefully reasoned argument about why school spirit assemblies were stupid. Surprised, delighted, she smiled. If ever there was someone born to be a philosopher—

So what happened? Why hadn't she become a Peter Singer? A Catherine MacKinnon? Or even someone close to?

She intended to go back through her life, through her journals, thirty-five years' worth. Not exactly one a year, but close. She'd read one a day. She needed to understand.

How did she get here—from there?

How is it that the girl who got the top marks in high school ends up, at fifty, scrubbing floors and cleaning toilets for minimum wage, living in a room above Vera's Hairstyling, in a god-forsaken town called Powassan somewhere in mid-northern Ontario?

She was the one who did all her homework and then some. She was on the track team, the basketball team, the gymnastics team. She belonged to the writers' club and the charity club. All of her teachers loved her. She was supposed to become something. God knows she tried.

What happened? Where did she go wrong?

And how did she end up so alone? There was no one she could call and say, "Hi, it's me." No one.

She read on. Two days later, she'd written a critique of her school's attendance policies and procedures. She'd argued for autonomy and against deterrence, though not in those words; she questioned the value of giving course credit for, measuring achievement by, attendance; she even pointed out the environmental irresponsibility of all those blue slips so laboriously filled out every forty minutes going to the dump, to be burned into air pollution.

Three days after that, she'd written about the fact that those students with a tenth period class couldn't attend the speech to be given by the newly elected premier.

She noticed, now, that it hadn't occurred to her to go to the speech anyway.

She looked up and stared out at the gently rippling water. Maybe that's why she'd become so very critical. If you have no intention of following the rules, you don't get upset by their injustice. Alternatively, if the rules prescribe what you would have done anyway, well, no problem.

So if she'd just been able to just break the rules—

Or ignore injustice.

But she was raised Roman Catholic. St. Louis was an impressive church, its ancient stone steps worn with use leading to a set of magnificently heavy wooden doors. The vestibule held a large marble font of Holy Water, and the church proper was glorious, with its high ceiling, its tall and narrow stained glass windows, its polished wooden pews.

She couldn't remember ever entering through those magnificent doors. They always used one of the side doors, as if they were the undeserving or uninvited second-cousins to the—no wait, she *did* enter through the centre doors once. When her sister got married.

Right. Of course. Because getting married was so fucking important. Made *you so fucking important.*

Not only did they always enter through the side, lesser, door, they'd always sit about halfway up. Never at the front, but never at the very back either.

She remembered putting on her Sunday outfit and walking to church for the eleven o'clock Mass. Every week. She remembered the Mass with all its rules about when to stand, when to sit, when to kneel—rules that were so very imperative and yet so very arbitrary.

So why didn't that, that insight, that fact, give you permission to break them, she wondered now about her younger self.

Well, she probably didn't see them as arbitrary. Then. She probably assumed she just didn't know the reason for them.

There were rules too about when to say something and when to be quiet. She remembered that at some point she thought it odd that you couldn't ask questions during the Sermon. So she went to the Rectory on a Saturday to ask her questions. The priest—Father Meilling, she still remembered his name—was amused. She'd been so disappointed.

Didn't know yet to be insulted.

She remembered her First Communion, her mother fussing over the new and very white Communion dress, as if that were the most important part of the ceremony.

Her First Confession, she remembered that too, she remembered waiting in the pew for her turn in one of the dark Confession booths. 'Bless me Father, for I have sinned, I argued with my sister twice last week.' She never had more to confess than that—

Wait—argument, a sin? Of course, she thought now. It made perfect sense.

At her Confirmation, as she walked back from the Altar, brimming with the presence of the Holy Spirit, she couldn't keep the beaming, beatific smile from her face, even though she felt that it was wrong, she was supposed to look pious instead.

Even so, she decided, then, to become a nun. The purity appealed to her.

She remembered the large bottle of Holy Water at home in the bathroom cupboard, from which they refilled the little vessels on the wall by the light switch in each of their bedrooms—actually, just her brother's room and the room she shared with her sister, come to think of it—into which they were supposed to dip their finger and make the Sign of the Cross, blessing themselves every time they left their room.

They also had to say their prayers every night, on their knees by their beds. They were supposed to say the Rosary as well, especially if they had trouble going to sleep.

Oh, that's rich. Religious belief as a sedative.

She went to St. Louis school, as did her brother and sister before her. So by the time she was eight, she learned that there were venial sins and mortal sins. There were sins of commission and sins of omission. There was heaven and hell, and purgatory, and even limbo, for those who died before they were baptized. Roman Catholicism was obsessed with sin. With right and wrong.

No wonder she went into Ethics.

No wonder 'should' had ruled her life.

(It would be decades before she realized that the ever-present 'should' was indistinguishable from what her parents wanted, which was, in turn, indistinguishable from habit and tradition.)

(Even so, it would take a lifetime to get out from under 'should'.)

She recalled now that much was made of impure thoughts. It was wrong to even *think* some things.

When even thoughts can be sins, being a philosopher is the highest rebellion, a supremely subversive act. She understood this only now.

What she understood back then, though not until her teens, was that she was the only one in the family to take it all seriously. Yes, her brother became an altar boy, but he didn't seem bothered by any of the dogma. In fact, he later became Baptist overnight. In order to marry his new girlfriend. And her sister probably didn't understand any of it. And her parents—her parents stopped going to church as soon as the three of them were in high school. (Public high school, not St. Mary's and St. Jerome's. Because they couldn't afford the tuition.) She never quite got that. Had they suddenly become non-Catholics? No, they said with irritation when she'd asked, they were just non-practising Catholics now. What did that mean? Did they still believe in the Catholic dogma then? The prohibition of contraception, for example? They shrugged off her questions. As if they were irrelevant.

But it had bothered her. Why did they suddenly think church attendance wasn't important? And why had it been important up to that point?

Why. For philosophers, the prime question was always 'Why?' But, she came to understand, it was a question most people weren't interested in. In fact, she realized now, accompanying her requests with reasons, with the 'why', made interactions worse, not better. People wanted to keep things simple, they'd rather not know— They'd just rather not know.

She supposed that going to church was her parents' way of instilling a sense of right and wrong, something apparently achieved by the time one reached high school age. And yet, whenever she wanted to *discuss* matters of right and wrong, they just … weren't interested. That was the best way to describe it.

Which meant her parents were either hypocrites or imbeciles.

Or both.

It was her acute sense of justice that in part led to her friendlessness. Groups by definition excluded people. And by the time she realized that such exclusion was at least sometimes justified, she'd refused to belong to so many groups …

Networks, she realized now. Far too late.

She looked out at the water, closed her eyes to the warmth of the sun for a few moments, then turned back to her journal.

She had written "awhile" and "alot" as single words and often ended with something trite, but all in all, she thought, with deep dismay, she hadn't come a long way in thirty-five years.

Those pieces too had gone unread.

Why didn't her teacher, the one who'd assigned the journal, suggest that she submit them to the school newspaper?

She turned a few more pages. Ah. Two weeks later, she'd written a critique of the school newspaper, describing what she would do if she were in charge: have a staff, regular meetings, regular issues, a standard cover, a table of contents, regular columns (sports report, student council report, library report), letters to the editor. She recalled then that the paper was haphazardly put out by a few of the cool kids. So even if she had submitted her pieces, they probably wouldn't've been published.

She really hadn't come any distance at all in thirty-five years.

So why hadn't she started her own paper? Because she didn't know anything about putting out a paper. But the cool kids probably didn't know either. They asked.

She never asked. How was it, she wondered, that she had become such a passive person, never actively seeking what she wanted, accepting, consequently, a life of frustration since it was unlikely that what she wanted, what she so badly wanted, would ever be offered to her?

She remembered then, she must have been four or five at the time, her mother had prepared the bath for her, told her to get in, then went to answer the phone. The water was hot. Too hot. But she stood there, her feet and ankles turning red, as her mother talked on and on. She didn't get out of the tub. It didn't occur to her to do so. It certainly didn't occur to her to turn on the cold water tap. Why not? She wasn't stupid.

No. She was obedient. She did what her mother told her. That's what good girls did. And she was a good girl.

She did *exactly* what her mother told her. Her mother had told her to get into the tub. She got into the tub. Her mother had not said, "If it's too hot, get out." She was doggedly literal-minded. Still.

Then again, maybe it wasn't about obedience or literal-mindedness, but initiative. She'd since read the studies. Infant monkeys, for example, who'd been able to control aspects of their environment, even for simple things like food and water, later exhibited more exploratory behaviour than did monkeys who hadn't had any control.

Her mother always made the supper. Then, at the table, she dished out the meat, potatoes, and vegetables. There was no need to ask.

Her parents looked after her. They knew best. They would provide. She trusted in that.

Which explains her immense anger when she realized they didn't. Look after her. Know best. Provide.

They should have told her. Yes, she supposed the illusion was necessary for a safe and secure childhood, but at some point during adolescence they should've told her the truth. They didn't know best.

As for asking for more, it just wasn't done. She learned to simply accept what was given.

More importantly, the simple act of helping herself, choosing how much potatoes, which carrots, was denied. And so, she never developed initiative. Initiative presumes one is *entitled* to have, to therefore seek, what one wants. Not just what one needs.

So there she was, five, ten, twenty years later, still waiting for permission. And crying 'No fair!' when someone else just went ahead and did what they wanted, to get what they wanted.

And it wasn't just that all was provided by her parents. All was decided by them. By her mother. What to do, when to do it, how to do it. She was never consulted.

Except on her birthday. Once a year, she got to choose what they'd have for dinner. But it was clear that she was supposed to choose from among two or three appropriate options. Roast beef. Roast pork. She couldn't, for example, ask for hamburgers or hot dogs. That was what they had on Sundays. Even meatloaf, which she loved, was for some reason inappropriate for a birthday dinner.

It was her sister, her 'slow' sister, who asked for cherry cheesecake instead of the usual chocolate cake. How was it *she* developed the daring, the imagination—and not her?

She wasn't bothered by 'should'.

She looked up—she'd just remembered something else. Months spent making a set of coasters, as a Christmas gift for her parents. She cut out twelve squares of cardboard and dozens of teeny quarter-inch-wide strips of coloured paper. Then she wove the strips criss-cross, and when that was done, she got a needle and some yarn and sewed a line around the perimeter, to hold it all in place. It was an impossible task because every time she tried to weave one strip into the whole, the ones she'd already done would shift and come undone. Each coaster took days of frustration. She has no idea why it occurred to her to make them. (Paper and cardboard for *coasters*? They'd get wet from the sweating glasses.) The thing is, it hadn't occurred to her to pin or tape the ends, to hold them in place, until she sewed them. Somehow that would've been cheating.

So, what—life was supposed *to be hard?*

And yet, she thought, it wasn't like she had an unhappy childhood.

She tried to think back to her first memory. After a moment, she laughed out loud. Oh, this is priceless. Her first memory, her very first memory, was of walking beside her mother—harnessed.

She must have been quite young. Two? Three? Old enough to walk, but too young to be on her own. She imagined now that many people must have thought her mother cruel to put her child in a harness, like a dog, but her memory is one of joy. When she had to hang on to her mother's purse strap, she had to focus on just that. Because what if she got jostled and let go? The very thought sent her into a panic. And it was awkward, uncomfortable, that reaching up and hanging on. But when she had the harness on, she could pay attention to everything, anything. More than that, she had the use of both of her hands and more range of movement. She felt free. And at the same time, safe.

She also remembered sitting on the porch, reading to her dolls. She remembered helping with the baking, kneeling on a chair at the table, stirring batter in the big bowl. She remembered getting to lick the frosting off the mixer beaters; she got one, her sister got the other. She remembered her blue princess costume for Hallowe'en—she wasn't crazy about the colour, but it was the one year they were allowed to have a real costume, one bought from the store, instead of having to put something together from what they had at home.

So not unhappy, no.

But fearful. She realized now that she'd spent much of her life afraid of not doing the right thing, of not doing what she was supposed to do.

She was afraid of being late for school, for example. If she was late, the world wouldn't end; she'd just have to go to the office to get a late slip. Still, it was unthinkable.

She even peed her pants once— She and her sister were doing the dishes. Her sister washed, she dried. "Hurry up!" her sister would scold with such irritation if she had to stop and wait before she could put more newly washed dishes into the still-full drainer. So if she'd stopped to go to the bathroom—what? It wasn't like she'd be left behind if she couldn't keep up—what was she so afraid of?

She was afraid she'd 'get heck'.

Where did that come from, she wondered, staring out at the water. It was such an odd phrase. 'You'll get heck!' What did that mean? She'd be yelled at? All that fear, just of being yelled at?

Well, yes. To be yelled at by her mother— Her mother was her whole world. If her mother got angry at her, if her mother didn't love her—

And, she realized now, she was afraid she'd 'get the strap'. The thick strip of leather was in the third drawer in the kitchen. She remembered getting a spanking, but she doesn't remember ever getting the strap. Still, it was always there, an ever-present threat.

Like hell.

And then she realized— *Our parents are our gods.*

She remembered having to sit facing the corner once, as a punishment, for something she didn't even do. She felt cast out.

So, yes, her mother's reprimands were to be feared. They were punishment enough.

There was no mechanism in their family for apology, for forgiveness, for reconciliation. Her mother certainly never apologized. For anything.

And they would never 'talk about it later'. Action, reaction. End of story. Any loss of love was permanent.

No wonder she was perpetually so afraid of doing something wrong, so afraid of her mother's disapproval.

So she was a good girl. *Such* a good girl.

And *still* her mother disapproved, she thought bitterly.

She closed the journal. It was enough for one day.

• • •

Ten minutes later, she was paddling past all the cottages again, basking in yet another beautiful, sunny day. Maybe she'd paddle up the stream today. It was calm enough. Or maybe she'd just keep going, all the way to the end again. Or maybe she'd do both. She smiled at the thought.

Her attention was caught then by movement at the last cottage. Oh, right. It was Friday. People would be coming up for the weekend.

Surely it was too cold for jetskis, she thought. Fishing boats wouldn't be quite so annoying, but their motors and fumes would certainly ruin her time out on the lake. Maybe even her time down on the dock. She hoped the forest wouldn't be overrun by dirt bikes and ATVs. Perhaps she'd go for a long walk instead.

3

She settled onto the lounge chair on the dock again and just stared out at the water for a while, cup of tea in hand. It was black, really. Not muddy or silty, but still, you couldn't see too far down. And that was what, she figured, made the sparkles so … sparkly.

There had been a lot of late night noise, most of it from across the lake, and dirt bikes had woken her up. It finally occurred to her that this was not just *a* weekend, but the *long* weekend. So she'd brought her earplugs, headphones, and portable CD player—all of which got good use when you lived beside the railway tracks— and loved music—down to the dock with her. Good thing. As soon as she sat down, a leaf blower started up.

Earplugs in, she pressed the play button, increased the volume, and Bach washed over her. Exquisite.

Eventually, she opened her journal to where she'd left off the day before, and saw a review she'd written of *Jesus Christ Superstar*. Although she hadn't heard it in decades, she recalled every note, every anguished inflection, of Murray Head's performance of Judas' song— She'd actually recorded the middle bit, when he breaks out into the painfully impassioned "I don't know how to love him," over and over, filling the whole side of a cassette, so she could listen to it, just that part, over and over. It was so … tortured. It—

It spoke to her. It spoke for her.

In a way Donny Osmond never had.

She read the review, and was pleased. She'd attributed the rock opera's success to its uniqueness; she'd called it a reaction to the religious brainwashing that had been going on for ages; she'd identified the humanity of Christ, and had said that the emotional quality was what was unusual, and attractive. It was pretty good, she thought. Well, except for the borderline appeal to ignorance in the middle—"At first we may scoff at the idea of Mary Magdalen as a prostitute, but there's no reason to think she couldn't've been". Mentioning that there's no evidence to the contrary was valuable, but not sufficient.

Despite her passion for ideas and argument, she didn't join the debating team. She'd tried once. There had been an announcement one morning that said the debating club would meet that day in Room 231. And after working up the courage to just walk into the room— She'd wondered why no one else seemed to find that difficult. She didn't realize that no one else walked into a room alone; they were always with their friends. People didn't stop and stare in that case.

When she entered the room, she saw the two Rothblatt brothers on their feet arguing with each other. She was so thirsty, it felt so right— And it felt so wrong. She couldn't quite put her finger on it. They were so loud, so cocksure. They glanced at her, then argued even more passionately. And she—she didn't say anything. Eventually she left. And never returned.

She realizes now that they were performing. Ostensibly for her, but really for each other.

You were never expected to join in, she told her younger self. About life in general.

She remembered discovering philosophy. One of the suggested topics for her grade eleven history essay assignment was "The Continuity between Socrates, Plato, and Aristotle." She was vaguely aware that they were philosophers. Certainly she'd heard of Socrates. Deep thought. Wisdom.

So she went to the library, found the shelf for Philosophy, and signed out all the books that had to do with Socrates, Plato, and Aristotle. There were seven. She also signed out three on Greek history and culture. And another four that were on the philosophy shelf that just looked interesting.

That weekend—

Her parents had bought a cottage on Silver Lake, and they went there every weekend from Victoria Day until Thanksgiving. She loved it. Going out in the canoe, going for a run on the dirt roads …

One of the first new things she'd done at high school was try out for the cross-country team. She'd never heard of cross-country before, but it sounded like something she'd like, and indeed, she fell in love with it: the distance running, the forest, the solitude.

She hated the evenings at the cottage though. Her mother would insist she join them after dinner to play cards. Canasta. Euchre. Something pointless. She had no desire whatsoever to sit at a table with a few other people, repeatedly subjecting herself to chance, having a near total lack of agency, engaging in something that required little intelligence, little skill, and for what—'I won'? But it was made abundantly clear that if she didn't play, she was being rude and selfish.

That memory triggered another. A few children's decks of cards in the drawer in the den. She had a favourite … Crazy Eights? No … Old Maid. It had the most colourful pictures, and—the picture of the old maid herself was horrid, she recalled now. A grizzled witch of an old woman, whiskers sprouting from her chin, a maniacal grin on her face.

God, it started so young, went so deep. 'See, that's what happens if you don't get married.'

She hadn't even known yet what 'an old maid' referred to.

That weekend, she set up a table and chair down at the water in the boathouse (after her chores were done), organized her fourteen books into three piles on her left, and set a pile of blank paper in front of her. She had her favourite pen (a BIC fine point with black ink) and she'd brought down a large glass of milk. She'd opened the door slightly, just enough to see the lake. Not the dock or any other evidence of other people.

One by one, the books moved from the pile on her left to a pile on her right. The sheets of paper became filled with her writing, her thinking. The breeze, the view of weeds, the water, the sun sparkling on the lake. She was *so* happy. In fact, she had never been happier. She knew then and there that that was what she wanted to do. For the rest of her life. Live alone in a cabin on a lake in a forest and just read, write, and think.

It was an epiphany.

When her mother called her up for lunch, she resented it immensely.

She'd never understood why eating at a certain time was considered sacred. So sacred that it took precedence to everything else. Was allowed to interrupt everything else.

Once she was on her own, she dispensed altogether with the concept.

"Why don't you come into town with us this afternoon to do some shopping?" her mother asked as she and her sister did the dishes from lunch.

Because she didn't want to. She wanted to go back down to the boathouse to continue reading, and writing, and thinking.

"You spend too much time alone with your books," her mother chastised.

Chastised.

She remembered one time she *had* gone shopping with her mother, to Yorkdale or Square One, one of the huge shopping malls in Toronto. Her mother had insisted. Because, at the time, she didn't have a coat; she just had jackets. Which was fine, as far as she was concerned, since she had stopped wearing dresses. But her mother was adamant. She needed a spring coat.

She'd said it like it was a rule. Like it was uncontroversial. And perhaps it was. For her. Perhaps all of life was uncontroversial for her.

That would explain a lot. Her anger whenever you wanted to discuss something.

She'd much rather have stayed at home. And had said as much. But her mother had persisted, so she had acquiesced. If it meant that much to her— She didn't want to hurt her mother's feelings.

When did her mother ever acquiesce to *her* desires? Took three decades to ask herself that.

Her mother picked out a pale blue one. She'd wanted the black one. But her mother disapproved. Apparently black was not an appropriate color for a spring coat. Or for a sixteen-year-old. Her mother purchased the pale blue one. It was her money. And she should have been grateful. But she never wore it.

Her mother was hurt.

And she felt bad about hurting her.

But her mother was hurt *whenever* she didn't like the same things, didn't want the same things. So it was inevitable that she would hurt her mother. Because she couldn't change what she liked, what she wanted. Was she supposed to?

She looked up from her journal, hearing the fluttery whir of ducks coming in for a landing, and saw a pair of mallards, the head of the one gleaming like a hummingbird. She watched them for a while.

She also remembered discovering consciousness. That is, she remembered the moment she first became conscious of her life—as a life. She didn't remember first gaining consciousness, which was odd, and a little sad, given how much she valued it. But she did remember her first moment of critical consciousness.

What was astounding to her now was the quality of her appraisal.

She was ten, it was a Sunday, and they'd all just come back from church. It was a bright, warm April day. They were milling about at the back door, by the patio where she often fed Chippy the squirrel, waiting for her father, already up the stairs and on the porch, recently painted green, to unlock the door. Just as she raised her foot to take the first step, to follow her brother and sister, she was … aware. Of her happiness, of her contentment. Simply put, life was good.

Well, you were ten.

She has since realized that not everyone develops such a self-consciousness. Not everyone reflects on their life. Not everyone is aware of their life, as a life. It's a second order consciousness. A squirrel doesn't have it.

Most of her neighbours haven't had it.

She idly turned the pages. More of the same. A scathing critique of television. Another of football.

It was the beginning. Correction: it *could have been* the beginning. All her life, people had criticized her for being too critical. *The irony.* But no one had ever suggested she become a critic.

Just as her mother criticized her for always arguing, but never suggested she become a lawyer.

I could have been good, she thought sadly, staring out at the water.

Better than good. You could have been, should have been, a Globe and Mail *critic by now.*

But no one celebrated her propensity for criticism, for argument. Instead, she came to apologize for it.

Besides, girls didn't grow up to become critics or lawyers. Not in the 70s.

And she didn't even know one could become, one could *be*, a philosopher.

She wanted to be a writer. She knew people became writers. After all, she read books. And although she'd written a few poems as a child, her passion to become a writer didn't solidify until high school. It was her Creative Writing teacher, Mr. Ledford, who had them start a journal: they were to write a page a day.

She would write several pages a day. For the rest of her life.

She joined the Writer's Club at school, had her work published in its annual magazine, and won or placed in the local library's literary competition every year. When her first poem was published in a 'real' magazine, she was thrilled. She thought she was well on her way to becoming a writer.

She actually thought she could become another Margaret Atwood.

She made the mistake of sharing her joy with her parents. Her mother asked how much she'd been paid for the poem. Not in a way that suggested that she thought women should be financially independent, but in a way that suggested that she measured value by price.

Her father asked "*Where* are they?" as if he knew, but had momentarily forgotten. And as if establishing the location of everything was absolutely critical.

Which it was, if you were a Neanderthal, foraging for your food and keeping away from predators.

Neither of them asked to read the poem.

She'd never make that mistake again.

And they never noticed.

>   later in the evening
>   long after the dinner and dishes were done
>   i came again to the kitchen
>   and this time
>   saw him.
>   our beloved budgie who delighted
>   in the flat chrome top of the fridge door
>   hadn't turned quick enough this time
>   his tail caught between
>   and with the closing jolt
>   he lost his balance
>   flipped over the edge
>   to hang helpless
>   as he hung still now
>   his little bird feet clenched
>   into stiff fists
>   his eyes bulged wide and still.
>   i opened the door
>   cupped him in my hand
>   and wept.
>
>   how long, i wondered—
>   when last did someone—
>   what does it feel like—
>
>   no, i need not ask about the pain
>   of dying
>   with the people you love all around
>   oblivious.

• • •

By afternoon, the long weekend was in full swing, so she did decide to head into the forest instead of out onto the lake. Halfway up the hill to the logging road that went into the bush, a pair of ATVs passed her and then turned in at the logging road. Covering her mouth so as not to end up with a headache for the rest of the day, she sighed and turned around. Part way down the hill, there was a newer trail, too overgrown to be used by ATVs. Not as easy a walk in, but clearly a better choice.

She'd also wanted to become a composer.

Her parents had started her with piano lessons at the age of eight, and she practiced every day like she was supposed to. One day, when she was about fifteen, she composed a piece. She called it, optimistically, Op1. No.1.

Her piano teacher, Mrs. Aldrich, had not assigned, or even suggested, let alone encouraged, any sort of original composition, but at the end of her next lesson, she mentioned, shyly, that she had composed such a piece. Could she play it for her? But, of course!

The piece was a little simplistic, but nicely done. It opened with a pretty bit in a major key, then moved to a dramatic bit in a minor key, then returned to the pretty bit in the major key. Mrs. Aldrich correctly identified Hagood Hardy as an influence. (Although she hardly ever went to a movie, she had recently seen *A Second Wind*, drawn by the running theme, and Hardy had written the score.)

Her parents were equally surprised, and even more impressed. They made such a to-do about hearing her play it for them, sitting together on the couch in the basement rec room, holding hands with such excitement, nodding to her to begin, then applauding wildly when she had finished.

Somehow they discovered that Hagood Hardy lived in Toronto, and was willing to take her on as a student of composition. Her father drove her, once a week, to Mr. Hardy's house. She quickly became his protégé, and by the time she was eighteen, had written a piece he felt was good enough to include in one of his concerts. Her career as a composer was launched.

In her early twenties, he introduced her to the wildlife sound recordist Dan Gibson, and they formed a partnership almost immediately: her piano pieces and his recordings of birds, streams, and so on. She found herself in the company of George Winston, David Lanz, and Paul Winter, on the cutting edge of the new age genre.

It could've happened.

It didn't.

She waited for a convenient moment, for when her mother was on her way up the stairs from the basement, having just put a load of laundry into the washer. "Do you want to hear the piece I composed?" she asked. Her mother wouldn't have to make a special trip back down to hear it; she could play it right then.

"Not now," there was irritation in her voice. "The supper's on."

Right. Supper was more important. And it couldn't possibly wait. Food always had priority. It certainly came before her daughter's first composition.

But the implied 'later' was never mentioned. By either of them.

It hurt.

Thus she learned early to hide her pleasures, her prides, her passions.

> burn victim
>
> i am always cutting flesh
> taking from one part
> to heal another—
> survival of the self
> sufficient.

She did play her piece, at her next lesson, for Mrs. Aldrich. Who said it was nice and then sent her on her way; the next student had arrived.

Her parents attended her piano recitals, but she felt that that was only because they had to drive her there. She realized now that they could have just dropped her off. Still, she didn't get the feeling they wanted to be there; she didn't get the feeling they wanted to hear her play.

After all, her piano had been put into the basement. And whenever she forgot to close the door when she went down to practice, someone slammed it shut.

She turned off the trail onto the logging road. After a short while, she got to the little brook and was delighted to hear its burbling. She'd expected it to have been almost dry by this time of year.

She realized, eventually, that yes, it was annoying to hear someone practice a musical instrument, to hear the scales up and down, and up and down, to hear the same phrase over and over, to hear the stumbles, the wrong notes—but the door was also slammed when she was playing a piece she'd mastered.

At first, she practiced the piano every day because she was supposed to, but she soon grew to like the simple accomplishment of learning a piece.

Then she grew to appreciate other, far more compelling, reasons for practising. Certainly for the beauty of the music, which was apparent to her even in some of the simpler pieces she was able to master—some Burgmüller, some simplified Chopin, and most of all, Bach's *Prelude I*.

But when she graduated to Bach's two-part inventions, the quality of her life changed. Literally. It was then that she became attracted to the attention to detail, and the precision—the precision of the composition as well as the precision required for its performance, not only in the reading, but also in the playing, in mastering the subtle response of the keys to perfection—

It's a pity she had just an old Heintzman. The first time she played on a grand, which was at her grade eight exam, she nearly wept. And was so distracted by the difference, she nearly failed the exam.

Many years later, she read somewhere about a budding pianist that "… money was found to buy a grand piano …." The simplicity of the statement stunned her. In so many ways.

She practiced Hanons for a solid half hour. Then a solid hour. Although her wrists would be on fire by the time she was done, she was swept away by the sheer physicality of it, the perpetual motion of the pattern up and down, the ever so slight change then up and down again, as she moved seamlessly from one pattern to the next.

One of her parents' friends, while visiting, heard her. "You should play Philip Glass," she said. "You were made for his music. I'll introduce you. Take you to New York next week, how would you like that? He'd love your technique."

As if.

Instead, one of her brother's friends, during one of his parties down in the rec room, set his bottle of beer on her piano. She'd come down to get something from the root cellar, potatoes she was to peel for dinner probably, and when she saw it, she asked him politely to please not put any glasses or bottles on the piano, please. Her brother scoffed and made fun of her concern. Well, at least she could close the cover, protect the keys. When she heard them banging away on it later, she sat alone in her room upstairs and cried. She couldn't say why exactly.

The word 'rape' had not yet entered your vocabulary.

She worked her way through the Conservatory piano exams, adding the theory component when it was required. She remembered writing her grade three harmony exam. She'd never written a three-hour exam before. When the proctor said "You may begin," she opened the booklet. *"Complete the following sixteen-measure passage with the given figured bass."* She was writing an exam in which you had to write music! It was an amazing thing to her. At one point, she happened to look out the window and saw for the first time gladioli, or what she figured out later must have been gladioli. Stalks of flowers. Flowers on a stick! she giggled. And the colours were so vivid! She'd never really *looked* at flowers before. But there, in the middle of writing that exam, her senses were heightened, her brain was so excited, neurons must have been flashing like crazy …

She also remembered the grade four counterpoint exam. It was a take-home: they had forty-eight hours to write a fugue. Unfortunately, it was a weekend and she had to do all of the dusting and her share of the ironing first. Then, later, she had to stop, right in the middle of the development section, to help get dinner ready, set the table, sit at the table, eat, then do the dishes.

Until she was around twenty, the only music she'd ever heard, apart from the pieces in her piano books, was the pop and rock played on the local AM radio station. The Partridge Family, the Carpenters, Barry Manilow, England Dan and John Ford Coley.

It never occurred to her to change the station. She hadn't known about the FM band.

She knew that her parents had some records in the stereo cabinet in the living room, but … Even so, she worked up the nerve one day to look through them. Among the Teresa Brewer and Engelbert Humperdinck, Glenn Miller and Boots Randolph, there was a James Last album—*James Last in Concert*. She put it on the turntable, careful not to scratch it. And— The music was so beautiful!

How was she to know there was more? She knew the pieces in her piano books were unlike what she heard on the radio, but it didn't occur to her that the people who had written those pieces would have written other pieces that were on records somewhere.

Kadwell's, the store at which she bought her precious 45s, must have carried more than the Top Ten, but she could afford only 45s. So she didn't even browse the LP sections. In any case, there were no listening booths.

Later, when she could afford LPs, she fell in love with the Beach Boys' "Lady Lynda," not realizing that it was based on Bach's *Jesu, Joy of Man's Desiring*. And Eric Carmen's "All by Myself" blew her away. Though it was really the second movement of Rachmaninoff's *Piano Concerto No. 2* in C minor that blew her away. Similarly Louise Tucker's "Graveyard Angel"—Albinoni's *Adagio*.

Once she showed interest in a Vanilla Fudge album her brother had bought, but he showed such contempt for her interest, she backed off. In any case, she wasn't allowed to play it.

Of course not, she thought now, lowering herself onto a fallen tree to just sit—she had come to the stand of maple trees, and the sun streamed through the trees, brightening the leaves. Teenaged boys listened to music for the rock; teenaged girls listened for the romance. That's why she'd listened to Donny Osmond instead of King Crimson. If she'd known about Stevie Nicks, Heart, Pat Benatar … No, she thought, even then … Girls are supposed to fall in love and get married. They're not supposed to become rock stars. Either.

4

It continued to amaze her how two people could live in the same house, for almost twenty years, and never say a word to each other. She thought about her relationship with her brother a bit before she opened the next journal she'd taken down to the water with her. It was another warm, sunny day, but a few clouds were moving in.

They sat at the same table for dinner. But her brother was on one side; she and her sister were on the other.

Right. Must maintain the sexism.

She thinks her parents actually had an agreement whereby her father was responsible for raising her brother, and her mother was responsible for raising "the two girls".

She'd hear him practicing in his room—the clarinet, and later, the saxophone— but despite the fact that she was also learning to play a musical instrument, they never talked about music.

Years later, when she saw someone her age talking and laughing with her own brother, she was astonished. She'd thought that that just happened on tv, brothers and sisters being close. Talking to each other.

She saw him occasionally sitting in his room at his desk. Their father had actually made a desk for him. The C student. While she, the A student, who brought home so many books every day and wanted to do nothing but study—she had to do her homework at the dining room table. Which meant she had to put everything away when she was done and get it back out the next evening.

They passed each other in the house as they went about their lives, but he never acknowledged her. She acknowledged him by getting out of his way.

And her parents didn't even notice. Or didn't care enough to do anything about it.

They certainly didn't walk to school together. Once, they happened to pass each other in the hall. She broke into an eager smile—and he pretended he didn't see her. She felt … shamed. But she … co-operated.

He got a chemistry set. She and her sister got dolls. She sat them in the old school desk in the basement and taught them something.

Like that would ever do any good.

He got Adidas. She and her sister got knock-off Cougars. Even though she was the one on the cross-country team and the track team.

He got an expensive Ingo sweater for Christmas. She and her sister got Warrens from the Sears catalogue.

He was entitled to so much.

They were entitled to so little.

Once he was sitting there, at his desk, on a Saturday morning when she had to do the dusting. That was Saturday's chore. She did the dusting; her sister, three years older, did the vacuuming. She also had to "dust around" on Tuesdays and Thursdays. That took less time because she didn't have to pick everything up, dust under it, then dust the thing itself before putting it back down; she just had to dust around the things. And on Mondays, she had to iron the easy things: the dishcloths, tea towels, and pillow cases. She and her sister also had to set the table before every meal, and then do the dishes after every meal. They took turns making the milk: they drank powdered skim milk, and whenever there were fewer than four quarts in the fridge, they had to make more in the big metal mixer bowl, bringing up the bag from the root cellar, filling the empty quart glass bottles with water to pour into the mixer one at a time, measuring out the powder, setting the mixer for a minute and a half, pouring the milk into the bottles through the funnel, waiting for the foam to dissolve, then capping the bottles and putting them in the fridge, and then taking the bag back down to the basement.

Her brother had to cut the grass once a week in the summer and shovel the driveway in the winter as needed.

She remembered clearly, that Saturday morning, his irritation when she'd had to disturb him so she could crawl under his desk, in and around his feet, to reach the baseboards.

She'd apologized.

Even so, she respected him. He was male.

And when he complimented her, she wrote about it in her journal. It was that noteworthy.

It happened twice.

It wasn't until she was thirty that she started to understand what a totally unremarkable person he was.

And an asshole to boot.

She had said once, at the dinner table, quoting some famous Olympic coach, and merely wanting to share her delight at a truth she had not to that point realized, that you didn't run with your legs, you ran "with your *arms, on* your legs." Her brother had scoffed, his voice full of contempt and disdain. Told her she was crazy.

This from a person who had never run a mile in his life. To a person who had been running since she was thirteen and who was, at the time, running thirty miles a week.

But he was male. Therefore, he knew better.

He was a guy. He especially knew better about sports.

Never mind that you were quoting an Olympic coach.

She was horrified, now, to realize all the times she believed her brother, and her father, and Craig, her only 'boyfriend'; whenever they said something, she accepted it as truth.

Years later, she realized they regularly presented their opinions as facts. Despite having no evidence whatsoever for those opinions.

She had been raised to think men were better than her. All men. They knew more. About everything. They were more competent. At everything. So she was intimidated by them, and impressed by them.

So every time she found out they *didn't* know more, they *weren't* better, she was not only disappointed, she was angry. Angry at them for lying, for pretending to know more, for pretending to be better. And angry at herself for her misplaced admiration.

She remembered her embarrassment when in grade nine science, as they took up their homework questions, she had proudly answered "How many gallons of water does it take to flush a toilet?" with "Twenty" because that's what her father had said when she'd asked him the night before. The teacher had laughed. She was mortified. A teacher had never laughed at her before. And, but, she was right! Her father had said so!

When she told him that evening that he'd been wrong, he brushed it aside. She was puzzled. Didn't he care that he'd gotten it wrong? Didn't he want to know the right answer?

It took a few years for her to understand that her father (a) didn't take her questions seriously, (b) didn't take her seriously, (c) didn't stop to think about things, or (d) didn't know fuck all about anything.

Or, of course, all of the above.

Shortly after that, when her parents went to Barbados for a holiday, her mother left laundry soaking in the tub for her to finish. She was to scrub it with the yellow soap, wring it out, put it in the washer, then hang it up to dry. The tub had contained her father's underwear.

Scrubbing the shit stains from your father's underwear is a real paradigm changer.

• • •

She decided it would be a good day to paddle up the stream. Five minutes out, someone revved up a jetski. Damn it. She kept close to shore, paddling hard to get out of earshot as quickly as possible. He drove in circles, around and around— Trying to put in one last afternoon for the year? Trying to use up the gas in the tank?

At the stream, she carefully negotiating the whirlpooling current, paddled past the first switchback, then the second, then, having reached quiet, relaxed again into thought.

Because her older sister was 'slow' (she'd failed grade four), her parents spent a lot of time with her. Helping her succeed.

She herself didn't need any such help (after all, she'd skipped a grade). And so didn't get any of their time.

The message was that even though her sister wasn't smart, she was just as important.

But the message received was that she was *more* important.

"I often said that of the three of you, you were the one I'd worry least about," her mother would say years later. Explaining fifteen years of neglect.

So despite her straight As, she grew up thinking she wasn't good enough. After all, she never got her parents' attention, let alone their praise. To praise her for her accomplishments would make her sister feel bad.

And we can't have that. Oh no.

It didn't help her self-esteem—though of course they didn't use that word back in the 70s—that according to the Roman Catholic doctrine, people were *born* in a state of sin. So even before you opened your eyes, you'd done something wrong.

Or were *something wrong.*

And even though she practically hid her straight-As report cards, lest they make her sister feel bad, 'You think you're too good for us' remained an unspoken accusation.

She was supposed to do her homework. But she wasn't supposed to acquire knowledge or competence.

Yeah, how does that work?

It was drilled into her: just because she herself was smart, she was not to think she was better than everyone else. *Anyone* else, actually.

So, since it was clear that effort *was* praiseworthy (they certainly praised every little effort made by her sister), she had to believe, then, that she was just born smart—that her being smart wasn't due to any effort on her part, that when she got As, she was just lucky.

And, so, true to her acute sense of justice, she felt guilty for her good luck, guilty that she'd gotten extra IQ points, IQ points her sister should've gotten.

But years later, when she was helping her sister with the material in her Early Childhood Education program, as she went over, and over, the stages postulated by Piaget, she became convinced that her sister simply wasn't concentrating, she wasn't even *trying* to process the information, she wasn't *thinking*.

She realized then that she had spent more time, *far* more time, doing her homework than either her sister or her brother ever had. Her sister gave up as soon as she had trouble. She herself persisted. On one occasion, with her high school physics homework, until tears of frustration welled in her eyes. Her brother went to Florida with his friends on spring break. She herself caught up on the assigned reading and her term papers.

Lucky, my ass.

And fuck the guilt.

Is it any wonder she actually chided herself every time she wasn't interested in a man who had barely graduated from high school?

So startled by this new connection, she stopped paddling. Think you're smarter than him? she remembered scolding herself. Think you're too good for him?

But then her mother called her a slut. Because she'd have sex with anyone.

She stared at the water rushing by. She'd come back to that.

Proclaiming everyone to be equal was also a middle class thing, she supposed, as she resumed paddling. And it was hard to argue with democracy.

And yet she did. Years later. When she realized it simply ensured a tyranny of the masses—the average, the ordinary, the unthinking. People like her brother and sister, people like her parents.

Because deep down, she *did* think she was better than everyone else. She couldn't ignore the evidence. She was the smartest kid she knew. And she didn't know anyone else who was an accomplished pianist, who'd had poetry published in a magazine, and who could run five miles in thirty-five minutes.

The sound of rapids broke into her thoughts. She looked ahead and saw that there was no paddling around them. The water level was too low. And it would be a lot of work to walk her kayak through them. No telling how far she could go once she was on the other side before a fallen tree blocked her way. Maybe another day, she'd find out. For now, she nudged her kayak into a patch of weeds and just sat for a while, listening. Such a pretty sound, the water pouring over the rocks, bubbling into below.

How did she reconcile having such a low opinion of herself and, simultaneously, such a high opinion of herself? She'd never noticed the contradiction before.

Ah. She wasn't better than *everyone* else. She was just better than all the *girls* she knew.

But then she would've had to have thought that the average man was, somehow, better than even the best woman. Which, she realized, was exactly what she had thought. It went without saying. All her life, growing up, it went without saying. Men were better than women; all men were better than all women. It was such a given, she didn't even *see* all the overwhelming evidence to the contrary until she was in her thirties.

So how did she reconcile the fact that she was the smartest kid in the class, the one who always got As, with the belief that a full half of the class, the boys, were all better than her? She didn't know. It didn't create any cognitive dissonance. At the time.

Most likely she assumed she must be missing something. She must be too stupid to see their superiority. It must be evident in areas closed off to her.

Imagine her rage when she discovered the truth.

. . .

After she'd returned and had a slice of the large pizza she'd brought with her, she saw that there was a fishing boat parked about twenty feet away from the dock, so she settled into one of the chairs up on the deck. It had a different, but just as pleasing, view. Less water, more curtain of trees, and the eye was drawn down rather than across. She opened the journal and continued reading through her life.

She didn't remember her mother, or her father, ever reading to her at bedtime. Which is probably just as well. It's an appalling thing to do to a kid: condition them to associate reading a book with falling asleep.

She also couldn't remember even one time she was comforted or soothed by her mother. Or her father. Not when she wasn't allowed to play Red Rover with the grade fives, not when she didn't make the basketball team in grade twelve, not when Scott dumped her, not when Craig didn't write back.

Well, they probably didn't even know about the last two. They took such little interest in her life.

They never hugged her.

The only touch she knew was sexual.

So no wonder—

She did remember that when they went to Church on Sunday, her brother led the way (of course), her sister followed next, and though sometimes she walked with her sister, other times she was just so happy—Sundays, going to Church, she felt the goodness of it all deep within her core—she insisted on walking between her parents, holding onto their hands and swinging between them, one giant step to their two steps. But she realized, even then, that she had to insist on doing that. They didn't offer to swing her, and they didn't seem to enjoy it. They tolerated her.

She learned she was someone who was tolerated.

Not someone whose company another person might actually enjoy.

Nor does she remember one serious conversation with her parents. Time to set the table, time for supper, what are you watching, time for bed … Nothing but daily trivia.

She turned the page.

> four grown human beings
> each half a lifetime used
> sit around the table;
> playing their new game of
> Triple Yahtzee
> because it's Christmas;
> triple strategy
> triple excitement
> triple fun;
> it says so on the box.
>
> they sit
> passing the bright shaker of dice;
> talking seriously
> knowingly
> of the best way to win;
> it matters.
>
> the properly-dressed woman of forty-five
> yells "Yahtzee!" in glee
> when the dice fall right;
> she carefully counts and
> records her score;
> she's happy now.
>
> she turns to me and boasts
> "I've had three Yahtzees this game!"
> and i almost answer
> i'm proud of you mom—
> but i bite my tongue,
> and my heart bleeds.

Whenever she approached her parents, about anything, they didn't want to discuss it, they didn't want to argue, they said.

To someone for whom discussion was lifeblood.

Or would be if she'd ever had someone to discuss things with.

And she wanted to discuss everything. But whenever they did discuss something, she'd end up hurting them.

How discussion could hurt someone, she never did figure out. Were they hurt by the mere fact of someone disagreeing with them?

Oh my.

No wonder she clung to the first person she met who *was* willing to discuss stuff. Her letters to Craig would eventually become forty pages long.

Later, her parents explained, "It's impossible to win with you."

She didn't understand why her ability to deal with all of their objections, her ability to have a stronger counterargument, would upset them. Wouldn't they be pleased? Maybe even proud?

It would be twenty years before she stopped accepting all of their admonitions: "You think too much," "You're overanalyzing it," "You always have to go too deep," "You're too sensitive."

No. You don't think enough. You don't analyze enough. You're too superficial.

And you're not, not nearly, sensitive enough.

Of course her parents never asked about her homework. The only time they showed any interest at all was when she'd mentioned the *Plain Truth* magazines of the Church of God that were appearing all over the city. She'd said she'd found the articles convincing. That is to say, she'd found their claims as convincing as those of the Roman Catholic church. Suddenly her father, pushed by her mother, set out to read the textbook for her grade twelve World Religions class.

But he never discussed it with her.

Years later, she realized he probably didn't understand any of it.

Which is probably why they were such ardent Catholics.

> nuns
> > habits of black and white
> explaining their faith

After her careful but unremarkable line of reasoning led her from Catholicism to Christianity, it led her on to theism, and from there, to atheism.

Unremarkable, but still, such a weight lifted when she realized there was simply no evidence, or lamentably insufficient evidence, for everything she'd believed about god and religion. She wasn't a sinner. She wasn't going to hell. She didn't have to believe "six impossible things before breakfast".

That oppression, at least, lifted.

One of the pictures in the living room, that she had to dust every Saturday, was of the four of them: her brother in his cub scout uniform, her father in his cub scout leader uniform, her sister in her brownie uniform, and her mother in her brownie leader uniform. She understood, cognitively, why she wasn't allowed to be in the picture. She wasn't a brownie, so she didn't have a uniform. And she understood, cognitively, why she wasn't allowed to join brownies. She had music and dance lessons. So she already had an activity. Two, in fact. They were already paying for not just one, but two, for her. But emotionally—couldn't they have let her be in the picture anyway?

You were only six, for godsake.

She remembered they'd said no.

She remembered having to stand off to the side all by herself.

She remembered crying herself to sleep that night.

Now, of course, she was glad, so very glad, not to be part of that family. She was an artist, an intellect, an athlete. A poet and a philosopher. A composer.

Not an office worker.

And yet, despite everything, she'd believed her parents did their duty as parents. They did what they were supposed to do. You couldn't fault them there.

She doesn't believe that now. She's raised her standards for parenting. It is, after all, a completely voluntary endeavour. And such a very, very important one.

She closed the journal, then watched twilight become dusk become night.

5

It rained the next day, so she curled up on the couch with the next journal and her tea, opening the windows so she could hear patter on the leaves.

Part way through high school, her parents decided to stop renting out the rooms in the attic. They suggested that she could have one of them. But she'd have to clean it first.

Three hours later, she had a room of her own. She was thrilled.

It had a large oak table she'd cleaned, waxed, and polished, then moved into the corner. She put all of the chairs but one into the other room, then covered the walls around the table, the desk, with cork billboard.

She sat at the desk, her desk now, six neat piles on the scrubbed linoleum floor beside her, one for each of her courses. Pen, paper, typewriter on the desk. Turntable and records in the corner by the old chesterfield. It was all she needed.

Every day after school, she'd get an oversized glass of milk—she used the brown plastic milkshake shaker that had come with the Nestlé Quik one year—and go up to the attic, not coming down until she was called to set the table for dinner. Then, after she'd spent an hour with her piano in the basement, and half an hour with her dance lesson, also in the basement, she went back up to the attic to work until she went to bed.

She loved it.

She loved being so far away from them. From their chatter, which was like radio static, sound with no meaning. From their very presence, which was a constant reminder of—deep mutual disappointment.

But "Come watch tv with us," her mother would plead from time to time.

She wasn't interested in watching *Mannix*.

And she hated it when they watched *All in the Family*. Her father laughed with Archie at Meathead and Gloria.

Which is worse, she wondered, that he didn't know or that he did? That she was Meathead. And Gloria.

And he was—he was Archie Bunker.

It would be one of the first times she was overwhelmed with inadequacy. Where to begin? To explain to him that he was—that everything Archie Bunker was—

She tried. And failed. And tried again. And failed again.

If she couldn't change her own father, if she couldn't make *him* see, how could she ever hope to change the world?

Every time he laughed at something Meathead or Gloria said, something perfectly reasonable, something important, about capitalism or pollution or equal opportunity for women, she screamed inside.

Then cried.

No wonder she'd put up a wall.

Without it, she would've been crippled with pain.

And anger.

> i wake.
> the sky is like soiled snow at a spring sewer.
> there are tears in the air.
> every morning we leave the house
> they go to work, i go to school.
> we walk along streets
> hearing the ebb and wash of the tide of traffic

as it sterilizes the pavement with carbon monoxide.
they go to buildings
that do not scrape the smog from the sky.
i go to a displeasing dome
by dubious decree.

and i remember
sitting in class
my gaze caught upon a cocoon
up where the ceiling is seamed
so pure and white
i felt its rough softness with my eyes
and when i saw it i dreamed
perhaps i will see
the butterfly burst out.

i listen to music
upstairs in an attic
that is my room of my own now
Beethoven boasts his beating heart and
Springsteen makes me move and
no one tells me turn it down.

last night, i listened to a song called "Sunrise"
the first few bars so wakened into glory—
in the morning, this morning
i rose
and bicycled six miles out of the city,
i saw gossamer glistening,
in the silver mist,
crystal veins dripping opal,
and as i sat in an open field,
i saw the sun rise!

and i thought,
                i feel
therefore i am.

> *i remember hope and i remember despair*
> *but i forget*
> *which is the key for life—*

Years later, reading *This Magazine, Kick It Over,* and *off our backs,* she discovered there were names for what she was. Social activist. Environmentalist. Feminist. Civil libertarian. Anarchist. Although it was sad, because she'd been trudging along, alone, in the soft, sucking sand, inventing the wheel when there were highways just a few miles away, it was also refreshing. To come upon a veritable oasis of kin.

But they were out of reach. They were theoretical kin. None of her friends—well, she didn't often have friends. Not really.

When she was at St. Louis, it was decided that she could 'accelerate': she was told she could finish the grade five textbooks over the holidays and then, in January, join the grade six class.

The grade six teacher welcomed her and showed her to her new desk, but she knew she wasn't really supposed to be there. She felt like she didn't belong. Again.

It was a feeling that would accompany her throughout her life.

But that wasn't all. Suddenly her best friends, Julie and Joanne, were no longer her best friends. She wasn't even allowed to play with them anymore at recess. She still remembered that first day, in January, going out at recess to join the Red Rover as she had always done—and being told she couldn't anymore, because the Red Rover was just for the grade fives.

And the grade sixes didn't play Red Rover. Well, the boys did; the girls just watched.

She ended up making snow castles with some of the grade four kids.

And so she continued to feel different, to feel like an outsider. That was bad enough. She would never feel part of a group, part of a team.

But the grade six kids were as ordinary as the grade five kids. They were just doing different stuff. So, also, she continued to feel felt smarter than everyone else. And she was right. She *was* smarter than everyone else. Everyone else she *knew*.

If she'd had the chance to be in an enriched class (St. Louis had only a 'special ed' class), she would have found herself in a room full of kids as eager as her and as smart as her, kids with whom she could've been herself, without fear of reprimand for showing off or standing out. It would've changed everything. Her entire view. Her entire life.

Because as it was, she would never feel like she could ask anyone for help. And expect them to be able to give it.

Worse, when she finally met people who *were* smarter than her, it would always take too long for her to recognize that. To recognize that she could learn from them. Even if she didn't ask for their help.

Asking for their friendship wouldn't even occur to her.

In grade nine, she became part of a group of friends again, Lisa, Colleen, and Sandy. And that might have developed into something. Something normal. But then a new high school opened up and all three of them, because of where they lived, were transferred to it, so in grade ten, she was, once again, friendless.

She became friends with Heidi then, who was, like her, a 'brain' and an athlete.

Friends? She realized now that she really didn't know how to 'be friends'. Heidi was just the person she hung around with during the school day, if they were in the same class or had lunch during the same period, and after school, if they had basketball, gymnastics, or track practice.

They never did anything together outside of school. Partly, she was too busy: she spent several hours each night doing her homework; by grade ten, she was up to an hour a day piano practice, and by grade thirteen, an hour and a half; and she was taking not only jazz lessons by then, but also ballet and modern, intending to take her Associate's exam; during the week she had cross-country and field hockey practice to go to or, later in the year, basketball, and then track; and on the weekends, and some after-schools, she had gymnastics, and a part-time job typing and filing at the insurance company her mother worked at.

In fact, she was so busy, so focused on her schedule, that one day—she remembered this with such guilt—while rushing to get to a class, or a lesson, or her job, on time, she saw a little girl who, while crossing a side street ahead of her, dropped a bag of pennies halfway across. The little girl wisely, or fearfully, didn't stop to pick them up. But once safely on the other side of the road, she broke into a wail and just stood there, helpless. She knew she shouldn't dare go back into the middle of the road and pick them up, but—

And she, the adult-enough who could have easily, safely, gone back and picked up the pennies for her, every last one of them, did not stop to do so. She just walked by. Left the little girl crying on the corner.

(Years later, she would atone, once stopping on a winter's run to push a stuck wheelchair-bound man up a ramp, another time simply picking up a child frozen with fear at the top of a crowded escalator, his mother, encumbered with baby and stroller, anxiously beckoning him from the bottom, and riding down with him.)

But, she wondered now, was it because she was so focused on her schedule or was it because she'd never seen anyone ever do something like that? She had no role models for stopping to help someone. Certainly she'd never seen her parents do anything like that. They always minded their own business.

And already you were rejecting motherliness. Though you couldn't articulate why, exactly.

The other reason she and Heidi never did anything outside of school was that she didn't know how to initiate such a thing. It never occurred to her to ask for Heidi's phone number. What would she do with it? Neither she nor Heidi were ever invited anywhere on Friday nights, so it's not like they could go to parties together. Neither of them liked shopping; they didn't want to hang out at the mall on Saturdays. Besides, she was saving her money for university. She didn't need any help with her homework. Practicing the piano wasn't something you needed a friend for. She supposed they could watch tv together, but what would be the point of that? And Heidi didn't seem to be the type to want to discuss things; she was into maths and sciences.

What else did one do with one's friends? She honestly didn't know.

She still doesn't, really.

But mostly, it just didn't occur to her to initiate anything with Heidi outside of school. That would have required an act of imagination. Not just imitation.

Because she didn't recall her parents ever going out with friends or having people over to the house. Or her sister. She didn't know how her brother managed it. And she certainly couldn't ask him.

All of which meant that she never had the opportunity to learn the norms of social interaction that would make such things easy.

Years later, when she moved, and some guys helped her unload, she didn't realize that she should have said thank you not just with words, but with a case of beer. She didn't drink beer. She'd never bought a case of beer in her life. She wouldn't even know how. So it just didn't occur to her. The men thought she was ungrateful.

And when, once, she was invited to someone's house for dinner, she had no idea she should have taken a bottle of wine.

• • •

It was still raining, so she decided to go for a walk in the rain. In the forest. It would be lovely.

She took off her glasses off and put in her contacts. They were old, prescription-wise, but they'd do. Actually, she'd see better in the rain with them than with her glasses streaming wet.

Back in grade seven, when she'd first put on her brand new glasses, she was amazed. She could see all the individual leaves on the trees. Before that, trees were just clumps of green fuzz.

But what really stopped her was what happened when she went to the tuck shop after lunch. For the first time, she could see the individual chocolate bars on display behind the counter. *That's* how everyone else always knew exactly what to ask for!

Years later, she realized that because of her myopia, she'd developed a habit of not looking very far around her. Why would she, since it was all out of focus? She'd developed a sort of tunnel vision, which would persist well into her forties.

In class, she saw the student sitting in front of her and the ones on either side of her, but that was it. She didn't see anyone else. (She wasn't supposed to turn around, so she didn't.) So her friends were, or were not, those three girls. If they were boys, she was out of luck.

When she played the piano at recitals, she literally did not see beyond the edge of the piano. Surely that had exacerbated her performance anxiety.

When she entered a strange building, she never took in much beyond ten yards. No wonder she got lost so often. No wonder new places were intimidating.

The physical reality became a social habit. She simply didn't consider what she couldn't see.

And it became a hopeless circle. She remained intensely shy, unable to socialize, because she couldn't 'see' others—and she couldn't 'see' others because she remained intensely shy, unable to socialize.

And no wonder she never saw the big picture. She would never develop control over the big picture of her life.

• • •

When she got back—and it had indeed been lovely, walking along the logging road, forest on either side, inhaling the damp and stretching out her hands to the dripping—she brought in some kindling and chunks of wood from the adjoining lean-to, made a fire, then curled up on the couch again, which yes, provided a fine view of the fire. She stared at it for a while. The flames didn't sparkle, but there was something similarly mesmerizing, similarly beautiful …

One day, out of the blue, Rick Bruendel, a boy who had been in the same grade at St. Louis, and then a grade behind her at St. David's, called her for a blind date. For his brother Arnold. He was going to be honoured at some banquet and would she like to be his date? She was flattered. Pathetic as that was.

Such a neat trick, she thought, gazing into the fire. Make all women feel inferior to all men, and any woman will feel honoured to be chosen—by any man. For anything.

She was also excited. A boy had called her for a date! Her first date! She was sixteen. It didn't matter that she had never talked to Rick. All she knew, really, was that he had several brothers. About six of them. Arnold was the oldest, she thought.

Her parents thought it would be okay. Her father vaguely knew of the Bruendel boys; they all worked at their father's plumbing shop.

Several of them arrived in a car to pick her up, and they drove in silence to a rented hall somewhere.

After they checked their coats, Arnold took her arm and walked into the banquet room with her at his side. He pulled out a chair for her, she sat down, and—that was the end of it. No one talked to her. For most of the night, they were off talking among themselves. And she was too shy, too confused, to initiate a conversation. Besides, her mother had warned her not to let her intelligence show. As if it were some unwritten rule for dating.

If men are so superior, why are their egos so fragile?

And what about your *fucking ego?*

So she just sat there. Ignored. All night.

No, that's not quite true, she remembered now. They did dance, once. Arnold took her hand, led her to the middle of the room, then turned her around and around while he pumped her arm up and down until the song ended. Then they sat back down.

She supposed she should smile. But she couldn't figure out at what. So she didn't.

She supposed she should be grateful. To have been asked to be his date. Sad thing was, she was.

You wouldn't think it possible for someone so shy feel any more awkward. No wonder she didn't ever again want to go to dinners, or dances, or parties, or any so-called social events. They just shone a spotlight on her social ineptitude.

Not once did he really acknowledge her. It was like he didn't even consider her a person. He didn't care what she thought. About anything. She was just this … thing. A body to fill the space beside him.

And despite her intelligence, it would take her several decades to realize—no, to accept—that that's how it was. How it always had been. And how it always would be.

At the end of the night, the boys pulled up in front of her house again and sat in silence while she opened the car door and got out. And then they drove away.

Years later, she realized they must have chosen her in some way. Chosen the girl least likely to say no, the one most desperate. She was humiliated. Years later.

The upside to social cluelessness.

Why didn't her parents say anything? Why didn't they stop her? Tell her that he just wanted to use her. That he wasn't interested in her at all. Were they as clueless?

Or did they think it was all very … appropriate?

That would be her only date during all of high school.

And yet of course she wanted a boyfriend. How could she not when every song every single song on the radio glorified having a boyfriend. Apparently, it was the best. And essential.

She never really understood why no one ever asked her out. She was attractive enough. And she was smart, she was artistic, she was athletic—

And all of that was why.

There were several boys she liked. At least, she liked the way they looked. She didn't know anything about them. She didn't know them. She never spoke to them. You just didn't.

Or at least she didn't. She couldn't just go up to a boy and start a conversation. She couldn't even do that to a girl. It's a wonder she had any friends at all. If the teachers had never put them in groups for various projects, she probably wouldn't've.

Boys were … out of bounds. Her brother never talked to her. Nor she to him. Her father never talked to her. Nor she to him. Boys hung out with other boys, girls hung out with other girls. In the cafeteria, boys sat on one side, girls sat on the other.

Who needs the Jewish mechitza? Or the Islamic rule about walking ten paces behind?

Unless of course you were married. Then that woman and that man could talk to each other. But the woman couldn't really talk to another man, unless her husband was present, nor could the man talk to another woman, unless his wife was present. It had to be the one couple talking to the other couple. Even then, the man generally directed his comments to the other man. Ditto, the women. That's how it was. How it is.

So she never spoke to the boys she longed for from afar.

And she didn't know how to show her interest without coming right out and saying—what? I like you? I'd like to get to know you? I'd like to become friends with you?

She certainly didn't flirt. Only bad girls flirted. That was teasing. In any case, flirting required talking to them. Or glances of a certain kind. Which she knew nothing about.

So instead she pined from a distance for boys who never even knew her name.

So why would any boy ask her out on a date?

Years later, she realized that most girls got asked out on a date after several group dates, occasions on which a bunch of girls and a bunch of boys hung out together. On these occasions, one particular boy might spend a bit more time with one particular girl, so after a few weeks, or months, it would be no big deal for that boy to call that girl. And ask her out on a just-the-two-of-them date. So she had been at a disadvantage, not being part of a group of girls that hung out with groups of boys.

Of course another way a boy and girl might end up dating is if they met at a party. Sort of the like the group date thing. But she was never invited to any parties. How would that have happened? She didn't know.

Not every girl gets asked to the prom.

The fire had burned down to embers, so she put in another couple chunks of wood. And made a note to herself to see if the hardware store had those packets that, when you tossed them onto a fire, made the flames multi-coloured. She'd have to drive into town at some point anyway, for another pizza and more half-and-half.

The typing and filing job at the insurance office where her mom worked was her first job. She was sixteen, it was an after-school part-time job, and although it paid only minimum wage, because of it, she was able to pay for her piano lessons and music books (which her parents had stopped paying for once she had a job), her dance lessons, her school books (in grade thirteen, they had to buy their own books), her track shoes, a pair of jeans, and a few shirts; she put the rest aside for first year tuition, hoping she'd have enough in two years.

But she hated it. Specifically, she hated the people. With their small little lives, the women talking on and on in the cramped little lunch room about dieting, everyone all excited when it was Friday, then all subdued come Monday, and endlessly anxious every day in between about whether the renewal policies would get out in time …

The actual typing and filing, she didn't mind. She was quick and efficient. And it was certainly better than being a waitress or working in a factory. The ability, let alone the desire, to wait on people with a smile was *not* an innate female characteristic, and the noise and fumes, not to mention the relentless repetition, of factory work would have made her ill.

She actually liked the attention to detail that her office duties required. Typing was a little like playing the piano. And filing was organization embodied.

But it was a mistake. Perhaps the first of a life full of You-can't-get-there-from-heres. She should've been an intern at *Ms.* Not a file clerk. But of course that wasn't an option in Waterloo. Or if it was, she certainly didn't know about it.

At the very least, she should've been a file clerk at a law office, not an insurance office.

But she was so grateful for what she got, she never thought to ask for more. Or different.

That was the way of her life.

The winter her brother went to Daytona Beach with his friends—

It was her father's "contribution" to his education, giving him the money for a little fun since he was working so hard.

He offered no similar contribution to her education.

Instead, once, during midterms, he helped her with the dishes.

She asked him, much later, why he didn't give her money for a similar bit of fun, because she too was working hard, but he just shrugged.

So she offered an explanation, her take on the matter, an exposé of his unexamined sexism, perhaps inherited from his own father, and was shocked by the vehemence of his response. "Oh now you're going to psychoanalyze me?!" he'd all but shouted at her.

Well someone had to.

Because you sure as hell didn't.

It wouldn't be her last encounter with the male refusal to develop any kind of self-knowledge.

The winter her brother went to Daytona, she took over his snow shovelling job. Without fail, everyone who saw her expressed surprise. By that time, she was doing one or two gruelling track work-outs a day, weight-lifting three times a week, and coaching gymnastics on Saturday mornings. But she couldn't lift a shovel full of snow? How insulting.

But what really made her angry was the discovery that he made twice as much shovelling snow as she did typing and filing.

"Well, it's outdoors. It's cold."

"So?"

She wanted to point out that at the office, the windows didn't open, so there was no fresh air. In the filing room, there weren't even windows. So you couldn't even *see* the outside.

But there was no point. She understood, on some unconscious level, that being outdoors in the cold wasn't the real reason for the higher pay.

And yet, her parents provided interest-free loans to him for his tuition year after year.

No such provisions were made to her.

To whom much is given, more is given.

There were so many more women than men in the office: Carolyn was on switchboard; Irene and another half dozen were the typing pool; Deb and Jennifer were in Accounts; Ruth was in Claims; her mother and Arlene were secretaries for Mr. Riley, the vice-president; Eileen and Georgette were secretaries for Mr. Peterson, the president. And yet the men ruled the place. Mr. Peterson, Mr. Riley, Mr. Eddy, who was Head of Claims, and all of the agents, who were all men, worked on the second floor. The women, all on the first floor, lived to please them.

Her father also worked at an insurance company. He was an accountant—

No, she realized just now, that can't have been right. That was probably just more of his 'loose talk', his lies. An accountant? With just a grade twelve education? And the stress he'd experience every year when he did the family income tax? She'd see the damp stains spreading under his arms … He was probably just one of the company's adding machine operators.

But her aunt—the summer she worked with her aunt, a whole new world opened up for her. It was the summer just before she started university. Her aunt was a manager at a small television station, and would she like a job as her personal assistant that summer? *Would* she?!

Over the course of the summer, she got to see how things were run. She went with her aunt to meetings with the City Council, the Chamber of Commerce, the

Rotary Club, and the Lions Club. She sat in on production meetings and helped schedule the various work streams so everything was coordinated. And saw, in the process, a number of jobs that were far more attractive than typing and filing. She was even allowed in the booth during a taping to watch the director direct the show.

Most important, she saw that anyone could get a tv show. People could come in with just an idea. No experience or anything. She listened to them pitch their idea, often badly, she thought, but then her aunt and various other people on the staff would work with them to develop the show, provide the graphics, and make it happen.

Which meant that later, once she'd graduated, *she* would pitch a show and—

Her aunt worked at the meat factory. On an assembly line. Stuffing wieners.

6

Next day, Tuesday, it was quiet again. All the people who had been up for the long weekend had gone home. It was also sunny again, so she took the next journal, and another excellent cup of tea, down to the water again. Before opening it, she just sat for a while looking out at the twinkling water, sipping her tea, contentment suffusing through her.

Eventually, she turned to the first page.

She'd agonized over what to take at university. Philosophy, certainly, and since she wanted to be a writer, English. That would also enable her to become a high school English teacher, part-time, so she could write. Teaching was the only job she knew that would pay enough part-time.

But she also wanted to change the world and had this idea not only that teachers were agents of social change, but that philosophy should be a high school course. (She had no idea that it already was in some countries.) She wanted to make that happen, somehow. If only people would think, she thought, the world would be a better place. Her writing too was intended to make a difference.

An A+ male student probably would have been told he was throwing his life away if he decided to become a high school teacher. But in her case, everyone seemed to approve.

She was also interested in Psychology. And of course Music. She'd also considered Social Work, Dance, and Kinesiology. Eventually she decided on a double major in Honours Philosophy and English Lit, with a minor in Psychology. She could continue her music and dance studies privately. Teaching would be her social work. And she'd keep running in any case. That way she could have it all.

She couldn't wait.

Of course her mother disapproved. Philosophy wasn't practical.

She loved books so much, she should become a librarian, her mother had said. But the very idea appalled her. Librarians were so prim and proper. That wasn't her at all! Didn't her mother see that? No. Like so many parents, she wanted to make her daughter in her own image.

The hubris.

Fortunately her high school guidance counsellor had a different opinion. "The University of Toronto has a good philosophy program," she said, "and with marks in the 90s, you're sure to get a scholarship. Actually …," she looked at her file, "with an average of 93% … and your sports activities … and oh my, you're president of Charitas, member of the Writer's Club—" She looked up at her, smiling. "Let me make some inquiries. You'll have to take the SAT," she continued, thinking out loud, "but that shouldn't be a problem … How would you like to go to Harvard? They'll love you."

She practically bounced down the hall, repeating to herself what the counsellor had said. "They'll love you." Harvard would love her! *Harvard!*

Everything changed when she went to Harvard. She met people as excited by the intellectual as she was. And as creative. It seemed everyone in her class at Harvard was a musician or an athlete. Or a chess champion or—

They got it. They got her.

She could learn from them. She could learn so much from them.

Everything *could've* changed.

Because what the counsellor actually said was "Philosophy is very difficult. " To the girl who'd gotten the highest marks in the school. Student body of 1,500.

She wondered, of course, if Mrs. Ellison would've said that if she'd been the boy with the highest marks.

Yes, they had separate categories.

She supposed that answered her question.

It also explained why fraternities at Harvard might, like those at Yale, chant "No means yes! Yes means anal!"

So, she realized, with a deep sigh, staring out at the water, nothing would've changed if she'd gone to Harvard.

Quite apart from the fact that Harvard makes politicians. *Oxford* makes philosophers.

And the fact that Harvard didn't become officially integrated until 1977, two years *later*.

She went to Wilfrid Laurier University. It was in her home town, which meant she wouldn't have to work another twenty hours a week to pay for rent and food; she could continue to live at home—her parents had said that she didn't have to pay room and board as long as she was going to school. She was grateful.

She didn't realize, of course, that many parents paid for their kid's room and board, for a dorm room, at a university away. *As well as* for their tuition and books.

She also chose WLU because her brother went there. And that was comforting.

God knows why. Given his total lack of acknowledgement of your existence.

And she chose WLU because UW, the other university in town, was much larger and therefore more intimidating. She had barely made it through her first day at the high school, she was so spatially-challenged, so easily disoriented. Years later, she realized that this was not only because of her tunnel vision, but also, perhaps even mostly, because she had never seen, had never been shown, a map of the school's layout. She'd never seen, had never been shown, a map of the city either. In fact, she didn't even know they existed. She'd seen only a highway map. It was in the glove compartment of the car. And only her father and brother were allowed to consult it.

Surely a metaphor.

Even so. She was thrilled to be going. To university! The ultimate intellectual institution! The place where people with fine minds hung out! People who were interested in ideas! There would be late night discussions about meaningful things—

Or not. No one in her classes seemed on fire for philosophy the way she was. Perhaps they were mostly General students. She didn't know. (The university was too small to have separate classes for its three-year General and four-year Honours programs.) She did know that once again she was not in the company of her peers.

She also knew that she was the only woman in the Philosophy program, Honours *and* General. Not only in her own year, but in the years immediately before and after her. For the entire four years, in all of her Philosophy classes, she saw only one other woman, Maureen, a general arts student who took Existentialism as an elective one year.

Certainly none of her Philosophy professors were women.

And, actually, now that she thought back, only one of her English professors was a woman.

Even so, her reading list was fascinating.

Though even there, she eventually realized—so few, so very few, of the authors were women.

But the library was huge! Three whole floors! She could spend days in it, wandering up and down the stacks. On several occasions, she did just that, simply pulling books out at random, amazed at what there was in the world.

There were bulletin boards full of notices about guest speakers, events, all sorts of things. She went to as many as she could.

The university had a well-developed music program, so there were weekly concerts, which she also went to. She'd never gone to a concert before. She'd never heard a live violin before. Or a cello …

She also went to her first dance performance. Her first theatre performance.

It was all so exciting! Her cup runneth over.

Shortly after the year began, the Philosophy Department had an informal gathering to welcome the new students. When she walked through the door of the two-storey brick house on a side street near the university, in which the Philosophy Department had its offices, she was bubbling with anticipation. People stood in small clusters talking, surely about intriguing philosophical problems. She approached one group, and the conversation stopped.

"Hi," she said to the group. "I'm Kris. First year."

A few of the men in the group mumbled their names. After a long awkward moment, she moved away from the group. And then heard the conversation resume.

She approached another group, this one containing one of her professors.

"You're forgetting that the correspondence theory isn't the only approach," someone said. "And given our inability to apprehend the nature of reality, my vote goes to the coherence theory."

They were talking about theories of truth. It was what Professor Mauritz had talked about that day in class.

"But the coherence theory is like a house of cards," she offered to the group. "Something might fit with all the rest, but what if all the rest is false?"

There was a silence. Surely they understood what she'd said. She looked from one to the other. Their faces were blank. What social gaffe had she committed, she wondered.

Dr. Mauritz spoke then. "Welcome, to our group. Kris, isn't it?" He leaned in to look at her name tag. "Would you like a glass of wine?"

"Yes, thank you," she said politely, as he reached around to the table and handed her one of several waiting glasses.

"I mean, if the rest *is* false—" she tried to resume the conversation.

"So, Kris, tell us a little about yourself," Dr. Mauritz smiled.

She received As on her papers, of course, but her brother mocked her achievement. Philosophy was useless, a bird course. Anyone could get As in Philosophy.

But she knew that wasn't true. Philosophy wasn't easier than Business; it was harder. Much harder. But what could she say in her defence? She didn't have the stats to support her belief.

Not that that would have mattered.

Years later, she would read that Philosophy students obtained the highest GRE scores. They were most able to handle abstract reasoning, most competent at the higher cognitive levels.

The Honours English program required that she take a foreign language, and since she'd taken French in high school, every year, she thought she'd take Latin instead (the only other option). Unfortunately it was offered at the same time as the first year Honours English course, ENG190. But the Dean, who was her advisor, said that that was no problem; she could take the General English course, ENG220, in her first year, then just continue on in the Honours stream in her second year.

When Dr. O'Reilly, the ENG220 prof, kindly took her aside near the end of the year to tell her that he thought she could handle Honours English, she should be going for an Honours degree, she was surprised. She told him she was. She *was* in Honours English. Of course she was an Honours student!

It was a small university. She had assumed the Dean would have sent some sort of letter informing her professors that even though she was in ENG220, she was an Honours student. Or that there would be some sort of list of incoming Honours English students, and she would be on it.

Apparently he didn't. And there wasn't.

So for four years, she was regarded by all of her professors as a General student who had stepped up into the Honours program. So of course they didn't expect her to get any A+s. A-s maybe. Perhaps the occasional, startling, A.

And we all know what Rosenthal and Jacobson demonstrated about teachers' expectations.

Also consequently, by the time she got into the Honours class, in her second year, she was an outsider. All of the students knew each other from having been together the year before.

So no wonder she sat at the back of the class. Unfortunately, it became a habit.

On top of which, she never felt confident enough to sit in the middle. And she certainly didn't feel like she deserved to sit at the front of the class.

In her fourth year, someone remarked about it, remembering one of the third year classes they'd both been in. "You always looked like you were just visiting, like you didn't really belong."

That's it exactly. She hadn't really belonged since grade five.

And so why would any of them engage with her? If she was just visiting …

But she made friends with Jen, one of the students in ENG220. She and Jen probably didn't have a lot in common, but their personalities meshed, and they got along well enough to go dancing at Jokers on an occasional Saturday night, and once a week they'd go up to the Student Union to shoot pool. Where the guys didn't know whether to hit on them or resent their presence. Mostly they did the latter, it turned out.

Hit on them. What a telling phrase.

They also played squash once a week. She liked playing squash with Jen. There was lots of hitting the ball, sometimes quickly, sometimes slowly, sometimes running for it, sometimes not. It was fun. So years later, when Craig asked her if she wanted to play, she said yes. But he constantly hit the ball into the most awkward, impossible places for her to get to. Whenever *she* hit the ball, she carefully made sure he could hit it back. When she finally realized that he was doing what he was doing *on purpose,* her appraisal of him went from incompetent to inconsiderate.

And she was angry. She'd thought that if you lose, you should lose because you're not as good, because your hand-eye coordination isn't as precise, because you're not as strong, because you're not as fast. Not because the other person intentionally made it difficult for you to be good. Competition for her was simple comparison. Not strategic sabotage.

Was this another gender difference?

Duh.

So even when women do *compete, they don't stand a chance. Not against men who'd been doing it, and doing it* that way, *since birth.*

Some time later, when Jen tried to set her up with Carl, one of her boyfriend's friends, both of whom were in Business, she suddenly realized—well no, she'd realized it before, but she hadn't fully understood the implications: WLU specialized in Business. Which meant it couldn't've been a worse choice for her.

But UW was her only other option, and it specialized in Engineering.

She should have gone to the University of Toronto. Why didn't anyone, especially one of her English teachers, insist she at least *apply* to the University of Toronto? She might have gotten a scholarship, one that might have covered the additional expenses.

But no, if going to UW would have been intimidating, going to UT would have been out of the question. She'd been to Toronto only twice, when her family went to Square One for a day of shopping. They'd acted like it was a trip to the moon, instead of just an hour and a half's drive.

And she must have thought—yes, she knew she did—that it didn't really matter. Wouldn't she get a good education regardless? Didn't that depend on the course material and the professors? And wouldn't the course material be pretty standard and couldn't excellent professors be anywhere?

She didn't even *consider* status. She didn't consider whether going to WLU would put her one up or one down. She didn't know that which university you went to could *do* that.

After marking her spot in the journal, she closed it. Then carried it and her empty cup back up to the cottage. She filled an empty water bottle with juice, poured some trail mix into a little plastic bag, and went out onto the lake. And thought about nothing for two hours, lulled by the rhythmic sound of her paddle in the water, the sparkles on the water, the breeze rustling through the stiff weeds …

• • •

She returned in time to watch the light sweep slowly across the cove, then had a bite to eat, then decided to finish the journal before heading out again for the sunset.

Part way through her first year, still searching for, still hoping to find, kin among the slush of Business students, she'd thought that maybe all those exciting all-night discussions happened in the dorms. Which she couldn't afford.

Or maybe they happened in the cafeteria. But since she couldn't afford lunch in a cafeteria, she never went there. She didn't even actually know how to get food, or a drink, in the cafeteria. All through high school, she'd brought her lunch to school. She didn't know that you went to one end, got a tray, and cutlery, then walked along and either asked for what you wanted, or helped yourself, and then paid at the other end. She'd never actually watched how people did it. They were always too far away to be in her myopic field of vision.

'Going to the pub for a beer' was similarly unknown to her. Since she couldn't afford beer, and in any case didn't like it, she'd never gone. And she did know it would be weird if she just walked in and sat down at a table by herself.

Besides which, she didn't have time to go to the cafeteria or the pub after class. As soon as she'd obtained her grade eight piano, at sixteen, she'd started giving piano lessons. She liked it. At least she thought she did. By the time she started university, she had a roster of about fifteen music students, in addition to her three hours of practice a day. She also taught some dance classes at the studio where she was herself taking lessons, and she coached gymnastics Saturday mornings. And the local Parks and Rec ran several youth drop-in centers during the summer, full-time, and again during the year, on Friday nights and Sunday afternoons. She'd been hired as a leader for the summer, then, much to her pleasure, been kept on during the school year.

So her daily schedule was something more or less like this:

> 7:00 get up
> 7:30 bike to … (or, in winter, run to …)
> 8:00 piano lesson
> 8:30 bike/run to the university, shower, and change
> 9:00 History of the Novel class
> 10:00 Milton class
> 11:00 library to work on term papers
> 1:00 Ethics class
> 2:00 bike/run to…
> 2:30 dance lesson
> 3:15 Jazz I class
> 4:00 Jazz II class
> 4:45 bike/run home
> 5:00 piano lesson – Andrew
> 5:30 piano lesson – Laura
> 6:00 practice (piano)
> 6:30 bike/run to …
> 7:00 drop-in
> 9:00 bike/run home
> 9:30 practice (piano)
> 11:00 course reading, term papers, etc
> 3:00 sleep

There were never enough hours in a day. Then.

Now, well, now there were too many. *Not* right *now, not here*, she smiled, watching the fluorescent green make its way across the cove, but back—no, it wasn't home—her room above the hairdresser's beside the railway tracks wasn't home, wasn't—

It was hard, those years at university, with that schedule, every day—but she loved it. All of it.

Perhaps the drop-in job most of all. The program had access to a large room and the gym at the rec center, so she spent the time playing ping pong with the guys, or basketball, or just sitting around, talking, just hanging out.

She'd never 'hung out' before.

Her mother didn't approve, of course. She didn't like her associating with 'kids like that'. She especially didn't approve when, a couple years later, she became a volunteer probation officer.

And yet when her brother became a Big Brother, he was commended.

Of course he was.

But, she realized, just as the cove lost the last of its light, if she'd had a family, or a friend, who *did* listen, understand, support, encourage what she did, what she was, she never would've become a writer. The need to express, to let it out, to get it out, to work through it all—that would have been satisfied with conversation.

Part way through that first year, she had discovered that there was a Philosophy Club—*there's* where she could have late night discussions about meaningful things! But she had been disappointed to find, once again, just a few guys in the room. They became silent when she entered. And remained silent until she left.

So she had discussions with herself, inside her head, non-stop, developing a sort of alterego. Alongside the notes she took in class, she scribbled reactions, responses, to Plato, Bentham, Kant, beginnings, middles, and ends of poems and stories, what would Milton's daughters think of that arrangement, ideas for essays, what did it really mean to have 'power over', ideas for books even, was free will a matter of degree, lines of melody to be developed at some later time, ideas for new pieces, a setting of Keats' *Ode to Psyche*—all of it was crammed into the margins in writing so small it was barely legible, but one idea led to another and another and the available space kept getting smaller and smaller—

Confined to the margins. Marginalized.

And every night she would transfer the bits and pieces into her journal every night. The very one she had in her hands.

She turned the page and saw another finished, neatly typed poem from that time.

(for my brother)

I

with a grunt of irritation
you condescend to be interrupted
and move your chair back a bit
so i can crawl
under your desk
(the one dad built special for you
now that you're at university)
so i can dust the baseboards
as is my job
(i've already done the rest of your room)

i'm quiet
careful not to disturb
because it's hard stuff, important stuff
you're doing
(i'm still only in high school
but you're at university now
it must be harder
you're getting only 60s)
i turn around in the cramped space
on my hands and knees
and see your feet

i think about washing them

i think about binding them

II

the guidance counsellor pauses
then discourages
"philosophy's a very difficult field"
and i thought
(no, not then, later)
i thought, she's telling the kid
who has the top marks in the school

it's too difficult?

III

it's true
i just find it easier
besides, compared to business
philosophy is such a bird course

no, that's a lie:
i'm smarter
and i work harder—
while you're out with your friends
friday nights
i'm at work
because *my* summer job didn't pay enough
to cover the whole year
and while you're watching tv
i'm at work
(at ten o'clock
after six hours of lectures
and just as many of typing and filing)
i move the set
so i can crawl
into the corner
to dust the baseboards
you lean and yell in irritation
because i'm in your way

because *i'm* in *your* way

7

It was another beautiful, beautiful day. The sun sparkling on the water, the gentle breeze, the quiet—she simply did not tire of it …

Just before her second year began, and quite unexpectedly, Craig contacted her. They'd been in a few classes together, and he'd also been on the Reach for the Top team, so they'd seen each other at a few practices and when they had competitions. She sort of liked the way he looked. His perpetually raised eyebrow indicated a certain inquisitiveness, an intelligence …

Jen saw a picture of Craig today. "His eyes" was all she said. Yes.

Her mother had said, seeing only his acne, "I wouldn't want to kiss a face like that."

He told her that he was going out west to attend UBC, in order to avoid having to take grade thirteen, which he thought would be a complete waste of time for him, and did she want to keep in touch? He said she inspired him to be better. To not be a screw up.

That should have been your first clue, she told herself.

Your second. The arrogance of assuming grade thirteen would have been a complete waste of time should have been your first.

She was flattered. And delighted. He was going to get a degree in Psychology, he'd told her, intending eventually a Ph.D. And he was a photographer. An intellect and an artist! Just like her!

She agreed to write. He wasn't exactly her boyfriend, they'd never actually gone out, but ... Within just a few months, their two-page letters became five-page letters.

Although she continued to make a point of going to all the university-sponsored parties—they were the only ones she was invited to—if you can call a notice in the student paper an invitation—she continued to find it difficult to just walk up to a group of people and join in their conversation. The few times she mustered the courage to do so, they nodded politely, then ignored her. She didn't know what she was doing wrong. She didn't know how you were supposed to act in such situations.

Well, first of all, you weren't supposed to be by yourself, remember?

She'd never been invited to a 'real' party. The only such party she'd ever gone to was her own birthday party, that her mom had for her when she was eight. They played musical chairs and pin the tail on the donkey. Then they had cake, all of them sitting at a table in the rec room in the basement. Danny Snoeder was there. And Davey Krebel. And Susie Dewinge. Her mother had invited everyone in her grade three class.

Otherwise, the only parties she'd ever gone to were the family Christmas parties, which were always fake with relatives she hadn't seen since the previous Christmas, didn't know, and, given what she saw at the annual get-together, had no interest in knowing. She hated going to these parties. But her mother insisted. She would've been so hurt her if she'd refused.

Every year, she felt nothing but uncomfortable. She didn't know how she was supposed to act, what she was supposed to do. The one time she actually enjoyed herself, she was dancing like crazy in the corner to a song that had come on that she really really liked, and her mother had told her to stop because she was showing off. She was deeply embarrassed and felt like she should go around and apologize to everyone.

For what, having fun?

She stared out at the water. How her mother had crippled her!

> we move
>
> with
>
> wooden
>
> spasms
>
> marionettes
>
> with
>
> umbilical
>
> strings

She came to believe that the parties she saw in beer commercials weren't real. People at parties, having fun, talking and laughing, that was a lie. A fantasy. Life wasn't ever like that.

And then she discovered that it was. There *were* parties like that. She just never got invited to them. A single girl, a girl alone, just somehow wasn't invited. Unless someone was specifically interested in her. A couple girls, or a small group, yes, but not just the one.

And then Dennis invited her to a party. Dennis! She'd met him at the small ceremony welcoming all the first year students who had received scholarships. So that meant he was smart. And he was friendly. To her.

That's all it took to sweep her off her feet.

She didn't realize he was friendly to everyone.

Whenever she happened to see him in the halls of the main lecture building, she tried to convey her eagerness to stop and chat. But he just smiled at her in recognition and kept on walking.

Then one day, he said "Hi." She made note of it in her journal.

She wrote down every little thing any guy said to her. Any attention whatsoever.

Jack said "looking good" as I lapped the track today.

Eric Preston asked me to sit beside him today in class.

She looked up across the water, appalled to remember how important they were to her. Men.

Then another time when Dennis saw her in the hall, he again said "Hi" and *did* stop to chat. He casually mentioned that a bunch of guys were having a party the next night, she should come by. He gave her the address.

Yes! Her first party! Her first party at university! See, it *was* happening!

She spent the next day in joyful anticipation. She washed her hair that afternoon, then put on her best jeans, a nice shirt, even a bracelet.

When she got to the house, it was dark. There was no party going on.

Puzzled, she walked around the entire house, trying to find a back door or something. But no. Had she gotten the night wrong? Impossible. He'd said "tomorrow night". Had she gotten the address wrong? No. She'd written it down.

She felt stood up. By an entire party.

Two days later, when she saw him in the hall, there was no indication that something had gone amiss. When she said, as casually as possible, "So I came by the house Saturday night, you'd said there was a party—" he sort of stared at her then said, just as casually, "Oh yeah, we had to change the location."

He'd forgotten he'd asked her.

So she decided to have her own party. If you want to meet people and have fun at parties, she thought, then just do it. Make it happen. She announced in her philosophy class that she was having a party at her place, and everyone was invited.

Why in the world did she think anyone would come? No one ever even talked to her. But it wasn't that they didn't like her, she thought, it was just that they didn't know her. And how do people get to know each other? You meet at a party, you talk to each other.

Maureen came to her party. And the professor came, but he left after an embarrassing five minutes of sitting with the two of them in her parent's basement, painfully hopeful music playing, a bowl of chips on the table, and a neat arrangement of empty glasses beside two large bottles of pop.

No one else came.

Her letters to Craig became ten pages.

"I need a harbour for my soul." Yes, that's it exactly.

At some point, unbeknownst to her, the word 'party' changed meaning. In her late twenties, she'd gone to a bar to pick up a man. Did she do this a lot? Not a lot, no. Just whenever she was really distracted—a few days once a month. She'd tried do-it-yourself, but it didn't satisfy. Having sex with men she just met didn't satisfy either (but then, she'd never had an orgasm with Craig either) (who made her feel like that was her fault) (and she accepted that because she had been unable to make herself come—how could she expect him to do it when she couldn't even do it herself?), but she kept telling herself the next one would be better. (Turns out most men aren't very good at it.)

Surprise.

Her sex education had consisted of a little turquoise booklet called *Mother's Little Helper* published by the Catholic Church. Each chapter wasn't to be read until you hit a certain age. She actually adhered to that until, at sixteen, she carried on and read the chapter for eighteen-year-olds. It wasn't educational in the least. It just told her that soon she'd be embarking on a wonderful journey, getting married and becoming a loving wife and mother ...

And the only thing her mother ever told her was "It hurt."

She'd gone to a bar and and a few guys asked if she wanted to go party. Of course she said yes. Here was her chance! Her second chance! Maybe she'd meet some interesting people. Women, men, whatever!

So they all got into the one guy's car, and half an hour later it was parked in the middle of a scrubby patch of bush. The three of them looked at her expectantly. Oh. This was their party.

Or maybe 'party' had always meant 'sex'—to men.

You'd think she would've stopped picking up men at bars after that. (Apparently they talked about it the next day; they couldn't figure out why she hadn't freaked out.) (It was simple really. None of them had a weapon, and she knew that she could open the car door and just take off. She was absolutely certain she could outrun them. None of them was in the least an athlete, and she was, at that time, still running five miles a day. So she'd just told them no, repeatedly, while they kept up their bravado, their insults, their mockery, their threats, then finally she said something like 'Look, this is boring. If you're going to rape me, go ahead and try, but know it will be rape, I'm not consenting, and I'll press charges. Otherwise, drive me back to my car.')

But no, she didn't stop until something else happened. One night she picked up a guy—they danced a bit, chatted a bit, then went to her place. Later, when she offered to drive him home, she discovered that he lived in a group home. For the developmentally delayed.

She hadn't realized. Because he was no worse, emotionally speaking, cognitively speaking, than all the other guys she'd ever picked up.

So, men in general— Instances of arrested development, every one of them.

She often saw Dennis at the pub that year—part way through the year, she'd started tagging along with Jen and her boyfriend—and one night she finally got up the nerve to ask him to dance. He smiled and led her to the floor. It was the last song of the night. Led Zeppelin's "Stairway to Heaven". Perfect. All those months, waiting. And now. It was happening. She was dancing, to "Stairway to Heaven," with Dennis! The song ended, he went back to his buddies at his table, and—

It suddenly felt like a pity dance.

Two whole years, she'd waited and hoped.

What a waste.

She finds it hard to believe, now, that she was so infatuated, so obsessed, with meeting someone, finding someone—but she knows that she was. Wasn't everyone?

She put the journal down, went back up to the cottage to make another cup of tea, then returned to her reading.

All through first year, she'd wanted to join the track team, but there was no women's track team. At the beginning of second year, it occurred to her that maybe she could join the men's team. So she went to the coach and asked him— would he be her coach? He told her to come out that afternoon, watched her run, and said yes.

Ten years after Switzer had had to do the same thing.

So in addition to the work-outs with the team four times a week, she started going to the weight room twice a week, just as she had with Heidi back at high school. (The high school weight room was a converted classroom and clearly intended for the boys, but they went anyway.)

Her mother disapproved. Girls weren't supposed to develop muscles. They weren't supposed to sweat.

She was always the only woman there. Some of the guys nodded a 'Hi', but they never included her in their banter.

Imagine everything you do, everywhere you go, you're not supposed to.

Or at least not expected to.

She continued to work at her various jobs, despite her mother's criticism that she should make up her mind about what she wanted to do. But it wasn't that she didn't know what she wanted to do. It was that she wanted to do it all. She loved it all.

She charged two dollars per piano lesson and was paid about five dollars per dance class, ten dollars for Saturday morning's gymnastics coaching, and minimum wage for drop-in. It worked out to around seventy-five dollars a week, for around twenty hours. During the summer, when drop-in went full-time, it worked out to about two thousand.

Her brother made four thousand. Working for a landscaping firm. Cutting grass.

Which meant that people (boys) got paid more to look after lawns than people (girls) got paid to look after kids.

So her brother's summer jobs always paid enough for the following year's university tuition and books, whereas hers never did. Which is why she had to work during the school year as well.

It also meant that although she could pay the cover charge to get into the clubs—often after a meet, the team would go somewhere—she couldn't afford the drinks. So she drank water. And when everyone went out for pizza after, she said she had to get home to work on something or other.

She certainly couldn't afford to go to Daytona Beach for Spring Break.

And she couldn't afford to buy a car. But she managed, over the course of two summers and the year in between, to save enough for a motorcycle. A second-hand Honda 350. Red.

Of course, her mother disapproved.

And, apparently, many people were surprised. Kris? A *motorcycle*?

But it felt so natural, so normal to her. She didn't feel at all as if she'd changed. Despite her social ineptitude, she'd always felt strong and capable. And despite her … demeanour, a bit radical. The bike fit that.

She liked the speed, the wind blowing past her. It was like running.

She liked the handling, taking the curves like a slalom skier. (That was another thing about weekends at the cottage that she loved: they could go waterskiing. They were allowed only two circuits of the lake, and they had to contribute for the gas, but she loved the motion of the slalom—the skidding across the wake, cutting hard on the edge, the lean, then the changing over, the letting go of one hand, to reach out, to extend, with her whole body, then the bicep curl, straining, pulling her body back in, to shoot across to the other side …)

And yes, she liked the cool. She felt oh so cool in her jeans, denim jacket, and boots (construction boots, purchased for the spring she worked on maintenance before drop-in opened).

She looked up from the journal and stared across the water. She missed her bike. Had missed it since she'd sold it.

She'd asked her brother to teach her how to do basic maintenance and repair. (In addition to a little MGB, that he never let her drive, he'd owned a Norton for years.) She'd wanted to be able to do what the guy in *The Art of Motorcycle Maintenance* could do. Going on a cross-country trip like he did wasn't out of the question either.

But her brother never managed to have the time.

She looked up again to see a squirrel scurry through the trees across the cove: it had a neat little route from one to the other, like it was playing Snakes and Ladders.

Of all her jobs, she especially loved drop-in. When she walked in, the guys (they were mostly guys) smiled and called out to her. Nowhere else was she welcomed with a smile. Her music students did that, and some of her dance students. But they were kids.

Technically, so were the drop-ins, but she didn't see them that way. They were high school kids. They were fourteen to seventeen; she was nineteen. So there was only two years' difference in some cases.

If she sat down at their table, one of them would easily offer her some of his chips. If she went into the gym to watch a game of basketball, those on the bench made room for her to sit beside them. It almost made her cry, the way they so easily included her.

It was her *Cheers*. The place where everybody knew her name.

It was a little like that with the track team—

> The meets are cool, the guys cheering me as I run, Ed saying "Run this one for Grigsby," Tim telling me he expects me to break sixty on the 400, Len calling out to me "Just do it!" …

—but she couldn't roughhouse with her trackmates like she could with the guys at drop-in. When she played basketball or floor hockey at drop-in—more often than not, they asked, or expected, her to play—she went all out.

They even went on a couple camping trips during the summer. She'd never gone camping before with a bunch of people. The hiking, the canoe-racing, the horsing around— It was all a lot of fun.

She'd never really had fun before.

And she was never to have that kind of fun again.

The guys on the team were supportive and encouraging. Yes, they cheered her on as she ran, they were okay with her tagging along after the meets, they even invited her to the dinner they gave the coach when he retired, and they'd had a plaque prepared, without her knowledge, that said "From the boys—and girl." But it was never quite the same. Something was in the way. The possibility of a romantic/sexual relationship. It's a pity, she thought, that the only physical touch 'allowed' between men and women is sexual.

But the guys, and the girls, at drop-in, they just … liked her. They thought she was cool, cruising into the parking lot on her bike, messing around with them in the gym, and generally hanging out.

It was the peer group she never had.

How pathetic is that, she thought. That she'd had to get her social needs fulfilled by fourteen-to-seventeen year olds at a drop-in.

But then again, it was completely understandable. Women her age seemed exclusively interested in being for, and with, men. Even Jen had had less time for her once she had a boyfriend.

And men her own age always had to assert their superiority, which she then had to challenge, resist.

That time Dan came to drop-in—he was a motorcycle cop that she'd met at the training course she'd taken—all the guys thought he was cool, they thought Kris with a motorcycle cop was perfect. But when he playfully, supposedly, put her over his shoulder and carried her into the gym, she was enraged.

To be treated like a child. A naughty child. He may as well have turned her over on his lap and spanked her.

She didn't see him again.

Furthermore, she thought, men her age had the power over her granted by society, such as it was; with men younger than her, there was a balance, their patriarchy-imbued power countered by the power of her greater age.

No wonder she would later prefer relationships with younger men.

Besides, she thought bitterly, it's not like guys her own age ever beat a path to her door.

Even though, and yet, she also had fun with the other leaders at drop-in, who *were* her own age.

She remembered Fox especially. One night, she was telling him about the latest frustration with her parents, and he offered to call them up and talk to them.

"Yeah?" she'd grinned at him. "And what would you say?"

"I'd say 'Mr. and Mrs. Muller, first of all, she wants to be able to cross the street by herself.'"

And she burst out laughing.

And the time he needed a ride to drop-in, she picked him up on her bike. He thought that was so cool. As did all the kids who saw them pull in.

> I don't come across as an authority figure, do I, I asked Fox tonight.
>
> No, you come across more like a degenerate. He laughed.
>
> But I'm responsible, right? I'm a responsible degenerate.
>
> Yeah. You're amazing, just incredible.
>
> What do you mean?
>
> I don't know, you as a person, I've never met anyone like you.

She tried to track him down years later. Remembering his warmth, his smile, the fun she'd had with him, she realized that she should've—that they should've—

She'd thought, hoped, maybe they could have a do-over. But she couldn't remember his last name, and although she had the university check every Barry known as "Fox" in Kinesiology and Environmental Studies … nothing.

She closed the journal, stood up, and stretched.

· · ·

Half an hour later, part way up the little river, she saw a deer come out of the forest. It hesitated on the bank, seeing her. She kept the kayak as still as she could, and then was rewarded to see it leap across, covering the distance with five splashing strides. How it kept its feet on the rocky bottom, she had no idea. It fled up the other bank and disappeared out of sight.

As in first year, she went back to her high school from time to time during her second year, walking down the familiar halls to visit her favourite teachers. Mr. Shepherd, Mr. Farnsworth, Mr. Ledford—they all welcomed her and, as during the five years she was a student there, made her feel like she was some kind of wonderful.

She must have known at some level that she would never have that again.

They weren't surprised at her apparent make-over. The jeans, the boots, the motorcycle. While the other students had always seen her as a shy good-girl brainer, they must have seen the independent and creative mind that would surely, eventually, assert itself …

When she discovered that Linda, whom she remembered as a quirky, radical classmate, and whom, years later, she recognized as a fellow feminist (it was not a word she knew in high school), had become affiliated with a local theatre group, she contacted her. Partly because she realized then that they had had so much in common and should have been closer friends, so maybe they could become friends now, and partly because she was hoping for some advice about how to get some of her material produced—she had just finished her collection of angry-young-woman soliloquies 'written' by Shakespeare's women protesting the role he had given them (Portia—you don't think someone that intelligent would be a little pissed at being bait and trophy? And Juliet, well, Juliet just wants to have—sex). But she was completely uninterested in reading her script, seeing only the person she'd seemed to be in high school and imagining no doubt some goody-two-shoes play.

When she'd told her, over the course of a brief catch-up conversation, about her experiences as a supply teacher, in particular, about a recent incident in which she'd been reprimanded by the principal for refusing to stand for the anthem, Linda had simply said, "I can't imagine you being called into a principal's office for anything but praise."

But her old high school teachers weren't surprised at all. They had paid attention to her questions in class. They knew she had a strong personality and a critical mind, and were not, therefore, surprised, to hear about such incidents. Nor to see her striding down the hall, helmet in hand.

Then one day, someone stopped her and told her that all visitors had to check in at the main office.

She stayed out on the water for the sunset, then leisurely paddled back in the starlight.

• • •

After a hot shower and a slice of cold pizza, she picked up the journal again. She'd finish the year, then call it a day.

She managed to continue to do it all—her courses, her jobs, track, piano, dance.

She also continued, during her lectures, to generate ideas, and more ideas, so many ideas, and insights, and poem buds, and melody bits, and every evening she'd continue to transfer the fragments from the margins of her notebooks into her journal.

And late into the night, when she did the assigned reading, she continued to talk to Descartes, and Berkeley, and Rousseau—well, mostly she fumed at Rousseau— and Mill, and Sartre—though mostly what she said to him was YES!

> "But whether or not one can live with one's passion, whether or not one can accept their law, which is to burn the heart they simultaneously

exalt—that is the whole question." Albert Camus

She turned the page and saw another poem.

    crease, flip, crease, flip, crease, flip,

    i fold the kleenex into an accordion
    then tie it with a tiny piece of string
    (it's important to tie it right in the middle—
    i have the strings all ready—)
    then i separate the tissue
    (don't pull it)
    ply by ply
    (it must be done carefully—
    the layers are so thin—
    they tear easily—)

    IT'S BORING
    AND TEDIOUS
    AND STUPID

    i pretend to fluff it up
    as if it's something important, something artistic
    then i toss it into the large flat box

    WE HAVE BEEN AT THIS FOR THREE NIGHTS
    my mother and i
    my sister's getting married

    and my brother's upstairs
    allowed to do his homework
    instead

    i feel again those tears
    of frustration and injustice

    and reach for another kleenex

It was right in the middle of mid-terms. And her mother expected her to do all sorts of stupid shit. Cheerfully. Which reinforced her view that her mother didn't know her. At all.

Nor did her mother *want* to know her. She didn't want to hear her views on marriage.

> When you get married, you're entering into a legal contract. You might be doing a few other things (promising your love to someone, making a deal with a god), but you're most certainly entering into a legally binding contract with another person. There are rights due to and responsibilities incumbent upon people who enter into a marriage contract. Some of these have to do with money, some have to do with children, some have to do with sexual services, and some have to do with other things.
>
> What I find so extremely odd is that even though well over 90% of all people get married, almost none of them read the terms of the contract before they sign. (Most people find out about these only when they want to break the contract.) Probably because the contract isn't presented when their signatures are required.
>
> Although this begs the question 'Is the contract, therefore, still binding?', the more interesting question is '*Why* isn't it presented?'

Her mother kept insisting that she too would get married some day.

Clueless. Wilfully *clueless.*

> when her mother explained
> what a hope chest was
> she didn't know
> whether to laugh or cry

She remembered having to go shopping for this and that—the wedding preparations seemed endless—and at one point, she waited in the car with her father while her mother and sister went inside for something or other. Earlier, during some disagreement with her mother, about what, she can't remember, her father was noticeably silent. So she confronted him about it. What did *he* think?

It irritated him to be put on the spot, but he finally confessed that he'd agreed with her, that, in fact, he often agreed with her, but couldn't say so. Her mother, his wife, would be here for the rest of his life, he explained. She, his daughter, would leave.

Which was why he didn't care what she thought.

He actually said that.

She was not impressed with their marriage. She pictured them leaning toward each other, each propped up against/by the other. So they stand together, yes, but if either one is taken away, the other falls.

She was surprised it lasted a lifetime.

> You can live with anything if you don't think very hard.

But then she always did underestimate people's capacity for denial, their capacity to wilfully delude themselves. Their lack of courage.

> I wonder how many marriages are kept together by pride. How many people simply refuse to admit it was a mistake, to commit for life, to that person (or any person). It is, by definition, such a huge mistake.

Angry at her for bringing it up, for expecting anything different, he also said that he had to support her brother over her because he was the oldest and his son.

Of course, she had to ask.

And yes, he would have been disappointed if he hadn't had a son. Because then there would be no one to carry on the family name.

What?

She didn't know where to begin.

Perhaps not with pointing out that she, despite being a lowly female, could carry on the family name.

Because at that moment, at that very moment, she decided not to. She'd use a pseudonym.

She set the journal aside, got off the couch, and made a fire. It took a while, since there was a backdraft—she had to heat up the chimney first by holding a torch of rolled up newspaper as far to the back of the insert as she could. Then slowly, she built the fire first with kindling, then added one or two small chunks, knowing that if she put a large chunk on too soon, the room would fill with smoke. Eventually, satisfied that all was well with the blazing fire, she returned to the couch.

Near the end of the year, she was sort of invited to a prom. Scott, one of Jen's friends from, and just finishing, high school, needed a date for the prom. She asked her on his behalf. "But he's just using you," Jen cautioned her. "He's gone through all the girls in his class."

She didn't care. She was finally going to the high school prom. Not her prom, and not while she was in high school, but still.

Or she didn't believe what Jen had said. After all, Scott was a musician. He wanted to be a composer, like her. She'd finally meet her soulmate. So what if he started out using her. Once he realized she was a fellow composer, and just as smart, once he realized she was someone with whom he could talk about Beethoven …

She couldn't afford to buy a dress to wear just once. Not again. She'd already had to do that for her sister's wedding. So she thought she'd just wear that dress. She actually liked the color. It was a bright, vibrant fuchsia. Her mother took off the puffy short sleeves and made a dark, short jacket to wear with it.

Still, she looked ridiculous.

But she had no idea. She was uncomfortable wearing dresses of any kind. So it didn't occur to her to get, and wear, something … sexier. In any case, sexy for her would have been black leather pants and a 19th-century men's shirt with a laced neck and ruffled cuffs. But this was the 70s. Young women wore dresses to the prom.

The first thing she said about music, on the way, in the car, he scoffed. Made her feel like she didn't know what she was talking about, like she was way off in her opinion.

Ditto for the second thing she said about music.

And then, she hadn't heard of *Yes*? But they were the best band ever! How stupid could she be?!

He refused to dance with her. All night. Because she looked like an idiot bridesmaid, he said.

The next day, he told Jen she didn't know how to kiss.

Even so, she pinned the corsage to her billboard over her desk and waited, hoped, for his phone call. Of course it never came.

Years later, she realized he didn't want his date to be someone who knew about Beethoven. *He* wanted to be the expert, the authority. He went on to get his B.Mus., then his Ph.D. Last she heard, he was a professor at some big music school, doing musicological analyses of rock bands. Like *Yes*.

Shortly after, her brother moved out—as soon as he'd graduated, he'd gotten a job in an insurance company in Edmonton—and they took in a roomer. It was odd to have a stranger living in their house. To see the man come out of her brother's room and go into the washroom. Once he stopped her in the hall to ask if she could sew, if she could repair his trousers. The question startled her. Her brother had never initiated conversation with her.

At the end of the summer, since drop-in finished two weeks before school started, she drove up to the family cottage. Just her. For two whole weeks.

It was amazing. To be able to eat what and when she wanted, not to be interrupted when she was reading, writing, or thinking, because it was 'Time To Set The Table'. She canoed or just sat outside at night, in the dark, without a light. Basking in the moon and the stars and the quiet. No one to tell her she should come in. Why, for godsake? No one to say, 'At least turn on a light.' No, damn it, I don't want a light! I *want* to sit in the dark! What the hell is wrong with that? She went for five mile runs. Then six. Then seven. No one to tsk tsk. She played the same piece on the record player, over and over, merging with it. No one to yell at her 'Enough!' And no one to tell her it was 'Time For Bed'. At eleven. Simply because that's when the prime time tv shows were over. So she stayed up until two or three. Then slept until ten or eleven. She worked better that way, well into the night.

She knew then that she wanted to live alone. Having to live with someone meant having always to give in to what they wanted, to go around what they wanted. Living with someone meant you could never do what you really wanted.

It also meant being constantly subject to criticism.

> "The greatest heights of self-expression—in poetry, music, painting—are achieved by men who are supremely alone." Colin Wilson

She closed the journal, selected a CD, put it on the stereo, turned out the light, and just listened. Malmquist. Such a delicate beauty …

8

Another sunny day. Another cup of really, really good tea. Another morning down on the dock, with the shimmering water, the gleaming water …

Her strongest memory of third year was that of impatience. She couldn't wait to work on all the bits and pieces she was accumulating, all the books she was planning to write, all the pieces she was planning to compose. She enjoyed all her courses immensely, did all the work, never skipped class, and she loved the track workouts, the running, and she loved her hours at the piano, her music students, and her dance studies, her dance students, and she really enjoyed drop-in—but she couldn't wait to have more time. To do her own reading (her list of books to read was now ten pages long), to do her own writing, to work on her own compositions …

She spent so much time on her studies. Struggling with the language in her Chaucer course, for example. She didn't know everyone else just went to the library and got a translation. She didn't know there *were* translations. And her History of the Novel course. She thought the reading list was compulsory, not recommended. She read every single novel on the long list, cover to cover.

And if I'd known then what I know now, she thought. Richardson, Fielding, Meredith—they were all such pompous pretentious twits thinking they were god's gift to the world, so full of wisdom, going on and on and on about the most trivial of things, so full of shit.

Susan Juby's Alice, I Think *is better than* Pamela *and* Tom Jones *any day.*

One warm, sunny day Dr. Spivey stopped her outside the library.

"Kris, hi, how are you?"

"Good, thanks," she said. Then added belatedly, "How are you?"

"I'm good too, thanks. Listen, I wanted to talk to you. I see you've taken a course overload again next semester. I hope you're planning on applying to graduate schools."

"Well, actually, I—"

"But you must! You of all of this year's students! Your work is excellent, and you've got the fire, everyone can see that! No one questions that you're Ph.D. material!"

Well, *she* did. Yes, she had the fire, but a Ph.D.? Her?

Besides, she had no desire to spend even one year, let alone three or four, studying some esoteric point of epistemology, metaphysics, or logic.

Nor the use of the semi-colon in T. S. Eliot's poetry or some such. Which is why graduate studies in English didn't appeal to her either.

He insisted she make an appointment with the Head of the Philosophy Department to get information and advice about where she might go.

"But I don't think I can afford it. I'm barely breaking even as it is," she said, looking at her watch. She was scheduled to teach a dance class at the studio in twenty minutes.

And she didn't really want to postpone her own projects for that length of time.

"But you'll probably get a TAship," he said.

She didn't understand.

"Most graduate students get a teaching assistantship. It's a guaranteed job."

Oh. She hadn't known that. That would change every—

"And there are probably a dozen scholarships you could apply for."

A dozen? Her high school counsellor had just told her about the entrance scholarships to the two local universities.

A week later, she was in Dr. Whittle's office, nervously telling him about her mother's comment that she'd make a great lawyer, because she was always arguing. On some level, in some way, she was trying to wrap her head around being in his office talking about doctoral programs. "But," she added, "lawyers are just intellectual cops. And I don't think I can put in all the years required before you get to be a judge. And even if I could, even if I *became* a judge, they're bound by precedents and rules too. So I *still* wouldn't be able to *question* the precedents and rules—"

"So you want to become a legal philosopher?" Dr. Whittle asked.

A legal philosopher? She'd never heard of such a thing. But yes!

"I would have thought you'd fancy feminist philosophy."

She hadn't heard of that either. She could spend three or four years studying the effects of gender on one's life? Hell, she could spend her *life* doing that! She wondered then if he'd heard about her Milton paper. She didn't have the tools, the language, to write a feminist critique of *Paradise Lost*, but she sure as hell knew what she'd say to Milton if she were Eve. So that's what she wrote. Filled ten pages. Apparently it had caused quite a stir in the English department.

In fact, one of the books she was eager to start writing was a collection of short pieces from the perspective of more women from the Bible, and from Shakespeare, fairy tales, and mythology—as if they, those women, *weren't* the creations of men. She thought that might count as feminist philosophy.

She also hadn't heard of philosophy of mind. And yes, the relationship between the mind and the brain intrigued her, the nature of consciousness …

That's when she realized just how poor her choice to attend WLU had been. Neither legal philosophy nor feminist philosophy was offered in the undergraduate program at WLU. Nor philosophy of mind. Nor social philosophy. Nor any applied ethics courses. Because yes, of course, she was also interested in questions about the morality of using animals for experimentation, of selling one's organs, of euthanasia … Apparently, any one of those could become her Ph.D. thesis.

"You need to put together a research proposal—"

"A research proposal?"

"And we need to get you a good set of recommendation letters …"

But instead, what Dr. Spivey actually said when he stopped her outside the library was "I see you've taken a course overload again next semester. Have you considered taking less than a full load instead? Spread out your degree over six years instead of four. It would enable you to focus on each course as much as you seem to want to do."

It was Kevin who received the grad school advice. And James and Robert.

> To My Philosophy Professors
>
> Why didn't you tell me?
> When I was all set to achieve *Eudamonia*
>   through the exercise of Right Reason,
> When I was eager to fulfil my part
>   of the Social Contract,
> When I was willing, as my moral duty,
>   to abide by the Categorical Imperative
> When I was focussed on Becoming,
>   through Thesis and Antithesis to Synthesis—
>
> Why didn't you correct me?
> Tell me that Aristotle didn't think I had any reason,
> That according to Rousseau,
>   I couldn't be party to the contract,
> That Kierkegaard believes I have no sense of duty
>   because I live by feeling alone,
>
> That Hegel says I should spend my life
>   in self-sacrifice, not self-development,
> That Nietzsche thinks I'm good for pregnancy
>   and that's about it—

> Why didn't you tell me I wasn't included?
> (Perhaps because you too had excluded me
>   from serious consideration;
> Or did you think I wouldn't understand?)
>
> (I do.   I do understand.)

If you don't know something exists, why would you go looking for it? So she didn't go to the Student Services office and ask, 'Hey, is there a university somewhere where I can get a graduate degree in gender studies? Environmental ethics? Biomedical ethics?'

Is there a grocery store where I can buy coconut mango juice?

All she knew was orange juice and apple juice.

Though, actually, she thought now, leaning back in the chair, soaking up the September sun, it's possible the fields of feminist philosophy, environmental ethics, and biomedical ethics didn't exist *anywhere* in the 70s. The word 'feminist' didn't even become common until the 80s; she remembers 'women's lib' from her youth, not 'feminist'.

Which just means she could've been, should've been, one of the pioneers.

In any case, she didn't want to be a university professor. She wanted time to write! That's why she'd already made up her mind to get a B.Ed.—so she could be a high school teacher, a part-time teacher, in order to *have* time to write!

She didn't know that full-time professors were required to teach only two courses. And would be paid about $40,000 to do so. And would be expected—*expected*—to write. In the remaining time.

In short, she didn't know that being a full-time university professor *was* being a part-time teacher.

And no one corrected her. Because she didn't talk to anyone about what she wanted, what she'd intended to do, what her life plan was.

She needed a mentor. It also wasn't a word used in the 70s, but she realized now that that was what she'd lacked.

And yet … maybe people had stepped forward to mentor her, and she just didn't recognize it. In grade eleven Math, Mr. Newcomb gave her a copy of *Flatland*. At the time, she assumed he just happened to have the book with him, saw that she had finished her work, and so gave it to her to read, to fill the time. But now, she wondered if he'd brought it especially to give to her, thinking she might find it interesting.

She did. She found it fascinating. But she never asked, after, to talk to him about it. It didn't occur to her that she could do that. So, again, it was her own— No wait a minute, he was the teacher, she was just a grade eleven student, surely the responsibility was on him to follow up.

She also remembered also being fascinated by the question posed in a Moody Blues song that Mr. Pendergrass mentioned in grade twelve Physics, equivalent to 'Is paint in a can a color before you open the lid and expose it to the light?' Truly fascinated. And he saw that. But again, no follow up. She didn't know what she expected—well, she didn't expect anything at the time, but now—surely high school teachers have a responsibility, a duty, to notice unusual interest and foster it somehow.

And yet, and yet. Twenty years later, when she went back and got her M.A., her thesis advisor asked if she wanted to go for coffee, she said no thanks. She didn't like coffee. She didn't see it as an offer of something else, a discussion of future possibilities, mentorship.

It might have helped if she'd gotten to know her profs. But she never went to see them outside of class; she never showed up at their office. That was for C students who needed help, not A students.

Who needed help.

How was it that had happened in high school though?

High school teachers didn't have offices. You just popped in if you saw them in their classroom during a spare.

Going to an office was far more intimidating. And she didn't want to bother her professors, she didn't want to impose.

She turned the page.

She'd entered one of her poems in the university's writing competition and placed second.

She didn't tell anyone. Lest someone see that glistening, iridescent bubble hanging so perfectly in the air in front of her, and then pop it with mockery or dismissal. She'd come to assume one or the other.

Except Craig. Who responded with a poem of his own. And she couldn't quite—wasn't that what she'd wanted? A fellow poet? She couldn't quite put her finger on why she was … upset?

She turned another page.

Jen went to Paris on an exchange program in her third year.

How did one find out about such things? She would've loved to have gone with her. She wanted to travel around Europe some day. When she could afford it.

Late that fall, she decided to drive up to the cottage again for the weekend. The trees would be amazing. Neither her parents nor her brother were going that weekend, and her sister never went by herself.

Her bike broke down halfway there, just as she was passing through one of the small towns on the way. So she called home, with the dime she always made sure to have on her for just such an emergency. But her brother was working that evening at the curling club and couldn't come. Her father was similarly occupied or didn't know anything about bikes, she can't remember. Nor can she remember why assistance by her mother or sister wasn't even considered. By her or them.

This was before credit cards were given to university students and in any case, she had no idea how to go about getting a room in a hotel.

So she went into a bar, which was the only place that was open, and watched people play pool until it closed at one o'clock. Then she rolled her bike to the nearest park bench and simply sat down to wait until morning.

Years later, when she regularly drove an hour to and from work almost every day, she was horrified to realize that she'd been only a forty-five minute drive away. And yet, not one of them—not her brother, her sister, her father, her mother—all of them could drive—not one of them offered to come get her, at midnight, if necessary, and then return in the morning to deal with the bike.

At the time, she didn't think that what they had done—what they had not done— was unusual.

No wonder she learned that if you needed help, you had to hire it.

But for most of her life, she couldn't afford to hire help. As a result, she became remarkably self-sufficient. And, so, remarkably limited.

More than that, though, her self-sufficiency became an invisible force field. Inadvertently, she gave the impression that she didn't need any help. So people never offered their help. And so her isolation, and by necessity, her self-sufficiency, increased. Around and around.

Also, because no one ever offered her any help, she never thought to offer anyone else help. Which only exacerbated her isolation.

Around and around.

Such a simple pleasure, she thought as she paddled. And such an intense pleasure. For her. She glanced at the cottages—the summer homes, she corrected herself— as she passed by. She hated them. They'd made life here impossible for people like her. And the people who owned them didn't even live here! They didn't *want* to live here. Not like she did.

• • •

Once back at the cottage, she had a bite to eat, then continued through her third year.

She met Matthew through Susan, who had also been on the cross-country team, in high school, though she couldn't remember now how they got in touch again while she was at university. Matthew was an Engineering student at UW who was renting rooms with two other 'gears' in a basement suite in Susan's neighbourhood.

She often stopped by on her way home. They'd invite her to stay for spaghetti. Then she and Matthew would sit on the floor between the two beds in his double room and talk.

They didn't have much in common, but he was open to her. He was interested in her. That was enough. Given.

That could've been, maybe should've been, everything. But he didn't—she had this list—and he—yes, he was clearly intelligent, but— He was an engineer.

She turned the page.

Part way through her third year, she discovered *Jonathan Livingston Seagull*. The book. And the soundtrack. The first time she heard it, she felt … buoyed by the wind of its exuberance. And realized then and there that she needed to learn how to orchestrate.

She also discovered Pink Floyd. And realized she needed to learn about … synthesizers?

One evening she was in the den watching a special program that she had begged her parents to let her watch—it was on at the same time as their beloved *Mannix*. Her mother was in the corner chair making out the grocery list, and her father was sprawled on the couch opposite her. When the commentator spoke of "a passion for music," her father asked scornfully, "How can you have a *passion* for music?" She stared over at him. At the derision on his face. Then tried to explain, saying something about an all-consuming desire. "I guess I've never felt a passion for anything," he said then, laughing.

Yes, she'd thought. That says it all.

> "How can you stand it, not to know [what you want]?" Ayn Rand, *The Fountainhead*

> They are flatlanders. Two dimensional.

> They will never be able to comprehend anything I do.

It was then that she had asked, hopefully, "When your kids, when I, was born—didn't you cry—out of joy?" Not exactly passion, but it would at least point him in the direction of overwhelming emotion.

No. He hadn't.

> i hurl my screams!
> they just strike the walls
> and ricochet in hap
> hazard madness
> within the space of my room …
> they collide, explode,
> or clatter empty upon the floor
> on and on
> within the time of my room …
> it's deafening.
>
> no,
> i know the sound of my own screams.
> this room is far too quiet.

She also discovered Janis Ian and Dan Hill that year. In a way, they saved her life. To know there were others that sensitive.

And still alive.

One day, she heard a piece of music on the radio, perhaps Alain Morisod, that had birds chirping in the background. She liked it.

So she asked to borrow a record of birdsong that her biology teacher had used in class one day, recorded it on her cassette recorder, rewound, then recorded the solo piano piece she'd composed, her Op. 1, No. 1, but of course in the process, erased the birds. She didn't know what overdubbing was. She figured she needed two more cassette players. One to record the birdsong, one to record the piano, then she'd play them both back at the same time, recording on third. But she couldn't afford two more cassette players. Yet. In the meantime, she started making notes for six more pieces in the set, that would feature wolf howls, rain, and ocean surf. She'd started composing in the new age genre. Before it had a name.

Much later, she wrote to Gibson, finding an address on the back of a record of nature sounds, suggesting a partnership: his nature sounds, her music. He said he already had someone. Fair enough.

Except that over the course of the following twenty years he'd add a dozen new composers to his roster. None of them you.

She turned a few more pages.

During the summer, when she was taking an extra course, Philosophy of Education, and had missed class two weeks in a row (first, because of an overnight camping trip with drop-in, and then, because her grade ten piano exam had been scheduled for the same time), Dr. Mauritz had asked her why she was taking the course if she couldn't get to all the classes.

"I want to be sure I get into teacher's college," she explained. Please don't kick me out, she worried.

"But you'll just have to take the course again. Philosophy of Education is probably a required course in every B.Ed. program."

Oh. She didn't know that. She hadn't thought of that. Maybe she could get an exemption and then take something else. She always wanted to take more courses than would fit in her schedule.

More to the point, the point he didn't make, there would be no question she'd be accepted at teacher's college. Given her grades, in the Honours program, and her extracurricular teaching experience? She was too good for teacher's college! Why didn't someone tell her that?! Why didn't someone tell her that teacher's college was for 'B' students, and conservative, unimaginative 'B' students, at that?

She was forever a victim of her low self-esteem, working so hard, so much harder than was necessary.

And yet it was never enough.

And she always seemed so sure of what she wanted. That's why no one tried to dissuade her, to tell her she should go for a Ph.D. or even an M.A. instead of a B.Ed.

She was so self-sufficient, no one thought she needed anything. Advice.

Friendship.

Love.

> "To want and not to have, sent all up her body a hardness, a hollowness, a strain … And then to want and not to have—to want and want—how that wrung the heart, and wrung it again and again." Virginia Woolf, *To the Lighthouse*

> When loves comes, I will be too weary with waiting.

She closed the journal while she watched the sun light up the cove. Inch by inch, the conifer green became neon. It was amazing.

• • •

Once she had a good fire going, she returned to the journal to finish out the year.

> OH HOW I HATE YOU! You, who are the measure of all things. You who would crucify me with your eyes—not for their power (alas, you have none), but for their pain—as I refuse to cross myself and pronounce the compulsory chant at the dinner table.

> You, so secure in your religion. Never asking a question unless you knew its answer. Roman Catholic you still insist. You have yet to explain how one can be born RC, born believing in some specific system—oh, but you were. And you sit snug, smug, in stability, the measure of maturity— while I, still the struggling *Adolescent*, friend of Fyodor, run.

Her mother's pain was her power. She realized this now.

And "Your intelligence is showing," she would say. Like "Your slip is showing," but much, much worse. It wasn't just a reprimand. It was a warning.

And her father would get such an amused expression on his face whenever she expressed an opinion he didn't agree with.

It was so fucking patronizing. Especially coming from some schmuck who'd spent his entire life working at an insurance company.

There is so much undoing to be done when people realize their parents are just ordinary people, just a couple of idiots who had sex and got married. Or got married and had sex. Just because that's what people were supposed to do.

> Parents are the most powerful people in the world. And anyone, anyone, can become a parent.

"You take yourself too seriously," they would say.

Yeah, well, you don't take yourself seriously enough.

Quite simply, she didn't like her parents anymore.

In fact, yes, she had come to hate them.

They were always criticizing her for nitpicking, for her attention to detail, to fine distinctions. It was like yelling at a kid for differentiating between fuchsia and magenta. Instead of nurturing the developing painter.

> It's like everything I am is in conflict here. Intellect, artist, athlete—
> Everything I am is stifled here. I'm suffocating. Here.

Her very *existence* imposed, interfered. No wonder she wanted not just to move out, but to live alone. So as not to impose on anyone. So as not to have to apologize to anyone—for playing the piano, for listening to music, for reading, for writing. For thinking.

That would be enough. Not to have to apologize for it. She didn't even consider the possibility of being appreciated for it. Let alone respected, or even praised.

> Why do I go on so, defending my hate?

Indeed.

She'd tried. She'd tried so hard. She suggested once that her father read one of her papers, so they could have a discussion. No, he said, he couldn't make out her handwriting. She offered to type it. No, don't bother.

Don't bother.

Of course she went back inside herself. Even further.

And yet he wanted bragging rights. Even as he mocked her. "My daughter, Einstein," he introduced her once to his boss.

> Why do you do it? Why do you mock me so? Are you jealous? Insecure? Threatened? I never thought I rubbed it under your nose. In fact I often tried to hide it, in between cursing it—what good was my intelligence if it separated me from the people I loved?

Thought you loved.

> And I must've done a pretty good job too: he actually thought Larry had 'more university' than me. Probably thought he had higher grades too.

Everything about living with them hurt. Their failure to understand, let alone support (encouragement was simply too much to ask for), her passions. Their failure to agree with *any*thing she said. No matter how well argued.

Her life had become so oppressive, their constant disapproving presence so overwhelming, she was afraid that if she suppressed, repressed, her self, her interests, her desires, any more, she'd lose herself altogether.

And she was realizing just how much energy it took to do that, to keep everything in, to keep everything hidden—energy she didn't have, given everything else she was trying to do.

So she decided to move out.

She'd had enough. She was twenty-one. Twenty-one!

> Even the trivial things— Everything I do must be done the way you want it to be done. My god, you even get upset when I untuck the sheet and

blankets at the foot of my bed. So, dancing in the rain? Out of the question.

In fact, she'd wanted to move out since part way through first year. She'd been becoming her own person since midway through high school. University, of course, intensified their differences, their distances.

It was only her reluctance to hurt her parents that kept her hanging on— If she could make it to the end of her fourth year— Her brother had moved out when, because, he got a job in a different city. Her sister had moved out when, because, she got married. What was her excuse, her reason? She wanted to. She didn't need to. She just wanted to. To move out when she didn't have to—she knew that would hurt them—

And why the hell did that matter so much? They clearly had no problem hurting you!

But she had come to hate their superficial and closed minds. The house with its mundane interiors, the ever-audible AM radio station, the tv always tuned to *Mannix*, Archie Bunker, and the like— All the assaults to her senses, all the assaults to her intellect—

> No wonder I closed in on myself, no wonder I became so overly focused on myself.

Overly *focused? You weren't any more focused on yourself than most men with ambition.*

And no wonder she wanted to move out.

Surely she'd waited long enough, tried long enough.

But no, apparently not.

"If you leave now, you don't come back!" her mother said.

She was stunned. To the core.

She had been such a good girl. Obnoxious, really. She'd always done her chores, without being told. She'd always done her homework, without being told. She'd practiced the piano every day. Like she was supposed to.

Except for that one time, having to sit in the corner, she couldn't ever remember being punished. Reprimanded, yes. Like that time she went with her brother and Danny through the cemetery, she must've been around eight, and they climbed the chain link fence, and on the way down, she caught her jeans on one of the pointy tips at the top and tore an eight-inch gash from the crotch to the knee. Her mother was so upset about having to sew up the tear. They were new! She had just bought them! And serves her right for climbing fences with the boys.

Only now does it occur to her that her mother was more concerned that she had torn the new jeans than that she might have torn her thigh.

> I didn't drink, I didn't smoke, I didn't 'run around with boys' or 'the wrong crowd'. When I went out, which was maybe once or twice a year, I told you where I was going and what time I'd be back. So I didn't even need a curfew.

> I never talked back. I never slammed my bedroom door. I never disobeyed you. I never lied to you.

> I was a straight-A student.

And yet—

And so—

So even though it was her choice to leave, she felt kicked out.

Her letters to Craig grew to twenty pages.

9

Matthew borrowed a vehicle from a friend and helped her move. The room, and it was just a room in a boarding house, across from the gun shop on King Street, was already furnished, so she didn't take much. Not that she had much to take. Given the circumstances, it was a 'You leave only with the clothes on your back' sort of thing.

But she loved it. She had a room of her own.

Without the crushing presence of her parents.

She would discover that that presence is a state of mind.

It would take thirty years to move out.

She had a desk, a chair, her books, her music, and a bed. In which she stretched luxuriously, all the way to her unbound toes.

No piano though.

So she bartered for practice time at her students' houses—she'd continue giving lessons, in their homes now (in the winter she'd actually run from one house to the next, putting in nine miles on Saturdays alone), and offer a discount in exchange for a half hour's use of their piano after the lesson. Many of them refused the discount, but allowed, even *wanted,* her to use their piano anyway. She agreed it would be good for her students to hear her practice; it hadn't occurred to her that her students' parents would actually enjoy hearing her play, at such an advanced level.

Tea was offered at one house, torte at another. And Andrew's dad—"Wanna beer, Kris?" It was nice. She felt more welcome in her students' homes than she ever had in her parents' home.

She subsisted on apples, potatoes (raw), pork and beans (straight from the can), and Shreddies. All of which could be eaten while she worked. Yes, she was often hungry, but ordering out for a pizza was out of the question, financially speaking. Even most of the stuff in the grocery store— Five bucks a week for food didn't go far. (Laura's mother never knew how much she treasured that weekly torte!)

Once when she was visiting her sister, she eagerly opened the fridge and helped herself. Not really thinking about it. Or just thinking of her sister's fridge like she'd thought of the family fridge. To which she had similarly helped herself. Yes, technically it was stealing. But she felt slapped in the face when her brother-in-law said so. She never helped herself again.

And she doesn't know why she even thought her sister would let her to do her laundry at her house.

Her parents later changed their minds and said she could come back, she could practice in the afternoons when they weren't there, she could even use the washing machine if she wanted.

But the damage had been done.

Despite the excitement of having her own place, by October she was running on empty. Very empty. Between her classes and all the reading lists and all the assigned papers, her practice time, up to four hours a day now working toward her Associate, her four jobs, her workouts—it was only her workouts that kept her going: she bounced from one endorphin high to the next. Whenever she missed a work-out, she slept for ten hours straight, rather than the three she was otherwise averaging.

Even so, she was exhilarated. Every minute, every single minute, was brimming over with life! With thinking, with feeling … It's just that she was tired. And starting to wonder about—Keeping up with the reading and the papers, mostly. Her practice too. She'd come to realize that she wasn't a very good pianist; it took far more work than it should have to master the pieces, but she'd come too far to stop now. So she dug in her heels … But it was the same feeling with her dance studies. She wasn't ever going to be a very good dancer, but again, the Associate diploma was finally in reach … And, of course, her B.A. She wouldn't throw that away, but really, did it make that much difference whether or not she actually slogged through *Beowulf*?

Kerouac and company started to appeal to her.

She went to Matthew's place more and more. It was nice to be there, to be out of her life, to let go of the intensity of it all for just a couple hours.

Jen was back from Paris, and they resumed playing pool in the student lounge once in a while, but she spent most of her free time with her boyfriend. At the end of the year, they went their separate ways. She tracked her down a couple years later, hoping to rekindle some sort of friendship, but she had married and their whole conversation was about her two lovely little boys.

She'd asked, when she told her she was married and had two little boys, why? In all the time she'd known her, she had never once spoken about wanting to have children. Why do so many people do that, she wondered. Have children when— It's such a long-lasting and all-consuming endeavour, wouldn't you want to be passionate about it?

> Maybe people have kids for the joy of watching something grow, for they themselves, alas, have stopped.

> Or maybe people want a distraction from their boring lives.

> Or maybe they have kids because then nothing else will be expected of them.

> Or maybe, at least for men, having a wife and kids is the perfect excuse. 'I've got a wife and kids' can justify almost everything. That is otherwise merely self-interested.

> Or maybe their biochemistry hijacks their brain. The selfish gene and all that.

Or none of the above. It's just a consequence revealing such gross stupidity (not using contraception) that most people simply pretend they wanted it.

By fourth year, she had several friends. They were individual friends, and mostly activity-specific: she played pool with Gary, Brian, or Don, whom she'd remembered vaguely from high school—he'd seen her there one afternoon and had come over to chat; she went dancing, occasionally, with Jen; she talked to Tim and Christy, a new member of the team, at track; and she spent off-time with

Matthew. So she didn't feel like a complete loser. (Plus, of couse, there was Craig. If she hadn't had all those long letters from Craig all this time …)

But she lost every one of them at the end of fourth year.

Perhaps it wasn't such a great loss, she thought now, since none of them were people with whom she could talk about important things. Except for Matthew, and Craig— Why were people so uninterested in talking about important things, she wondered, things of substance?

Her social *group*, the only place she felt like she belonged, continued to be the drop-in. In her fourth year, she ran a second drop-in at the local YMCA on Thursday nights, in addition to the main center Friday nights and Sunday afternoons. She was promoted to supervisor for both.

It was the highest position of authority she'd ever have. In her life.

She stared out at the water for a while then turned the page.

Susan invited her to have Thanksgiving dinner at their house. She hesitated, because Thanksgiving dinners had always been such an unpleasant charade, but who was she to turn down an offer of friendship? Not to mention a free meal.

The dinner table discussion at the Krimmler house was like the proverbial water in a desert to someone dying of thirst. Susan's father was an anthropology professor, and her mother was a biologist. The experience was such a revelation. She had no idea families could be like that. Could interact like that. They smiled, they laughed, they argued.

It made her so sad.

Then after dinner, she and Susan went into their living room—Susan wanted to show her something—and she was so surprised to see her parents just sitting there, each in their own chair, just reading and listening to music. It was so very different—

Her parents used the living room for their after-work drink (a 'do not disturb' situation) and on Christmas Day, because they'd set up the tree there and so would unwrap the gifts there.

Where they sat in the evening was the den, which had the tv. So whenever they were there, the tv was on, and she wasn't allowed to talk.

She turned another page.

Her Shakespeare prof took her aside one day to talk to her about her essay. Forty footnotes, he exclaimed, in a ten page essay! She didn't understand. Wasn't that good? She'd done a lot of research. She'd been thorough. She had, in fact, signed out fifteen books and read every single article in every one of them that was on her topic.

You could have thought of a lot of these arguments yourself, he said, seeing that she was confused. Well, yes, of course she could have. Wait—she *could* have? Her essays could be about her *own* thoughts on the matter? Then why were they called *research* essays?

Quite apart from that, it was like he was giving her permission. To think on her own. To think for herself.

And she suddenly realized how handicapped she'd been to that point with*out* that permission. She suddenly realized she'd *needed* that permission.

She wanted a do-over. From grade eleven on. Certainly from first year on. (Yes, she'd been thinking on her own, thinking for herself, since grade eleven, but those thoughts went only into her journal, never into her assigned papers.)

And yet, ten years later, she was told by her advisor in the Masters' program that students weren't expected to do any original work at the Masters' level. That was expected only at the doctoral level.

I'll bet he never told that to any of the male students in the program.

She drained her cup, went up to the cottage for another, then resumed.

As for the boyfriend thing, just wait. Mr. Right will come along. Isn't that what everyone said?

> How incredibly implausible. That there is one, and only one, person who is right for you. And that that person, that one person in six million, will miraculously find you.

And yet, she remembered one of the lunch concerts— Some guy had chased after her once it was over and she'd left the building, and when he caught up to her, he blurted out, "What book are you reading?" She told him, "*Tristam Shandy*." And then continued walking. He turned away and did the same. And why not? She'd brushed him off.

No, she'd just totally missed the subtext.

But what should he have said? "Would you like to chat, you look interesting, I'd like to get to know you a bit"?

Well, why not?

She probably would have told him that she had to go work on an essay that was due in two days. Which would have been true.

But how often does that happen? It was straight out of a movie. Boy sees girl, falls in love at first sight, runs after her. It *does* happen! It *did* happen—*to her!* And she totally missed it.

No doubt there were other misses. She remembered now that Don had told her that when he first saw her on her bike, he'd thought "That can't be Kris." He was impressed. He was delighted. He was definitely interested. And Brian had asked her once, "What are you doing this weekend?" She'd told him. "Sounds busy," he'd said. And Tim had asked her once if she wanted to go to a game after one of the meets. And Matthew. Certainly, Matthew.

But no, those weren't exactly misses. She simply wasn't attracted to any of them. She enjoyed Don's company, and Matthew's, but— Their interest wasn't enough to make her fall in love with them.

Nor should it be.

And then she met Peter.

He was an artist, a painter. She'd often see him in the cafeteria, sitting alone, legs crossed primly. She can't remember now how their friendship began, but she can remember talking all night, literally, in a 24-hour donut shop. About philosophy. About art. About the meaning of life.

"'To be closer to believing,'" she'd quoted to him once.

"'To be just a breath away.'" He'd known the next line.

A week after they met, he asked if she'd come to Europe with him.

Yes. *Yes! Oh my god, yes!!*

She didn't have the money. But he did. Somehow. Not a lot, but enough.

And it was everything she'd ever hoped for.

They spent a month in Paris. A whole week in the Louvre. An afternoon in the Musée Rodin. She saw *The Thinker*. They went to the Paris Opera House. The building itself was so opulent, so beautiful … she'd never seen anything like it before. They spent almost an hour on the grand staircase, pausing on each stair, to drink in the perspective, the perfect lines. One night, an opera, the next, a ballet. They walked along the Champs-Elysees, gathering chestnuts. Each night, a different café, talking, just like Sartre and Beauvoir. The month was full of late mornings, leisurely afternoons, long evenings, and even longer nights.

Then they drove south, through Bourges, and Limoges, to the coast, to Marseilles, Toulouse, Nice. They spent a week on the Mediterranean, just staring at the impossibly blue waters.

Then over to Italy, south along the coast. They couldn't get enough of Michelangelo and da Vinci. And the houses built right into the cliffs.

After Italy, a month in the Greek islands, going from one to the other, whimsically. The white houses, again the crystal blue water, the life, the food …

Then back up the other side of Italy, to Florence, and Venice. More art, more beauty, more— More.

They finished their trip in Salzburg, attending a Mozart concert, performed by musicians in period costumes. On period instruments. She was delighted.

But no. She'd already planned to go out west after her fourth year. To be with Craig. They'd been writing for three years now. During the day, she'd often make a note of something to tell him; he was always there, in the back of her mind. She'd eagerly read his letters in their entirety as soon as they arrived, and then respond to a few pages at a time in the evening. Their now-forty-page letters were ongoing, like a conversation that never ended. She told him everything. Understandably.

She knew Peter was her soulmate, but she had to give Craig a chance. He wrote poetry. He played the guitar. He was a photographer. He was getting his Ph.D. in Psychology. Maybe he was the one. She had to know.

Even so, her first time was with Peter.

She didn't want to be a virgin when she went out west to Craig. He wasn't. She didn't want him to have the power, the advantage, of experience over her.

And yet, she wanted her first time to be special. Matthew was willing, as were Gary, Don, and a few others. But she wanted Beethoven and candlelight.

"Have you seen the moon?"

"Yes. Yes, I have."

So she started taking the pill. She knew you had to be on it for three months prior.

When her mother found out, did she commend her for being responsible about having sex? Of course not.

And when other people found out, they were horrified that she had planned it, so logically. She didn't understand. How was that a bad thing?

She didn't want a baby, a child. What she wanted was to experience the bliss of sex, the ecstasy of orgasm. Whatever. She didn't know really, since she'd never done it before. But everyone said how good it was, how great it was, how it was such an intense physical pleasure, the earth moves, and all of that.

It was none of that.

She was in love with Peter. That wasn't the problem. Though years later, she came to realize that that's never the problem. You can have great sex, she suspected—for she'd never had great sex—with someone you don't love. And you can have bad sex, she discovered, with the person you do love.

So, her first time. He lit the candles. She put *The Moonlight* on the stereo. He said, lips trembling, as she stood by the window, silhouetted in the night, that he wanted to paint her.

and you.
    upon my soulscape
            i have touched
oh i have touched—
        a child, discovering,
your brow, your cheek,
        in the candledark
      the prelude of our eyebeams
                            reaching out
                    intermingling
            and merging adagio our mouths
seeking, hungrily, sought.
        trembling your touch
                upon my face, my neck
    flowing along the sands of shape
a sculptor, knowing.
            exploring gently
                    probing then finding
—a quick breath at the dormant quickened—
            finding again
          and again
                rising as you enter,
                    crescendo, climax.
        and ah, the floatfall after
      into warmth, washing
    between the spaces not there
            between
        us.
    upon my soulscape
so have i touched.

As soon as he was done, he muttered something like "If that's all there is, what's all the fuckin' ruckus about?"

He asked if she came. She said she didn't know.

"How can you not know?" he asked.

"Well, when you have nothing to compare it to …"

"Did you just say what I think you said?" he said after a moment.

And then he got dressed and left.

She was confused.

And completely—   No, shattered is too loud.

She had dissolved.

> i grasp
>   and clutch
>   the bleeding roses.
> you hurl me aside
>   and i lay alone
>   cast upon my virgin snow.

Later, Jen told her he was gay, didn't she know that?

Well, he's bi now, she'd said to herself.

She hadn't told him she was a virgin. Why would she? It was an embarrassment. A vulnerability. A subordination. She didn't want any special treatment.

Though maybe she should've. Maybe she needed special treatment. There should be men you can hire, men who know.

At the very least she'd expected, she'd wanted, to spend the night together, the whole night, touching.

Instead, she spent the night, her first night, curled in a tight little ball. Crying.

"On the crest of this elation, must I crash upon the shore?" Greg Lake

The disappointment was—   There are no words for it.

    stay   need   want

    i thought—

She hurt so much. Not physically. Not physically at all.

She had been waiting, hoping, imagining, believing, holding out, holding in, for years.

And he didn't even stay the night.

    Tell me it can be better.

    Tell me love can be.

It's not like she had any sexual confidence before. Now …

Well, no wonder she went out and fucked every man she could.

She didn't know why he'd left. He wasn't in class for several days after, and when she made subtle inquiries, she found out he'd gone to Montreal. Eventually she obtained an address and wrote to him. She tried to make him see that he was, that they were— She had shown him her poetry, he had shown her his paintings, they had quoted Emerson, Lake, and Palmer to each other, and T. S. Eliot, all of their conversations were meaningful, he eschewed small talk as much as she, they wanted to go to Europe together …

He didn't write back.

    "I'll be dying slowly till your next 'hello' …" Neil Diamond

He could've been Ted Hughes to her Sylvia Plath, she'd thought.

Right.   Look how that turned out.

• • •

Two hours in to the forest, when she rounded a bend in the logging road, she happened to glance to her left and pulled up to a sharp stop. At the far end of an open meadow, a bear was foraging. She stood absolutely still, trying to determine if she was upwind or downwind. The bear didn't even look up, so probably the latter. She continued to stand, motionless, watching it, as it rummaged in the bushes. It was such a rare thing, to see such a large animal in the wild. She continued to watch, treasuring the moment …

A few minutes later, it wandered out of sight, and she turned around to head back.

• • •

By the time she returned, the wind had died down, so she decided to finish the journal, the year, then go for a moonlight paddle.

By the end of the first term, everything had started falling apart. She'd been doing too much for too long—the pizza dough was spread too thin and gaping holes started appearing. She'd somehow misread her watch or got the time wrong and showed up to one of her dance classes exactly an hour late. One of the classes she taught. She dutifully kept up with all her course reading, but absorbed none of it. She fell asleep between heats at a track meet.

So when her brother returned from Edmonton at Christmas with his happy-time flirty friend, who said that while he was here he'd like to see Toronto, did she want to come, she said sure. She hadn't seen Toronto either. Not really.

"You went to Toronto with Dale?" her mother asked stiffly a few days later. Her father was in the den sitting in his lazyboy chair. A metaphor if there ever was one. Her mother was standing in the doorway, as if unwilling to fully enter, unwilling to fully engage in any discussion. Another metaphor.

"Yes." She'd come by the house to get her metronome.

"You stayed in a hotel together?"

"Yes."

"You shared a room?"

"I won't lie to you," she'd said at that point, "but please think carefully about the questions you're asking."

Heedless, her mother continued, thinking, no doubt, that it was her business.

"Did it have two beds?"

"No."

"Did he sleep on the floor?"

"No."

And then her mother called her a slut.

She who had waited until she was twenty-one, and safely on the pill, to have sex.

She who had waited until Peter.

> "If you can't stand the truth, don't force me to speak it." Simone de Beauvoir

Was she supposed to be a virgin for her entire life? Apparently she wasn't the kind of girl or woman that boys or men asked out on a date. And she had no intention of getting married. Quite apart from making promises about the rest of your life, the whole institution of marriage was sexist through and through. The word 'wife'—she eventually wrote a piece she titled "Here Comes the Bride" that juxtaposed Wagner's "Bridal Chorus" with a recitation of the history of marriage and statistics on wife abuse—the word 'wife' first referred to women who were captured after invasion and conquest, and taken home to be slaves; marriage was a degradation.

She'd read *Jude the Obscure*.

And anyway, what exactly did her mother mean by 'slut'? And what, exactly, was wrong with being one?

"Can we talk about this?"

Silence.

Well that was nothing new. She'd never been willing to talk about anything of importance.

"Mom, please, look at me."

"I can't." It was clear her mother felt disgraced.

Right. She'd made it all about her. As usual.

> Is that why I must write it down, in painful detail? To purge myself of its power, to exorcise myself, to expel it from my mind by sentencing, committing it to forever to paper?

Turns out it wasn't an exorcism, but a solidification.

Was she attracted to Dale, had she *wanted* him? Not particularly.

But she'd learned she didn't have a hope in hell of getting the man, or anything really, that she wanted.

Over the next few months, she added others to her list. Matthew, Gary, Don—all became friends with benefits.

There were also a number of so-called one-night stands—men whose names she couldn't remember, or hadn't even known.

In short, she had a lot of sex. With a lot of men. She wasn't a snob. They didn't have to have to be intellects. They didn't have to be artists. They just had to be willing. She wanted to feel sexually attractive, she wanted to feel that men would, could, want her.

She didn't realize, then, that being sexually attractive had nothing to do with it.

That most men were willing to fuck anything.

And so she never really healed.

She continued to write throughout her fourth year. She had to. Long poems full of passion and pain. Piano solos in minor keys.

And she continued to be alone, loving it and, at the same time, not.

The piano was a solo instrument. But did she choose it because she was solitary or did she become solitary because she had chosen it?

Well, she didn't choose it, her parents did.

But it did suit her.

The Loneliness of the Long Distance Runner. That title probably had as much a part in her decision to become a distance runner as did her love of the forest. But yes, it suited her too.

Reading, writing— All of her passions, they were all lone endeavours.

But was that cause or effect?

> "Crazed/by love and feeling and internal thought/protracted among endless solitudes ..." William Wordsworth

> Yes. That's it precisely.

At least she still had Craig. She could tell herself there *was* someone special. When he'd suggested she come out to B.C. at the end of fourth year, she'd been ecstatic. Their relationship *was* everything she'd thought, hoped, it was.

She turned the page.

Between her own five mile runs, and running to and from her piano lessons and drop-in, she was putting in twenty-five miles a week. Her coach upped her to thirty, then thirty-five, then forty. Soon she was running ten miles at a time. Then fifteen. He contacted a colleague and obtained some information about training for a marathon. He entered her in a university competition, and in April of her fourth year, she ran her first marathon in just under three hours.

Several American universities contacted her, offering full scholarships; she could enrol in the graduate studies program of her choice. She accepted one of the offers, and went on to become part of the Olympic team, when women were finally allowed to enter the marathon event, in 1984. She finished about ten minutes behind Joan Benoit.

Either that or she didn't run her first marathon until she was forty-three.

Because at the time, in the late 70s, women weren't running marathons. The 3,000M was the longest event women could enter. At any competition. So it didn't occur to her. Or to her coach, apparently.

She hadn't seen Kathrine Switzer run the Boston Marathon in 1967. And if she had, it would not have been encouraging.

She certainly couldn't afford a subscription to *Runner's World.*

And this was before the internet.

So she didn't know anything about training for a marathon. She didn't know she was ready in her late twenties, once she was running forty miles a week, with longest runs of twenty miles. She didn't know she could be ready in four months.

She had started running at thirteen, and didn't feel ready until thirty years later.

That was how long, how hard, she thought you had to work at something before you could be good enough.

Talk about a metaphor.

She also didn't know that fifty miles a week was too much. So she kept overtraining and injuring herself. She didn't know about good shoes. She didn't know about carbohydrates and protein and glycogen. She didn't take a water bottle with her when she ran, and certainly didn't have anyone who would agree to be at certain spots with water. After one particularly scary dizzy spell ten miles from home in the middle of nowhere, she started planting water bottles at certain spots along the way, but it took time to stop and get them from out of the ditch.

But she did it. She measured the distance in her car, out in the country on gravel and dirt roads. And on one perfect summer day, she ran a marathon. At forty-three. In just under four hours.

Just her. No one to push her off the road, no one to scoff at her from the sidelines.

Or cheer her on.

What *did* happen that April was an athletics awards ceremony at which, after a long line of young men had been called to the stage, applauded, slapped on the back, and given large letters they would presumably have sewn onto their jackets, she was called to the stage. And given what looked like a tiny lapel pin. She could hardly hold it up to the audience to invite more applause. Should that have been her inclination.

She was puzzled, curious as to why someone had thought women wouldn't also want a letter, but she wasn't angry. Her coach was, however. The whole team was pissed off, apparently. (Which was, she admitted, kinda nice.) They'd seen the insult she had not. She hadn't associated bigger with better.

She tried to remember now what the award was actually for. Surely not Female Athlete of the Year. Yes, she'd set several track records at the university but only because, she thought, she was the first woman in the university's history to have run those events. Her times were decent—she was always in the top quarter of her field—but not exceptional.

Yeah, but none of the football players who'd received awards were exceptional either.

Near the end of April, her sister became pregnant. And though she herself didn't want to be a mom, she was looking forward to being an aunt. She happily suggested to her sister, and Dick, her husband, that while they took care of bowling and baseball, she could take care of books and ballet. Or something to that effect.

They told her she was to have nothing to do with their kids.

Her brother didn't even contact her when he had kids. They hadn't had an argument, there was no formal parting of the ways— That he didn't contact her, that he had, in fact, no way of even doing so, was an indication of just how distant they had been from each other their entire lives.

How was that possible? It was a question she'd asked from time to time. How can two people live together for twenty years as if the other didn't even exist? Brothers in Islamic countries pay more attention to their sisters.

Even if is just to kill them.

She managed to finish the year, although she got her first Cs, one in a Psych elective, and the other, horribly, in one of her Philosophy courses. She also received a C on her English Comprehensive exam. She understood the other two, but was surprised at that one—she'd spent months preparing, reviewing her entire four years' worth of notes, and had, she thought, written an especially good answer to at least one of the three questions.

Years later, she would find out that two of her profs had given her an A and two had given her an F. Hence, the C. The first two thought her discussion of the nature of literary criticism remarkably insightful, getting to the philosophical heart of the matter. The other two thought she had bullshitted her way through it.

She passed, barely, her Associate exam in piano. Ditto, her Associate in dance.

By the time she finished her degree, she knew what her first novel would be. A portrait of the artist as a young woman. A coming of age novel—about a *woman* coming of age. Something that would show the artistic, intellectual, and emotional interiors of a woman.

Surely it was time.

The novels in her high school English courses were all about boys—*Catcher in the Rye*, *The Apprenticeship of Duddy Kravitz*, *A Separate Peace*, *Lord of the Flies*. And, of course, *Portrait of the Artist as a Young Man*.

And she had just spent her four years of university reading more books written by men about men. And apparently for men. Because they sure as hell didn't speak to her.

So *surely* it was time.

10

Two days after she wrote her last final exam, she was on the three-day train out west. To meet the love of her life, the boy/man she'd been writing to for three years, her one hope.

She'd found a good teacher for her music students. Laura, one of her students, had asked, several weeks prior, whether, if she didn't finish the sonata she was working on (her first sonata!) before she left, she could send it to her? She was touched.

She'd said her good-byes at drop-in. She would miss it dearly.

There were several other people she'd miss—Matthew certainly, the guys on the team, the guys she played pool with, and Diane, in the English program, to whom she had just started talking and had discovered was a kindred spirit—all too late, all too little, for any exchange of addresses and promises to write. Not that she had an address to exchange.

In short, she was ready. Oh so ready, standing at the train station with her new backpack containing a few clothes and a few necessaries, but most importantly, her journal, all her works-in-progress, and a few essential books.

Two nights after she arrived, she was in Craig's room in the apartment he shared with another guy, waiting and waiting, in anticipation. It would be their first time. Finally, she got dressed and went out to see what was taking him so long. He'd decided to make applesauce.

Well, she thought, trying hard not to be angry or hurt, people don't always do what you want when you want. She wouldn't have it any other way. She could wait for what she wanted, she wasn't a child.

An hour later, she dressed again. Apparently making apple sauce was a two-hour activity. He was irritated at her impatience.

She should have left. Right then and there. The apartment. The relationship.

But—

> I had this idea of what he was, formed more by what I wanted him to be than by actual evidence, of which I soon had much to the contrary, and I couldn't let go of that belief. Didn't want to let go of it. All very pedestrian, really.

She couldn't—

He turned on the radio when I was talking …

She should've—

The Brownings fell in love writing letters.

The first time she saw him play the guitar, she … stared. *That's* what he meant when he said he played the guitar? He just sat there for fifteen minutes, fiddling rather aimlessly, unable to even tune it.

And yet there was something—his attitude, the way he sat, his face—all implied that the action was far more serious than it was. And she must've bought it. At least initially.

> The first time he happened to hear me play, Beethoven's *Pathétique*—

'Happened', note. He never asked to hear you play.

And you never expected him to.

> I've gotten a job teaching piano at the Point Grey Community Center, and they have a grand piano in the Oak Room, a spacious, elegant room into which the sun streams through tall windows, and twice a week, when the room isn't in use after my classes, I stay and play.

He expressed surprise. He didn't know I was that good.

What? What did he think?

He knew she practiced every day for hours, he knew she took the Conservatory exams, had just passed her Associate, so— What did he think? How could he possibly have thought that his aimless fiddling every now and then with the guitar was even *remotely* comparable?

You were an accomplished musician, he was fuck all.

She didn't see any of that, at the time, as accountable to gender. As men overvaluing their accomplishments, undervaluing women's accomplishments.

Worse, he interrupted. "There you are!"

Peter would have just stood, quiet in the corner, in reverence. Not for me, but for the music. He would have empathized, understood how it felt, how I felt, to be a conduit, to be so in the music. In that beautiful room.

...

And tonight, I ask, softy, "Do you wanna make love?" and he jokes "With you?"

How that hurt. Oh god, how that hurt.

Why didn't she leave?

Because she didn't know any better. He was her first boyfriend. Her only boyfriend. She had nothing to compare it to. Not even the shared experiences of girlfriends. Because she didn't have any. Girlfriends.

And compared to her parents, her brother, and her sister, her relationship with Craig was good. Or at least normal.

One night she was *so*—she was actually covered in sweat, lying beside him in bed, almost panting, trying to control the desire rushing through her body. But he was too tired, he said. He wasn't interested. She tried to make him interested. He pushed her away.

> I came to you practically begging like an animal in heat and all you can do is say 'Yeah, life's a bitch.'

She stared out at the water. This journal would be hard, she realized. Even now, after all these years. She thought about going for a walk in the forest, but then decided to push on.

> a rush of flames
> at the core
> and all of me is melting, down
> there's nothing left
> but the hot liquid
> in a pool upon the floor
>
> soon,
> i'll harden.

There was no chemistry, as they say. She knows that now. But at the time, she concluded she was undesirable.

> And yet, and yet, after he heard one of my pieces, he said to his roommate, 'Yeah, she's gonna be famous some day.'

But then when they looked up at the stars one impossibly clear night, he said, comically, "Starry, starry night."

And she knew then, she should have gone to Peter instead.

> "If the stars in the sky mean nothing to you, they're a mirror." Rod Stewart

There was no affection. No warmth.

But it didn't bother her because it wasn't any different from what she'd been used to. There had never been any affection or warmth in her life.

Susan commented once that it didn't sound like a good relationship. "Destructive," she'd called it. She should have listened.

"You will crawl without bending your knees." Leonard Cohen

But beggars can't be choosers.

After she broke her arm—as soon as she decided to stay for the year, not just the summer—god knows why—she arranged to have her bike crated and shipped out, and then had an accident speeding through a yellow light rather than risking a stop in the rain—and she had trouble making a sandwich for her lunch, he grudgingly put it together, but then didn't even slice it in half.

Oh Matthew—god, how I want you!

How could I have turned away from the love you were offering?

Because you didn't feel it in return. No matter how much the mind wants … If it's not there, it's not there.

Years later, seeing Greg wordlessly help Janice put on her sweater when her wrist in a cast, she knew then, it wasn't her. It was him.

Or maybe not. Maybe she didn't, doesn't, elicit tenderness. Maybe it was that whole self-sufficient vibe she gave off.

Because after all, he drove all the way to Patty's apartment to kill a spider for her.

No, he drove all the way to Patty's apartment for a quickie. You know that now.

The problem was, there were good times. They went hiking in the mountains. They went to Kitsilano Beach, Stanley Park, Granville Island. She bought a used bicycle, and they toured Saltspring Island.

They went to parties. And she suddenly realized how being part of a couple— There was a whole social world out there that until now she had no idea even existed. People invited couples. They didn't invite singles. All this time, she'd thought it was her. It was, but not her personally. It was her status, her lack of status, as a singleton.

She turned the page.

He told me tonight that I didn't love him.

What?

It had shattered her.

Was he right though?

your words scrape across my skin

nerve-strings recoil, stretch, twist

trying to phrase a melody

trying to

wrench beauty from truth.

She'd been trying so hard.

She tried several times to ask about his work, but he never wanted to talk about it. Five years later, she still wouldn't know the point of it, wouldn't know what hypothesis he'd set out to investigate.

Once he asked her to be a subject in one of the experiments he was conducting. She was delighted. As she recalled, he handed her a pair of headphones and asked her to listen, after which he would ask questions. When she realized there was one thing in the left ear and another in the right, she asked which she was to pay attention to. He became angry. Just listen! I can't tell you any more! But, she protested, it would make a huge difference to the results if she paid attention to the left or the right. Just listen! he repeated, even more angrily.

She'd been appalled. How could he get any reliable results if he didn't tell people what to listen to? Even an instruction to try to divide one's attention would have made a difference. Surely the only conclusion one could draw from his experiment would be about the tendency of people to listen to the right or left channel.

She eagerly accompanied him when he went to various conservation areas to photograph rocks, trees, and the like, but it soon became clear that she was, essentially, to tag along. She was not to ask any questions, she was not to suggest places to go to, places *she* wanted to go to. She took a book and whatever piece she was working on at the time, whether poem or prelude, but it annoyed her to have to get up and move on whenever he said.

> counterpoint
>
> two lines of melody
> refusing to coincide
> collide
> again and again
> with each beat
> they twist and tangle
>
> leaving all my notes
> in knots

No, he wasn't talking about love. He was talking about devotion.

> And when I'm catatonic, rocking myself in the cold white porcelain tub, absolutely numbed by your declaration, struggling to rewrite four years of my life, you do not say, 'Come back to bed,' but 'Can I get you something?' And I take that as love. That meagre, minimally decent response.
>
> …
>
> You can make it through this pain. Breathe. In out in out.
>
> …
>
> I used to be so alive, so cool, so sure …
>
> My students, drop-in—they wouldn't recognize me now.

And that was just the first year, she looked out across the little cove. My god, I stayed with him for four more.

I need to do something alone soon, something totally alone, ride to the beach and sit all day with the seagulls, read, write, swim—

Always this need. To be alone.

She was stronger that way.

"Who's Botticelli?" he asked.

And then she got a letter from Peter.

Was he too late, he asked? He'd been a fool, he said, he still loved her, had he lost her forever?

No! she wrote back passionately. Realizing by then that her relationship with Craig was no intertwining of souls at all …

Realizing by then that Peter's invitation, not Craig's, had been the 'Come live with me and be my love' she had been waiting for …

But then again he didn't write back.

He reads the postcard from Peter.

"Quite the romantic. Do you want someone to say to you I need you, I want you, I love you?"

Well, yes.

"I hope it's more than that," he says.

That would be enough, I think. It's way more than you've ever said.

"Those are easy things to say," he says.

You seem to find them difficult enough.

"Why did you come?" Craig had asked her then, irritated.

Why did she stay? she'd asked herself. Later. Much later.

Too much later.

Why didn't she leave and go to Montreal, to Peter? She didn't have the money. She couldn't change plans so easily. She should give Craig a fair chance.

Should?

Months passed. And still Peter didn't write back.

> I'm weary with waiting, I'm weary with wondering, but most of all, I'm weary with writing these words to myself.

Twice, she and Craig decided to separate. They were much better as friends, they realized.

> I have lingered on beaches, hoping …

> I have wandered through libraries, looking …

But then, they'd drift together again.

If she'd been back home, if this had been in her third or even fourth year, if she'd been anchored firmly in the lattice of her life, perhaps she could have resisted that drift—

Because then it would happen all over again.

> It was always me to suggest getting together, and when we were, it was always me to reach out and touch. You made me sit up like a puppy, begging to be petted.

She marked her place in the journal, went up to the cottage, changed, and went out in the kayak.

• • •

The lake had such an interesting shoreline. It was delightfully complex. Weeds here, waving in the wind, reeds there, stiff as sentinels, a dozen different kinds of bushery, another dozen different kinds of trees, all in various stages of growth, some jutting out, some receding, most in one green or another, a few in a lovely russet. The combinations were infinite. As she paddled, she noted the contrast, the interest, provided by a white birch and, a bit further along the shore, a few grey skeletons of dead evergreens. There was so much detail one could attend to. Escher couldn't have done better.

And blissfully, it was all without meaning.

• • •

She returned to the dock well after the sunset. She secured the kayak, watched the moon glimmer on the water for a while, then went up to have something to eat before continuing where she'd left off.

Despite her disappointments and difficulties, it was an amazing year. She smiled, now, remembering all the energy and passion, the excitement of being in B.C., in Vancouver. She'd rented a basement apartment on a street that, shortly after she moved in, burst into fuchsia cherry blossoms. Everything she needed was within biking distance: a couple used book shops, a used record store, the university campus with its endowment lands, several beaches, sunsets. She still had a photograph she took while astride her motorcyle, the mountains in her rear-view mirror.

She'd started immediately to make her way through the accumulated bits and pieces of poems, stories, plays, compositions that she had brought with her …

Inspired by her Eve essay, she started reading *The Bible*, looking for more women who needed to have their say, and she began writing monologues, half essay, half story …

> Is that why bibles typically don't have an index? It would make it so much easier to recognize the ridiculous inconsistencies.

She finished a play and entered it in a competition for a local festival. She told Craig, excited about completing her very first play and maybe, just maybe, seeing it performed. "You haven't got a hope in hell," he said.

> Taking stock: in the eight months since I've come here, I've finished three stories, fifteen poems, three monologues, and one play; I've finished four

of the seven pieces of Opus 1; and I've sent stuff out to almost two hundred journals and magazines …

She'd also started on the reading list she'd been keeping for when she had time to read books that weren't on her required reading lists …

"Franz [Kafka]'s mother loves him very much but she has not the faintest idea who her son is and what his needs are. Literature is a 'past-time'! My God! … All the love in the world is useless when there is total lack of understanding." Yes!

"… but the woman who accepts a way of life which she has not knowingly chosen, acting out a series of contingencies falsely presented as destiny, is truly irresponsible." Germaine Greer

Lessing's *The Golden Notebook* …this is going to be a good book for me …

"It takes a tremendous amount of courage to be young, to continue growing, not to settle and accept." Robert Henri

Huxley, Kesey, Hess, Rand, Mann, Dosteovsky, Wollstonecroft …

A couple months in, she applied for a position at the university; a professor was looking for an editor to help him with a book he was writing. She was hired. He liked that she had a degree in English and was actively writing herself. She rewrote his manuscript in two months, easily turning it into something clear, coherent, cohesive. He was amazed. And terribly grateful.

So grateful, he spread the word, telling his colleagues about her. Soon she had requests to edit half a dozen manuscripts. The money—good money—poured in.

And when that didn't happen—instead of posting the position on the job boards she regularly checked, he'd mentioned his need for an editor to a colleague, who mentioned it to someone else, who mentioned it in her class, and a first-year Comm101 student got the position—she got a job with Office Overload. She was dismayed to be working in offices again, surrounded by stern and sour faces.

Oh god. I cannot live this way, I cannot spend my life working in an office.

She decided to take a few courses, courses she'd been unable to fit into her schedule at WLU: a fine arts studio course, a history of art course, and a music composition course. The last mentioned started with an assignment that required going to the Music Library.

It was like walking from a room with a dripping tap into a waterfall.

She still remembered getting Philip Glass' *Glassworks* from the desk, taking it out of the sleeve, putting it on the turntable, sitting down, putting on the headphones, and—

She was stunned. Absolutely stunned.

The music was amazing. She hadn't heard anything like it before. The movement, the harmonies, they cascaded over her, they ran through her …

She discovered that one could sign out records, like one signed out books. She lugged home the maximum allowed every week for the whole year.

And then, five years later, studying at the Conservatory for her Associate in Composition, one of the books she had to buy was a book full of scores. She didn't know such books existed. It occurred to her that she could listen to a piece of music *and read along*. She could *see* the music!

She chose carefully her first experience doing so. Beethoven's *Fifth Symphony*. It wasn't in the book she'd had to buy, but she discovered that not only were there bins and bins of records at the University of Toronto Music Library, there were shelves and shelves of scores. She found the score for Beethoven's *Fifth*, then found a recording of it—she had no idea that some of the dozens were better than others—then walked to an empty carrel, put on the headphones, opened the score to the first bar, and carefully set the needle on the record. It was like tasting colour.

While she was out west, her parents sold her piano. Like it was a piece of furniture.

When she read that news, so casually written in one of her mother's letters, it—

Yes, it was an old piano, and only a Heintzman. And yes, like them, she anticipated being able to afford a better one at some point in time. Still.

They also sold the cottage.

When she expressed her dismay, they were surprised. *Surprised.* Did they have no idea how much she loved it? That she wanted nothing more than to live in such a place? There was a high school thirteen miles away. She could have taught there. While she wrote at the cottage. Looking out at the lake. Surely they had known—

They spoke of the increase in taxes. The lease. They pointed out that she wouldn't have been able to afford it. That she was not one but two years away from having a regular job, now that she'd decided to stay in Vancouver before returning to go to teacher's college.

All true, she conceded.

Ten years later, she realized that some parents would have just given the cottage to their kids. At the very least, they would have willed it to them.

She closed the journal, selected a CD, then turned out the light. *Pink Floyd* was best in the dark.

11

Next morning, she sat for a while on the dock with her tea, simply breathing in the beauty.

Near the end of the second summer, she sold her motorcycle (she would buy another; truth be told, it had been leaking oil since the accident) and packed up everything else (the typewriter she'd bought, the several boxes of records and books she'd accumulated, and all of her work, finished and still in-progress), loading it into the van she and Craig had bought for the trip back east. He'd been accepted into the graduate Psych program at McMaster, and she—she went to teacher's college. Not grad school. Not for Philosophy, not for English. She wanted no more assignments to keep her from her first novel.

If she was so eager to be a writer, why didn't she enrol in an MFA program? It was *because* she was so eager to be a writer. No one explained that in an MFA program, her first novel could *be* her assignment.

Or that MFAs got published.

And B.Eds didn't.

No doubt the feedback could have been valuable, but given the feedback she'd received to that point— Her Milton professor called her Eve piece cute and quirky, not feminist scholarship. And the people in the writer's club she'd joined after she won the local library's writing contest seemed to her to be just a bunch of people getting together once a month to chat about what they were working on.

Furthermore, she'd thought that to get into grad school, you had to have straight A+s through your undergraduate years. And although that's what she'd started with, by fourth year, she was scraping by with B+s mostly.

Imagine her surprise when several years later she scored over 2000 on the GRE.

Imagine her anger.

And then the horror.

All those Ph.D.s *weren't* smarter than her.

As it was, suddenly all the people she knew, Matthew, Don, Craig, even Tim from track, they were all past the piddly little B.A. and getting TAs and RAs, while she was typing and filing. Again. She was far more intellectually inclined than they were! None of *them* read nonfiction, *textbooks* for godsake, in their spare time!

> *A Literature of their Own*, Elaine Showalter. *The Politics of Reproduction*, Mary O'Brien. *Mind and Matter*, Bateson.

"At least you're getting back into something regular," her mother had said in one of her letters, when she'd told her about now being in teacher's college.

> Why must we all be regular? God damn it don't shove your boring, routine mediocrity on me!

In one of the letters she had from the beginning not welcomed. They were chatty letters. She replied, to be kind, but as briefly as possible. But eventually the superficiality of it, the fakeness of it, wore her down.

> Do I have to wait until you die before you get off my back?

> You are the measure of all things, you've made that very clear. Mother dearest.

She'd intended to effect a severance with her parents upon her move out west, but when she realized how much her mother depended on her letters …

But everything she wanted, everything she wanted to be, everything she thought and felt, seemed to hurt her mother. Or meet with disapproval. So either she could keep hurting her, again and again, or she could keep exposing herself to disapproval, or she could suppress, keep to herself, her self. She chose the latter. After all, she owed her mother life itself.

But then "Let me in," her mother cried. It was a lose-lose situation.

What do you say to your mother's pain?

You tell her to fuck off and give up the martyrdom.

And then one weekend, they were discussing, god knows why, whether the whale in *Moby Dick* was just a whale—the book had arrived as part of a book club subscription, to be put high on the bookshelf with the others—and when her father finally conceded to give her the benefit of the doubt, she lost it.

> How fucking patronizing! *You'll* give *me* the benefit of the doubt? On *this*? What an insult. What a fucking, though truly representative, insult.

> How would you feel if, over an elementary income tax issue, I differed with you but patronizingly allowed you the benefit of the doubt?

It got worse.

> And then you said that 'probably' or 'possibly' I wasn't a child anymore. I'm twenty-three.

> I suspect you'll continue to see me as a child until I have the standard trappings of adulthood: husband, children, career.

She was absolutely right about that. Thirty years later, he'd toss her a twenty to buy a pizza. He'd been tossing interest-free loans to her brother for decades. For adult things like buying a house.

Did women not need a house? Were they supposed to live like trolls under a bridge somewhere?

And so she divorced her parents. She didn't like them. If she met them somewhere, she wouldn't want to spend any time with them. They were boring, self-righteous, smug, shallow, stupid. What sane person would continue to spend time with people she didn't like?

> Did you ever take an interest in them, Gary asked. Good question. No.

I'm not interested in what color the upholstery is. I'm not interested in how to make a good casserole.

Would it be so hard to pretend, he asked then.

Why should I pretend? I respect them too much to pretend, to lie to them.

And why should *they* pretend? She wasn't interested in what they were interested in, and they weren't interested in what she was interested in.

They seemed incapable of joy.

They were also incapable of looking beyond themselves. Her father had said once, "If it doesn't affect us, why should we bother?" Bother to read, to find out about it, let alone do something about it.

He is such an asshole.

And it took so long to get there.

Because it's such a long way, from hero to asshole.

Especially since 'hero' was formed at six.

Worse, their constant dismissal, even mockery, of her interests and opinions was devastating. Because they were all she had, in terms of 'family and friends'. Except for Craig. If she'd had friends who had the same interests, the same opinions … But she didn't. It would be hard enough to go it alone, without anyone's support, with no one caring one damn bit whether she finished that poem, had that story published. But to do it in the face of constant mockery—of that poem, that story— she wasn't sure she'd be able to continue writing in that case.

One can end a marriage, leave a lover, break off a friendship. Why is the relationship with one's parents expected to be permanent? One should be able to end that relationship too when it dies or becomes destructive.

And, so, she sent a letter informing them of her decision. To divorce them. A very carefully worded letter. She thanked them for the first fifteen years of her life. They had, after all, provided food, shelter, security. Music lessons for ten years, dance lessons for five. Clothing, books, and so on, until she turned sixteen and got her first job.

> "You continue to see yourself as figure of authority, minister of approval …
>
> "I once tried to interact with you as equals, as one adult to another, but you refused …
>
> "In any case, I'm not really interested in interacting with you on that basis. I don't really like you. We have different interests, different values, different opinions, different beliefs, different behaviours. It's all different. Would you be friends with people with whom you have nothing in common?
>
> "Do not think me thankless in my rejection — I recognize and am grateful for what you did and or intended to do for the first 15 years of my life. But a love of gratitude can only go so far, and I have gone as far as I can go. The rest of our relationship rests on a shared past. A past which is dead. And can't be revived. I am no longer what I was 10 years ago. Further, to forgive and forget would be to deny reality. So let us finally end the fight by recognizing and accepting this parting.
>
> "With as much love as I can give, goodbye."

Besides, she was tired of hurting them. Her very existence was apparently a problem, a disappointment. Certainly every time they interacted, there was conflict.

> I will never become the kind of person they want me to be, and they will likely never become the kind of people I can grow close to.
>
> If they showed interest, it would be insincere because they really don't like Bach or whatever, and if they don't show interest, I accuse them of not caring. It's a no-win situation. Best to let it go. Walk away.
>
> I'd be an irritant. If I forced them to think about things, they'd end up unhappy. What right do I have to rip off their rose-colored glasses? My questions expose truths they'd rather not face. Inconsistencies. Delusions.

Of course they wrote back, upset. Her father said something like 'This is the thanks we get for supporting you all these years?' Her mother said something like 'You have misunderstood and twisted everything.'

You supported me all those years? Please. You tolerated me. At best.

You say I have misunderstood and twisted much, but you don't want to explain exactly what or how.

So be it then.

Even so, she wrote yet another letter.

"You complain that you always lose when you argue with me. Well yes, that's probably true. And rightly so. Larry has something to show for his business degree: he knows about administration, marketing, accounting, he has a job selling insurance, he's moving up in the world. You see all that. Concede all that. But you're blind to what I have gained from that 'useless' degree you say I threw my intelligence away on. That honours degree in philosophy and literature. As a result of it, I'm a damned good thinker. And I'm well-versed in positions and counterpositions, attitudes, opinions, on all sorts of topics — truth, beauty, right and wrong, life, death, love. But you're right. It is useless.

"You say I'm causing you pain. I know. I'm sorry. But then again, I'm not responsible for the pain caused by your inability to accept what I am and what I do.

"I don't want you to be a part of my life anymore. I don't want you to be my mother anymore. I don't need mothering anymore. I feel no affection for you. Or from you. I don't love you. And I wish I didn't have to keep saying these things to you.

"'I loved you the best I knew how', you say, 'but that wasn't enough. You wanted love on your terms.' Yes, I suppose I did. I still do. Don't we all?

"So you offer love on your terms and I don't want it; I offer love on my terms but it's not enough. It's a sad, sad story. Let it end here."

Neither her sister nor her brother contacted her. Neither of them wrote to say, what's wrong, what's happened, can we help?

Which, in itself, was … revealing.

But what is even more revealing is that it took thirty years for that to even register.

> "I want you, I need you, but there ain't no way I'm ever gonna love you … We can talk all night, but that'll never change the way that I feel … You've been cold to me so long, I'm crying icicles instead of tears."
> Meatloaf

Years later, she would dream that she'd been frying her parents and had forgotten—and had come back into the kitchen to find them black lumps in the pan.

They were dead to her.

She looked up from her journal, noting that it was starting to cloud over. If it didn't completely cloud over, the sunset would be gorgeous. She decided to read on through that year at Western and then go for a late, long paddle.

Early on, she wrote again to Peter, in case he had replied to her address in Vancouver after she'd left, and gave him her new address, in London.

The first time she went to Craig's apartment for the weekend, he didn't come to pick her up at the bus station, insisting that it was an easy walk from there to his apartment. He had a baseball game to go to; the Psych department had a team in the University league, and he had joined. But it was night when she arrived, and she got lost. And she had a suitcase full of books. She was soon exhausted, wandering around in the dark, looking for the right street, lugging her suitcase. It was a residential area. There were no phone booths. She finally decided she'd have to just leave the suitcase somewhere and come back for it. She didn't blame him. In the daylight, it *was* an easy route, and he had no way of knowing she was going to bring fifty pounds of books with her. And miss a turn at the bottom of a steep hill.

Years later, someone, just a neighbour, offered to come pick her up from somewhere, and it blew her away. That people would do that. For her.

That weekend, she met one of his friends, Daniel—they'd been invited over for dinner—and part way through a really interesting discussion, he seemed to simply abdicate, saying it didn't matter, he didn't really believe in what he was saying.

It had irritated the hell out of her. That he (men?) were so careless with words, ideas.

He was probably about to lose the debate.

When she talked about it with Craig, later, he accused her of taking the discussion too personally.

Another deflection of defeat.

It occurred to her then that discussions between the two of them were unsatisfying for the same reason. He often just suddenly seemed to lose interest. Or he got angry at her for taking it too personally.

Conversation is competition. For men. It doesn't matter to them whether what they're saying is true or whether their argument, if they're making one, is a good one. What matters is winning.

She turned the page.

> Read Jane Rule's *Theme for Diverse Instruments*. I like her style.

> And Susan Sontag's *I, etcetera*. I'm very intrigued by her form. Not at all 'short stories' but rather fragments, pieces of literature.

> Diane Arbus' photography puts my work to shame.

> Saw NFB's *Not a Love Story*.

> And the Twyla Tharp dancers. Springsteen to Bach! Yes!

Another page.

She'd dress for him, and he made fun of her. "Are you trying to be sexy?"

She'd put on music for a bit of slow dancing, and he'd mock. "You expect me to be romantic with your shitty 45s?"

And then suddenly she asked herself, Why do you assume it's *your—*

Because it's always the woman's fault.

Why isn't *he* thrashing about wondering 'What's wrong with me, why can't I respond to a sexual come-on without joking?'

> please Craig call me
> please Craig touch me
> please Craig fuck me

> I hate what I've become with you.

> I want you to want me. Matthew, Gary, Don— Hell, even Dale wanted me more.

> Okay, so don't look to him for sex, don't ever want it. If he wants it, consent, but don't express, initiate, or ask—that opens yourself to the charge of childishness if it ends in frustration or disappointment. He's never told you how to show him you want him, and you've tried several ways, so just stop. Just stop trying.

She came to realize that he wasn't an artist at all. Sure he'd written some poems and he fooled around with a guitar, but he didn't have an artist's soul, an artist's sensibility, an artist's sensitivity.

> to Craig

> no more shall i quiver
> as our eyebeams twist and thread
> upon one double string—
> you have made me too aware
> such conversation is in the ear of the beholder.

> winds no longer whisper
> waves do not reassure—

that is personification
a literary technique
a pathetic fallacy.

the moon was once a marbled orb—
now it is pockmarked
with named craters.

my music is not the voice of my soul—
it is organized sound
synthesized by neurons.

and if some gypsic minstrel should beckon
come live with me and be my love
i shall have to answer
it is too late—
my passions are but chemicals
bleeding through my brain.

She also came to realize how much of her thought, and emotion, how much of her *energy* was focused on Craig one way or another.

"They exhaust each other and they have to separate to recharge." Linda Newman, *A Share of the World*

That's it, exactly.

I am much better on my own. You bring out the worst in me. This relationship is too exhausting. I'm getting out.

And yet, again, she didn't.

And still there was no letter from Peter.

The hardest thing now is curbing the hate. I rehearse our meeting, I polish my cruel lines, my complete and controlled indifference, I assign myself the strength to leave your love letters unanswered for weeks, months, as you have done. It has been too destructive, expressing passionate protestations of love to a wall. It has been too exhausting, I am drained, waiting and hoping, hoping and waiting.

Did you know intense love and intense hate could reside so side by side? I cried over you last night. I actually cried.

I have been such a fool.

Goodbye.

I can't care anymore.

Only an idiot sits beside a dusty road under a barren tree waiting. For two years.

…

How do I hate thee, let me count the ways. I hate thee with the fire that once flamed as love. I hate thee for making me ask, again and again, and I hate thee for turning your back months on end. I hate thee for the crowning touches you put on my romanticism, on my idealism; they are now submerged inextricably in cynicism and realism. I hate thee for failing; you were the one person to whom I could bare my beautiful soul without apology, without self-consciousness, without fear of mockery, and you slapped it. Not once, but twice.

Most of all I hate thee for the mirror you hold to me: I see a weak, dependent, destroyed person.

…

The daily rise and fall of hope. Daily, I say.

The excitement, the anticipation as I go to the mailbox; the destruction as, once more, my hand holds nothing from you.

…

you will wash over me
      like the waves of the sea
            till the stones in my heart
                turn to sand
there you will build castles
      in the sun
         and the wind …

–but the moon changes
and the night–

          … then as the tide rushes in
      it recedes
leaving shells along my shores
      that hold nothing
    but the sound
of you

…

You egotistical bastard, you will not take on step to cross that bridge I built. I have swum in the turbulent waters trying to reach you—

So fine. Having gone under once too often, I am gone now.

The failure of our two solitudes to meet, once in a while, rests on you.

Proud? The word is too small for you.

How to play the fool #246a.

She remembered that she went to the keyboard. And composed a piece she never titled. It was painfully beautiful, a piece of longing, and loss, and in the end, nothing.

I can survive. And I can do it beautifully.

She flipped through the rest of the pages.

Other than divorcing her parents, and continuing angst over Craig, and Peter, there were only three things that stood out about her year in London.

Her friendship with Greg: he had a pink rat's tail, he was into teaching for the same radical reasons as she was (they were in Man-in-Society together, her second teachable), he was enthused about life (enthused!), they talked about everything as they walked to class together, they did stuff together—and he was in a relationship with someone who was in Toronto getting her Master's, and he wrote just once after they graduated, from a small school in northern Manitoba where he was having the time of his life.

The MacBeth moment: the English class was going to perform a scene from *MacBeth*, and when the prof asked 'All right, who will be MacBeth?' she thrust up her hand. And he hesitated, he actually stuttered, as she looked steadily at him, both of them knowing that men used to play women's parts, which was irrelevant in any case—

The sospiro moment: she was walking quickly down a hall from one class to another, or maybe to the library, and someone was inside one of the rooms, obviously a room with a piano, playing Liszt's *Un Sospiro* and she just—stopped. The music, the beauty—it literally arrested her. She stood motionless until the piece had finished. And wondered, if music could do that to her, what the hell was she doing at teacher's college, getting a degree to teach English to high school students?

But she carried on, got the degree, and while she waited for a job offer, Craig suggested she move in with him. It made sense. She didn't know yet where she'd be living. That depended on where she got work. So there was no point in renting until she knew. One year lease and all.

So she didn't have a piano. She'd sold the one she'd bought for her year at Western. It was cheaper to do that and buy another one later than to store it for the interim.

She remembered sneaking into a practice room at McMaster to work on her first sonata. Time passed. She didn't notice. She was oblivious to everything but the music. And she was so content. To be there, at the piano, pen in hand, score paper in front of her, writing out the notes, working out the melody, the harmony, oh, god, it was going so well, the second movement—

Craig eventually found her. And interrupted. He was worried. It was well past supper time. She knew then that she wouldn't stay with him. She didn't need him. She didn't need anyone. Or she needed someone to just find her, set a fresh cup of tea beside her, smile, then leave. But, she thought, she would never find that person.

And she was right.

12

She slept late the next day for some reason. Perhaps it was getting just a little bit colder and her body was starting to go into winter mode. Sure enough, when she looked out across the lake that morning, she saw that the trees were beginning to change, the scarlets and tangerines emerging ever so slightly. It was almost the middle of the month. She was running out of time.

No, she sighed, she'd already run out of time.

She took a sip of tea, then opened the day's journal.

It was the 80s. Teaching positions were few and far between, but by mid-summer, she'd been hired by a high school near Barrie. It was a half-time position. Just what she'd wanted. A secure income and enough time to finally write *Fugue*, her portrait of the artist as a young woman.

> I teach three days a week to pay the rent and spend the rest of my time, my life, at my will—I read, I write, I compose, I study. Far cries from a husband, two kids, and a house around the corner.

Teaching was *nothing* like she'd anticipated. The hostility on the part of the students, the disinterest on the part of her colleagues—it hit her like … a ton of bricks? No, like the pile of boulders at a stoning. By the end of September, she had completed "The English Teacher" and was sending it around to journals and magazines.

> Shit, I'm on time for "O Canada" again. First time I sat through it in a classroom, I was called down to the office. "You aren't setting an example for the students." Damn right I'm not. I'll be no model of hypocrisy. 'The true north strong and free?' Right. 'I'll stand on guard for

thee'? I will not, I'm pacifist. 'With glowing hearts—' "You don't have to sing it, you just have to stand for it. It is our national anthem." Nationalism is an infantile disease, I footnoted Einstein.

And then "The Lord's Prayer." Oh god. I stand and look out the window at the garbage blowing in the wind, so they don't see the derision on my face. Quote for tomorrow's writing exercise: Religion is the opiate of the masses. Marx.

Then the announcements come on. I don't submit any announcements. I tried once, at the beginning of the year, but they censored it, can you believe it? It was to start a debating club, and it read something like 'Does God exist? Is capitalism good? Is abortion murder? Should attendance be compulsory? If you're interested in issues like these, come out to Room 204 at 3:30 for the very first meeting of LCI's new club, the Forum.' They read, instead, 'A new club for debating will meet today after school in Room 204.' Too controversial, they'd said when I inquired. I mean what the fuck. What about the pursuit of knowledge, the freedom of— I don't understand.

I teach wearing jeans, a shirt, and track shoes. (I could tell you what kind of socks too, but it might not matter. I'm not sure anymore. What matters.) My attire seems to pose a problem. I was called down to the office, this was in September, and I was told that I was to "Set an example by dressing properly." What's improper about my clothes? "Well maybe 'inappropriate' is the word." What's inappropriate about my clothes, they don't seem to hinder my ability to teach, I don't suddenly forget the material when I put on my jeans, my evaluation standards don't decline if I have track shoes on— "Well there is an accepted convention regarding dress for teachers." Is an Accepted Convention kind of like a Commandment? Are you saying it's mandatory for staff to wear uniforms? Why?

A teacher in this department, they still talk about it, confessed to me the other day that he was very grateful for his suitcoat and tie during his first years of teaching because they gave him the authority and respect he needed to control the class. So that *is* why. I thought so. I said to him, "Every day you wear your suitcoat and tie, you're teaching the students that it's what's outside that counts, and you thereby discourage them from looking beyond the facades, from reasoning; you perpetuate the mentality of evaluation on the basis of appearance, of 'You are what you look like', of 'Judge a book by—' I once knew a white mouse that acted on much the same basis: response patterned by sensory stimuli." He didn't understand me. My colleague. Not the white mouse.

I mean I could wear a suitcoat and tie too, but then they'd all wonder if I really was a lesbian, and then I'd have to shave my legs pierce my ears pluck my brows curl my hair paint my face and varnish my nails to prove that I'm normal.

Oh, and in defence of giving one of my students the finger? Certainly I respect him. And it's because I do that I'm trying to communicate with him in a way he'll understand.

On the issue of not standing for the prayer, she offered to just wait out in the hall instead of visibly not participating in front of her students (she'd already had a class discussion about the separation of church and state), but apparently she was required by law to be *in* the classroom.

She pointed out that teachers in the staff room didn't stand. Nor were they required to.

One of the vice-principals told her she was too rigid. The other one told her she was too flexible.

I was explicitly asked *not* to change things. But I'd been hired to teach not only grade ten English and grade twelve Business Communications, but also the grade eleven *Society, Challenge, and Change* course.

I was told not to bring values into the classroom. As if standing for the prayer and the anthem isn't doing just that.

And all the novels she was required to teach? They were the same ones *she'd* been taught. *Lord of the Flies, The Apprenticeship of Duddy Kravitz, A Separate Peace.* Books by boys about boys for boys. Every one of them. Women have to change sex to even be a part of the world. Unless they wanted to be somebody's mother, somebody's wife, somebody's secretary, or the town belle. Who was, apparently, everybody's.

Half of her Business Communications class walked out during a business meeting simulation exercise, and she thought great! There will lots to debrief at the next class. (Lesson one: don't walk out of a meeting when you're frustrated with a lack of leadership …)

But apparently they walked straight to the principal's office to complain that she wasn't teaching. Priceless, she thought. But the principal didn't agree.

The principal didn't understand.

> The failure rate of my classes last term was 45%. I was called down to the office for that too. Apparently it's supposed to be no higher than 20%. "Justify your figures," the principal said. Well, I said, twenty-nine of the thirty-six students who failed didn't hand in at least ten of the twenty required assignments. As well, all failing students were absent at least fifteen days during the term. That's three weeks of missed school. "Well we can't have a failure of 45%, that's too high." Oh. "Perhaps you could raise all the marks by 15%, would that bring the rate down?" Yes, it would. "Fine then." (What language are you using?) It would also give six students a mark of 105% or better. "Oh no, that's too high. We can't have that. The computers can only handle two digits." (What language did you say you were using?)

> It's my job to teach, I announced in class one day, and I intend to do just that to those people in this room who are students. It is not my job to entertain or babysit. Half the students walked out. I let them. No, that's not right. How could I have stopped them?

> Students think nothing of coming to class ten minutes late, as if my prepared lesson were a soap opera, something you can miss part of to no detriment. Todd echoes everything I say in a tone that drips with derision. Ian sits at the back, silent, smirking at anything I do that doesn't work, like ask a question that no one answers or discuss a story that no one has read. Mark simply got up out of his desk and turned off the overhead projector as I was talking. Sanford screamed at me when I miscounted the completed pages of work in his disorganized file, 'If you're gonna do it, at least do it right!', then slammed the file drawer shut. After I told the class for the 98th time that if they talk and miss the lesson, it's their fault, Donna hurled at me 'You're supposed to control the class, that's your job, not ours'. They know teachers are allowed to send only one student to the principal's office per day.

> Perhaps it has to do with being the youngest child. I never felt older than,

and therefore wiser than, or therefore an authority over, anyone. I have to remind myself I'm older than—well, everyone who's younger than me.

Early on, she'd mentioned to the principal that she wanted to introduce a philosophy course into the curriculum. His response—well, there was no response. She was puzzled. She had expected, and was prepared for, questions as to specifically what she had in mind.

He probably didn't take you seriously.

She mentioned it to the vice-principal as well, but he rejected the idea, and that was that. After all, no means no.

Years later, she discovered that there was a team at the University of Toronto that was designing not one, but two, Philosophy courses for the high school level, and going through the process of getting Ministry accreditation. Her dream. Happening. Right beside her. And she had no idea.

> How, why, did I fail yet again when I was, could've been, so far ahead of my time? That was my idea, my reason for getting a teaching degree! And it happened! And I was oblivious.

How were you to know? You're not telepathic.

And they were men. The U of T team. All of them. Again. How often does that have to happen before people recognize it's not coincidence?

> I never asked anyone the process for getting a new course introduced into the curriculum.

The vice-principal should have told you. He didn't. Guess why.

When she found out about the U of T thing, she'd felt so—frustrated isn't quite— Nullified. She'd felt nullified.

It was like wanting to run in the Olympics and training so very hard, becoming very good, but then when you mention to people that you want to compete in the Olympics, they just look at you. You don't know there are Olympic trials, you don't know that you have to enter certain competitions to qualify for the trials, you don't know that you have to join certain organizations—you don't know there's a clear path from here to there. You just assume that if you're good enough—what?

It seems stupid now, when you can just google, but how was she to know, then? How are we to know how to fulfil our dreams?

Despite probabilities to the contrary, she managed to make it through the year.

> Today I received the evaluation of the Department Head who sat in on one of my classes last week. "Observations: The class began at 10:31 a.m. A few students came in late, one as late as 10:37 a.m. Many of the students were sitting towards the rear of the classroom, fourteen of nineteen. Attendance was taken by the teacher. A definite homework assignment was not given. The class was generally well-behaved."
>
> Content is irrelevant, I see. We may have been discussing the function of the cilia in a two-toed paramecium on rainy days in February. However, what we *were* discussing was a story's theme: the desperate extents to which being an alien can drive one. The character in the story, able to understand and be understood by no one, starts talking to dandelions, and then kills himself.

She hadn't realized that high school teaching was such a conservative field. For her, high school had opened up her world, it had changed her, it had *saved* her. All those new ideas, all those discussions in class, all those books in the library! She considered teaching to be the most radical act possible.

She hadn't realized that high school *teachers* were, generally speaking, quite conservative. Hers hadn't been.

And it was the most conservative ones that aspired to become principals. Not the Humanities teachers, but the Business, Math, and Phys-Ed teachers. Which made it even more likely that she would fail to receive any support whatsoever.

On top of that, it turned out that Simcoe County had the most conservative board of education in the province and was the last place she should have looked for a teaching job.

But even if someone had told her that— It was such a broad generalization, how can you say that about whole county? Individual and independent, she would always underestimate the effect of peer pressure, socialization, enculturation. The truth of generalization.

At the end of the year, she was declared redundant.

Teaching is the saddest story of unrequited love.

She sent a letter to the school, offering an Award for Independent Thought, a book prize to be given annually to a graduating student, but the offer was declined; apparently it would be too difficult to administer.

Apparently inquiring minds don't give a fuck.

She looked up from the journal. Well. That didn't take long. Ten months. To find her dreams of a career in pieces. She was not going to be Sidney Poitier's "Sir" or Gabe Kaplan's "Kotter" or Richard Dreyfuss' "Mr. Holland" or Robin Williams' "My Captain!"

All male, note.

She marked her spot and went for a long and deeply peaceful walk in the forest.

• • •

On her way back, just past the little creek, she stopped and stood very still. A doe and fawn were browsing at the edge. She watched, barely breathing. The long-legged little fawn still had its spots. After a few moments, they moved on, out of sight. She waited a bit longer, so as not to alarm them with her scent, or her steps, then carried on.

• • •

By the end of that year, *Fugue* was done. Three days teaching had meant four solid days writing. And she wouldn't've survived the former without the intensity, the passion, of the latter.

Fascinating. That's what Nora, one of the full-time English teachers, said about it. She said the minor characters came alive. Good. That's hard to do when it's all in first person. And she said so much rang true to her. Good. So it's not self-indulgent. She said others have done the same thing, but their work comes across as polished; yours is appropriately raw, you've got the adolescent angst down, she said. She wanted more when she was through. She had actually put off finishing it.

Even Craig said some parts of it were brilliant.

She prepared a query letter and started sending it around to agents.

> In the far past, most female characters have been minor, supportive, mere appendages; then they started moving into the spotlight, but the focus has been on the pain of the often futile struggle for maturity and for selfhood, which ended in, if not a total giving in of self to others, at least a compromise of self with others. What I want to achieve is an accurate and just as realistic presentation of the female struggle from adolescence to adulthood, which ends not in rejection but in celebration of the self, as significant individual.
>
> Though perhaps much of my attention in *Fugue* is given to the male/female antagonism, I hope not to have its interpretation limited by this reality. And, as in the past, when female readers have often had to undergo a sex change in order to identify with heroic figures, so, now, male readers will have to do the same.
>
> This "passionate record of realization during a period of transition" is comprised of journal entries, letters, poems, stories, and even music compositions.
>
> The manuscript is 1,090 pages (double-spaced) in length. I enclose an excerpt; if you would like to read the complete manuscript, please let me know.

No one was interested. The mainstream publishers wanted only books by men about men. No that couldn't be true, she thought. There were more female authors than male authors. Yes, but J. K. Rowling had written about Harry Potter. Sue Townsend had written about Adrian Mole. And both were published twenty years later.

In the 70s, people were reading John Fowles (*The French Lieutenant's* Wife—the woman couldn't've possibly been a lieutenant herself), Erich Segal (*Love Story*—

yes, a woman in that—she falls in love and then dies), Arthur Hailey, John Updike, Robertson Davies, Harold Robbins … In the 80s, it was James Michener, Robert Ludlum, Sidney Sheldon, Stephen King, Ken Follett. And Judith Krantz and Danielle Steele.

You didn't have a hope in hell.

And the feminist publishers— She hadn't been sending her stuff to feminist magazines and journals, the few there were, because she wasn't feminist in the sense of being pro-female; she was anti-sexism. And she didn't want to be pigeon-holed as a feminist writer. But eventually, she realized that pretty much everything *not* identified as feminist (that is, everything in the mainstream) was pro-male.

By the end of the year, she'd sent queries to every feminist press she knew of. Still, no one was interested. It seemed their mandate had narrowed. They wanted to publish lesbian authors and authors of color. Somehow it was assumed that if you were a heterosexual white woman, you had a place in the patriarchy.

And of course you did. It just wasn't the one you wanted.

13

Fortunately, the teachers in Toronto went on strike that June, and suddenly their schools were scrambling to staff their summer school and night school programs. She was hired for two summer school courses and, when the strike showed no sign of ending, three night school courses for the fall.

Did she feel guilty for crossing the picket line? No. Why should people who already have a full-time job get first dibs on the leftovers?

She was qualified. Probably more qualified than many of the older teachers who got their jobs before a B.Ed. was required.

And she was experienced. She'd been teaching since she was sixteen.

She'd already decided to move to Toronto because she'd discovered the Conservatory had an Associate Composition program. She could study privately with various teachers to learn orchestration, history, and, most importantly, composition. There would be twelve four-hour exams in all.

She also signed up for lessons with Alexina Louie, whose music she'd heard and, of all the contemporary composers, actually liked.

And she was delighted to discover that there was also someone at the Conservatory, Wes Wraggett, who taught electronic composition. So she signed up for lessons with him as well. She needed to know how Tangerine Dream and Pink Floyd achieved their sounds.

By the end of her year in Toronto, she'd acquired the basics of her own studio: a Tascam 244 four-track, a Roland JX-3P synthesizer, a drum machine, and a reverb unit. All used equipment, but still. The indie cassette culture was just getting started and if she couldn't get her stuff produced by 'real' record labels, well, hell, she'd do it herself.

She composed a lot that year. Not only the assignments required for the many courses she was taking, but her own stuff. But when she composed a piece she did it by ear: she knew the notes she wanted when she heard them out loud, but didn't have perfect pitch, so she had to search by trial-and-error, her fingers on the keys, for each one, for each arrangement of notes for each beat.

No wonder her stuff was on the minimalist side.

Only after, maybe, she'd figure out what key the piece was in and insert a key signature. Until then, she used accidentals as if it was a twelve-tone piece.

Of course, it never was. She'd been exposed too long to mundane music, to major and minor. It's hard to imagine what you've never heard.

But she suddenly understood why it had taken her so long to learn the pieces required for her piano exams: two years for the grade ten pieces and another two years for the Associate level pieces, even though she had spent four hours a day at the keyboard. As far as she was concerned, each note could be any one of the twelve in an octave. Up to five notes for the right hand, and five notes for the left— the number of possible combinations was staggering. And with each beat, each quarter beat, the constellation would change.

She understood harmony, and she'd practiced scales and chords to perfection, but she'd never put it all together, she'd never applied those scales and chords to the pieces she learned. She never *thought* through the piece—this opens in D major, so all the notes in the first bar or even the first few bars will probably be d, f#, or a, then it goes to the dominant, to A major, so the notes will be a, c#, e. That would have narrowed it down considerably. From random to a pattern.

She recalled one of her later teachers yelling at her, "Is it so hard to play the right notes?" Well, yes. Since she was learning them by muscle memory, she had to rewire her brain for each piece. With each new piece, she was like a brain-damaged person learning to walk again.

She did okay in the Conservatory courses, achieving an 89% in her Orchestration I exam, a 91% in Orchestration II, and about the same in the other ten exams. But it didn't translate. She still didn't know how to orchestrate her own stuff, how to fill out the solo piano with strings, how to make her music soar. Eventually she realized that it wasn't because she was stupid, it was because she'd never had the chance to *hear* what she'd written. She'd had no idea how it sounded. Any of it. So she never learned how to write what she heard in her head. She should've studied scores with recordings—*beat by beat*. Pink Floyd scores, Emerson, Lake, and Palmer scores, Tangerine Dream scores.

Once, having finished a beautiful solo for sax, she went walking through the city, looking for a sax player, and found one busking on the street corner. Armando. She told him she was a composer, had just composed a piece for solo sax, would he be willing to play it, so she could record it, eventually release it on one of her cassettes. She couldn't pay him, she explained, but she'd credit his performance on the cassette and give him a copy. "Sure," he said, and followed her back to her place.

She also put notices up at the Conservatory, for the musicians she needed to perform the pieces she was composing.

Gerard, the cellist, didn't hear the flaws in his performance.

Or just didn't bother to correct them. For you.

I did, but didn't say anything. Why not? Because I'm uncomfortable making the same demands on others as I make on myself.

Because heaven forbid you should correct someone, be an authority about something.

Just as Alain Morisod had sent her into new age (she eventually set the sax piece to rain and had plans for duets with wolves and loons), the albums of Rod Serling's poetry with Anita Kerr's music inspired her to set her own poems to music. Then Simon and Garfunkel's "7:00 News/Silent Night" and Hardcastle's "19" led her to become even more creative with both the text and the accompanying sound … she started creating what she called social commentary collage pieces.

She hadn't known about Laurie Anderson.

She should've, could've, become a Laurie Anderson.

If she'd married a Lou Reed.

Who became more known than Anderson.

Of course.

And, motivated by her classes with Wes, she started composing pieces for, or to, a series of photographs Craig had taken, black-and-whites of rocks and trees, synthesizing sounds from scratch—essentially *creating* sounds, not just replicating them, not just arranging them …

By the end of the year, she had four different albums in-progress: a classical piano album, a classical/new age cross-over album, an electronic soundscapes album, and an album of sound-text collage pieces.

Even so, by the end of her year in the city, she wasn't moving in musicians' circles. She knew individuals, the ones who'd responded to her ads, but they came to her little 'studio', played her music, then left. She didn't know how to become 'connected', how to insert herself into some established network.

They were men. You were a woman. Unless you became someone's girlfriend, you weren't ever going to be admitted to the club.

She did meet another woman, who had booked the time slot in Wes' studio right before hers. Turned out she was a member of the Parachute Club. And she invited her to a rehearsal at the end of the week.

It was so cool, seeing Lauri on keyboards, Lorraine on vocals, Julie on percussion. They didn't need a second keyboard player, but they were open to hearing some of her collage pieces. They particularly liked "Always Carefree" which juxtaposed ads for 'feminine hygiene' products with rape statistics. It didn't quite fit their in-progress album, but they talked about maybe releasing a separate album, under a different group name, featuring that piece and several like it.

But no, she didn't go to the rehearsal. She had been exploring Toronto, and had found libraries, galleries, theatres, and dance studios, as well as gatherings of indie film composers, playwrights, choreographers … But invariably it took her forever to find the place, and then, in the latter case, she had to work up the courage to walk in, by herself, into a room full of people she didn't know, who would stare at her. She didn't have any friends, there was no one she could call up and say 'Hey, d'ya wanna …?' And she'd run out of courage by the end of the week.

She looked up at the water as the wind blew a patch of silver across the rippling blue-grey gleams on the black water. It was a moving pointillist painting.

She turned the page.

> Vangelis is today's Beethoven.

> And he can't read a note? Really? So he composes totally—like I do? Playing by trial and error until he gets the sound he wants, the sound he hears in his head?

Alexina was impressed with her work, her "theme and variations" for piano and, a year or so later, the "lament" for solo viola.

"That's so very sad," she said, admiringly.

"You have a good ear," she'd said on another occasion.

For a while, it seemed that Alexina may have considered her a protégé. It looked like good things could happen. She had a mentor, she would be introduced to people, she would have opportunities, she could become a member of the next generation of Canadian composers.

But—what? She didn't ask for help, guidance, advice, direction? She never said to Alexina, 'How do I make it as a composer?'

> Are men more likely to do that sort of thing, talk to their professors, their teachers, about their future?

Probably. Because they think what they want, what they want to do, is so goddamned important.

On the other hand, they don't need to ask.

Why didn't she ask? Because she didn't think Alexina, or Wes, or any of her professors could give her advice? No, she didn't think that.

It was because she didn't know she needed advice. She thought she knew how to make it as a composer: study composition at the conservatory, write music, submit it to performance groups and record companies. Similarly with making it as a writer: get a degree in literature, write, submit it to journals and publishers; in the meantime, apply for grants. She didn't understand that being a composer wasn't the same as composing, that being a writer wasn't the same as writing.

But besides all that, Alexina was writing contemporary classical music, and she didn't want to go in that direction, except to write solos. And apparently one had to write big music, symphonic stuff for orchestras, in order to make it as a composer.

Yeah, guess who established that path to success.

Shortly after her year in Toronto, she discovered the music of André Gagnon. Not the showy, pop stuff, but the beautiful, solo piano pieces that were Chopinesque. *That's* what she wanted to write. She discovered he lived in Montreal, so she wrote to him, asking to study with him.

He never replied.

So it's *not* that she didn't ask for what she wanted. It's that— *What?*

She went up to the cottage to get a second cup of tea. And a slice of cold pizza. The perfect breakfast.

Fortunately, teaching summer school and night school was different than her experience teaching day school had been. *Way* different. It was like drop-in.

The students loved her. They loved her style, they loved her dry humor, they loved the discussions they had, in class, during break, after class, outside sitting on the grass …

Turned out most of them were from the nearby private school, unsatisfied with the As they'd gotten, wanting to up them to A+s.

I'm in the *gifted* class! I'm *teaching* the gifted class! What an honour!

She became such a popular teacher, her students actually told others to try to transfer into her class from the other grade thirteen English that was offered.

Tonight when I arrived, I saw that they'd written "HI TEACH" on the board. I *am* Kotter! I *can* be their Captain, oh Captain!

At both night school and summer school, she could choose which works of literature she wanted to teach. So she taught Myrna Lamb's play, *But What Have You Done for Me Lately*—in which a man finds himself pregnant and has to decide what to do about it—by having the students role play one of the scenes, two at a time, one of the young men stretched out on the examining table, three desks shoved together, being interrogated by one of the young women, the doctor.

And she taught Camus' *The Plague* with a simulation, each student in the class secretly assigned a role—doctor, philosopher, reporter, parent, kid, business owner—dealing with the plague, each minute signifying a day, ending with the announcement that another person had died, that student to leave the action and move to the edge of the room.

She assigned a journal, and they willingly wrote a page a day. It was fascinating reading. She had ongoing conversations with each one of them through her comments.

Even now, she remembered so many of them. Miriam, who was going to become a doctor. The three musketeers—three young women who always sat at the front and were so bubbly, but in a passionate-about-life way, not a trivial, dramatic way. Jon, who wanted to become a dancer and whose answer to some question about Godot and Atwood—"a corrected human being"—blew her away. Isaac, who asked to meet with her in the park one night—he needed to talk about the pressures he was facing at home, wanted to ask her how she had carried on when it all got too much. Richard, who intended to get a Ph.D. in Philosophy as a result of having taken her class. Seth who asked her about the feasibility of maintaining a long-distance relationship that was on his horizon. Todd, who had a wicked sense of humour. Aaron, showing up unembarrassed in a pink suit he had to wear for a wedding. And Gino who'd said she reminded him of Prince: you've got that cool, tough style, he'd said, along with that sensitive and thoughtful side; you write poetry and drive a motorcycle, just like him.

From Prince to a cleaning lady living in a room above the hairdresser's.

She stared out at the water. *What the hell had happened to her?*

Her students' end-of-course evaluations had brought tears to her eyes.

"The most important thing I learned is that I have ability and determination. I cannot thank you enough for that."

"I like the way you're crazy."

"I think I have gotten more intellectually out of this course than I did out of all of high school."

"You are, hands down, the best teacher I've ever had. Please do *not* give it up."

Well, I didn't, she looked out at the water again, sadly. *Not willingly.*

When the strike finally ended, all of the regular day school teachers wanted their night school and summer school courses back. She was left with the table scraps of supply teaching. A day here, a day there.

She tried to apply for a position at one of the alternative schools—during the year, she had made a niche for herself among them as a supply teacher—but there simply weren't any: every disillusioned radical idealist in the regular system ran, didn't walk, to an alternative, any alternative, as soon as such a position became available.

Even so, her foot in the door might have, perhaps should have, led to something … but she floundered at the subtle process of making that happen. One day when the staff went out together for lunch, she didn't assume she was invited and so busied herself with a score she'd brought to work on, so her exclusion wouldn't make her look so pathetic. But when Raymond lingered in the doorway, asking her whether she was coming, she pretended not to hear. She didn't have enough money for lunch, and didn't quite know how to ask someone to lend her some. She also didn't quite know how to go out to lunch with a bunch of people, and was embarrassed to be so socially awkward, still.

She still remembered the time in high school when Mrs. Baron took the girls' cross-country team out for dinner to celebrate the season's end. She didn't know how to order. When the waitress asked "What dressing?" she had no idea what she meant, so she just said "No dressing, thanks." And then there was a big fuss as to whose salad was the one without salad dressing. Part way through the dinner, she reached toward a dish with her fingers for a piece of cheese, but the dish had held small squares of butter. Everyone stared at her. She was mortified.

She regretted immediately not having the social courage to say to Raymond, 'Sure, where are we going?' She liked him. He was a sculptor, always taking days off to exhibit or, he confided, to work on a piece. And Brenda, who had listened to some of her songs and then thought about how to perform them—early Joni Mitchell, she'd decided. And Randall, who was the funkiest principal she'd ever met. All of them were like her. Misfits who had fled the institution of the regular school system. Intelligent and creative people with ideas of their own about education.

Except they had jobs. Teaching jobs.

The upside of the sporadic teaching was that she had lots of time to read.

> Adrienne Rich, Robin Morgan (*Going Too Far*—I love her tone), Patricia Meyer Spack (*The Female Imagination*—D. H. Lawrence as a chauvinist? Yes, of course! And "to be 'good' as a woman I usually to embrace limitation") …

> Just reread Shelley's *Defence of Poetry*. What a bunch of pompous and vague shit.

> Celine's *Journey to the End of the Night*, "Everything is allowed inside oneself." Maybe that's it. People who lack imagination and ability to think are denied the one salvation, the one legal harmless total escape.

> Saw *The Turning Point*. Excellent.

> And *My Dinner with André*. I could write something like that.

> Julian Jaynes, *The Origins of Consciousness and the Breakdown of the Bicameral Mind*. Fascinating.

> Rilke, *Letters to a Young Poet*. Simplistic shit.

Perhaps it was just as well that she was a loner. A full peer group, a social group, would have provided too much input, too many stimuli, each one sending her running on a rich path through a lush forest.

• • •

Half an hour later, she bobbing gentle at the mouth of the marsh, paddle resting across her knees. The remains of broken trees stood in the shallow water—complicated cathedrals with brittle spires, castles with weathered turrets. In some of the larger ones, the cores had rotted away, leaving craters full of water. A few were sprouting new growth, saplings clinging, somehow, to the wreckage.

Other trees had fallen over, uprooted, unable to hold on, their tangled fingers curling around air.

Two black birds, perched on one of the gnarled roots, flew away at her approach.

Further along, a heron, a small pterosaur, took lazy flight.

She looked in vain for the otters. Perhaps it was still too soon.

• • •

She docked the kayak, had a slice of pizza, made another cup of tea, then picked up where she'd left off.

Peter, you are a tumour in my side.

"Faith" was accepted! With payment! (And not in copies!)

Bertrand Russell, *Why Men Fight*. Gwynne Dyer, *War*. Michele Landsberg, *Women and Children First*. Marilyn French, *The Women's Room*. Lynne Sharon Schwartz, *Disturbances in the Field*. Linsey Abrams, *Charting by the Stars*. Gail Godwin. Jane Rule.

On one of her supply teaching days, she met Joel. He taught English, and he was directing *Jesus Christ Superstar*. Her jaw must have dropped. And he was having trouble with the choreography. Dropped further.

"I can help," she said. "Can I help?" she asked, ever so hopefully.

"Sure. You know how to dance?"

It was—*amazing*. His direction, her choreography. They worked well together, their ideas gelled, she loved the excitement of working through the scenes with him, planning the blocking, the moves, the break-outs into dance. They spent several evenings combing the more interesting parts of Toronto, looking for the right prop, looking for costume ideas … It was so exciting, genuinely one of the highlights of her life. They could have, should have, formed a long-term partnership.

That's what men do.

Instead, at one point he suddenly just—shut her out. Literally. Forbid her from coming to the rehearsals. Said she'd forgotten who was the director.

She went to the opening night performance with Craig, and felt sick to her stomach when she saw that her name wasn't anywhere on the program, and, worse, that he had all but eliminated every trace of her influence. Every idea, every move— Judas' dance, of which she had been most proud—they'd put a lone student on a rise, the lights making it look like she was in a cage, her movements choreographed to be as tortured as the vocals— He'd cut it all.

She tried to get backstage after, to congratulate the students and, truthfully, to make sure they knew she hadn't simply quit on them two weeks before opening night. The looks on their faces when they saw her indicated that that's exactly what Joel had told them. And as soon as he saw her there, mingling, he stomped over and practically shoved her backwards out the door. She asked if she could at least have one of the JCS shirts that had finally arrived. As a memento. He denied ever receiving her payment for one.

> I'd rather soar and crash and soar and crash than spend my whole life flying at low altitudes.

And yet here you are, crashing at low altitudes.

She closed the journal, and retreated to the beauty of fire and music.

14

She opened the next journal; she was still in Toronto. And she was still, again, on the dock, looking out across the cove … As the sun hit the ripples just right, the sparkles would suddenly flash, then disappear …

Saw *Equus* last night and was actually in tears with Alan when he is eventually tranquilized after re-enacting the mutilation scene. When his passion is extinguished.

What determines significance? Why are some events more important than others?

I'm drifting into mediocrity. It's so hard to retain the fire, the intensity, the devotion to my work, my purpose. I am nowhere near writing something as powerful as *Equus*.

I leave off my ruminations and go for a walk in the park because I feel like it and it's quiet, and two guys stop me to tell me 'You better be careful.' 'Of what?' 'Well you never know, you're alone.' You don't think I know that? From the moment I saw you, two hundred meters away, I've been ready to run.

She and Craig limped along. They split again. Then got back together again. One step forward, two steps back.

Why do you close your eyes when we make love? he asked.

Because we're not making love.

At least *she* wasn't. She knew that now. He'd been right. She hadn't loved him. Not really.

It occurred to her one day that they didn't act as a team. She hated people, couples, who acted like they were joined at the hip, but she and Craig didn't seem joined at all.

Was she unable to be part of a group, even a group of two?

Once when he was coming to her place in Toronto for the weekend (usually she went to his place in Hamilton), she was feeling particularly fragile, so she put a sign on the door, "Please don't criticize me this weekend." Any derision or mockery would have tipped her over the edge that weekend. She felt so pathetic having to do that.

And it was years before she realized how awful it was that she *had* to do that.

She can't believe how much shit she took.

She sent another letter to Peter, with her Toronto address. And was elated to have it returned, unopened, inside another envelope, with a note indicating that he now lived in Toronto!

She called the number on the note. He seemed pleased to hear from her. So she went to see him.

Just 'pleased'?

They picked up exactly where they'd left off that night she'd asked him if he'd seen the moon. Yes. *Yes!*

But then she started noticing things. He was living above a laundromat which he managed, he said, and was in the process of renovating so it would serve his purposes. He needed more light, for example, here, and here, but it couldn't be fluorescent or even incandescent, he'd need to put in a couple windows, casements. He was going to install plumbing, a double sink for his paints and brushes, with a swing faucet. He went on and on about his plans, so specific with their hardware details …

And yet she paused, recognizing kin, when she saw the corkboard above his small desk, covered with quotes, notes …

She tried to update him on *her* life, *her* plans, to continue teaching part-time while she finished the four albums and the themed collection of poetry she'd started. And was surprised— No, that's an understatement. She was stunned when he reprimanded her for giving in, for becoming part of such a conservative establishment, for compromising, for not spending *all* of her time on her art.

> I come to see you, after two long years, and you tell me my life is all wrong? Who the fuck do you think you are?

He was the laundromat manager.

She suddenly realized that he saw her as some sort of student, not a lover, not an equal, not kin. He was going to help her, poor thing, along the path of fulfilment as an artist.

She'd asked about the notes on the corkboard. It was his credo, he said, humbly, his manifesto-in-progress. But no, of course, he couldn't explain it to her, not in just an hour.

He was just another Christ looking for a disciple. Good thing you didn't go to Europe with him.

> I told him his long looks were melodramatic, they were saying nothing to me.

She was surprised to read that. She had forgotten she'd said that. Out loud. To him.

Yay you!

When she asked why he had disappeared, after that first night, he shrugged, and said that he couldn't afford to support her.

What? *What?* She'd never expected him to. *When had she ever asked him to support her?* That wasn't— She wasn't— He didn't know her at all if he thought she was looking for a breadwinner, a husband.

He didn't know her after all. At all.

• • •

She decided to go for a long paddle. It was a gorgeous day, and, since it was Wednesday—or no, maybe it was already Thursday—in any case, it was not yet Friday—there was unlikely to be anyone else on the lake.

She made her way along the shore toward the small inlet in the distance. Its composition made it so beautiful— It wasn't just an inlet; there were three islets across it, each with a tree on it, arranged, left to right, medium, tall, and short (short, medium, tall would have been less aesthetically pleasing); the few bushes in between added just the right level of complexity. And behind the trees, there were two layers of depth, two different clarities, the distant forest more misty than the closer forest …

• • •

While she was still in Toronto, her parents contacted her. Out of the blue. She can't remember how they'd come to have her phone number; they'd probably just guessed Toronto at some point and looked it up. She refused to invite them to visit.

> You always made me feel apologetic, and so self-conscious, about my abilities. It's taken me a long time to feel good about what I'm good at, and I'm not about to expose myself to a setback from you.
>
> I left? You'd already abandoned me. Years before. Emotionally, psychologically, cognitively, financially. I just walked away.
>
> "[Being a mother is] a fucking self-indulgence … in responsibility, in guilt, in sorrow, in pain, and finally … in power…" Marilyn French, *The Bleeding Heart*

One day in December, she happened to see Kathy, one of the students who had been in her Phil of Ed course at Western, leaving OISE. They stopped to chat. She was getting her Ph.D. in Philosophy. She also met Anne-Marie, another Ph.D. student. They were both working on gender issues. How was it they had found out they could do that, at OISE no less, and she hadn't?

It turned out that Anne-Marie's husband was a poet, he'd probably love to read some of your stuff, she'd said, you guys could exchange feedback or something.

What does this line mean, I ask, his poem in hand.

No answer.

Why did you write it, I try again.

It sounded good, he says.

What? That's such a mockery of words, such an insult to intelligence— It's so irresponsible, so damaging—

Perhaps everything I've ever read that I didn't understand— Perhaps there was nothing to understand.

Years later, Anne-Marie landed a job out west. Her husband got a job at the same college. "What are the odds!" she wrote to Anne-Marie.

She hadn't known. She'd really thought it was happy coincidence.

A few years after that, Anne-Marie's husband got his poetry collection published.

Probably by the college press. Happy coincidence.

"... with all your dark unheeding illegible male authority ..." John Updike

Shulamith Firestone's *The Dialectic of Sex*, Aritha van Herk's *The Tent Peg*, Mary Daly's *Beyond God the Father*, Betty A. Reardon's *Sexism and the War System*

broadside, off our backs, herizons, otherwise — I splurged on subscriptions for them all. So much more interesting than mainstream stuff!

The following June, as soon as her night school courses were over, and before the start of the summer school course she'd managed to get—every now and then, there was a course none of the day school teachers wanted—she spent a week by herself on the Bruce Trail trying to figure out where she'd gone wrong, what she could do to salvage the relationship with Craig.

After a long day's hike along the challenging trail, she came to a breathtakingly beautiful cove, and upon implausibly, but certainly, hearing Bach's *Air*, she shrugged off her backpack and danced an impromptu ballet, still in her hiking boots. The beauty of the music, the unbelievably turquoise water, the expansive sky, and the sun— When it ended, she was startled, and delighted, to be applauded by the two fellows at the other end of the cove from whose cassette deck the music had come. She nodded acknowledgement, then proceeded to set up her tent.

She looked out, now, at the lovely dark water, the sky, the sun— She had recalled that moment often over the course of the intervening decades.

She turned back to her journal and read the insight she remembered coming to at some point on her trip: if she had to work that hard at the relationship, something was wrong. Fatally wrong.

She also came to understand that for Craig, life was something to be coped with. She saw that it wasn't just the stress of his undergrad program, or then of the graduate program—he would always be stressed, he would always be 'coping'. It was not an attitude that fit well with someone for whom life was to be passionately lived.

Once she realized these things, she was able to make the final break. Perversely, it helped to realize that Patty was waiting in the wings; she didn't want his nervous breakdown on her conscience.

And then she realized that the past four years of learning so much about herself, out west, in London, in Barrie, and then in Toronto, was not that at all. It was, rather, a painful process of internalizing Craig's perception of her and destroying her own.

> I cannot believe I didn't leave that first year in B.C.

> Or the second in London.

> Or the third while I was in Barrie.

Why did I stay, why did I take such emotional abuse?

Well, she looked out again at the dark water, we didn't call it that then. We didn't call it anything. It's hard to recognize something you don't have a word for.

He was upset. "Don't leave. I don't want to lose you."

Not 'I want you.'

Or 'I love you.'

She stared out at the water.

Why have I been so unloved? Why am I so unloved?

Am I unlovable?

"I need you," he said.

Why is it that when men need, it doesn't undermine their power, it seems to reinforce it. But when women need, it infantilizes them.

Is that why I couldn't love? Because love is having your needs looked after, being looked after?

So love enhances a man, but demeans a woman. Hm.

Maybe no one loves. Or is loved. Maybe you're just one of the few people honest enough to recognize that, to admit that.

Or, third possibility, maybe love doesn't exist. Maybe there is no such thing. Maybe what we call love is always just something else.

He was also surprised. That alone proved that she should leave him. She'd worked so hard to make their relationship work, even asking Ruth, Daniel's wife, whom she didn't like, at all, for advice, thinking maybe she had some insight about living with someone in a Ph.D. program ... When Craig found out about that, he couldn't believe it. He was surprised not only to discover there was something wrong, but something so wrong she'd talk to Ruth about it.

Oblivious. Utterly oblivious.

> He asked why I didn't ever suggest we try together to work it out. Good question.
>
> Because of my family. It was like it or lump it. Deal with it. If you can't stand the heat, get out of the kitchen. There was no working it out together, no compromise, no yielding, no changing.
>
> Besides, you were always busy, you had to work on your precious Ph.D. or you had to meditate or you had go swimming …

It had taken eight years to realize, to accept, that her image of him had been wrong. All wrong.

To realize, to accept, that he had been not the love of her life, but an imaginary friend.

Once she left, she felt the same relief she'd felt when she finally declared, realized, she wasn't a Roman Catholic, and more, that she was an atheist. It was the elation that comes with freedom from a straitjacket. One cognitive, the other emotional.

> Being with him was like running with ankle weights on.
>
> And you know what happens when you take them off.

Still, it hurt. For a very long time. She'd failed at her one and only relationship with a man.

> leave.
> a decision.
>
> sever.
> quickly done.
>
> but as i walk away
> each fine tendril drags out slowly
> back through its burrow
> (mined through the days and years and effort and love—)

singeing exposed nerves at each millimetre
                    pulling
            retreating
        extracting

leaving.

and finally,
the fibres dangle
tingling,
        twitching at the harsh cold air
then,
lifeless,

15

Although she loved all the opportunities that living in a city offered, she craved to be living in a cabin on a lake in a forest. Days she'd walk on the sidewalks, wishing they were trails; she'd be surrounded by buildings, wishing they were trees; escalators seemed alien.

Also, she was starting to feel more alone in the city than she would all by herself in the middle of nowhere. The constant presence of people she *didn't* know, hundreds of people who *weren't* her friends or even her acquaintances, thousands of people who *had* friends and acquaintances—it intensified the absence of such for her.

She'd met Marilyn during her year in Barrie. An art teacher at the same high school, she was also an active artist working in watercolors and doing mostly landscapes; years later, she'd start doing some really interesting stuff with hands. More importantly, she was an ex-hippie who had retained her social activism and her feminism, a radical teacher, an avid writer of letters to the editor.

> For the first time in my life, someone who gets it.

They didn't go out anywhere together or do things together, but that was fine. She genuinely enjoyed just the talking—the visits, the phone calls, the letters.

It was Marilyn who found a great little house on Georgian Bay for her to rent. She'd have to vacate at Christmas and during the summer, but that was no problem: Marilyn needed a dogsitter over Christmas when she flew to visit her family in the States, and she'd rent a room in Toronto during the summer, teaching as much as possible and doing the city thing for those two months.

The house was on a dead-end road, with a few nearby houses, none with permanent residents. Sand dunes across from her, forest beside and to the back of her, and the beach just a two-minute walk away. It wasn't quite her cabin on a lake in a forest, but it was close. Perhaps as close as she'd get.

And it was just a two-hour drive from Toronto, which meant that not only could she keep up her weekly lessons at the Conservatory, she could also keep a couple night school courses, making the drive twice a week.

In addition to the work in Toronto, she convinced the local Y to offer some dance classes, and as soon as she bought, finally, a piano—she couldn't afford a grand, but she fell in love with a gorgeous Kawai upright that had such a silky touch—she advertised for music students. She also registered with the region's high schools for supply teaching.

She moved in, made the space her own, and then suddenly felt very alone.

The idea that ending it with Craig was a mistake gripped her.

No, she told herself, they could still be friends. She wanted that, she'd said that.

Eventually, she healed.

Modern Math

1.

unlike those in relation parallel'd
we two are as lines intercepting:
therefore, covering more, we are close less,
yet, our separate distances upon the other
do not depend for measure,
and our facility to direction change
rests, perhaps, unparallel'd;
so let us love our intercepting lines
forgetting not that parallels
in touching doth self-negate.

2.

1 + 1 =
it depends:
there's so much to consider:
i mean sometimes it equals 2

but if one of them is negative
you end up with nothing at all

and in base one
it equals 11

and anyway
perhaps the more important question is
what is 1 + 1
greater than

or less than

3.

why is the circle
the symbol of love?
  because it's never-ending
so is the square—
and it has corners to hide in.

4.

the shortest distance between two points
is not a straight line—
it is a line that detours around dreams
lest it get caught or confused
in their multicoloured spirographics
and either change direction or never come out,
it is a line that encloses broken promises
with the deliberation of an etch-a-sketch

before moving on,
it is a line that arcs around conflict
and crisscrosses over canyons of pain,
no, the shortest distance between two points
is not a straight line—
it is a line of curving tangents
that never connects

5.

they say the line is an illusion:
solid, continuous—
but only points, here and there, seen together
make it seem so

how appropriate, therefore,
that we sign today
on a dotted line

6.

we were binary
an ordered pair of single values
and even as we grew complex
each of us a string of values
for a long time
we were even an identity

but then
exhausted by conflicts of range and domain
    frustrations of circular functions
        delusions of rational and transcendental functions
i attempted transformation—
but it always stayed the same.
through translation, rotation, reflection
it was always still the same thing, really.
but then what can you expect from
such rigid motions?

so i stretched, and sheared,
mapping myself into new territory
—you didn't even notice the ellipse—
>   broke open a bit
and found myself a perfect parabolic!

(i dream of hyperbolas
of becoming two by myself
each curve extending into infinity)

Or so she thought.

Sometimes I'm so slow. Didn't you say you didn't ask Patty to look after your cat because you didn't want to impose on her for three weeks?

Patty, note. Not Pat.

Because you didn't know her that well? What a fool I was. The real reason was that she was going with you!

You fucking bastard! That time I commented on the looks Patty was giving you at the party and told you she liked you— You just grinned, 'Is that so?' You already had a full-blown affair going on! Just how far back did it go?

All the while, laying all the blame on me: I didn't care, you said, I didn't give you any emotional support, I no longer wanted you (yeah, you're right about that one, my body knew before my heart, before my head)—

And to think I postponed leaving you until I saw that she was in the picture somehow, waiting in the wings, so maybe you wouldn't have a complete nervous breakdown, wouldn't totally fall apart.

Another thing about the house was that it was close enough to Marilyn's for her to just drop in for a visit. She'd never been able to do that before—just drop in on a friend. It was nice. They'd gotten together once in a while that first year, and again from time to time during her year in Toronto, since Marilyn was taking courses for her M. Ed. at OISE, but it was only once they lived close enough to each other for impromptu visits …

Unfortunately Marilyn bore the brunt of her postmortem over Craig.

> How can he have the time and energy to give to Patty when he was too stressed, too preoccupied for me?

> He says he loves Patty now, so he can't talk to me now, he can't be friends with me. What?

Funny how being in a relationship with you didn't stop him from 'talking' with her.

> In August you're telling me you're not close enough to ask her to look after your cat, and then in October you're marrying her? What the fuck!?

Talk about being utterly oblivious. Waiting in the wings. Right.

> So after all those years, *for* all those years, he lied.

She should've left two weeks after she arrived in Vancouver.

> Given such a low standard for attention, interest, support, affection, *for love*, it's no wonder I stayed with Craig for eight years. I'd go to his place (yes, far more often than he came to my place) and not once did he stop what he was doing to hug me or, god, make love to me. I always had to wait until he was done whatever it was he was doing at the time— meditating, picking at the guitar, cooking, doing his laundry. I was never first. I never felt—cherished.

> Given my family, I thought that was as good as it got.

Turned out, it was.

Instead she spent eight years with him, up and down, up and down. And why? Because she'd invested three years, writing those long letters—it was so hard to say, to accept, that she was wrong, all wrong.

> Patty's more into being a couple, he said.

No, she just knows how to do it.

Then again, I would never even *think* of telling him what to wear. Let alone buy his clothes for him.

I remember when we were all at the Phoenix, Patty had her elbow casually, comfortably on his shoulder. One, I never did that, I never felt that coziness. We never did that couples-in-love stuff. We never even held hands. Two, how did I miss its significance? They were seeing each other. Already. *Months* before I left.

The fucker.

Going over to her apartment to kill a spider, my ass.

…

'I needed someone,' he says by way of explanation.

And, what, we're interchangeable? Anyone will do?

Pretty much. Apparently.

…

I need to keep things simple, he says, and you're not simple.

I'm 'difficult'. How am I difficult? Why am I so difficult?

Because things matter so much.

Life isn't difficult with someone who doesn't really care about anything one way or the other.

No, and, it's a gender thing. Women who think are dismissed with that label.

You're the one who could never say 'I love you', *you're* the one who said there was no real caring between us—so why didn't *you* leave?

A year later, he and Patty had kids.

I remember now he said once that it'd be neat if we had a kid.

Neat?

She'd told him from the beginning that she didn't want to have kids. So if he did, why the fuck did he waste eight years of her life?

He probably didn't take you seriously.

And if he didn't want kids, why did he go ahead and have them?

"… families mean support and an audience to men. To women, they just mean more work." Gloria Steinem

Same goes for relationships.

She was, truly, glad it was over. Still, it hurt.

He didn't even try to keep me. I said 'bye' and he essentially said 'okay'. 'I want her instead anyway.'

She looked up, hearing a motor in the distance. A small fishing boat was starting to circle the lake, trawling.

Even so, she tried to maintain some sort of contact. After all, he had been— She'd known him, more or less, since they were sixteen.

"How's Patty?" I ask him.

"Fine. She's always fine."

…

He mentions being friends with Rob, he's become part of a citizen's action group, they get together, sit, talk, smoke up, and then, my god, he tries to get me on board with environmentalism. What? He has no idea. How can he have no idea? I've been 'on board' with environmentalism since the 70s. Stopped using spray cans when the relationship between their CFCs and the ozone was first announced. My second published poem, written at fifteen, was titled "Pollution". (I know, real imaginative…) I've been re-using plastic bags since forever.

It's someone from the group who wants to hang his stuff, and they help people get jobs, he says, and they have all these contacts with people interested in arts, people with money— All these years, I've had to research, to query and submit cold, to finally get to where I am, which is clinging to the bottom rungs of ladders, and he walks in to a social network crawling with connections he's all too eager to take advantage of.

All her life, she'd tried to make friends; she'd never, like he seemed to be doing, cultivated a relationship for purely utilitarian purposes.

Maybe men don't distinguish between the two, she thought. That would explain why they so easily form useful relationships.

Maybe for them, useful relationships are the only kind they have.

Even their relationships with women.

Perhaps especially their relationships with women.

The boat had stalled. Then started again.

Then he asks 'What do you do? All day.' What? What?! I tell him. I give him a rundown of my typical day. And he's so surprised at the hours I keep, the evenings I spend teaching, then the nights I spend working on my own stuff … I do what I've been doing for years, Craig, since before you knew me, since during when you knew me— I am stunned at his obliviousness. About what I do!

He says Patty has three (three! he emphasizes) courses to teach, she has to prepare every lesson, he is amazed at the work she has to do. What? Again, what?! What did you think I was doing when I had that half-time position in Barrie, when I had all those courses in Toronto?

It wasn't my imagination, my selfishness, that made me accuse 'You're not interested in what I do, you don't care, you don't support'—it was true. Because he didn't know. He had no idea. How could he have had no idea??

She is stunned to this day.

> Reading his dissertation (too bad he had to wait until we split to give it to me) …
>
> I'm struck by how mundane it is. The material, the writing— In short, it's nothing special. *He's* nothing special. I'm simply not interested in it, not intrigued one little bit. And there are so many papers I *would* be interested in, so many papers I *would* find fascinating.
>
> Then I'm struck—five years for this? What a waste of the best years of one's life.
>
> So then again, I was right not to pursue a Ph.D.
>
> And 'Craig F. Garruthers'. Oh my. The middle initial. How utterly pretentious.

She'd asked why he hadn't given it to Patty to read. "She's not interested," he'd said. And she almost choked on the incomprehensibility of it all.

> I am so glad I left. He didn't get any better. Even with Patty, he's smoking up every night, he's even started to stutter. Still 'coping', still dealing with stress, still unhappy.

She sighed angrily, then flipped ahead impatiently—she had filled an entire journal, 200 pages, with ups and downs, regrets then resolutions, she missed him, she missed him not.

> Why do I go on and on … Why such a need to relive every moment … To assign blame?
>
> No, not to assign blame. To answer the question. The only question that matters. The one most people avoid, pretending there is no answer. Why?

To determine cause.

Cause becomes blame only when the moral element is added.

When he sent her a picture of his newborn son (she hadn't asked for a picture; she had no interest in seeing a picture; and she was yet again appalled that he was so very ordinary, bragging about his kid like he'd found a cure for cancer—and "My son!", and as if Patty had had nothing to do with it), she saw the same raised eyebrow. And she just stared at it, trying to— He had been *born* with it. That raised eyebrow that had so attracted her *wasn't* an indication of inquisitiveness or intelligence. At all.

Marilyn let her rant and rave. Eventually spent, they moved on, or back, to other issues. She'd update her on the responses she'd received to the submissions she'd made to various journals and magazines, she'd ask to see Marilyn's latest work, they'd talk about what annoying sexist thing was in the news that week, they'd enjoy *Cagney and Lacey* together …

Having Marilyn made it easier to not have Craig. She realized that simply being able to show and tell was almost as important as to whom one was able to show and tell.

Though … she was always the one to drop in on Marilyn. Marilyn never dropped in on her. This would bother her for the duration of their friendship.

Why am I always the one to initiate?

Why am I always the one who has to maintain the relationship?

The fishing boat looked like it was going to come into the cove, in which case its fumes would likely trigger a headache. So she quickly closed the journal, went up to the cottage, put on her jacket, and headed into the forest.

• • •

In addition to teaching whatever courses she'd managed to get, she took some AQs, additional qualification courses for teachers: the Honours English Specialist certificate; Music, Parts 1 and 2; and ESL, Part 1. All in the hope of becoming more employable. And all in vain.

She'd thought that if she just was good enough, qualified enough … but then when she wasn't hired because she was overqualified, she didn't understand. Why would being *more* qualified than you need to be be a reason not to get hired?

Marilyn explained: it meant they'd have to pay her more. The day school teachers were unionized. And that was one of the rules. Suddenly her whole life seemed to backfire.

At one of the interviews—she continued to apply for steady, though not necessarily full-time, positions—she was told that her cv was too long and it looked too cluttered. After a brief moment of surprise, she replied that that was how long it had to be to include all the relevant information. She could add white space to make it less cluttered, she explained, but then it would have been even longer. It was a bizarre conversation.

At another interview, a vice-principal her told her that she should've dressed up a bit. She replied that since she intended to wear jeans to teach, she thought it honest to wear jeans to the interview. She totally missed the patriarchy's booming voice, "You're a woman, you must wear a dress and make-up …" Only later did she find out that airline attendants are *required* to wear make-up. But only the female ones, of course. Apparently men are not incapacitated in the performance of their duties by not wearing it.

Later, that voice would practically deafen her. Acquiescing would have been like being in drag. It would have been as uncomfortable for her to wear a dress and high heels as it would have been for a man to do so. Not because she felt like a man. But because she didn't feel like a woman. She just felt like a person.

> "A great mind is androgynous." Coleridge

Several of her Toronto students had said that she should teach in a private girls' school, she was wasted doing one or two night school classes a year in the public system. She tried to explain what would happen if she taught in a regular day school again, but they insisted that a private school would be different. Maybe, she thought.

So she looked into it. Turned out one of the performing arts schools in Toronto was looking for an English teacher. Her background in dance and music wouldn't be needed, since there were people on staff far more qualified in those areas, but they liked that she was a serious artist. They thought it would give her real empathy with the students. And they *loved* her idea of introducing Philosophy into the curriculum. They ended up creating a position just for her: three English classes; a Society, Challenge, and Change class; and two Philosophy classes, one for grade twelve and one for grade thirteen.

She was ecstatic. Absolutely ecstatic.

It would mean moving back to Toronto, but with the full-time income they were offering, she could afford a place in the Beaches area. She'd also have a more-than-adequate pension by the time she retired.

It would be the beginning of a brilliant teaching career.

The philosophy courses were immensely popular. The students *loved* being able to talk about things that mattered, they loved learning how to be critical, how to be *seriously* critical, about all the stuff that was happening in their lives, and in the world at large. They lingered at her desk after class, and even sought her out during her spare, her lunch, and after school, in order to continue the in-class discussions.

Within a few weeks, she started a philosophy club to meet the extraordinary interest. She called it a philosophy café, and they met in the common lounge area. So she finally got her late night discussions about things of substance, things that mattered! Well, not quite late night, though certainly often into the dinner hour, when they just ordered out for pizza and pop and kept talking. It was amazing. Even the custodial staff joined them from time to time.

In fact, so did students from other schools. She was surprised, and delighted, to discover that her own students had told their friends at other schools, and they were just showing up. Covertly at first, but when they realized she didn't mind, overtly. With more friends.

They went back and told their teachers about it, and soon she was receiving invitations to teach guest philosophy classes at other schools. Her own school gladly provided the time off, with pay, to accept the invitations.

And soon after that, she was fielding requests to hold workshops for teachers at other schools so they could develop and teach their own philosophy courses.

Again, her school was all too happy to facilitate such workshops.

Being able to teach the same courses year after year reduced her prep load considerably. As did not having to also teach a roster of private music and dance students. Her drive time was also considerably reduced. So even though she had a full-time teaching job, she continued to have time to work on her own writing and composition. Somehow, being affiliated with the school gave her status that opened doors which to that point had been closed. So not only did she develop a brilliant teaching career, she became a reasonably well-known writer and composer. Who knew?

Well, she didn't. Because there were no teaching vacancies at any of the private schools. And it didn't occur to her to apply anyway. Private schools were for the rich and well-to-do.

16

She continued to write, feverishly, adding monologues by women from mythology to those by women of the bible. Then, inspired by Judy Chicago's *Dinner Party*—which had stunned her so much she couldn't speak—

> I remember standing on the sidewalk with Craig outside the gallery and just crying, silently. He didn't know what she was crying about. And said as much.

—she embarked on a crash course in women's history, having decided then and there to add pieces by real women, women who might have said, quite possibly would have said, but who couldn't, or didn't—or did but their words didn't survive for anyone to read.

> Discovering Lou Salome— It's like I have a degree in men's studies and now I have to go back and do it all over again, with a different framework, a different context of consideration, understanding, judgement …

Soaking in Diane Juster's music, she started to work on "Amelia's Nocturne," the nocturne mentioned in her monologue by a fictional contemporary of Chopin who is patronized, ignored, then banished to the garret for her 'hysteria'.

Her rage.

She took "I am Eve," one of the monologues she'd written, and set it to a collage of sound, including a church organ that became more and more distorted as the piece went on, as Eve revealed more and more problems with the Judaeo-Christian story. She wrote it, performed it, recorded it. When she finished the last take of the last track, then the last mix, and then listened to the whole, for the last time, as the sun rose, she thought, with such quiet excitement, this is *good*.

She would often work late into the night, into the morning.

Or she would avoid her work altogether for days at a time. It wasn't good enough.
It wasn't … something.

> Portrait of the Artist, Struggling
>
> unarmed i loiter at the edge of the field
> casting nervous glance at shreds of flesh
> still sticking to bones of those before
> i falter at this fear of mediocrity
> turn and dally, dally and turn
> (there is hope, there is safety,
> in potential, in becoming—
> a battle unfought is a battle undefeated)
> coward, i stall confrontation
> i crawl from my anxiety into shaming naps of negligence
> but awake, always, in apprehension and despair
>
> and still, i do not dare
> i do not dare

She continued to have this incredible need, this desire to express—because she felt
so much, thought so much.

> I imagine Craig calling and saying 'Hi, how are you?' 'Vibrant!' I would
> answer. I wouldn't've said that a year ago. When I was with him. Woven
> in to him.
>
> But here it is Sunday night, and I'm feeling strong and lean and free, I
> make a fire, I dance in the sand to Rod Stewart, under the starry sky on a
> warm summer night, my bike is parked out front, this house where I live,
> my music studio with my compositions all around, my works in progress
> on my desk by my typewriter …
>
> …

A small panther. I like that. The animal I remind Marilyn of. Because, she says, I'm muscled, compact, and focussed. The intensity.

What food? (I was reading some magazine article.) Trail mix. That made me laugh. But she's right!

She continued to send her stuff out, and she continued to be published in magazines and journals. Nine rejections for every acceptance, but still. "The English Teacher" was published. A few of her monologues. Several of her poems.

Vinnie

my idol
my starry starry night
my symbol of the misunderstood
you are all too easy
to understand.
i've looked at each painting
i've read every letter:
it is a portrait of a young man
as a commercial artist.
you're not trying hard enough to sell

my pretty flowers and sceneries,
you scold your brother as he supports you
too incompetent or too greedy or too selfish
to support yourself, to support your own art.

and that bit with the ear—
the madness of genius?
hardly.
a childish tantrum is more likely
or the madness of syphilis.

Her music started to be played on radio stations. Mostly college stations and international stations dedicated to classical and electronic music, but still. Two pieces were accepted for inclusion in a concert series in Toronto. That was exciting. Arranging the performers, doing the rehearsals, seeing it, hearing it.

Suzanne Langer's *The Problem of Art, Selections from the Notebooks of Da Vinci, Beethoven: Letters, Journals, and Conversations*, George Sand's *My Life*, Shulamith Firestone, more Beauvoir

She was invited to present a paper at a Feminist Poetry conference. She was invited to speak at a high school during Writers' Week. She continued to receive Ontario Arts Council grants. And the reviews! She smiled as she re-read them.

"Weird! And I like it. Take 'Some Enchanted Evening,' for example: a horribly mellow rendition of the Rodgers/Hammerstein tune with people being asked the question "Where did you meet your spouse? Would you say it was love at first sight?" on top. One of the replies: 'I thought he was the most egotistical, self-centered asshole I ever met.' See what I mean? This cassette often borders on theatre. 'Rub-a-Dub-Dub' suggests that the three men in the tub were gay and goes on to discuss the sexual semantics of putting three other people in the tub. 'Let Me Entertain You' is altogether upsetting: between snippets of the song, women describe various social manifestations of the ways women are degraded by men, ranging from child molestation to gang rape. Controversial feminist content. You will not be unmoved."

That was from *Option* magazine, one of *the* magazines.

"We have found *The Art of Juxtaposition* to be quite imaginative and effective. When I first played it, I did not have time to listen to the whole piece before I had to be on air. When I aired it, I was transfixed by the power of it. When I had to go on mic afterward, I found I could hardly speak! To say the least, I found your work quite a refreshing change from all the fluff of commercial musicians who whine about lost love etc. Your work is intuitive, sensitive, and significant!"

"Liked *The Art of Juxtaposition* a lot, especially the feminist critiques of the bible. I had calls from listeners both times I played 'Ave Maria.'"

"We have your *Juxtaposition* cassette and I particularly enjoy 'I am Eve'. Every time I play it (several times by this point), someone calls to ask about it/you."

"Thanks for the tape…The work is stimulating and well-constructed and politically apt with regards to sexual politics. (I was particularly impressed by 'I am Eve.')"

Her electronic soundscapes were also well received.

"Kris is truly a master of visual music."

"*Rocks and Trees* is excellent! One person who heard 'Rocks (1)' thought it was new Philip Glass. And I found 'Trees (1)' to be very reminiscent of John Mills-Cockell."

"The *Rocks and Trees* album is really cool. Soundtrack material!"

And yet, and yet …

"We found that the music was unique, brilliant, and definitely not 'Canadian'. She is a very talented individual. We were more than impressed with the material. *The Art of Juxtaposition* is filling one of the emptier spaces in the music world with creative and intelligent music-art."

… was from a rejection letter from a record company.

What does it take, she wondered.

A few years earlier, she had the idea of composing original music for figure skating routines. As far as she knew, skaters typically performed to something spliced together, often from three different pieces of music, in order to get the fast-slow-fast sequence they needed; the splices were often bad because each section had to be a certain length, and the high points of the music seldom seemed to match the high points of the skating. What if someone composed something from scratch? The tempi, the durations, the climaxes—all of it could be made-to-order. If a skater needed an extra two seconds before the jump, you could just go back and put it in, lengthen the rise to the peak. You could even compose specifically for the spins, the jumps, the spirals …

So she approached a relatively well-known coach in Orillia with the idea.

He could've said sure, what a great idea, why don't you work with Jeannie, the little eight-year-old? She would've composed a piece, something appropriate for an eight-year-old, something with obvious changes in volume and speed, and a few playful moments. It would be good. Then Sally's mother would see it and ask her to do one for *her* daughter. Word would spread, and by the time she was composing for the teenaged skaters, she could be charging a good fee. Then one of the skaters she composed for might make the nationals, her name as composer of the music would be on the program, and the phone would really start ringing.

Instead the well-known coach just looked at her and said, doubtfully, "Do you think you can?" She was so discouraged at his all-too-apparent lack of confidence, and interest, she just turned and walked away. He didn't call her back.

She should have been more … insistent, she thought now. Instead, if anything, she had downplayed her abilities, her qualifications.

Of course she did. She was raised Catholic, she was raised female, and she was raised with a 'slow' sister.

How many lessons in self-sacrifice and martyrdom can one have and still come out assertive enough to get what you want? What you so intensely want?

She started to work on a series of short stories, each about a young woman's first year of university, each in a different discipline.

And she suddenly realized she would always have more ideas than time to actualize them.

During the summers, she lived, really lived, in the city. She took a wendo course, found an indie video house and put up notices, took a recording techniques course, saw a couple dance performances, went to a couple concerts, went to some dance clubs, discovered U of T's Women's Center archives …

She can't remember how she came to visit Jacqueline's house. She can't remember how she met Jacqueline. Perhaps Marilyn had mentioned her as a fellow writer.

She does remember how stunned she was. The beautiful rosewood dining room table and a little side table for the phone. Her desk, a polished rolltop begging for an inkpot with a quill pen. Bookcases, gleaming wood full of books—

The house she had grown up in had never been full of such beautiful things. Antiques, she learned to call them. She grew up with rec room panelling, formica tables—everything came from Beaver Lumber or Simpsons Sears. She didn't know other stores existed until she was on her own. And couldn't afford anything but K-Mart.

—and a piano. It was a grand. It was the first time she'd seen a grand in person except for her grade ten exam. She hung back. It was a sacred thing.

Jacqueline must've seen—   Of course she did.

"Do you play?"

"Yes. I have my Associate."

"That's quite an accomplishment. Most people get to grade eight and then stop," she said. "Play something for me." It wasn't a polite request. She genuinely wanted to hear her play.

No one had *ever* asked to hear her play. She almost cried.

"I don't have my music—"

"What would you like?" She started going through the music that was stacked on another little side table.

"Bach. *The Preludes*?"

"Here you go."

She took the book, opened it onto the stand, and sat down. And almost cried again.

As she played the first prelude, time stood still.

There was a moment of silence after the last note faded.

"You have such a gentle touch."

She did? She hadn't known. How would she have known? Neither of her piano teachers had ever said so. They didn't believe in praise. The absence of criticism was the most she could hope for. She didn't think it odd. Since it was the same at home.

"Very beautiful. Very rare."

And then Jacqueline said, "Play it again. I'd like to hear you play it again."

Never again would she meet someone who *wanted* to hear her play. Who truly *enjoyed* hearing her play. Who appreciated— Who thought she played beautifully.

But it did happen. Once.

She looked up from the journal, holding back the tears.

Eventually, she continued through the journal.

She was particularly annoyed, but pleased to have her decision to leave validated, since it confirmed that he was such a sleaze, when Craig called her a couple years after she'd finally left, for good, to ask if she could put in a word for him at 'her' college. (She had gotten a single Business Communications course at the nearby college—just one night a week, but it was something.) He was trying to get a job teaching photography.

She was stunned. For so many reasons. One, he didn't have a teaching degree. Or any formal credentials in photography.

Two, he had no photography career to speak of. Not like, say, her 'career' in composition: by this time, her cv listed a few concert performances, airplay in several countries, and half a dozen self-produced album releases; she'd even presented at a few conferences and had had a short interview with the leading magazine in Canada, *Canadian Composer*. As far as she knew, he had some pieces on exhibit at the office of that environmental group he'd joined.

Three, how was she to "put in a word for him"? Even if she was inclined to do so, which she was not, did he think she was friends with someone in HR or the Dean or whoever it was who made hiring decisions? And, so, he was willing to get in through the back door, to take an unfair advantage if he could get it? He didn't think jobs should be awarded purely on the basis of merit?

It occurred to her years later that men must 'work' the workplace much differently than women did. Why else would he even think she could do what he was asking?

And not just the workplace. She would read, later, in Babcock and Laschever's *Women Don't Ask,* about a man who recalled that "'his father had taken the boys out and … taught them how to slip the maitre d' money for good tables or give some money to the guys who were in the band to play a good song … *how to circumvent the system' to get what [they] wanted.*" It explained so much.

Craig told her that he'd put together a proposal, a course outline. As if he'd written some sort of masterpiece. By this time, *she'd* put together over a dozen course outlines; every time she was hired to teach a course, she had to put together a course outline. It was a lot of work, but no big deal really. A paragraph about purpose, half a page of objectives, several pages of syllabus, and a page or two about assessment.

He asked if she'd take a look at it. Partly out of curiosity, she said sure. And she was amazed. My god, but it was impressive. To anyone who hadn't actually taught. He'd filled it with stuff teachers take for granted, expressed in the most pretentious language possible. It was thirty pages long. He made teaching sound like rocket science.

And perhaps it was. Certainly it was a lot more difficult and a lot more valuable than it was given credit, or pay, for. Because women did it. She was reminded of the job description for housewife she'd read somewhere, in association with an argument that housewives should get paid. Six-figure salaries. If you outsourced the cooking, cleaning, laundry, childcare, sexual service, and secretarializing, it would indeed add up to six figures.

And if you described teaching in words and phrases used by those in Business, perhaps it too would support a six-figure income.

Men have a way of making themselves, what they're saying, what they're doing, seem important. Women have a tendency to do just the opposite. After all, that's the way they were raised, respectively: to think of themselves as important, and not.

She resented not being taken seriously, but the way she presented herself, as nothing special, *said* don't take me seriously.

> And his course outline—it angers me, it's so damn impressive, he's used all the superficialities of professionalism, the grandiose diction, the polite acknowledgements— It's just teaching! But people will be impressed. More impressed with him than with me. Me with the B.Ed., the AQs, the years of experience, and course outlines too many to count.

But she also wondered—is that how it's done? If she didn't see an ad for a teaching position in her field, she assumed there wasn't one. End of story. It hadn't occurred to her to pitch a new course to someone.

So she put together a proposal for a Music Appreciation course. She had a teaching degree, and the two AQs in Instrumental Music. She also had, of course, her Associate in Piano from the Conservatory at the University of Western Ontario, and an Associate in Composition from the Conservatory at the University of Toronto. And she'd taught piano for fifteen years. And she was an active, somewhat successful, composer.

She submitted the proposal to half a dozen colleges in the area. No one even replied.

And if she ever found out Craig had gotten a job teaching Photography, she thought she'd scream. For a very long time.

• • •

She paddled past the cottages, noting that some people had already arrived for the weekend, past the stream, the marshy part, the stretch of crown land, past the next cove, someone there too, and around the curve.

A flock of geese honked overhead. They'd be heading south soon, she thought.

She circled the little island, noting how the view, the composition, changed with each stroke—the proportion of rock to water to distant shoreline, now pleasing, now not quite so much, the lines, the angles, the shapes …

• • •

Once back at the cottage, she had a hot shower, made a cup of tea, set a fire, and continued reading.

Patty didn't read his photography course outline. What? And I did? Even now, when we're no longer together? And he says she supports him like I never did? What the fuck?!

And she's a teacher even.

"She doesn't like reading," he says.

What? He bought that? She has him wrapped around her little finger. *And* he's an idiot.

And she took his photographs somewhere and presented them as hers. What? Without asking his permission. My god. I would never.

And here I am asking politely to use his rocks and trees set in a concert, waiting politely for him to give a set of copies to me.

I give up. It makes no sense at all.

…

It bothered me so much that he'd read when I was there. I was there for only a few days a month, and he'd often just sit there with his nose in a book, completely shutting me out. I accepted that, though—if he needed alone time, okay.

Apparently Patty says 'Why don't you put that down?' He wanted me to do that? He wanted to be coaxed, cajoled?

I assumed he knew what he was doing and did it because that was what he wanted to do. End of story.

It's called assuming, granting, autonomy.

She turned the page. Oh. She'd forgotten this. They'd had, what, goodbye sex? After she'd left, after he was with Patty, he'd called, said he missed her, said he missed her intensity, her intelligence …

And I bought it.

She'd really thought that he might be changing his mind, that *she* was the one he really wanted, that he was discovering that Patty lacked …

It was only several days later, when he quickly ended a call with "Patty's here, gotta go" that she realized—

> The little shit.

She stared at the water. She had been so naïve. About so many things.

She got up for a slice of pizza, put another chunk of wood onto the fire, then finished the journal.

In her late twenties, she decided to get neutered. She'd never wanted children. She didn't want to look after a child twenty-four-seven. For ten plus years. It just wasn't something she wanted to do. End of story.

She was surprised to find that it wasn't going to be that easy. Her family doctor— scratch that—her personal physician, as well as the surgeon to whom he referred her, seemed to think she should have children first, before she had herself sterilized.

> Sure there's a possibility that one day I'll want children. There's also a possibility that one day I'll want to be a nurse.

One actually said something about wanting the fun without the responsibility.

> What?

Another asked why she didn't want kids. And was she married.

> What?

She wondered whether a man seeking a vasectomy would be subjected to the same sort of interrogation.

> I'm denying my femininity by not wanting kids? Seriously? How much arrogance does it take for a man to tell me this?

She didn't want to reproduce, to replicate. That should have been all that mattered. Why are women's wants always so challenged? Or so irrelevant? It was her body, her choice. And not even a *potential* human being was going to be killed in the process.

Eventually she found surgeon who understood he was just a surgeon. Not her Father-Knows-Best. He asked whether she wanted ligation or cauterization. End of story.

At least you lived when and where it was legal.

Several months after she'd read his photography course outline, she called Craig. She had to know.

"How was your summer," he asks.

"Great," I say, "and yours?"

"Fine. Well—it could've been worse, I guess—well yeah—I'm getting better."

Still coping, still recovering. From what, I have no idea. The Ph.D. program? Life?

He says he blew the interview to teach at college. He couldn't say what standard deviance was and why it's used. "The questions were so basic," he explained.

Right. Sure. That's why you blew it. (He got an interview?)

He probably came across so stressed and nervous, they couldn't imagine him in front of a class.

He says he's changed his mind about getting a college job. It's so much teaching.

Well, yeah. Duh.

He now says he intends to teach a course at Dundas Valley Art School.

"Oh," I say, "you got a good response to your outline?"

"They haven't gotten it yet."

Then how the hell does he 'intend' to teach there??

We talk again about collaborating for a grant application for *Rocks and Trees*.

"I know some people at Artists Inc." he says.

So?

He talks on and on, meandering, diverting, repeating, but he will not be interrupted, so now I don't even try.

I tell him I'm not strong enough to carry us with the Canada Council application, since it's for multimedia.

He objects to my use of 'carry us'. So I ask him point blank: "Have you had any showings? Any publications?"

He stutters.

He has no idea.

No fucking idea.

She turned the page.

I'm sorry I ever met him. More sorry I wrote to him all those years. All those exciting years, my university years, I was emotionally and psychologically bound to him.

And then all that time—spent with someone who kept fucking up, compared to my image of him. I was so unable to change my image of him. I wanted to have someone and he was it: he was intelligent, artistic, sensitive. On paper, he was what I wanted. I couldn't accept him as he was. I kept insisting that the reality was just a temporary aberration, and I kept getting angry with him for those aberrations.

What I resent him now for, among other things, is not leaving me. If he knew what he was, and he knew what I thought he was, why didn't he leave?

Because of exactly what he was. Weak, passive, perpetually coping with life. It was *my* mistake. A mistake that lasted eight fucking years. A mistake fuelled by the romantic myth.

And maybe he didn't leave because he was doing to the same to you. Struggling with an image he had that was wrong … refusing to believe it was wrong, insisting to the end you'd want kids, for example.

And, paradoxically, my persistence was fuelled by the contra-romantic myth that said persist, real love has to be worked at, it isn't ideal.

I was stupid to want him. That's the long and short of it.

We see what we want to see. Also the long and short of it.

She turned the page.

And you know what? I'm not interested. In collaborating on the grant. In this friendship. It hurts too much. Because you're not really interested. I asked for your photographs for *Rocks and Trees* to display at a concert in Toronto. You couldn't be bothered to prepare them—i.e., to get framed enlargements. I was giving you exposure! After all this, I was doing you a favour! But no, all you had ready was the one for "Rocks (1)" and that took you three fucking months.

And if everything in society hadn't pushed her toward the expectation that she would be, should be, with someone, she might have realized early on that she'd rather be solo.

She closed the journal. After a while, she made a cup of tea, then went down to the water to watch the magic, remembering, since it was the weekend, to take her earplugs, headphones, and CD player with her. And Bach's cello suites.

17

Since the lake was noisy, she drove into town Saturday morning for another pizza. Two more large should do it, she calculated. She also picked up more half-and-half, more juice, more trail mix, some fruit, some yogurt, and a couple chocolate bars. Dark almond.

When she came back, she decided to sit up on the deck instead of down at the water.

Although she thoroughly enjoyed her friendship with Marilyn, she thought it would be nice to have a few friends she could do stuff with. So she tried to meet people who lived in the area. She kept her eyes open at the library, at the post office, at the grocery store, but there was no protocol for getting past a smile and a friendly nod.

All the female friends she'd ever had had dropped her after they'd gotten married and/or had kids, and all the male friends she'd ever had had dropped her when it was clear she wasn't romantically or sexually interested.

She'd split from her family, and the nature of her work meant no collegiality.

And, of course, there continued to be the whole couples thing. She wasn't part of a couple—not even a roommate couple—so inviting her was always perceived as awkward. Couples don't invite singles, and singles don't invite other singles unless they're seeking to become a couple.

> Never included, never invited, so always alone, so people assume I want to be alone, so I'm never included, never invited …

> Maybe I should say 'Hey, can I come?' but that would be imposing. And what if they say 'no'—or want to say 'no' but are too polite.

And she think of the less direct, more diplomatic, 'Got room for one more?' to which people could always say 'Sorry, no, we're full up, maybe next time.'

The only place it seemed you could meet people was the local bar.

> It's hard to walk into a bar alone. Not knowing anyone. But I did it. Time and time again. Walked in. Started a conversation with someone.

> The women thought I was a lesbian. The men thought I was a prostitute.

Given that, she *was* able to meet fuck buddies. She'd just ask some guy if he wanted to come back to her place.

> "So, do you come here often?" he asked.

> "No, only when I want sex," she replied.

> "Really? Me too!"

> "So, your place or mine?"

They'd walk out. It was that easy.

Men are such sluts.

> we who have cast off polite camouflage
> dare to move in undressed desire;
> sleek and restless in our naked need,
> we slip through social labyrinths
> crammed and crowded with stiff costume,
> easy in urgent search for kin, we seek.
> perchance we collide or coincide:
> in our fugitive couplings we grapple and clutch
> desperate flesh screaming from the heat
> leaps pulsing into exultation—
> stilled, slaked, we lay then,
> we who are free,
> laughing.

Of course she knew it was unconventional, but she didn't want to ask them out on a date—she wasn't interested in sitting at a table, having dinner, and engaging in boring conversation, nor was she interested in going to a movie theatre and watching a movie 'together' (who with any brain at all can sit through a Hollywood-made movie without commentary?). What she was interested in was having sex. She wanted to have sex just for the physical pleasure. Like a man. She didn't want to make love.

Men don't have sex to experience pleasure. They have it to experience conquest.

And to satisfy their primitive brain, the part that urges them to replicate.

> in the night, your mouth at my neck
> a long passionate kiss arches my back
> then stronger, hungrier, more purposeful—
> i wonder how close you are to my jugular
> do you mean to suck at my core?
> but you stop
> and i am still alive
> so i think of leeches instead of vampires.
>
> the next morning, i stand at the mirror
> from behind you wrap your arms around me
> i am looking at my neck
> and seeing the truth of your intent:
> a territorial claim to ownership.
> then i look at your face and see more
> the arrogant leap from brand to birthmark.
>
> during the day, someone asks about it
> and realizing the truth of accomplishment
> i turn and say to you
> it is merely a bruise,
> and therefore, nothing permanent.

She eventually decided that orgasms were just a myth. Or, at least, if what she experienced was an orgasm, highly over-rated.

I thought I was so cool, so strong and independent, no fear of flying here. But, truthfully, I just ended up having a lot of really bad sex. It barely took the edge off. Nowhere near satisfying.

Maybe it wasn't bad sex. Maybe it was ordinary sex. Maybe ordinary sex is bad sex.

It's bad enough that due to my Roman Catholic upbringing, I had to contend with the deep-rooted feelings of shame regarding anything sexual. Add to that, all the men didn't really know what to do or didn't care enough to find out. Then the one who should've cared enough made me feel like a spoiled child whenever he did just for/to me. No wonder I never came.

And when a woman doesn't come? She's either a nympho (it's impossible to satisfy her) or she's frigid (it's impossible to satisfy her).

It's never that the man's inept.

And yet if she does to him and he doesn't come, that's exactly what she is.

And yet— Kevin tossing the pillow at her, Darren wrestling with her in the snow— It was seldom a cold wham-bam-thank-you-m'am thing. Often, there was a friendliness, a consideration, a 'drive safely' camaraderie. And when she saw them subsequently at the bar, there were no cold shoulders. They'd invite her to sit at their table, offer to get her a drink.

And when I asked later, to confirm, "Still want me to come over?"

"Yes, I'll be waiting."

Yes.

I'll be waiting.

...

He opened his arms for me. God, in eight years, Craig never did that. Not once.

...

But when I told Alex that a radio station in the States said they really liked my piece and asked if I could send more, there was the oh so familiar lack of interest and lack of understanding that disappointed and hurt. Better not to have told at all.

And only now, thirty years later, does she realize it's jealousy. She wasn't supposed to be more successful than them. So of course they wouldn't celebrate, or even acknowledge, her successes.

So it's over with Derek already. Why?!

She flipped ahead through several, a great many, pages. She remembered those years ...

He'd said "Let's get together again"—

"Let's get together again" means nothing of the sort.

Once is not enough!

Once is exactly enough. To score. To do her. To notch the bedpost.

And had no desire to relive them.

This agonizing, relentless agonizing, about male attention—do I have it, did I have it, how do I get it, what did I do to get it, what should I have done to get it, will I still have it tomorrow night—my god, such a waste of energy.

She stopped at a spot several months later.

People say I'm not a relaxed person—I'm intense about everything.

I don't *feel* particularly intense. Anything less than what I feel would be boring.

I care about stuff, yes. If you have desires, interests, you do care about stuff. And I want life to be fair; I care about injustice.

Is that what people call 'intense'? Caring about stuff? Is it that most people don't care? About anything?

How can one *not* care?

And I'm judgmental. Apparently.

You'd be judgmental too if you saw, noticed, realized what I do.

She turned another page.

Today was a very good day. Spent three and a half hours writing six pages of "Ophelia," then went for a walk on the beach, lay down on the sand in the sun, then went back and worked on my choreography to Phil Collins' "In the Air Tonight," then ran four miles, read Jasper's work on existentialism, then worked out the melody for a new song.

Isaac Asimov, Arthur C. Clarke, Ursula Franklin, Munroe's *Journeys Out of the Body*, Pearce's *Explaining the Crack in the Cosmic Egg*, Balzac, Bookchin, Turgenev, Illich's *Deschooling Society*

She tried not to be elitist. Jim's boasting that he could pick up a dime with his backhoe, it was an attention to detail, a skill, an art …

I bend myself backwards to make and keep friends, the things I don't say, the things I try to ignore—shallowness, stupidity—

The acceptance of mediocrity.

I'm afraid it will become a habit I won't be able to change some day.

And not only with regard to others.

…

He said he didn't have the time.

She didn't know anymore who the 'he' was.

Does it matter?

> Eight months and nine men later, I have no friends, not one person to just hug, talk with, be with, go dancing with, have sex with—they all stopped wanting to see me, sooner or later, most sooner, soon after they got what they wanted, I guess. Been there, done her.

> …

> Salome was a brilliant woman whose company was brilliant men. She knew, hung out with, Wagner, Tolstoy, Nietzsche …

> I know Perry, Gordon, Jim.

> Yeah, but at the time *they* were just Bob, Leo, and Fred …

> Well, no, they were Peter.

And so she thought about Peter again.

> How is it we became opponents, we who seemed to start so kin? Alas, I know. I feared that to win your attention, I had to convince you of my worth, I had to justify my existence. And you, seeking to improve, or examine, or justify your own existence, seemed to object, to criticize, and fling me further away.

> So I imagine our future interchanges to be stormy debates, attacks and defences. It's not what I want.

> But to feel secure of your friendship, to not need to win your attention, is impossible when it has always been I to beckon you.

Even so, she wrote to him once more, now that she had yet another address, trying to understand what went so wrong, trying to salvage the friendship, perhaps the relationship. She asked him point blank, "What do you think of me? What do you want of me?"

His response cut to the bone: "Absolutely nothing."

She stared out at the water for a few moments, then turned the page.

> to peter
>
> once
> misunderstanding my fascination with flame
> i saw myself moth
> dusty descendent of maggot
> fluttering blinded to your light.
>
> later
> i flew to you as firefly
> misbelieving i recognized kin
> in your intermittent flashes.
>
> now
> i burn alone, taper
> dying as i live
> at peace with my passion
> and phoenix.

She marked her spot, closed the journal, then paddled up the river to the rapids. She sat there for a long time, lost in the sound of the relentless force of the water as it coursed over the rocks.

• • •

Shortly after she returned, she made a fresh cup of tea, put on an extra sweatshirt, then went back out on the deck.

During that time—after Craig, while living at the beach house, during her early thirties—she continued to compose. A quick and fun Xmas album of re-written standards—Rudolph's nose was red from Chernobyl's radioactive fallout, "Here Comes Santa Claus" became "Here Comes an Army Tank" in honour of Tiananmen Square … A new set of piano solos. A mournful piece for piano and vocalize. A solo for cello. When she finished "lament," the solo for viola, she thought, I can die now. This piece is perfect.

Still in love with the Romantics, and Emerson, Lake, and Palmer, she easily finished the setting of Keats' "Ode to Psyche" once she heard, in her mind, Greg Lake singing it; his "C'est La Vie" and "Lend Your Love To Me Tonight" had continued to move her.

Somehow she tracked down his manager's address and sent the score. He sent it back saying Mr. Lake was on tour at the moment and couldn't look at it. She was puzzled. Why didn't he just wait and give it to him when he returned? She wrote back and suggested as much.

Next thing she knew, she got a letter saying "Mr. Lake has asked that you not contact him any further." That really puzzled her. What kind of response is that to the submission of a score?

She didn't realize until many years later that she'd been perceived as some sort of love-struck groupie. Not a serious composer. And she didn't know why. What had she done wrong?

Eventually, she realized that such submissions would typically be made through an agent. But she didn't have an agent. She'd sent her writing to a great number of the literary agents listed in the *Writer's Market*, but so far to no avail. It hadn't occurred to her to do the same thing with her music.

> Yes, okay, my approach screamed amateur, but even so, surely some of my stuff was good. Could no one look past my fumbling attempts to see that?

They would have if you'd been a man.

She continued to flip through the pages, bits and pieces catching her eye.

> "Double Soliloquy" was rejected because "Jasmine argues her case too strongly and thus loses my sympathy."

> Why does arguing too strongly make you lose sympathy?

> …

> Heard the *Flashdance* song, "What a feeling … I can have it all … " sung

by a man today. The lyrics had been changed to "She's my lady … I can have it all…" What the fuck? All her exuberance and ambition is thus turned into something *he* can own. Men's inability to accept us as human, like them, with our own energy, our own effort, our own achievement, is disturbing. Very disturbing.

…

Watching Skate Canada … Albert Schram did the choreography *and* the music for Craig Henderson.

…

The visual artist both conceives and performs his or her conception. (If others perform it, it's called copying and considered illegitimate.) But the composer and the choreographer just conceive; others typically perform it. Why the difference? Paintings and sculptures exist in space; they can be committed to space once and for all. But, via recording, the same is true for music and dance compositions. Is it because music and dance compositions are often not solos? But we don't expect the composer or the choreographer to perform their compositions even when they are solo. Why do we expect that of the visual artist?

…

Am I going home for Christmas? I am so sick of that question. I am home. Do you mean am I going to where my parents live?

…

I've been on my own for nine years now and have saved only $3,000. But when I work it all out, it's all accounted for—rent, heat, gas, insurance, food, courses, the difference between what I got for my bike and what I had to pay for a used car, and the occasional splurging on used records, used books, a new typewriter, some electronic equipment (all second-hand), and an upright piano.

…

Listening to Vangelis, I realize that my music doesn't soar. I am moving from pretty to beautiful, and I'm getting power, but it's not … expansive. It's focused like a laser instead of filling the sky with its brilliance.

What am I missing? Length? Complexity? Depth? Yes, it's orchestration I lack. I don't know how to make everything fuller, richer, more developed. Verbose. It's all too bare.

How do I learn what I need to know? I took Orchestration I and II, but— Study scores, listen along. Yes, I should have been doing that since day one.

Even so, if I write something like a Vangelis piece, it'll never get performed, so what's the point?

And to perform it myself, I need more equipment—more synths, more processors, an eight-track …

At about this time, she received her first bit of studio work. Someone who had found out that she could play the piano called and asked if she'd come to his studio to lay a track for a commercial. Reluctantly, she agreed. She didn't want to use music to sell shit. But, she thought, go, see where it leads.

"Fuller chords," the guy said.

"Not so staccato," he said.

"A bit slower, you're two seconds short," he said.

Then, "Hey how about that thing from Beethoven, you know, DA-DA-DA-DUM, can you use that?" To sell locks for a security company.

She said no.

And thought again about becoming a prostitute. It would be easier to sell a part of herself she didn't particularly care about.

The studio guy pointed out the Conservatory logo at the bottom of my scores (I buy my pads of score paper at the Conservatory store) and said that I should get custom-made manuscript paper, like letterhead. So, what, all this time my submissions have been dismissed out of hand as student works? Is no one able to discern artistic quality?

A bunch of dirt bikes roared along the road across the lake. Then they roared back. She decided to move inside and make a fire. It'd be dark soon, and she was getting cold.

By the end of her twenties, she'd gotten published in dozens of magazines and literary journals, and she'd received ten Ontario Arts Council grants—nothing big, five hundred dollars here, a thousand dollars there—but enough to make her think she was good. Good enough. On her way.

And yet, she hadn't managed to get any of her book-length manuscripts published. *Fugue* had failed, and she knew poetry and short story collections were hard sells, but … She had sent her stories to mainstream publishers, but they rejected them, saying they didn't publish science fiction. Which confused her, since she hadn't identified her material as science fiction. It wasn't what she'd come to think of as science fiction: heroes and villains fighting battles in outer space. One story was about a society in which it had become mandatory to suicide at sixty, to make room for the ever-increasing population. Another was about interactive tv, in which viewers voted on the outcome, and it turned out to be a real story. Yet another was about the sexual revolution during which intercourse would fall by the wayside except for reproduction (this was just as HIV/AIDs started to show up and everyone thought it was a gay disease; she remembered the difficulty she had getting answers to her pointed questions—if it's transmitted blood-to-blood, then she, heterosexual female, *was* also at risk, right?). Another story imagined a time in which one's 'tour of duty' would be environmental, not military.

But okay, science fiction it is. But then sf publishers rejected it as well. It wasn't really science fiction, was it, they said.

Eventually she stumbled upon the label 'speculative fiction'. *That's* what she was writing, she thought. A sort of philosophical subgenre of science fiction. So she went back to the mainstream publishers with it. Then they said they didn't publish feminist stuff. A women's press might be interested, they said. She hadn't identified her speculative fiction as feminist: just having a strong and independent woman as the main character didn't make it feminist, did it? But okay, she sent her stories to all the women's presses. They said they didn't publish speculative fiction.

She didn't realize that a novel, a *conventional* novel, was a mandatory ice-breaker.

Had she thought to write a feminist sf novel, she would have. But she hadn't yet discovered Le Guin, Tepper, Piercy, Butler, Russ, Gilman …

> Someone said I should be enclosing a list of previous publications with each submission. Why? Whether, and where, and how often my work has been previously published is irrelevant to the quality of the work in question.

Not to people who can't determine quality for themselves.

But that's how it's done. That's how success leads to more success. It was a phrase she'd never understood. She hadn't realized that it assumed one *mentioned* one's past successes. Because that would be bragging. (Which is why she would list her degrees on her resume, but never her GPA.)

She hadn't even been including a cover letter. It was unnecessary; her name and contact information was on each poem or story. (And even *that* is feeding the *ad hominem* fallacy; all submissions should be anonymous until the decision is made.)

And so, again, she had been dismissed as an amateur, a neophyte.

She was told by someone at some point that applications to the Canada Council were rejected out of hand if they didn't come with letters of recommendation. She was so angry. All that time spent applying … wasted. Why didn't the guidelines *say* that letters of recommendation were compulsory?

It meant another dead end. Who did she know who would, who could, write a letter of recommendation?

Oh no, the person said, you didn't need to know the person, you could just write to someone, some author you admire, care of their publisher, and ask for a letter of recommendation; send along a sample of your work with your request.

Really? She was dumbfounded. That was such an imposition. It would never occur to her to do such a thing. Years later, she happened to see Margaret Atwood at a book fair—by this time, she had published her collection of monologues herself and had bought a table at the fair—and she really wanted to stop her, introduce herself, and give her a copy of *Satellites* as a thank you for *The Handmaid's Tale*. But she would never presume. Let the woman walk through a book fair in peace, without being badgered by fans every ten feet.

Instead, she tracked down the address of Atwood's publisher—which required driving to the public library and looking in several 'big city' phone books—and she sent a copy by mail.

She never heard back. Not even a thank you.

Then someone at the Council said that Al Purdy did that sort of thing, wrote letters of recommendation for poets, she could contact him. The woman gave her his phone number. She called, and his wife told her he didn't do that sort of thing anymore, sorry.

She turned the page. And would have smiled—

> Why am I so delighted with Randy? Because he's such a contrast to Craig. The energy, enthusiasm, joy, exuberance, playfulness, relaxation, youthfulness … He wants me. He likes me. He initiates—he calls, he drops by. The warm affection, the tenderness, the care, the caring, that's what separates him from all the men I've picked up. And he's interested in me. Not my art, okay, you can't have everything, but he wants to hear my opinions, he wants to know what I want.

> So now are all my ideas about love and sex changing? Because I have for the first time, because I'm feeling what it's like to have for the first time, sex with real tenderness, real warmth, real liking? (Was there *never* this with Craig? My god, what was sex with Craig like? Like sex with Perry, Gordon, Derek, Troy?)

> Perhaps I interpret tenderness as chauvinism in older men. Randy is younger. If he were thirty, the same gentle caress would be felt differently. Hm. This is disturbing. Isn't it?

> Marilyn finds it hard to believe that I've never felt like this before, but it's true. A letter from Craig would make me buoyant for a while, but no—

I've never felt like this before.

—but she knew what was coming.

Two weeks. Two weeks in ten years. Is that all I get?

Marilyn thinks I'll find someone else. But I know better.

And she was right.

How many more short-term things can I bounce back from? If you don't meet the love of your life by the nth guy—

Each time this happens, I get just a little less willing, a little less *able*, to become emotionally involved. So I hang back, aloof. Soon I will be just a cold hard piece. Of ass.

Men have been nothing but a disappointment, she realizes. Craig. Peter.

Then Derek, Jack, Nate, Darren, Chad, Gordon, Troy, Kurt … Randy. Her conclusion was not drawn from too small a sample.

With all of them, she wanted a friendship that included sex and they, every one of them, were incapable of that. If she was at all sexual, then she was only sexual.

huddled into the corner of the room sobbing

call me

somebody

please call me.

But there is no one, she thought. No one who will call me. Not then. Not now. Probably not ever.

She stared at the flames, then out at the dark night.

I am so alone. Emotionally, socially, artistically, intellectually. After all.

> solitude on the steppes
>
> wolf wanderings
> pacing to and fro
> and fro and fro
> silverlight on snow
> g listen.
>
> soul scavenging
> contenting with fleshscraps
> m eager.
>
> sacrisufficing self.

Then turned the page.

> Went to Harbourfront to see Margie Gillis perform. And started crying when she did Tom Waits' "Waltzing Matilda". She was performing me. That was my life. My whole life. So hopeful, so eager, then so crushed. So very—   crushed.
>
> ...
>
> People all over the world have such wounds. Far greater than mine. How do they go on?

But she did. Go on. She began a new set of monologues, this time mining fairy tales for women whose stories she'd tell as if they had a feminist consciousness. Snow White, Cinderella, Little Red Riding Hood, Sleeping Beauty—my god, the pieces wrote themselves.

> And yet if a woman kissed a male sleeping beauty to bring him back to life, I'd say 'Yeah *she* has to service *him*, keep *him* alive, *we* are responsible for *their* lives.' There's no winning.

She also started a new series of soundscapes, titled *AudioVisions*. And a volume two of *The Art of Juxtaposition*.

And she continued to send her stuff out into the world, to journals and magazines, and publishers, to radio stations and record companies …

She closed the journal, having reached the end, and stared again at the flames, the vibrant orange flames—

She ached, how she ached, to be there again. So full— Full of becoming, full of excitement, full of passion. Full of hope.

But she'd been wasted and wounded.

And the wounds had never healed.

18

And then her dream, one of her dreams, came true. She got her cabin on a lake in a forest. She'd had nineteen addresses in ten years, and as many jobs, dead-end and low-paying, every one of them, but then she got lucky: there was a long-term temporary teaching position at one of the high schools in the area, and the person who'd been hired had received, shortly thereafter, an offer elsewhere for a permanent position, so the principal called Kris—she'd been their second choice, was she still available, was she still interested?

YES! She started the day after.

It was worse, much worse, than her first teaching position. She wanted to quit. Every day. But she didn't.

Which, no doubt, disappointed the principal. Who wanted to fire you. Every day.

She also continued teaching her four dance classes and her ten music students, and accepting relief shifts at the women's shelter and the child services residential program … Some days she'd teach from eight-thirty to four, then have music students from four to seven, then dance classes from seven to nine, then an overnight night shift from eleven to seven, then have to be at the school again for eight-thirty to four … She'd sneak naps in her car or in the girl's locker room during lunch … She kept living at poverty level, on her patchwork income, and put the Board of Ed paycheques straight into the bank. And five months later, she had $15,000 saved. Enough for a down payment on a cabin on a lake in a forest. Her dream. Come true.

The cabin was on a small cove at the end of the lake and crown land curved around, so it was—solitudinous. Nothing but trees and water. The beauty was a sedative and a stimulant at the same time. It was perfect. She loved it.

The main space of the cabin was open concept except for a counter that marked a separate kitchen area. She tore out the counter, making room to dance.

There was a fireplace with a large window on either side, facing the lake. One of the windows was cracked, so she had it replaced, then set in front of it the couch that one of her students had given her (it had a broken spring, and it was easier to give it to her than take it to the dump). She spent most of her time there, looking out at the trees, at the water, reading, writing, thinking.

She put her mattress on the floor on the other side of the fireplace and opened the window every night, so she could hear the loons.

The back corner behind the couch and across from the kitchen area, she turned into a study. She set her large oak table there, the one she used as a desk, then put her filing cabinets on one side, her typewriter on the other. She recycled the wood from the counter and built bookshelves onto the walls.

Past the main space, there was a washroom and then two small bedrooms. She took out dividing wall between the bedrooms and turned the space into her studio. Piano, synthesizer, four-track …

Every day for three months, she'd work until she was exhausted, with flea market tools and trial-and-error skills, then go for a long walk in the forest or just sit down at the water.

At the end of the summer, she bought a red kayak, a discontinued model on sale for clearance.

She was cold for most of the first year, having learned that a fireplace is not a source of heat and that the two baseboard heaters were inadequate to the task of heating the entire cabin. And she went without running water for half the winter three years running until she could afford to have a trench dug in order to bury the line. (She'd thought 'winterized' meant you could live in it during the winter.)

But oh, the lake. It was dark and lovely and the sun set it sparkling. And the forest. Mostly evergreens, but also white birch, bits of bark hanging off like parchment waiting to be written on.

Miles of lake to paddle on. Miles of bush to walk through.

Oh Virginia, I had a cabin of my own.

For years, every spring when the lake became liquid again, she danced outside to Loreena McKennitt's "Tango to Evora".

She stared sadly out at the water, remembering that. It had been a long while since she had danced simply to celebrate … life.

Within a year, she'd managed to put together a new patchwork of jobs—in addition to the occasional supply teaching day (it was convention at the nearby high school, apparently, that the wives of teachers be called first) (she didn't know if the husbands of teachers were called second), she had a few piano students, a few dance classes at the local arena, and occasional relief shifts at a residential program run by the mental health association.

> I was reading Popper and Eccles in the staff room, *The Self and its Brain*, and someone asked "Are you studying for something? Or taking a course?" One can't be reading just for the intrinsic value of doing so? In the staff room at a school? An institution of learning?!
>
> No, not an institution of learning.
>
> A school.
>
> …
>
> Seeing Cheryl's bracelet, I read the name 'Duane' engraved on it—even she has someone. And yet I want to … warn her.

When she was working at the mental health home, she considered becoming a philosophical counsellor. Her conversations with the residents indicated to her that their problems were often due to their acceptance of unexamined assumptions. Darlene's intense anger with her life, for example, seemed primarily due to her acceptance of her husband's presumed superiority. When she tossed that out, when she recognized that he was as incompetent as she was, a whole bunch of stuff became … irrelevant. Similarly, whether or not to quit your job, whether or not to have an abortion, whether or not to kill yourself—these were all philosophical questions. Even trying to determine why you feel depressed involves philosophical skills—to uncover and clarify not only your assumptions but also your perceptions.

She had realized, when she'd thought about it, that, at least in Canada and the U.S., when people were advised to get counselling, what was meant is *psychological* counselling. But, she had discovered, when she'd looked into it, there was also such a thing as *philosophical* counselling. It was a well developed field in Europe, with its own competing schools of thought and its many journals; one could become a certified philosophical counsellor and hang out a shingle for business. As a parallel to psychoanalysis, it made perfect sense. After all, philosophy *is* analysis.

But then she realized, when she thought about becoming certified, that she didn't care enough about other people. Not really.

So she just continued doing her best on her relief shifts. One night as she was reading through the day staff's reports, she was puzzled for a good ten minutes by the recommendation that "we access the resident's anger and develop a management plan." She was surprised at the notion wondered, how could that work? How exactly does one *access* another's anger, and how would that be sufficient or even suggestive of a plan to manage it? Part way through the rest of the report, which was riddled with spelling mistakes, she realized that the person had meant "assess" not "access". So she corrected the mistake to save others the time she'd wasted trying to figure it out. While she was at it, she corrected all the other mistakes as well.

Next time she was in, she was summoned by the supervisor. And reprimanded. The reports could be subpoenaed for court use, he explained, and a corrected report would look doctored. The staff member in question had had to rewrite the entire report.

> "There's no surer way to destroy a man than to force him into a spot where he has to aim at not doing his best, where he has to struggle to do a bad job day after day ..." Ayn Rand, *Atlas Shrugged*

Only a woman would say that. Only a woman would see that.

She remembered then reading *The Anthologist* by Nicholson Baker, a delightfully clever poetic collection of odd bits, like "'Marseilles' is a mattress of a word". And suddenly she envied, no, she *resented*, men's freedom to be clever, to be good at what they did. To not self-censor.

After a while, a full-time teaching position opened up at the nearby high school and she applied. When she walked into the principal's office for the interview she'd been granted, she saw the vice-principal sitting there with a copy of her letter to the editor of the *Toronto Star*. The one in which she'd praised Russia for introducing critical thinking into their high school curriculum, saying it was a pity such thinking wasn't taught here in Canadian schools and providing several examples of the absence of said critical thinking.

She didn't get the job.

> Ray told me that he took a proposal for a new program to his interview. I wouldn't *presume* to do such a thing! Even once I've been hired, such initiatives on my part have been met with 'Who do you think you are?'

> Is that a(nother) male-female thing? Men can get away with telling someone how to do their job, how to do it better, when they haven't even been hired yet, but women? God no. You'd have to be CEO before you could do that.

> …

> So fucking angry!! We were in Hoover's office, Brasson, Hoover, and I, were talking, having a serious conversation about pedagogy, I thought— he'd called me in to discuss a complaint one of the students had made the last time I was in to supply. I was surprised to see Brasson, the VP, there as well, but hey. Then after about twenty minutes, Brasson looks at his watch, stands up, and says to Hoover, "We should go—"

> They had a meeting to go to. They were just killing time. Chatting with me. When it was time for them to leave, I was dismissed. No not even that. I was just expected to smile and leave, my role as intermission entertainment over.

> …

> "They construed my use of gender neutral language to be 'shoving my politics down students' throats.'" Yes! And surely using male-dominated language is doing the same thing. But whose politics are more inclusive?

Eventually, she stopped being asked to supply.

> In the staff room today, someone expressed sympathy for Claude because he's getting so few days of supply teaching, his wife has to support him. What about me? I'm not getting enough supply teaching days either. A man whose wife has to support him is worse off than a woman who is unable to support herself? What?! At least *his* bills are going to get paid!

> We are invisible. Women who are self-supporting.

Perhaps it was just as well, she sometimes thought.

> I'm so tired. Ever since I started teaching, in schools, in regular day schools, I've been hassled by the students, by my colleagues, and by the administration, just for being different, *moderately* different. I've become so sick of teaching. And I used to be so very enthusiastic. Philosophy into the high schools! What a laugh.

> What makes it even more frustrating, even more defeating, even more sad, is that I used to be such a good teacher. I used to love teaching. It's not like I chose the career because of the summer vacation and the pension.

> If it was just a job, I'd say fuck it, I'd wear whatever they want me to wear and let them call me whatever they want, but it's precisely because it's *more* than a job to me that I care so much, that I refuse. I'm so concerned about the consequences of a dress code, gendered titles, daily Christian prayers, daily displays of patriotism …

Anne-Marie told her about a group at OISE that was developing a website for the new high school Philosophy course. She contacted them, so very eager to finally be part of that dream, and made the three hour drive to Toronto to attend their next meeting. One of the guys (they were all guys) showed her what they'd done so far, and she was horrified to see that the iconic figure on the main page was clearly male. She suggested that another, clearly female, figure be added or, better, that they use a single androgynous figure or no figure at all.

She was not informed of any subsequent meetings.

How many anecdotes make proof?

We need a study. That can never be done. Because it'd be a Schrödinger's cat thing: our observation would affect the results.

…

March was car insurance, April was property taxes, May will be car repairs—there is no end, no month I can get ahead, tuck a little more away. No wonder it took me nine years to save $3,000.

And it's not just the money, it's that someone like me, someone with my resume, can't get a good job. Hell, I can't even get a bad job.

All I can get are the table scraps of relief work.

It bothered her that everyone in the neighbourhood had more money than she did. Even the grade twelve dropouts, apparently. How is it, she wondered, they can afford all their toys—their pickups, their ATVs, their snowmobiles, and their beer and their cigarettes—and kids as well?

She found out when she had to call a plumber.

And yet, if you'd charged that much, you wouldn't've had any piano students.

Still. She had a cabin on a lake in the forest. Every day she wasn't working, she could be out paddling or walking. And every night, she could watch the moonlight glimmer, she could listen to the loons, she could stare up at the stars.

She started a set of pieces that were intentionally dissonant, trying to break out of the major-minor box she was in. She also started a set of 'paintings'—composed, electronic backgrounds for improvised, acoustic foregrounds. She'd find the musicians somehow …

If you're a classical composer, you seek performances of your work, for which you get paid a commission, and maybe eventually you release a CD of some of those performances and receive a royalty.

But if you're an electronic or new age composer, you're expected to do the performance yourself. Jean-Michel Jarre, Vangelis, Winston, Yanni.

I'm an electronic and new age composer (as well as a classical composer and social commentary collage artist) who doesn't perform. Well, I do, but not comfortably. So it really limits my composition. I can compose only what I can perform.

The Art of Juxtaposition continued to receive good reviews.

" … mixes biting commentary, poignant insight and dark humour while unflinchingly tackling themes such as rape, marriage (as slavery), christianity, censorship, homosexuality, the state of native Americans, and other themes, leaving no doubt about her own strong convictions upon each of these subjects. Her technique is often one in which two or more sides to each theme are juxtaposed against one another (hence, the tape's title). This is much like her *Christmas Album* with a voice just as direct and pointed. Highly recommended." Bryan Baker *gajoob*

"Thanks for the cassette … it really is quite a gem! Last Xmas season, after we aired "Ave Maria" a listener stopped driving his car and phoned us from a pay phone to inquire and express delight." John Aho, CJAM

And in fact, the album was in the top ten of the year at CKLN, Toronto's flagship station for independent music.

Sales hit thirty-two.

She stared out at the lake. That disjunct still amazed her. Eventually, she turned the page.

Oh god, to have had an engineer! Like who was it, Luba? Siberry? That artist interview and studio clip I saw. She knows what she wants and *someone else* figures out how to get it.

Then she learned that many composers didn't even do their own orchestration. She'd been appalled to discover that, for example, Neil Diamond probably *hadn't* written the score for *Jonathan Livingston Seagull*, that he probably just wrote the words, the melodies, and the basic harmonies, and then said to someone, someone *else*, 'Make it more lush' or something. Composers of classical music do it all. The 'arranging' is the composing. So how was she to have known, guessed, that was how it was done?

> Can you imagine some painter saying 'I want a picture that's like this' and then getting someone else to make it so? Or a choreographer walking in, showing the dancers a few moves, then saying, after watching it, 'It's too empty here, do something more here'?

> ...

> So how do I find an orchestrator?

> Even if I could answer that question, how do I pay him/her? When I've managed to save just $3,000 in nine years, when I make $800 a month and rent is $450?

She paused at the next page. She couldn't believe that she'd forgotten this.

Narada had read a review of her sampler tape in *Option* and requested a copy. She'd sent one, and they wrote back within a month saying that *for Amelia* and *Ruby Rose* were most in line with what they did and could she please send those two tapes. But she didn't have them ready yet; her sampler had (optimistically) featured one or two pieces from each of her *in-progress* projects. When she sent the two albums four years later, they weren't interested. They were huge by then. Probably didn't even remember her, probably accepted agented submissions only by that time, same old same old.

She'd missed the chance to get in on the ground floor. She stared out at the water. The ground floor of one of *the* new age record companies.

I must've interpreted it solely as a distribution offer, she thought. Like getting her albums in some catalogue. Which she'd been able to do on numerous occasions, with no results whatsoever.

Because otherwise, surely she would've—*should've*—stopped everything and finished both albums right then and there. Well, 'right then and there' would've taken a while even if she *had* stopped everything else.

Then again, they'd said "We encourage you to send any future recordings to

Narada." So she had no reason to think it was a time-sensitive offer. If they were interested in her work now, they'd be interested in it later.

It was the only time a huge recording company (a huge anything, actually) had contacted her. And she'd simply, and stupidly, written back saying 'Sorry, I have only those four pieces, I'm working on the rest.'

She should have called, she realized now. She should have spoken to someone.

But she didn't have a phone yet (the phone company wanted several hundred dollars to run a line across the bottom of the lake). She was cold, she had no running water (again), she had no money, she was scrambling for work …

No, wait just a minute. They could have said 'Okay, we'd like to include these two pieces on one of our samplers now, and we do want to hear the rest. How much time will you need to finish the albums?'

No, she thought, who am I trying to kid? I didn't miss the opportunity of a lifetime. The finished *Ruby Rose* and *for Amelia* albums weren't *that* good. They would've said 'pass' when they heard them.

But they could have been. That good. The sax pieces, with rain, wolves, and loons, they were good. And "lament" was on that album. And a very good cello solo. If David Darling had gotten hold of it, he could have made it, he could have helped you make it, breath-taking. If you'd had access to an arranger…

Maybe, she thinks now. And surely Narada's artists are given such support. Surely none are expected to do everything on their own …

So why did I think that I had to do everything on my own?

Because you're a woman.

And, so, because it's true.

When she submitted her stuff later, not only to Narada but also to Private Music, she hadn't progressed far enough from what she had written in her early twenties. And besides, she didn't have a demo tape, a professionally produced demo tape. How could she afford that?

Virginia, a room of one's own is just a starting point. A necessary condition, not a sufficient condition.

She turned the page.

Finished my choreography to Vangelis' "Alpha"—god, what I'd pay to see a real dancer perform it!

She also choreographed "Back on My Feet Again" for Elvis Stojko and "Unchained Melody" for Underhill and Martini, wrote out the choreography, found their addresses, then sent them her work. She'd started to learn formal choreography notation, but they wouldn't know Laban or Benesh anyway, so she just used stick figures and notes inserted in the space between the lines of a score with lyrics.

They didn't respond.

It's difficult, exhausting, to live without support, without encouragement. To keep doing what I'm doing, what I'm trying to do, without cognitive and emotional sustenance.

She was delighted when Andrew, her very first piano student, four years old to her sixteen, tracked her down and called her.

And Andrew tells me, when I mention the non-response to my idea, my offer, to compose for figure skaters—he's been hired to edit existing music for figure skating programs—that there's no budget for music.

But I didn't ask for money, I didn't expect money, I just wanted to do it!

Is that also part of the problem? Because I didn't expect to be paid, they, men, thought I wasn't serious and/or wasn't very good? Go figure.

I thought if I offered it for free, that would increase, not decrease, the likelihood of acceptance. I saw it as a matter of being affordable.

Besides, she was so used to *not* getting paid for her work. Writers typically *don't*. All those magazines and journals paid in copies. Academics similarly don't get paid for the papers they publish.

How is it that such important stuff—art and analysis, beauty and wisdom—isn't valued?

She glanced up at the sky. A thunderstorm was looming, but for now the air was … quiet. She marked her spot, closed the journal, took it and her empty tea cup back up to the cottage, changed, then paddled out.

• • •

She could always get onto shore somewhere and wait out the storm, should that be necessary in the event of lightning. Rain, she could paddle through. It was actually quite neat to do that, surrounded by the heavy drops plopping on the water.

She remembered one time she *had* gotten caught in lightning. She'd paddled as fast as she could to the nearest shore and took refuge in someone's gazebo. It was a fantastically exhilarating experience, standing there, soaking wet, right in the middle of the storm, the thunder rumbling all around her, the all around her being lit up again and again by the lightning.

Once she got past the other cottages, she lost herself in the beauty. The horizon in the distance was layered: the steel blue-grey sky above mirrored the steel blue-grey water below, the marbled clouds contrasting with the horizontals of the moving water, and in between, the verticals of green reached from far left to far right, trees behind weeds, tall spires of dark green behind short strokes of light green.

She paddled on, keeping an eye on the sky, and by the time sheet lightning started flashing at the far end of the lake, she was ready to turn and head back.

• • •

Once back, she settled inside, windows open to the still-approaching storm.

It took years to— She'd started with nothing. Most people set up their household, their home, with a bounty of gifts. Ostensibly called wedding gifts. Dishes, small appliances, large appliances, even furniture—they were all household gifts, really. But since she hadn't gotten married, she'd had to start from scratch. She'd had to buy … everything. All because she chose not to enter into a legal contract with a man.

And because her parents, of course, had given her nothing. In lieu of.

But on top of that, she hadn't expected to scrape by from one paycheque to the next for ten years.

Thirty years.

First, she fixed the water situation. It took a year to finally afford to have the trench dug, but even then, three winters in a row there was a problem with the valve and each spring she'd have to dive down into the icy cold water to fix it, one year coming dangerously close to— She'd started to feel so 'at one' with the lake, convinced she could breathe under water because water was partly oxygen, right? The effects of anoxia, she later found out.

Then the cold. She bought a freestanding woodstove, but then had to have a separate chimney installed because it couldn't be used with the existing one, and the guys from the stove place actually charged her for the half hour they'd spent standing around in the busy hardware store waiting to ask for directions since they'd gotten lost.

Over the course of the next few years, she discovered that everyone she hired—not only plumbers, but also carpenters, electricians, even general do-it guys—charged more per hour than she made. So she did most of the work herself.

Explain again how a grade twelve graduate with, yes, sometimes, a few years as an apprentice, makes more than a grade thirteen graduate with five years of university.

Another problem with the guys she hired was that other clients always seemed to get priority. Once she had to do without a functional toilet for a whole week. The men acted like they were doing her a favour by coming out to do whatever it was she'd hired them to do.

> "No man is required to relate to a man as a woman is required to relate to a man ..." Dale Spender

It was then that she started to realize that life as an unmarried woman was considerably different from life as a married woman. She suspected that if the plumber had given one of her neighbours the run-around, her husband would've just called and said 'Hey, we need it done now!' and it would've gotten done. Now.

And neither he nor his wife would even have known what the problem had been. The real problem.

> Impossible today to get any real information about snow tires versus all-seasons. The guy next to me had all his questions answered in full.

Or maybe her neighbour wouldn't even *have* a problem because the plumber would know there was a husband in the picture. That was far more likely, she thought. So when, if, she'd tell another woman, a married woman, of her troubles, the other woman would just think it was her, that she wasn't being assertive enough or something.

Married women have no idea how much their husbands provide 'protection' against second-class treatment.

And kids. Another advantage. She'd noticed that kids clear a sort of right of way for women.

Yet another problem was that the men always left a huge clean-up job: cigarette butts, mounds of sawdust, bits of wire, handprints … Would they have done that if she'd been a man? Would they have expected a man to clean up after them the way they obviously expected her to?

She turned a few pages.

She kept underestimating how much time and energy it took to sustain a patchwork of part-time employment. By the time she added in all the prep time and travel time, none of which was paid for, she realized she'd be further ahead with a simple nine to five. At least that way she'd be guaranteed every evening and every night, all evening and all night, as well as every weekend, all weekend, for her own work.

So she tried that. She got a maintenance job at a summer camp. But at the end of the mind-numbing eight hours, she wanted only to read or watch tv. And she didn't have any more money to show for it, since it paid much less per hour than the part-time jobs she'd had.

> Cleaning the outhouses and shower rooms with a couple degrees in my back pocket. Does not feel good.

So she tried to get something better.

> When they interviewed me for the assistant coordinator position, they said, and this was their first question, 'Look at all of this [they held up my oh-so-impressive and yet severely edited resume]— why on earth would you want this job?!'

> Because, I said, I can't get any other job. And would've added, but for the tears, and it's a hell of a lot better than the job I have now, cleaning toilets.

It was like those last few interviews for teaching jobs, when she was competing with the freshly minted B.Ed.s. Only someone completely out of touch with reality would go in as shiny and bright after ten years of failure. The longer you're unemployed, the more likely you're to stay that way. They can smell despair. And don't-really-give-a-fuck.

> Teaching was such a wrong turn. I mistook my love of the subject for a love of teaching. I am so not interested in nurturing. Or policing.

> But what other job can one do part-time and be paid enough to be self-supporting? Waitressing? I'd never get any tips.

It was a wrong turn in more ways than one, she realized now. It had led people to yet another set of completely wrong assumptions about who she was, what she was like. She may as well have been a librarian.

> But if you'd gone straight on into academia, where presumably those who love their subjects go, you would've ended up an adjunct. Still underpaid and overworked with nothing to show after ten years but student debt. Certainly no cabin on a lake in a forest.

But whatever else, through all that scraping by, there was the joy of her music and writing. She was, she was becoming, at least, a composer and a writer.

She finished *ProVocative,* the follow-up to *The Art of Juxtaposition,* as well as *AudioVisions.*

> I've scaled down my conceptions because with the equipment I have— I

have to choose between small and actualized or large and just-in-my-head.

She finished *for Amelia, Ruby Rose,* and *Paintings,* then started a set of preludes, inspired by Bach, but, unlike his, starting in one key and ending in the next. It was an intriguing challenge. She also continued to work on various solos—for violin, cello, flute, sax …

Atwood wrote *The Handmaid's Tale* at forty-six. So much superb excellent brilliance to look forward to from me! After forty! And I still have almost ten years before I get there!

Right.

Sean called. He's in Winnipeg now. Someone asked him to write music for a video. What? Him? Music for a video? He's not even a composer. Yeah, he plays guitar, he and his friend and I got together one night, had some fun laying tracks, but he's never composed anything. So how—

It occurred to her then that the cool kids had been *asked* to put out the school paper.

Big difference. Between that and *asking. Huge* difference, she was starting to understand.

I mean, here I am, I have several albums to my name, I'm getting reviews, I'm getting airplay, and no one asks me. No one knows me.

Well, Sean knows me. He could've asked me to collaborate. We could have become partners.

No, it's like Joel. Men don't consider women as potential work partners.

"Statistics on women's progress in the professions," Virginia Valian would write, years later, "back up the idea that a succession of small events, such as not getting a good assignment, results in large discrepancies in advancement and achievement."

It pisses me off that people like him get such invitations.

People don't advertise, they ask 'someone they know'. *That's* the way in—to invitations, to opportunities. And if you aren't someone people know, you won't be asked. Knocking on the door won't work—no one's there to hear you. Having a key won't work—there's no lock, the door only opens from the inside. They call you and when you show up, they'll be there to open the door for you.

So all that effort, all that knocking on doors, had served only to exhaust her, impoverish her, demoralize her. Things happen to those who don't do anything to make things happen.

But women can't be friends with men. And it's mostly men that are inside.

I asked my supervisor out to lunch one day, just to get to know him, and it was perceived as so odd. Then a new guy was hired, and the two of them started having lunch together all the time; it wasn't seen as weird at all, despite being supervisor and subordinate—they were just two guys having lunch. Male bonding trumps. Everything.

...

You keep thinking of yourself as, and chiding yourself for being, so passive and asocial, and you keep seeing that as a reason for being professionally and socially unconnected, but you've probably made more initiating moves than most gregarious people. Someone approached Sean about writing the music for that video. He didn't send out a dozen queries. Someone approached Ben about writing that textbook. He didn't send out a dozen proposals.

'Gregarious people'? Or 'men'.

It's like I'm in a deep dark well, and I'm digging into the stone with my bare and bloody fingers, to make steps up and out, and after ten years, I realize that ropes, and even ladders, are dropping in and people are being pulled up or just climbing out.

Still, she kept trying. She joined the Canadian Electroacoustic Community and was delighted to be invited to present a paper at their next conference, in Ottawa.

She was so excited.

She'd assumed the invitation meant that accommodations would be provided (she'd never been invited to speak at a conference before), but when she got there, she found that no, that was not the case. She could afford only a room at the Y. Everyone else was staying at the hotels near the university, where the conference was being held. Outsider once again.

She met one of the organizers, a guy her age, and also, of course, an electroacoustic composer. He'd had his first studio, a whole studio, at eighteen.

> I didn't even get my synth until my mid-twenties, then only later the four-track, then the other bits and pieces, one at a time, always used, always low-end. At eighteen, I didn't even know places like Long & McQuade and Steve's Music Store *existed*.

And when she *did* finally discover, and go to, Long & McQuade and Steve's, it was wall-to-wall men. The salespeople, the customers ... And every one of them was so full of confidence and swagger.

And shit.

> He'd listened to, bought, his first Tangerine Dream album at fourteen. I didn't buy my first TD album until, again, my mid-twenties. And it was such a radical act for someone who was supposed to be, and who *was*, listening to Barry Manilow.

You also had to fight the whole 'girls don't plug things in' thing.

> How many guys thought of buying a sewing machine? Then went to the sewing machine store and bought one? Then read the manual and figured out how to use it?

> They don't understand. They call it derivative of Mills-Cockell, but I wrote it before I'd even *heard* of Mills-Cockell.

She'd discovered Vangelis only because the *Chariots of Fire* theme song made AM radio.

She also met, at the conference, guys her age who had formed their own groups, had played in Austria, had become university instructors, had become president of this and that association. She had missed so many trains. How had that happened?

> Here I am at thirty-two, with what others had at eighteen. I really can't even call my pathetic set-up an electronic studio. It's nothing like the professional studios that other composers have. Other composers *my age*.
>
> ...
>
> I see their albums so nicely, pricely, done, and the back cover photographs of their studios, their bios mentioning a nice house, two cars, and three kids, or whatever, and I think even if I had a full-time job— How did they all manage to get not only full-time jobs but full-time jobs paying *three to four times* what I make (because that's what it would take to have bought all that)? And still have the time and energy to do those albums? What am I missing?

The full-time job was doing *those albums. Like the professors whose job is writing books.*

> "The piece involves a writer, a woman, and a young pacifist." What? So neither the writer nor the pacifist is a woman? So why not say 'This piece involves two men and one woman.' Or 'This piece involves a writer, a philosopher, and a young pacifist.' I mean, the woman does, *is*, something, isn't she? Besides a female?

Nope.

> "I wrote this piece to represent Radio-Canada in the Prix Gilson competition." Excuse me? Who the hell are you to take it upon yourself to write something to represent a national radio station? Did they commission you to do that? How?
>
> Another program note explained that the compositional method used was essentially improv, with no prior design. Doesn't anyone have a purpose or plan anymore? Is intent, forethought, dead?

It turned out she'd joined the wrong group. It was dominated by university affiliates who had access to Faculty of Music electronic studios and who were composing esoteric electronic music like Xenakis. She hated his stuff. It wasn't beautiful. It wasn't moving in any way. It was cerebral. Sound organized by mathematical principles.

It was dominated by men.

She turned the page.

    electronic studio

    it's getting so i can't work:
    every time i patch a connection
    i'm reminded of confinement, restraint,
    bondage, forced entry—

    holding the plug
        —any plug, they're all the same,
        RCA, quarter-inch, mono, stereo,
        all little silver phalluses
        visibly active, everywhere—
i move toward the jack
        —any jack, they too are all the same,
        input, output, mic, headphone,
        all fixed vaginas, immobile,
        necessarily passive, in their units–

            (oh i know why it's like this:
            the female part is stationary
            instead of the male
            because it has more energy, more power—
            but this knowledge only makes it worse.)

    unable to rape
    i stand there, unconnected,
    without any sound.

She found out about the Bourges competition and, later, entered a piece. Not realizing that winners were electroacoustic Ph.D.s writing in what she came to call the academic style.

She wondered if the same was true of publishing. Were winners of the Giller Prize, for example, those with MFAs who wrote in some sort of academic style? A style she was oblivious to?

But she didn't write in any popular genre either.

So where did she fit in?

> Overheard a guy say that prior to joining a certain band, he'd never played a guitar before. A woman would, could, never do that. She'd never even *consider* doing that. When I auditioned for that band, in Toronto, I wondered whether my keyboard skills were good enough. (They weren't.)

They would've been if you'd been a guy.

> Seeing a picture of 23-year-old pianist, hand in pocket, leaning on piano, in a suit, smiling—what makes him so confident at 23? The experience of being male? What makes me *not* come across like that, not at 23, not at 33, probably not ever? The pose implies an arrogance, an attitude of 'I know everything I need to know, I'm worth listening to, you will want to hear me'—what kind of life would he have had to have lived to be like that, at 23?

> …

> He writes only two pieces a year? Well, I suppose if they're 60 minutes long … Still.

> But at \$200/minute, that's \$24,000/year!

> If I'd gotten paid for *any* of my 60-minute long albums…

> …

> Nicholas is the Artistic Director of the Inter Arts program at Banff! And he graduated two years *after* me! And I can't even get into the damn program as a student!

She remembered applying. Leafing through the brochure, seeing the photographs of those who had been awarded residencies. All four of them were bearded white men.

> How do people become directors? He doesn't have a business degree; he has a music degree. What *is* an Artistic Director?

> I assume no guidance. If I don't know on my own what's involved, I don't apply. These people who get these positions, are they *told* what to do, are there some policies and procedures manual they just follow?

> Or do directors just tell other people what to make happen—they themselves don't do anything, they just make decisions and give orders.

> Well that's easy. If all I had to do was make the decisions and say 'Make it so'!

When she got back home, she read about an André Gagnon concert in North Bay. She drove up and approached him at the meet-and-greet after. She didn't tell him that she'd written to him years earlier … Just gave him a copy of *for Amelia*. She'd credited him in the liner notes as an influence.

She thought, hoped, that maybe once he heard her stuff …

He never responded.

She started to get the feeling that the world had mistaken her for a loser, some deluded wannabe. Not since high school had anyone considered her destined for success.

Even so, she continued to read and think. She continued to write and compose. She continued to go for long walks in the forest and long paddles on the lake. She continued to listen to music.

> Koestler makes Harriet, the only female scientist at the event (*Call Girls*) a lesbian, so male-tagged are intelligence and independence that women possessing these must be made into pseudo-males.

> …

In John Fowles' *Ebony Tower*, the first mention of women is when the narrator sees two young ones nude in the sun. And of his marriage, the narrator says "It was successful." Not happy. Not exhilarating. "Except for one brief bad period when Beth had rebelled against 'constant motherhood' and flown the banner of Women's Liberation."

I know the main character is not necessarily endorsed by Fowles, but.

…

"Causality is merely an old-fashioned postulate of a pre-scientific philosophy." Robert Heinlein, *Methusaleh's Children*

No, I don't buy that.

…

"You forgot to put on your make-up," this strange young man said to me at the concert. I was stunned. Speechless. Stuck between his expectation that all women wear make-up, his assumption that a woman who doesn't have on make-up has forgotten to put it on, and his presumption that it's his place to make such a comment.

…

December 6. Some guy walked into an engineering classroom in Montreal, told all the male students to leave, then proceeded to kill thirteen female students and one female staff member, leaving a note screaming that feminists have wrecked his life.

The scary thing is not that he was so fucking crazy. It's that he was so fucking normal.

And the scarier thing is that in the staff room at the high school, they acted like it was a point of contention, whether or not it was a hate crime, whether or not it was femicide. No, they all said, it was just one crazy guy.

How can so many relatively intelligent people, *teachers* for godsake, the very people who are supposed to be teaching toward a better world, a non-sexist world, deny that it had anything to do with sexism in our society??

...

> Leona Gom, Postman and Weingartner's *Teaching as a Subversive Activity*, Tolstoy, Gide, Antony Flew's *Body, Mind, and Death*, Robertson Davies, Kurt Vonnegut

Then one day, one week, one month, she stalled. Couldn't get past the fourth bar. Of any of her pieces in progress. Was it because she knew no one would ever hear it? Was it just too much work for nothing?

Used to be, she *had* to compose, had to get the feelings out, had to express what she was feeling, it was so overwhelming. Well, no surprise, then. Her emotions weren't roiling in a cauldron like they had been. She'd finally vented all her pain. It wasn't quite that she'd gone numb, emotionally: she felt deep peace, joy, and contentment living in her cabin on a lake in a forest. It was that the turmoil from various relationships had finally … dissipated.

Also, cassettes gave way to DAT which quickly gave way to CDs. She couldn't afford to re-release all of her cassettes. Already on the fringe, she fell even further to the wayside.

And, truth be told, once she'd discovered Vangelis, Eno, Jarre, Darling, Kater, and so many others, she realized it wasn't necessary. To compose. Other people had written the kind of music she was writing, trying to write. So she didn't need to. She could listen to what *they'd* written. Which was much better than most of what she'd written anyway.

And so, one day, she realized she wasn't a composer anymore. A month passed, then six months. Then suddenly it had been a year since she'd composed anything new. It was difficult to accept.

She knew it wasn't the same, but she felt like the woman in *The Other Side of the Mountain*, the skier who'd had an accident and become a paraplegic. The hardest part, she'd said, was when she woke up—and remembered she was no longer a skier. It had been who she was. And wasn't anymore.

19

She clung to her writing. She wasn't a composer anymore. She had to admit that. She never really became comfortable with it, but she had to admit that it was true. She walked around, trying to adjust to the change in her identity, the change in how she thought of herself.

> It's not fair, Martin Rugenen, Alastair Coover, even Darlene Lambiel, all B students at high school, now making headlines, as musicians, as composers, and me …

She'd seriously over-estimated the significance of being an A student.

But then it's not like she'd coasted on that. She'd continued to work as hard to 'make headlines' as she had for those As. *That's* what wasn't fair.

How many of *them* took their art so seriously it determined that they didn't get a full-time job?

She continued to listen to music. Every day. For hours. And it hurt sometimes, to think when she heard David Lanz, George Winston, Hennie Becker, Kim Malmquist, 'I could've composed that. I could've played that. That could've been my album, maybe even my career.'

She continued to work on her 'first year' collection of stories.

> When Russo's first person narrator says it, it's impressive, but when my first person says it, I'm afraid I come across as 'Look how clever I am!' Why didn't Russo fear that?

Are we back to my reluctance to be the best, the smartest, I can be, my habit of holding myself back—

Or are we back to the double standard—men are assertive, women are pushy; men are competent, women are—show-offs?

...

I have a problem with the omniscient narrator stance, with presuming to know more about my characters than they do.

Isn't *that* interesting.

...

"...Marie R. was Carson's literary agent, a choice Carson made carefully after several interviews." Patricia Spacks, *The Female Imagination*

Several interviews? Have things changed since then or is it just me? I write a letter, they send a form rejection letter, end of story.

But then one day, as she started the process of applying for a grant, she just—stopped.

There's something very disheartening about finding, after almost twenty years, that you're still an "emerging writer."

At that point in her life, she thought she'd be one of the jurors. Or at least an applicant in the "established writers" category. At the very least, in the "mid-career" category.

What does it take, she wondered. Again. She'd been published in *Alpha, The Antigonish Review, Ariel, Atlantis, Bite, Bogg, Canadian Author and Bookman, Canadian Dimension, Canadian Woman Studies, Contemporary Verse 2, event, Existere, (f.)Lip, grain, Herizons, Herstoria, The Humanist, Humanist in Canada, Hysteria, Interior Voice, Kola, Mamashee, The New Quarterly, Next Exit, Onionhead, Other Voices, Poetry Toronto, Prism International, Rampike, Shard, The University of Toronto Review, The Wascana Review, Waves, Whetstone, White Wall Review, Women's Education des femmes.* She'd had a few poems published in

Tom Wayman's anthology, *Going for Coffee.* She'd had a broadsheet published by Ouroboros Press.

She'd written *Fugue,* three collections of poetry, two (almost) collections of short stories, and *Satellites Out of Orbit,* the odd, but intriguing (she thought) collection of monologues giving a feminist voice to women of the Bible, Shakespeare, history, mythology, and fairy tales.

But it had been rejected. All of it. Rejected by agents. Rejected by publishers.

> So why do I bother? It's like shouting in an empty room that has no doors. If I can't be read, there's no point in writing.
>
> …
>
> But what would you do if you quit? Seriously. That's the question I've been asking. What if I stopped being a writer? I've already stopped being a composer. That was upsetting enough, but at least I was still a writer. Being a dancer was never really an identity, I wasn't that good. And being a choreographer never even got off the ground. I'm still a runner, but that's not how I identify myself primarily. But what if I wasn't even a writer?

She turned the page.

> "This is almost flawless stylistically, perfect in form and content, etc. etc. It's perverse: satirical, biting, caustic, funny. Editorial revisions suggested? None, it's perfect. Market potential/readership targets: Everyone—this is actually marketable—you could fill Harbourfront reading this probably. General comments: You could actually make money on this stuff …"
>
> "You are clearly a writer of considerable talent, and your special ability to give expression to so many different characters, each in a uniquely appropriate style, makes your work fascinating and attractive …"
>
> "The pieces are often funny, sometimes sensitive, always creative. But they contain an enormous load of anger, and that is where I have problems … I know at least one feminist who would read your

manuscript with delight (unfortunately she is not a publisher), who would roar with laughter in her sharing of your anger …"

"Your writing is very accomplished … authentic, well-written, and certainly publishable … read with more than passing interest …

"You're a talented writer … I note your ability to write and to write well …"

She sighed. She'd forgotten all those wonderful things publishers had said about her work. In their rejection letters.

" … engaging and clever …"

"… well-written, imaginative, intelligent …"

"… original and intelligent …"

"… well-crafted …"

"… enjoyable and provocative …"

"… appealing and unusual … interesting idea for a book …"

What does it take? she asked yet again.

It took knowing someone who knows someone who knows someone. And she simply didn't know anyone.

Besides, such cronyism wasn't fair. And so she wouldn't support it, wouldn't engage in it. People should get opportunities, grants, jobs, publishing contracts because their work was good. Failing that, because it would sell. Not because they were friends of the acquisition editor.

She didn't want to join writers' clubs or go to author association meetings (should she eventually be eligible to join) in order to become 'friends' with the people she might meet there who might be able to do things for her. It didn't occur to her that she could do something for them in return. Perhaps read their manuscripts. Such a conscious reciprocity was as abhorrent.

But it also didn't occur to her that she might genuinely become friends with the people she might meet there, simply because they were also writers: they would 'get' her.

Furthermore, once she was published in a journal, she never submitted to that journal again. She'd thought the idea was to get published in as many different journals as possible; such widespread recognition would be proof of her worth. She didn't realize that if she published in the same journal over and over, her name might eventually be recognized by its readers, one of whom might be an agent or worked at a publishing company who would then contact her and ask if she had a manuscript. So, instead, people, readers, possibly important people, thought 'Oh she can't be that good, they published her only once, it was a one-off, a fluke.'

> "… grants spawned grants because all granting agencies wanted you to be certified by others first so that they wouldn't be risking anything." Marge Piercy, *Summer People*

> So *that's* why they ask about previous grants? I thought it was because they want to spread the grant money around. Make sure every deserving writer got at least a little something.

How much she missed because she kept thinking in terms of justice. Or at least merit.

> So grants are stepping stones?

But the grants she'd obtained to that point *hadn't* led anywhere. She'd stepped off them into deep water.

> It makes me so angry that most of those who 'make it'—just listen to the radio or watch tv—are producing mere entertainment. Surely my purpose is worth more attention, more support. I'm writing to change the world, to make ordinary people start thinking about things…

> So why don't you just become a preacher?

> Besides, if that's your purpose, you should be writing for the masses.

But I am! That *is* who I'm trying to reach.

Well, they're not reading you.

So, what, I should write mysteries or romances? Mysteries with a message? A mystery series with a kick-ass feminist protagonist whose sarcastic asides carry the torch? Into Plato's Cave?

But truth was, she was getting tired of it.

If I could just write, and send everything to someone to do the rest—

She'd probably spent more time and energy trying to get her stuff 'out there' than she had creating it.

So maybe you *shouldn't* write for the masses. Maybe you should write for the people who might actually read you.

But it's the masses I need to reach. They're the ones who … need to change.

If I'd gone into politics, I could have effected change that way.

Right. Like women in politics are able to effect change.

The journals and magazines started saying her work was too didactic, too polemic, she was sending a message, making a point.

And that's a problem because …? What about *Gulliver's Travels* and practically every other work of great literature?

Oh, well, if it's written by a man—

And yet, Ayn Rand, Margaret Atwood …

But Rand's first novel was rejected by twelve publishers before it was accepted, and although it became a bestseller, initially it received largely negative reviews. How incompetent that proves the publishing world to be, that such a bestseller, such a *long-running* bestseller was rejected and reviled by so many …

She turned the page.

> I discovered *This Magazine* today. Not at all a feminist magazine, but I notice it's run almost completely by women and almost all of the articles are by women. They're superb articles. Imagine the world …

That's how men experience the world.

> Asimov wrote 466 books. 466!!! That's 10 a year for 50 years. Almost one a month. How can he write one book a month? He obviously doesn't write like I do, agonizing over each and every sentence for clarity, each and every paragraph for coherence. And yet they aren't harlequins.

> Then again, if I didn't have to work at a bunch of jobs, twenty hours a week, and if I had a cook, a housekeeper, a typist, an agent, a publisher, a publicist, a business manager—

> Yeah, but he surely didn't have all that from the beginning.

> …

> Thirty-five years and look what I am, look what I have done. Well, take away the first twenty. So fifteen years. Give or take. Still. That's a long time. 131,400 hours. Well, minus one-third spent sleeping, that leaves 87,600 hours. Take away 20/week spent acquiring food and shelter, plus 10/week hustling, looking for, preparing for, driving to and from, that leaves 64,200 hours.

> 64,000 hours. What have I done with 64,000 hours? I've mastered, at a rudimentary level really, and only for a short time, one musical instrument. That leaves 55,000 hours to account for.

> I've composed, performed, and produced nine albums, that's about seven hours of music, each of which maybe three or four people, a dozen tops, have heard.

> I've written 1,500 pages of stuff, most of which has never been read by more than a hundred people. The editors or agents who rejected it.

You assume they read it.

Tanya Huff was born in the same year as me and really just wrote one novel a year since 1988. If I'd done that, just from the time I got my cabin— And I *could've*—because that's not so much, right? What did I do instead? *What have I spent all my time doing?*

Let's say I've spent a couple hours a day composing and the same writing. So minus 22,000 hours leaves 33,000 hours.

I've read maybe 1,000 books, that should account for about 5,000 hours, so we're down to 27,000 hours.

Four hours a week for runs, two hours a week for miscellaneous, that leaves about 22,000 hours.

Okay, yeah, minus the time getting degrees, diplomas, certificates, what have you, five years of 40 hours/week, that's 10,000 hours.

That leaves 12,000 hours. Unaccounted for. Wasted.

What I could've, should've, done in 12,000 hours.

She took a long swallow from her cup of tea and then noticed the loons. They had come into the cove to fish. She watched for a while as they paddled around, every now and then dipping their heads under the water to take a peek. When they started making dives, she tried to anticipate where they might reappear, impressed, as always, with how long they stayed under. One came close to the dock, and she stood up, slowly, hoping to see it flying underwater, but the sun was in her eyes.

She sat back down and turned the page.

Although she struggled with all of the other aspects of her life, she continued to love her cabin on a lake in a forest with such a passion. She loved the feeling of being away, alone, separate. It—fit.

She often wondered whether she had voluntarily exiled herself in order to avoid the pain of being shunned. If you don't participate, you won't feel left out.

But no, she truly did love it. She loved everything about it. Every day, she went for a long run, a long walk, or a long paddle. Every day, and every night, she sat down at the water and stared out across the cove.

A flotilla of diamonds coursing across the lake.

She looked up across the lake. Yes. *Yes!*

Reading reviews of two recent anthologies of Canadian women poets— The frustration— How do I find out about anthologies like these in order to submit?

She didn't know they were by invitation only.

She didn't know how to get invited.

Same old, same old.

"It hangs somewhere between a treatise and a story." Exactly! So I'm succeeding! I've succeeded, I've created the hybrid prose form I wanted to! But it was a rejection. "The piece exhibits a failure to work within the framework of the genre." What? What!?

And later, from another journal, about the same piece. "The piece sits uneasily among three stools: essay, prose poem, and short fiction."

And another. "I think you need to decide which way you want to go with it."

And another. "It's neither a story or an essay."

But—

She recalled reading an interview … yes, she had made a note about it.

The Clichettes' interview about how difficult it's been for them to get their stuff out there: "It's not really theatre. It's not really a play. But there's no question in our minds—if men were doing this, they'd say 'how innovative, how incredibly interesting!'" Yes!

Even so, she continued to send *Fugue* out every now and then. One of the rejection letters said they had enough autobiographical writing by women.

Who said it was autobiographical?

She discovered that was a common complaint.

Complaint.

They say that women's writing is typically autobiographical, that we write about what we know, and that all that we know, since our lives are so limited, is our own personal experience, and therefore our scope is small. Whereas (of course) men write about the big issues, political issues, they write with a wider scope.

That's partly because men don't know themselves. They *can't* write about their personal experience. They're simply neither that reflective, nor that expressive. Perhaps that's why their characters are so flat, so two-dimensional.

Men value what they have; they belittle what they don't have.

And/or they don't, they *still* don't, understand that the political is personal. When they write about those political issues, they're actually writing about themselves.

And when we write about our personal issues, we're actually writing about the political.

She also continued to send out her poetry collections and *Satellites Out of Orbit*.

Beauvoir had three unpublished books before her first publication.

I have seven now. At what point do I stop?

Today one of my neighbours referred to my writing as a hobby. I was speechless, shocked at the gap of understanding. It was reminiscent of the prof who thought I was a general student, not an honours student.

When you structure your entire life around it, when you do it four or five hours a day, when it is almost all you do, that's not a hobby.

So what was she using as a criterion? Being published? But she didn't even know whether or how often I've been published. Being a household name? That rings more true. But her entire knowledge of the world is formed by what she sees on tv and reads in 'the paper' (there is only one, no doubt, as far as she knows). So while Margaret Atwood is a writer, since she may have occasionally been mentioned in the forementioned paper, or, more likely, is a name she remembers from school, I am not.

But of course, several pages later …

But maybe she's right. Maybe I am just a hobbyist, having mistaken myself, all my life, for the real thing.

How long can I go on believing I'm something special, believing I can write a *Handmaid's Tale* or compose a soundtrack, go on believing I'm not just an amateur, not just a hobbyist.

She couldn't even join the Canadian Authors Association. She had been published, but the rules required that you had received payment for your work. All of the journals and magazines that she'd been published in—that is, all of the literary journals and magazines she knew of—paid in copies.

Nor could she have joined the Canadian League of Composers. She didn't have "three professionally-presented public performances by three different performers, ensembles, or organizations". If she could get those three performances, maybe she could join, and if she could join, maybe she could find out how to get those three performances.

Didn't matter. She couldn't afford the membership fees anyway. They didn't accept payment in copies.

She did splurge and buy the *Writer's Market* one year, then submitted her material to every listing that accepted the kind of stuff she wrote, spending weeks typing cover letters, photocopying manuscripts, preparing the SASE enclosures, then addressing and stuffing the envelopes. Nada.

So she dismissed any writers' guild or association newsletters that provided the same market information. Not that she had access to them. Since she couldn't join.

But then instead of spending the money on associate memberships, sometimes offered, she'd spent money on wild goose chases.

In either case, money she didn't have.

The same was true for composer resources.

And philosopher resources. She didn't even *know* about *The Chronicle for Higher Education*. How would she—unless she'd had a university position?

The one day she realized with horror that Lorrie Moore and Sandra Shamas were both the same age as her. She was the same age as them. And look.

At thirty, I could tell myself that the successful people were older.

Now, they're my age.

Wait until they're younger.

I'm still planning for a future that's come and gone.

Whole careers have been made in the time I'm still waiting for my break.

So she decided to publish her books herself. To put her money where her mouth was. She'd done that with her music, but there was a well-developed indie subculture in music. In fact, *real* musicians went the indie route; they didn't sell out to Sony or RCA; it was understood that the big companies were just in it for the profits.

Not so in literature. Writers didn't seem to recognize that the big publishers were also in it for the profits. They naïvely assumed that all good material got picked up by a publisher.

But, she eventually asked herself, how could that be when there were only a few publishers in the country that published the kind of stuff you wrote? And none of them accepted unagented submissions? And agents accepted you only if you already had a publishing contract?

Such a catch-22: you can't get published unless you have an agent, and you can't get an agent unless you've been published.

But if you self-publish, everyone cautioned, you'll announce to the world your stuff *isn't* good enough. You'll lose all credibility.

Well, she didn't have any credibility anyway. At least this way, people would be able to read her stuff.

> Jimmy Smits and god knows how many others, because I never really took notice before, are executive producers of their own series—which means they put up the money. That didn't make *him* lose credibility.

And of course way back, weren't many of the great literature works of literature essentially self-published, self-financed? T. S. Eliot. Gertrude Stein. Beatrix Potter. G. B. Shaw. Even Margaret Atwood, she'd discovered.

Some of the publishers were starting to ask that you to submit a marketing plan. So why not self-publish? Apparently, either way, you have to do your own marketing. And that's what success comes down to. Now. Maybe always.

So she re-typed up *Satellites*, setting it up so the same page appeared on the left and right side of an 8.5 x 11 piece of paper inserted long-wise, then photocopied fifty copies, double-sided, carefully working out the backsides, then cut them down the middle. Marilyn designed a cover, she went to a printer for 100 copies of the right-sized cover stock, then took it all to a binder.

She then had 100 copies of the book, her book, in hand.

> If writers and composers were paid as much per hour as steelworkers and carpenters for their work, no one would ever read a book. They'd cost too much.

> Yeah, but we write one, and it can be copied, duplicated, a hundred times.

> Still. The guy who prints and binds a book gets paid more than the person who wrote it.

She worked hard to get fifty copies out to reviewers, directories, book stores, libraries ... But so many magazines didn't review self-published books. Most bookstores didn't carry self-published books. No libraries bought self-published books.

She had to sell them at readings and book fairs. And that cost money. The gas to make the drive. The fee to buy a table.

She slept in her car at the side of the road to save on the hotel. At most, only a dozen people would show up. Once, the host forgot to advertise the reading. So no one showed up.

> "The lecture circuit for poets had not yet become the big business it is now. I simply wrote to 50 colleges and offered to read for $25 if they'd put me up for a few days." May Sarton

> Really? If I did that, if I named a figure and expected accommodation, they'd say sorry, no. Which is exactly what they said when I *didn't* ask for payment or accommodation.

And, unlike men, you took 'no' for an answer.

> Proposals for poetry readings. Compositions for figure skaters. Submissions for concert performance. Every time I didn't say what my fee would be, people dismissed me. All this time. All my life. I never asked for pay. It was offered or not. End of story.

> Why do I have to ask? Do men ask? Is that the difference?

The other fifty copies sat in her garage. Or would have if she'd had a garage. They sat in her study. A clear reminder of yet another failure.

Time and time again, she had no idea how to turn her work into a career.

You should have stuck with one thing and perfected it, she told herself, staring out at the water. Instead of trying to be a writer and a composer and a philosopher. And, in that one thing, you should have stuck with one genre. Instead of trying to be a poet, a short story writer, and a novelist. Instead of trying to be classical, new age, electronic, and avant-garde.

But no, she knew, that would have been too boring. More to the point, it would have denied too much of what she wanted to do. She wanted to do what she wanted to do, write the poem and the monologue, write the social collage and the viola solo; she never stopped to consider what genre it was.

Of course, it could be—the reason she could never turn her work into a career—that her stuff was just pathetically bad. But the rejection letters, the grants, and the reviews said otherwise.

She marked her spot, closed the journal, stood up, and stretched. It had been a long morning. Actually, she noticed the sun, it was already mid-afternoon. Definitely time for a paddle. Or a walk. She considered the wind and the sky—clouds were in the distance, moving toward her—and decided on a walk. Maybe she'd go out on the water for the sunset.

• • •

As she approached her late thirties, she had a nagging suspicion that she was no longer becoming. She was. She had become. And what she was, what she had become, wasn't what she'd hoped to become.

Most of her music was unremarkable. She had composed maybe six really good things: "lament," the three sax pieces, and "Amelia's Nocturne." Most of her writing? Also unremarkable. She could call 'excellent' a handful of poems, a few of the monologues, and just one or two stories. And *Fugue*? She didn't know. She really didn't know whether it was even good. Let alone excellent.

It stings. To have the sentiment but not the skill.

It wasn't happening.

So what's my excuse for not being brilliant? I have had no husband, no kids, no full-time job sucking awa my time, energy, and attention.

All my sacrifice has been for nothing.

Well it wasn't really a sacrifice, not getting a full-time job.

Given the full-time jobs you knew about.

And the no husband, no kids? No sacrifice at all.

So why *haven't* I fulfilled my potential? Because despite no children, no husband, no full-time job, I've been so busy, too busy, making ends meet?

The thought that maybe she *had* fulfilled her potential—

Maybe they were right. Maybe she was some deluded wannabe.

It became a struggle to keep writing, to keep being a writer.

I've spent twenty years climbing this ladder, one rung at a time, only to find it doesn't go anywhere. It just sort of ends in mid-air, leaving me hanging

She'd never found her Forrester.

Janet Evanovich has been at it for twenty-five years, and no one heard of her for the first fifteen. Then she switched from romance to the Stephanie Plum series.

So I need to switch. To something.

But to what?

...

I'm tired. So very tired. Of doing it all myself. Of supporting myself, financially, emotionally. Everything is so fucking difficult.

The only dream that ever came true was my cabin.

And now even that—

It's not idyllic anymore. I found myself agreeing with an author who said how nice it would be to have a shed, a desk, and a chair, and just write, and I thought Yes! And my heart leapt at the thought and then I realized—I *have* that.

But the psychic space here has become so full of my bitterness, my weariness, my frustration and anger, my hopelessness, and the shift schedule for next week and it's the middle of winter and the lake is frozen and the pump is starting and stopping again for no reason

like my heart

now

…

How many times can you pick yourself up after you've run headlong into a brick wall?

She sighed. She hadn't quite finished the journal, but decided she'd had enough for the day. The sunset was imminent.

• • •

The paddle dipping rhythmically into the water was like a slow metronome. It soothed and steadied. She drifted for a while. And felt such a beautiful lassitude. The water, the trees, the sun …

Suddenly she heard the chirrup of otters. She eagerly looked around, then saw two sleek little heads bobbing high in the water, looking at her. She smiled and paddled toward them. They slipped serpentine out of sight, then popped up several yards away, chittering at her again, snufflesnorting their curiosity at her presence.

• • •

She paddled back in the lovely dark, then made a fire, and decided to finish the journal after all.

She opened it to where she'd left off, turned the page, and— Time's wingèd arrow froze, hung motionless for a moment, as if confused.

dreaming of kaleidoscopes

whirls a storm
   of scarlet and crimson
            the cobweb drips
         and black and blue

black blue shrouds
      the bleeding petals
                  torn
                     ragged
scabs and scars
            blowing across the snow

desert voices
in a white room
stark and naked
      i
         walk slowly

twisted grey and sometimes purple
rarefied and far too dense
i walk
         i walk
                  and every now

and then
      i pick up a piece
like shards of glass
                  some mirrors
and i don't know
            if i throw it away
            if i lose it
            if i store it for sustenance
                        to inflict
                        to understand
                              who.
who.

standing on a cliff
in a silent blizzard
  crumbling
and dreaming of kaleidoscopes
all the pieces always fit

and i don't know
   i won't take the one with the sharpest edge
and make the cut
to end all cuts.

20

Next morning, she was back down on the dock, with the almost-done journal of the day before and the next one. And her cup of tea. It was a bright, breezy, sunny day. As she gazed out across the cove, the wind blew the dancing sparkles this way and that, and then held them in one place for over a minute—it was like watching Chopin's *Etude in A flat.*

Shortly after she'd gotten her cabin, Marilyn came up and painted starry skies on her bathroom walls. But that was the last time she visited, saying it was a long drive.

It *was* a long drive, which was why when she visited Marilyn, she stayed for a couple days, breaking it up a bit, giving Marilyn her space, by making a trip to Toronto while she was there, checking out the used CD stores, the used bookstores, maybe going to a dance performance at Harbourfront …

So even though they still wrote, long letters, and even though they still spoke on the phone, long conversations, both of which delighted her, it was she who did the visiting.

She got so tired of—*she* was always the one to call, write, drop by. *She* was always the one to ask about the other's work, the other's interests.

It never occurred to her that, like her relationship with Craig, if it was that much work, something was wrong.

But then one day, several years later, when she called Marilyn to suggest a visit, Marilyn said 'Not this weekend. The kids are coming over.' She was going all grandmothery with Roy and Vicki's kids. And again, next time she called, no, a friend was coming to visit. Third time, it was something else. She decided she would not call again. It has to be reciprocal, she thought. She would not beg for friendship.

Marilyn never called. Not to invite her down or even to say 'Hey, long time …'

She actually cried when she realized their friendship was over. They had been friends for over ten years. But more than that, Marilyn had been the only woman she had been able to connect with. What had she done wrong? She'd thought Marilyn had enjoyed her company, her conversation, despite the age difference.

She took Marilyn's name off her 'in case of accident' cards.

Now there would be no one to call in case of accident.

One day when she went into town for groceries, when she said 'thank you' to the cashier, she realized that that was the first time she'd spoken to anyone all week. And it would be that way for—

> This must be temporary. This not having anyone to— It can't go on forever like this. I can't go on forever like this.

So she kept trying. To make friends.

Soon after she'd moved in to her cabin, on her way to get the mail at the group box up the road, she met a woman doing likewise. She smiled and eagerly slowed to chat.

"Hello."

"Hello, I'm Suzanne. And you are … ?"

"Kris." She introduced herself.

"Oh, you're Cal's girl?"

"No, I'm—"

"Don's wife!"

"No—"

"Those two little boys I see out and about … yours?"

"No."

And then the woman had nothing more to say. Certainly nothing about music, poetry, dance, beauty, passion. Let alone the patriarchy and gender politics.

> "Most housework, Friedan suggested, could be adequately performed by feeble-minded girls or by eight-year-old children." Barbara Ehrenreich, *The Hearts of Men*

No doubt, if she *had* been somebody's girlfriend, wife, or mother, she would have made friends easily. And if she'd been a lesbian, she could have joined the region's LGBT group; if she'd been a senior, she could have joined the Seniors' Club. But she had no community. Where is the community for straight white solo-by-choice childfree-by-choice women?

> I want to shout to Jane Rule, not all women who live alone, who are strong, and who refuse to play Nora, are lesbians or divorcées. (But indeed, where *are* all the single heterosexual women?) (The single middle-aged heterosexual women?)

Once, one of the teachers at her school-for-the-day, asked Kris why she didn't have kids. It was a common question. She was in her late thirties and still people asked. 'Don't you want to have kids?'

> No, I'd tell them, I'd be a bad mother. I'd be one of those parents who slammed their baby into the wall if I couldn't get it to stop crying.

> Everyone smiled, as if I was kidding, and assured me I'd never do such a thing, I'd fall in love with it.

> But I wouldn't. I know. And if I didn't kill the kid, I'd spend so much energy resisting the desire to do so— I'd resent its presence. Its noise. Its imposition. Its relentless *neediness—*

> Why is everyone so hell-bent on everyone else having kids? Why can't they just accept that some people *don't want* kids?

No one explained that the reason I'd fall in love was because of chemistry.

Oxytocin. It rewires the brain. Permanently.

Yet another reason not *to have kids.*

Speaking of which, why aren't any of the evolutionary biologists writing papers about that?

Oh, right. Because they're male. And that would be a women's issue.

She swore that if they were still asking when she was in her forties, she'd ask back why they were so eager that she make a kid with Down's Syndrome, and if she did make one, would they look after it?

> Everyone glorifies being a parent. As if it's something important, something *as* important as any one of a hundred careers. Truth is, it's not. Because we don't need more human beings.

> It could be, though. We need more *special* human beings. But the human beings most people raise aren't special. They *think* they're special, because they have their DNA. Which just means they think *they're* special. Either because they're that egotistic, that arrogant, or because some primitive part of their brain overrides their rationality— Maybe we're hardwired to think that about our kids because otherwise we'd kill them pretty damn quick.

> Then again, we *don't* need more special human beings. The system would just kill them.

> Or rather, we need a *number* of, *a critical mass* of, special human beings, all at the same time, to revamp the system. To save the planet.

> No we don't. It's already too late.

> ...

> Also, because becoming a parent is such an investment, only the most courageous, only the most honest, would admit they made a mistake,

would admit they voluntarily derailed their life for nothing. Or at least for nothing special.

And yet, *because* she wasn't married, didn't have kids, she didn't feel like a grown-up. She was approaching forty, and still she always felt younger than … well, everyone. Women in their twenties seemed more grown-up, with their hair, their make-up … She felt like some perpetual teenaged tomboy.

Once when she was in a fabric store, looking for some felt to cover her keyboards, she felt like a kid who was there to get something for some school craft project. She certainly didn't identify with all the other women there, who were looking at the fabrics, looking through the pattern books …

She'd felt the same—like she didn't belong, there among the women—the one time she went to get her hair cut.

And she would never even consider getting her nails 'done'.

In fact, she even felt 'wrong' in the women's restrooms if there was another woman there, touching up her lipstick, fluffing her hair, preening at the mirror.

And yet there was no question about her sexuality. She wasn't a lesbian—she wasn't sexually attracted to women at all.

She just didn't come across as an adult. Why? Because if you're female, the only way to be, or feel like, an adult is to be a woman. (Females aren't allowed to be people; the word for person is male: 'man'—'Every man for himself …') And she never was. A woman. She didn't wear make-up, heels, a dress; she never had a boyfriend (she never considered Craig a boyfriend, but a partner), husband, kids. That could explain why she was seldom taken seriously.

So, what, women have to wear make-up and heels in order to be taken seriously?

The more make-up a woman wears, the harder *it is to take her seriously.*

Not having a full-time job, and still reading, writing, and thinking—activities traditionally associated with being a student—didn't help.

Reading, thinking. Activities associated with being a student.

She could count the number of times people, not including her students, had come to her for advice. Three. Melinda, the bus driver at the summer camp, asked her whether she should pull over when the kids refused to stay in their seats, Shelley, one of her colleagues at the mental health home, asked her what to do when she failed the firefighter test, and Marilyn once asked her about the way she was going to hang her paintings in a gallery. Three times. No wonder she didn't consider herself an authority. Apparently no one else did either.

She'd started noticing that when men speak, they never started a sentence with 'I think'.

> Without that, their opinions sound like facts. A handy habit if you want to sound like you know it all. And don't want to be challenged.

> Not only do they, therefore, speak with such authority, they speak as if what they have to say is important and as if they're the first person or the only person to say such things.

> By comparison, my delivery is so casual. I assume the other has come to the same insights, and I'm just reminding them of what they surely already know. After all, I'm nothing special, I'm no genius, I don't have a monopoly on insight. But no wonder people don't stop and listen.

She'd noticed too that women who were mothers seemed to have nailed that authoritative manner, that easy ability to tell others what to do, and the expectation that they'd be listened to. She herself hadn't developed that ability, and she certainly didn't expect to be listened to. Given her life, it was a realistic expectation.

> And then, since I assume they know what I know, I'm so appalled at what they do anyway. Enlist in the army, for example. Surely they know what they're signing up for. Any thinking person knows it's not for the opportunity to be all you can be. Soldiers are pawns in someone's greed for money and/or power. And any thinking person knows they'll come back broken.

> But no, apparently they don't know what I know, so it's not 'anyway'.

But she suspected there was more to it than not having the conventional trappings of adulthood. She suspected it was also because she was always hiding her competence, her knowledge—remnants of handicapping herself lest she make her sister, her parents, feel inadequate.

I've been so careful not to make other people feel stupid—

Given that constant cover-up, is it any wonder everyone has thought *I'm* stupid? Damn you to hell, mother!

And yet, if you'd hadn't covered up your competence, you would have been accused of arrogance. And still not asked. For advice. Still not invited. To participate.

The only time it was permissible was in class. Who knows the answer? My hand shot up. I do! I must have irritated the hell out of all my teachers.

She's spent her whole life waiting to be acknowledged, waiting to be recognized. Pity she couldn't just raise her hand.

Over time, she met more people who lived on or near the lake, but they were people like Suzanne, people like her mother, her father, her brother, her sister—they were the world, they were *her* world. And so the wall between her and everyone else grew. And one day she realized it was all around her.

She flipped through the remaining pages in the journal, then started on the next.

Her interactions with the men in the area were even worse than her interactions with the women. She'd asked one of the snowmobilers, politely, if he could just turn around a minute earlier, *before* he got to her end of the lake. She so loved looking out at the beautiful white snow, the pristine— He told her she didn't own the fucking lake and then made a point of driving back and forth, and back and forth, right in front of her cabin, criss-crossing until the entire cove was a mess of soiled tracks.

It wasn't the first time such a thing had happened. And it wouldn't be the last.

It's like they hate me without even knowing me. It's like I'm some sort of affront.

Of course you are. Unmarried women challenge their view of the world—that a woman needs a man.

She heard that some of the men in the neighbourhood thought she was a bitch.

> Men expect women to pay attention to them.
>
> (Women don't expect men to pay attention to them. Except sexually.)
>
> And if you don't pay attention to them, they get angry at you and call you names.

She eventually realized that an unmarried woman is a target. When she's no longer a target for come-ons, she's a target for hostility.

And it's because *she's no longer a target for come-ons, she's no longer 'available' for sexual service, that she's a target for hostility.*

She finished her tea, but wanted to sit for a while longer, so she carried on.

> In the german language, every noun has two forms, the male and the female. It is absolutely amazing, and appalling, that sex is so important, so very fucking important, that every word must have a sex assigned to it, that even words must be identified by sex.

She found out that there was an all-comers basketball game at the high school every Tuesday, so she showed up. She genuinely wanted to play basketball again, but also thought maybe she could meet some people there, make some friends. She discovered she was one of just two women. The other woman was someone's mother who seemed to dismiss her at a glance.

It was convention that they played one-on-one, which was fine, but the guys assumed the two women would always guard each other. Indeed they were always put on opposing teams for just that reason. Shouts of 'Switch!' occurred every time one of the women replaced someone. It was confusing. And annoying. And completely unnecessary: she was quite capable of guarding male players, most of whom were boys, not much taller, not any faster, and definitely not more coordinated than her (they couldn't run backwards, for example) (at all). The guys never threw the ball to her, even when she was in the clear with a good shot. When one of the guys, one of her own team-mates, physically pushed her out of the way so he could catch a rare throw intended for her, she'd had enough.

You couldn't've come up with a better metaphor for your life if you'd tried.

> "I was having lunch with some friends, all of whom were lawyers or feminist legal scholars, and … " It was said by the character so easily, so casually, but it stopped me. My heart just did a flop. What I'd give for *one* friend with a university degree. For *one friend.* How does one get *several* friends, all of whom are lawyers or feminist legal scholars?

It took her breath away to think, now, about how much of a difference that would have made.

> Well, if I'd had lunch today with Linda, Jen, and Diane, I could well be having lunch with a production manager, an economist, and an esteemed Professor of Literature. So maybe it wasn't that that person had met those four; maybe she knew them from way back, and that's just what they had become.

> So my problem is I didn't cultivate friendships way back. Partly I didn't quite know how. And partly I didn't have the time! Not with all those part-time jobs to put myself through university, and all the course work, the four hours of piano, the track workouts—when was I supposed to hang out with my friends?

And then at a book fair in Toronto, she met Jeff. He had a table, like her, and was peddling a sort of 'Why I'm not a Christian' book that he'd written and self-published.

And she allowed herself to get excited once more. Because still she hoped to find someone. Someone with whom she could live together, apart.

He was just about to defend his dissertation, in Philosophy; he was a classically trained musician; he was supporting himself with a bartending job; and he did a lot of weight training. In many ways, he was her double. She thought there was a lot of potential in their common interests, their common abilities …

She was rudely awakened when, on their subsequent get-together (their first date, she supposed), he started explaining his thesis, an explanation she had invited, and when she started interjecting with questions and comments, he angrily told her she should wait until he was done before she asked questions.

Well, fuck you.

Of course at the time, she apologized. Profusely. Followed up with a phone call and a letter even. She swallowed her pride. She begged for another chance. She must've known it was her last.

But even as she grovelled, it felt wrong, so wrong, to be doing so. It was only her misplaced desperation that had kept the 'fuck you' deep inside.

And when he didn't return her call or reply to her letter, something broke. For good.

And she gave up. For good. She had wasted far too much time and energy on the romantic illusion.

Not just on that, but on simply trying to establish a relationship with a man.

> What was that line from *A Life Less Ordinary*? "Love is merely an emotional adaptation to a physical necessity." Perhaps it's a good thing then that I never had an orgasm. I remember Diane saying something like 'Now I know why people get married. It's the sex.' If it's that good, that addictive …

Truthfully, it wasn't that difficult. To give up for good.

She'd already become celibate. In the late 80s, AIDS/HIV had come onto the scene, and it was a no-brainer that sex wasn't worth dying for. Even if the man said he wasn't HIV-positive, there was simply no way she'd ever trust anyone, let alone a man, with her life.

> If they lie about the little things, they'll certainly lie about the big things. Like test results.

> Who am I kidding, they won't even bother to get a test; half the time they don't bother to get a condom.

What she had missed more than having someone special was simply having kin— people with whom she could be herself and people with whom she could have fun.

She did wonder, though, if there was something wrong with her. If she was simply incapable of having, being in, a relationship.

"Every woman in the world is ready to believe everything is her fault if you just tell her it is." Sheri S. Tepper, *The Gate to Women's Country*

She knew she wasn't affectionate. She didn't exude warmth.

You exude passion, intensity—that's not enough?

Once when she was teaching a kinderdance class, she decided to force herself to hug her students. She thought maybe that way she could get over her inability to be casually affectionate. She figured they wouldn't notice, little kids being so comfortable with hugs, with being hugged by adults, and since they didn't really know her, they wouldn't think it strange, look, Kris is actually hugging someone. She thought she'd get used to it with them, then maybe graduate to other people, other situations. So at the end of class, when they were all milling about, all happy and dancey, she gave each one a hug goodbye.

And felt nothing.

Was she incapable of feeling? No, that can't be right. She felt. She felt too much. That was the problem.

So said others.

Who didn't feel nearly enough.

Was she incapable of feeling, of caring, *for other people*? Perhaps. In the specific. In the particular. But in the abstract, humanity at large— Well, no, even that. Now.

She used to care for humanity at large. Which is why she tried so hard to make the world a better place. With her teaching, her writing …

Though maybe, she wondered, it was just that she felt she had a duty to do so. Roman Catholicism plus idealism equals.

Or maybe it wasn't because she cared about the people at all, maybe it was just the principle of the matter, the injustice of it.

In any case, now she didn't give a flying fuck. About the people or the principle of the matter.

Is that why she was so alone in the world? Did everyone pick up on that?

No, that can't be right. Lots of people don't give a flying fuck.

It suddenly occurred to her that most people were just their family away from being as alone as she was. Beyond family, people were just acquaintances, neighbours, colleagues they'd stop seeing as soon as they moved or lost their job.

And she'd walked away from her family.

And doesn't regret it one damn bit.

A lot of other people would probably have done the same thing if they hadn't've made a new family, and well, it's useful to have grandma and grandpa to help out.

> Perhaps another reason I'm not very affectionate is because it's quintessentially feminine. And I so eschew everything feminine because to be feminine, to be female, is to be subordinate.

Research was starting to show that oxytocin was also related to the inclination to seek social interaction, even to fall in love. A link with Asperger's and autism, neither of which she'd heard about back then, was also suggested. If she had low levels of oxytocin, that could explain her difficulty with social attachments, her inability to have romantic relationships. So her coldness, her inability to cuddle— it was chemical-based?

And if *she* had low levels of the stuff, maybe her mother did too. Which would explain—

Not everything.

Before, with so many men, she'd thought the problem was that she was smart, strong, competent. Men didn't like feeling inferior. She'd just have to wait until she found an equally smart, strong, competent man. But after Matt, she realized that even the smart, strong, competent men didn't want an equal. They wanted to feel superior too. They all wanted to feel superior. To women.

She also wondered whether the problem was that she didn't appear to need anyone. Do men, all men, want, as well, to be needed? It's not enough to be wanted?

She knew she didn't appear to need anyone. She realized now that she didn't appear to want anyone either. She didn't dress the part, and men, like most people, judged by appearance, negotiated the world by stereotype.

She stared out at the water. And suddenly realized that Craig was just like Matt. Or Matt was just like Craig. Tweedle-dee, tweedle-dum. The intellectual discussions that weren't, really. Because he didn't think she would or could understand. Or didn't want her to. For the longest time, she'd thought she *didn't* understand, because when she did, the matter at hand didn't seem that difficult or that special, so she thought she must be missing something. Turned out it simply *wasn't* that difficult or that special.

It had been a bit mind-blowing to apply this to all the men she'd studied—Plato, Shakespeare, and so many others. They were primitive men, they'd lived in primitive times, so it was far more likely that *they* had missed something than that *she* had. When she didn't understand them.

It was a logical fallacy: men's belief that since they themselves were special (being male), what they do must be special. If anything, it goes the other way around.

She turned the page. One of the magazines to which she'd submitted "The Pietà"— a story rising out of her relationship with Peter—had rejected it, dismissing the main character, Jonathan, as a cliché.

No, he's real, she'd protested at the time. But it hit her now. He was real *and* a cliché. So was Craig. A cliché. And Jeff.

And then, she realized with sudden, and devastating, clarity, that she herself was a cliché.

Not just not exceptional, but a cliché.

21

She didn't read from her journals at all the next day.

22

She considered not reading from her journals the day after as well.

But after a very long walk, she realized that it was *because* her life was so cliché, so commonplace, that she had to keep going, had to figure out what had happened.

If Craig, Peter, Jeff—if they're all clichés, how is it that intelligent women fall for them?

The answer, she thought, was that intelligent women tend not to have much experience with dating, with boyfriends—we don't *know* they're clichés. You need context to form that judgment.

But it wasn't just that. In fact, that was the least of it.

She needed to understand why *her whole life* was all too common.

Why was it all too common that hard-working, high-achieving, goal-directed young women just … never … made it? Where are all the girls who got straight-A in high school? The straight-A boys, they're everywhere. Hell, even the B-achieving boys are everywhere.

It had become cold overnight, and the sky was overcast. She hoped there were a few more warm, sunny days left. She could still kayak when it was cold and overcast—in fact, she'd always called November silver, the water like mercury, the sky like smoke, and the forest full of bare grey branches—but she liked the warmth and the sparkling water better.

She drained her cup of tea, then opened the journal that lay limply on her lap.

At some point she realized she also wasn't a writer anymore. She hadn't written any poetry or short stories in over a month. Then in over a year. She hadn't written a second novel.

She told herself that she had to accept the fact that she wasn't nearly as creative as she'd thought. She really didn't have much of an imagination. If she had, she *would've* written a second novel.

Then she told herself that that wasn't true. If people knew what she'd grown up with, and how socially isolated she was, they'd realize that her whole life was an act of imagination.

So why had she stopped? Romantic angst had fuelled her endeavours through her twenties, and hope got her part way through her thirties, but surely there had to come a point at which one recognized—what's that saying? Insanity is doing the same thing over and over but expecting a different outcome.

So now what? she wondered.

She had to recreate herself.

She decided to give academia another try.

It would take a while to save enough for tuition and books. In the meantime, she decided to apply to Concordia and McGill; it'd be nice to live in Montreal for a year, she thought. She wrote the GRE—not realizing that people prepared for months before doing so, not realizing that there was an entire GRE-prep industry. She received a score of 2100, which put her in the top 5% for verbal, the top 5% for analytic, and the top 25% for quantitative (which, she was amazed to discover, was above the average for engineering candidates). Her score put her in the top 2% of the population at large, which meant she was smart enough to join Mensa. Should she be able to afford it.

As soon as she was accepted, she found someone to rent her cabin for the duration, since she couldn't afford rent *and* her mortgage, and then went off to Montreal get an M.A. in Philosophy.

> Having to get a job to pay rent means I won't be able to focus exclusively on my studies and thus distinguish myself to get a scholarship for Ph.D. studies at Rutgers or wherever … and so another dream crumbles and it's

all such a fucking shame. My GRE score puts me in the top 10% of all grad school applicants from the last fifteen years and yes, yes, I know Einstein worked in a patent office, and Eliot worked in an insurance company, but it's still all a fucking shame, what the hell is wrong with our world?

She thought that maybe once she had the M.A., she'd try to obtain a few courses as a sessional; there was one university an hour's drive from her cabin, and another a two hours' drive. She didn't know that the relationship between professors and sessionals was the same as that between regular high school teachers and night school teachers. Worse, actually, because for one-third the pay, she'd be given the classes with twice the marking load; there was no cap of thirty at the university level.

Regardless, she was excited. She felt like she was just continuing where she'd left off fifteen years before.

But, of course, she was that much older than most of the other students. Which made a difference. Worse, many of her fellow students were married with kids.

And so, despite her attempts at conversation with the strangers in her classes, she found herself once again without any friends. She knew that many of the students headed to a bar after class—many of the male students—but she never found out which one. As for the other female student—yes, singular—she paid far more attention to the male students than to her. So again, there would be no late-night discussions about philosophical issues.

She tried making friends with some of the younger profs, since they were more her age, but, well, she was 'a mature student'—she didn't realize that there was such a stigma attached to that, such a stereotype. She tried to make them realize that she *hadn't* been a wife and mother for the last fifteen years, that she had been reading, writing, and thinking, just like them …

But they could not recognize, there was no mechanism for recognizing, an independent scholar.

So I'm at one of the computers at the end of the semester during the final paper rush, and this male student comes in, importance throbbing at his temples and streaking through his beard. He stands over me and asks "Are you going to be long?" "Oh no," I say, "I'm just doing my Christmas card list." He's silent. "It was a joke.   Apparently, about you."

One day, her thesis advisor asked her if she'd be interested in co-authoring a paper with him. She said 'No, thanks'. She wasn't particularly interested in the topic. And she already had a lot of work to do. As during her undergraduate program, she had not just one, but several part-time jobs in addition to her course work and thesis work. Rent in Montreal was higher than she'd anticipated.

She didn't realize that many of the students in the program had been given teaching assistantships. She'd never seen an advertisement for such positions and so had never applied.

When she'd gone to the university job office, she was told that one of the local schools needed tutors, so she applied for that job. And got it. She ran the two miles there and back, even through the winter. It didn't take any longer than waiting for and taking the bus anyway. But the student she was assigned to tutor kept 'forgetting' the money to pay her. This reduced her to tears one day. There she was, in her late thirties, a degreed and experienced high school teacher, tutoring some kid, running two miles through the snow to do it, and not getting paid. And so not being able to afford even the day-old stuff in the grocery store.

She also said 'no' to her advisor's query because 'group work' had been the bane of her scholastic existence. Whenever she'd had to work in a group, either she ended up doing it all herself or she accepted a lower mark than she would have gotten if she *had* done it all by herself.

That reasoning didn't apply in this case, but not because her thesis advisor was less competent than her: it didn't apply because she wouldn't actually be working *with* him. That she would be doing the paper mostly on her own and sharing credit with him didn't occur to her. That he would be 'lending' her his name, his status, didn't occur to her.

She'd been helping other people with their work since grade two. She was the student who was always done first, so she was forever being put into service as teacher's helper. 'Krissie, would you mind helping Roger with his reading?' 'Krissie, why don't you help Danny, he's having trouble with long division.' And none of the kids she helped had *their* status increased by needing, having, help. So why would it occur to her that having her advisor's help would somehow increase *her* status?

She'd thought that doing it *on your own* meant getting more credit, because you had done it all *without* help.

> Men see everything in terms of competition, in terms of win/lose. Every action, every gesture, every word is measured in terms of rank—'Does it put me one up or one down?' Women don't think that way. In fact, since infancy, *we've* been *co-operating*. We see everything in terms of helping others.

> So it's not that women compete and lose. It's that we don't compete. We don't know how. (We know how to work hard. But apparently that's irrelevant.)

How many women like me, she wondered, have gone through life sabotaging their success by not seeing the competitive subtext to all the decisions, all the choices, we make, understanding them instead either at face value or with a completely different subtext?

> 'How does it affect my status?' simply isn't a question we ever ask.

Because women are exempt from status ranking. To put it bluntly, we don't count.

So it didn't matter that you declined the co-author invitation. Your status wouldn't have increased anyway. It would *have been just more work.*

> Furthermore, if you don't recognize the hierarchy, you don't recognize the ladders.

A problem not only because you won't use them, but also because you might bypass them. The penalty for trying to pole-vault is fierce.

She thought about getting another cup of tea, but then decided to read on.

> "Ninety percent of answering questions is anticipating which ones will be asked …" Richard Russo, *Straight Man*

No wonder I didn't get straight As. I never did that. It was so strategic.

And I thought it was somehow cheating.

Not until now did I even know people *did* that.

And not just 'anticipate' the questions, but—one of the profs here actually advised us to go to the Department office and consult the comprehensive exams from previous years; he told us it was possible some of the questions might reappear on this year's comp exam.

Was that the case even back in my undergraduate years? Did everyone but me know that?

She flipped through the rest of the year in Montreal. She'd enjoyed her year there, much like she had her years in Vancouver and Toronto, but to *really* enjoy living in the city, one had to have money. More money than she ever had.

Even so, the libraries, the used book shops, the used record shops, the free concerts, the pay-what-you-can theatre shows …

At the end of the year, her advisor said he'd like her to continue; he'd make a place for her in the Ph.D. program. It was tempting, but he didn't guarantee any sort of scholarship or even a teaching assistantship (she knew by then to ask), so it'd be an expensive, and exhausting, three years.

And for what? Neither of the two universities near her were hiring in the Philosophy Department, nor were likely to do so in the near future, so a Ph.D. wouldn't've had any value unless she moved. Which she had no intention of doing. After just the one year away, she was eager, so very eager, to return to her cabin on a lake in a forest.

Besides, she didn't need to be formally enrolled in an academic program to keep reading, writing, and thinking about the issues that intrigued her.

And she was right not to go on to the Ph.D. She loved thinking too much, she was too pure, she was— During her oral examination for the Master's, she'd said to her three inquisitors, happily, because she was finally getting the intellectual discourse, the exchange, she'd been seeking all year, "This is fun, ask me another question!"

And that stopped them. Every one of them. They'd all forgotten how they had, at one time, loved to think.

It started to rain, so she headed back up to the cottage, made that second cup of tea, then settled on the couch. Perhaps she'd make a fire in the evening, she thought. Or, if it cleared, she'd go back down to the water to watch the moonlight.

When she returned from Montreal, she was able to resume her relief position at the mental health home, but she'd lost her music students and her dance classes. She doubted she'd get any supply teaching. It wouldn't be enough to pay the mortgage, let alone the hydro and phone bills. She had enough—no, she didn't have enough wood to get her through the winter.

One night when she walked in to the office for shift change, her colleague was reading the paper.

"Hey, Kris, here's a job for you! The university is looking for someone to teach remedial English."

What? Really? She rushed over to read the ad. Her eyes widened. It looked too good to be true. They were actually looking to fill two positions. One was to teach a remedial English course; the other was to run their Remedial Writing program twenty hours a week. She was well qualified for both positions. Her heart started to race. A position at a university. A foot in the door. Who knew what could happen from there?

So she applied. And was called for an interview. And was hired. They were very pleased that she had high school English teaching qualifications and experience *and* a Master's degree. *And* she was local. Perhaps that meant they didn't have to pay for her moving expenses, but she doubted they would've anyway. Part-timers don't get that sort of assistance.

She eagerly entered the lunch room on her first day, intending to get to know her colleagues as soon as possible, and stopped dead at the doorway. All of the men were sitting at three tables on left, and all of the women were sitting at one table on the right. It was just like high school. Not only like the high school student cafeteria, but also like the high school staff room.

Well, enough of this shit. She approached the table on the left that was occupied by her supervisor, his supervisor, and the Dean. All men. But then halfway there, she just nodded and changed direction. She'd recognized that one of the other tables on the left held members of the teaching faculty. So she sat there and introduced herself, making sure to mention not just her Remedial English/Writing position, but also her Masters in Philosophy and her hope that she might be able to teach a couple courses as a sessional.

She'd be damned if she was going to sit with the secretaries, the women at the table on the right.

She didn't realize she was already damned.

A week later, she started approaching individual people in the English and Philosophy departments and asking them out to lunch—not to use them, but just to meet fellow intellects. She started with Carrie, one of two new English faculty members. During their lunch together, she came to realize that she'd been asked to move her office from the portable (which she loved because it had a window that opened, onto greenery) because Gerard wanted it. She also found out that he'd been given English 1500, one of the 'real' courses she'd had her eye on. Carrie told her that her acceptance had been contingent on there being a position for Gerard as well. He was her husband.

The unfairness of it all made her lose her appetite. And nice as Carrie was, she couldn't be friends. She just couldn't.

She also approached the head of the Philosophy Department and asked if there were any courses she might be able to teach.

He wasn't really paying attention. After all, she was just the remedial English teacher. She told him she had a Master's in Philosophy. It didn't seem to register. After all, she was just the remedial English teacher. She told him she'd prepared a course in Environmental Ethics as part of her studies. Perhaps, she suggested, they could offer it in the spring or summer session. Just as a three-credit course. See how it goes. She'd come prepared: she handed him a copy of the outline.

A few days later, he contacted her to tell her that he'd decided an Environmental Ethics course would be a good addition to the Philosophy Department. The

University had a strong Environmental Science department. Woohoo!

That course led to several others.

A few years later, during which she continued to live at the poverty level to which she'd become accustomed, she was able to pay off the mortgage on her cabin. She couldn't believe it.

And then she bought the land that curved around the cove. So she wouldn't wake up one day and see cottages there. She also bought the empty lot beside her. So she wouldn't wake up one day and hear ATVs next door.

Or she didn't. Because when she told Walter she'd like to buy the cove, he just smiled and shrugged. What kind of an answer is that, she wondered.

Same thing happened when she told Bruce she'd like to buy the lot beside her.

Years later, after Walter had died and the land went up for sale, she called to inquire: could the cove be severed from his house lot? The real estate agent didn't know. Well find out, she wanted to say. Did he think she was asking just out of curiosity?

A few years earlier, when there had been some excavation going on a couple lots down from her, from eight in the morning until dark, she'd asked if they could stop at five, when her piano students started arriving. But, again, they just smiled. As if she'd made a joke? As if she was just some middle-aged woman blathering on about something or other? Look, you fuckhead, TAKE ME SERIOUSLY! she wanted to shout. This is my work, my livelihood, I can't do it when you're banging away. Did she really have to sue him for loss of income before he'd take her simple request seriously?

When she prepared a proposal for another new course, a Bioethics course, the department head suggested she contact the local hospital to offer her services to the Ethics Committee. What a wonderful idea! She called the next day and was appalled to discover that they didn't already have a philosopher on the committee (how can you not have a philosopher on what is, essentially, a philosophy committee?), but was delighted to hear they would love to have her join their group.

Over the course of the next six months, she initiated a Research Subcommittee that would assess all proposals requesting the hospital's participation in research studies, according to a detailed protocol that she designed (she'd obtained the protocols that were in place at several other hospitals and put together a 'best of' composite, adding several missing components about informed consent and cost-benefit assessment); an Education Subcommittee that would hold seminars for hospital staff on all sorts of issues (she was horrified to discover that most surgeons and nurses made ethical decisions according to the 'If it feels right, it is right' model); and a Consultation Subcommittee that would be available to anyone who had an ethical issue they didn't know how to handle.

At the end of that six month period, she was offered a permanent part-time position at the hospital. She was floored at the salary they proposed. That it was well over minimum wage was an understatement.

Either that or they would resent her presence and resist her teaching. They were adults, after all; they already knew right from wrong. They certainly didn't need someone from the university to tell them how to do their job.

On top of that, she would discover that she was the only one *not* being paid for her committee work. Eight of the members were hospital employees and so attended, and did their committee work, while on hospital payroll; the ninth was a lawyer, and he was paid a consultation fee. Two hundred dollars for each meeting he attended.

And she was doing most of the work.

And it was very good work. She later found out that the Chair of the committee had taken their (her) Research Committee protocol to a province-wide meeting and many of the other hospitals were so impressed, they asked for copies so they could use it as well. She hadn't put her name and contact info on it; why would she?

The Chair would have replaced it with the Hospital's name and contact info anyway.

And the flowchart of questions she'd prepared for consultations so impressed one of the surgeons, he nearly wept. She had identified (untangled) the (many) ethical issues involved (consent, harm, allocation of resources, quality of life, and so on); articulated, defining where necessary, the applicable values and principles; anticipated the relevant consequences … This is what I have needed all my life, he said: an organized, thorough way to figure out what to do in these sorts of situations.

If she'd been a man, he would have recommended her to conference organizers; she would have been invited to do show-and-tells with her ethical decision-making flowchart. And she would have been paid handsomely. Each and every time.

Handsomely.

Or it might have occurred to her to publish it in a medical ethics journal or newsletter, which would have led to huge reprint payments.

As it was, the surgeon simply photocopied it and passed it around. At every subsequent conference he attended. He didn't take credit for it, but nor had he put *her* name on it.

And near the end of the year, the Chair invited someone from Toronto to come speak about ethical decision-making. The man was no more qualified, no more skilled, than she was. What's that all about, she wondered. Why do they think he's something special?

Not only had she been dismissed because she was a woman, she had been, no doubt, dismissed because she was a philosopher. Most people didn't understand that philosophers aren't the *least* rigorous thinkers—visions of zen monks wondering about the sound of one hand clapping come to mind—they're the *most* rigorous thinkers, the ones obsessed with logical thought, with the progression from premise to conclusion.

In fact, she thought, people dismiss important questions by calling them 'philosophical'—as if to say that if it's a philosophical question, it can't be answered with any certainty, so there's no point in even considering it. Which of course makes all *ethical* questions not worth considering, unless you subscribe to some theory of objective morality, such as the divine theory. Or unless you see the value of having reasons that are more, or less, adequate, the value of determining which actions are more, or less, wrong, or harmful …

It doesn't help that at first glance, it seems like anyone can 'do' philosophy, just as anyone can 'do' ethics. The problem is that only those who can do it well can tell the difference between that and not doing it well. If we taught people to see mistakes in reasoning just as we teach them to see mistakes in arithmetic, which is, of course, just one kind of reasoning, the easiest kind …

She suddenly realized why people so often rejected scientific opinion: they didn't understand evidence—relevance, adequacy; they didn't understand how scientists reached their opinions.

At the end of the year, she submitted a paper to the World Congress. It was a gendered analysis of environmental ethics. She postulated that the male tendency to externalize waste disposal—a tendency encouraged, even conditioned, by an upbringing in which Mom, female, does the cleaning up—explains, in part, the dire situation we're in. If companies had, from the get go, taken responsibility for cleaning up the messes they made, for being aware of the messes they were making … The paper was accepted.

She was so excited! She'd never been to Boston before. She'd never been to a philosophy conference before. And here she was, at the World Congress! She'd had to pay for her own airfare, of course, and for her accommodations, as well as the registration fee, because sessionals, like supply, night, and summer school teachers, don't count, but four days! Four days of discussing ideas with intelligent people as passionate about said ideas as she was!

She was smiling broadly as she walked down the hall toward the large conference room for the keynote address. Then she saw in the distance, the head of her department. She'd seen his name on the program. As she got closer, he recognized her, and just as she opened her mouth to say 'Hi', he opened his.

"What are *you* doing here?"

There was something about the tone, and the question, that spoke for all men to all women.

Once she recovered, she replied, in a smaller voice than she would have liked, "Presenting a paper. Just like you," she thought to add.

He seemed unable to process the information. How can the remedial English teacher be presenting a paper at the World Congress in Philosophy? He seemed to have totally forgotten that she had a graduate degree in Philosophy and was, in fact, teaching a few courses. Philosophy courses.

She presented her paper. There were several interesting questions, one of which had to do with the equally male tendency to 'take out the garbage'.

"That's a good point," she said. "I hadn't considered that." There was a sigh in the room that she didn't understand. And no one seemed to hear the rest of her response. Which was about the difference between taking out the garbage and collecting it, the difference between a single, discrete chore that takes a minute and an ongoing responsibility that lasts a lifetime. About the gendered patterns of littering: women don't toss their beer cans out car windows. Her attempt to reconcile, to integrate the additional fact into her framework seemed, for reasons she didn't understand, irrelevant.

She didn't know it would be different, very different, at the SWIP conference. She had joined the Canadian Philosophy Association and the American Philosophy Association, but not the Society for Women in Philosophy. She didn't know the first two were misnamed, misrepresenting themselves, as they did, as gender-inclusive.

At the SWIP conference, speakers from the floor did not challenge; they questioned, they elaborated, the group collaboratively moved toward something more cohesive, something more complete, something more valid; consequently, speakers were open and receptive, not defensive; concession was not an admission of defeat; there were more smiles, more laughs, no pretensions of sobriety (men's cover as presumed synonym for intelligence). Even the frowns on faces were different: where the men were criticizing, evaluating in order to compete, the women were trying to understand, evaluating in order to improve.

What if her entire education had been at women-only schools?

What if her entire life had been in a women-only world?

Or maybe, just maybe, she presented the paper, and later, at one of the many social events, someone approached her.

"I attended your paper," he'd say, then introduce himself and reach out to shake her hand. "I'm Dr. Jensen. At Berkeley."

She'd shake his hand, "Pleased to meet you, Dr. Jensen. I hope you found my paper interesting."

"I did," he'd reply. "We have an opening in the Fall. Applied ethics. Might you be interested?"

Yes! She was very interested! But she wouldn't've known she could negotiate her opening salary, or she would've, but was so glad to have a job offer she didn't dare. Either way, it would mean that she made $4,000 less than her male colleagues. In her first year. By the time she retired, given interest rates and the practice of making raises proportionate to salaries, she'd have some $500,000 less than her male colleagues. According to Babcock and Laschever.

And why are men so much more apt to ask for more? Because they want more. And they think that what they want is important. And because they feel entitled to more. Or at least entitled to get what they want.

Note: *feel* entitled. Because Babcock and Laschever would discover that unlike women, men didn't really *think* about whether they deserved this or that.

But of course what Dr. Jensen said instead was "Would you like a glass of wine?"

Or maybe someone who hadn't been able to attend her paper, but who had read the abstract and her bio, would contact her with an invitation to co-present at the upcoming APA. He'd sound really, really interested, and enthusiastic, so she'd agree to meet for coffee and discuss the idea. The second she walked into the café, she saw it in his eyes: the instant he saw she was a middle-aged woman, his interest wilted. Completely.

Or maybe, while at the Congress, she went to the book fair, looking for a better text to use in her Environmental Ethics course. She stopped at a table.

"Can I help you?"

"Yes, thanks, I'm looking for a text to use in an Environmental Ethics course."

"Ah. It's a fairly new field, and I'm afraid we have only the one to offer." He picked up a reader from the table and handed it to her. She quickly skimmed through it.

"I'm afraid my students need a lot more introductory material. They will be mostly science majors, not philosophy majors, so I'm looking for a book that has a fairly extensive introductory section. Something about how to think about ethics, an overview of the major theories—that sort of thing. I've seen some good primers, but they don't have readings. So they'd have to buy two books, the primer and the reader. I'm trying to avoid that."

"Ah." The man smiled.

"Plus, I'm afraid they'll need study questions to accompany the essays. Something to guide their reading. Most are rather unable to— They're unused to the rigors of philosophical inquiry.

"And it should emphasize Canadian issues. Most of the books I've seen here have an American focus."

"I see. You sound quite clear about what you're looking for—"

"Well," she said, apologetically, "I've given it a lot of thought."

Apologetically.

And, after all, she knew a thing or two about pedagogy.

"Yes, it sounds like you *have* given it a lot of thought," he replied. "We might be interested in publishing the book you describe. Can I interest you in submitting a proposal?"

What? She wasn't sure she heard correctly.

"Yes!" she said eagerly. "Are you serious?" she asked then, somewhat unprofessionally.

He grinned and explained that he had explicit instructions to solicit proposals for textbooks in three areas, one of which was Environmental Ethics. And as they were a Canadian press, they too wanted a Canadian focus. He handed her a business card and pointed out the publisher's website address.

"We have proposal guidelines on our site. Send something, and I promise we'll take a good look at it."

When she went home, she prepared a proposal immediately.

A week later, she received a phone call. They'd accepted it.

She couldn't believe it. Fifteen years of sending her manuscripts to agents and publishers, and now an unsolicited invitation had led to a book contract. Not for a collection of poetry or a novel, but still.

Suddenly overwhelmed by the task she'd taken on, she spoke to one of the Environmental Science profs at the university, asking if he'd be willing to work on the text with her; what a cool textbook they could write as a team, she'd thought, a scientist and a philosopher. A week later, he agreed to "help her out".

'Help me out'? How fucking patronizing, she thought. She'd offered him co-author credit and royalties.

So she retracted that offer and approached another prof, asking if he was interested in writing just the case studies. For a flat fee.

He agreed, but they were so poorly written, she'd had to redo them. She was amazed. He was a full professor, with publications in various journals, and he couldn't even write a coherent 500-word case study. It didn't occur to her that he'd probably had one of his grad students write them.

Both profs, she would see, co-authored books a few years later. One with a younger woman, the other with a man.

She was so pleased, so proud, when her complimentary copies came in the mail. She opened the textbook, her textbook, glanced at the now-all-too-familiar table of contents, flipped through—wait a minute. There. The bit on J. S. Mill. She'd taken care to feature Harriet Taylor. She'd even insisted they replace the suggested caption under her picture, a comment about her relationship to Mill, with a quote from her work. They'd changed it back. Un-fucking-believable.

Marketing didn't seem to give the book much attention.

Surprise.

Complimentary copies were sent to professors who asked, but that was about it. Sales weren't great. A second edition wasn't forthcoming.

Or, amazingly enough, it was reviewed. In the *New York Times* of all places. By someone who somehow thought *she'd* written all of the included essays and then harshly criticized her for her incoherent view.

She didn't know that she should've written a response correcting the reviewer's mistake. She thought that that would come across as overly defensive, an accusation she'd heard so many times before.

But of course. 'Methinks the lady doth protest too much' is slung at any woman who protests at all.

The book had taken a little over two years to write, pretty much full-time. Without access to the faculty support services, she'd had to search for, request, scan, then proof every article herself. Then write the accompanying questions. And then introductory material. That alone, over 100 pages, had taken six months.

She'd received a $10,000 advance, which was paid back in three years. at which point the book went out of print. It worked out to $2.00 an hour.

But, because of it, she received invitations to be a guest speaker, even to be a visiting professor, at a few of the larger universities.

Or not.

Because she didn't realize that textbooks had no prestige whatsoever in academia. In fact, those who wrote textbooks were looked down upon.

Like those who had to teach.

Had to.

She also failed to receive such invitations because she didn't know that she should have gotten a publicist to arrange such things.

Or maybe, when she passed that publisher's table, at the Congress book fair, the rep was on a break. She browsed the books, didn't see what she was looking for, and moved on.

Which would be too bad, because the next course she taught would not go well.

She knew how it would end:

> Dean of Arts:
>
> Please consider this as comment/rebuttal to John Smith's allegation of unfair treatment in SOSC 2107.
>
> 1. I don't fully understand John's first point that "with a considerable amount of commentary and another rewrite, [his first paper] was worth at least a pass." Students were not allowed to submit rewrites of their first paper (not one, and certainly not "another"); furthermore, any "commentary" he wanted to include about his paper would have been, should have been, in the paper itself. Further still, he seems to think that effort rather than achievement is the criterion I used for assessment.
>
> 2. I did not, as he claims, grant an extension to another student for the second paper [and thus should have granted an extension to him]; I certainly did not do so to a student who "simply forgot about the due date."
>
> I did allow a student to hand in the *third* paper a week after it was due: I had changed the due date, moving it earlier by a week, and she apparently was not present when I announced the change.
>
> Also, I did allow two students to *resubmit* their second paper: this was clearly not permission to rewrite, however; while both students had identified the secondary source they used, they did not include quotation marks wherever they quoted that source—I merely refused to mark their papers until they inserted the quotation marks (so I could clearly see what was their work and what was not). Believing that John, and perhaps others, misunderstood that as permission to rewrite (and therefore evidence of unfairness), I explained at some length to the class as a whole exactly what I was permitting those two students to do; unfortunately, that was a day John arrived late (as was his habit), and I therefore had to

repeat the explanation—it is possible my repeated explanation was abbreviated, leaving John not fully understanding the distinction between 'rewrite' and 'resubmit'.

Further, I'd like to point out that with regard to the second paper, students were required to submit an extensive outline four weeks before it was due. I provided extensive feedback two weeks after submission (meeting with students individually), leaving them two weeks to rework (if necessary) and write up the paper—I, thus, 'built in' the rewrite option. John, however, did not take advantage of this: he did not submit an outline; he simply submitted a completed paper on the final due date. (Such preliminary feedback was also allowed for the third paper; again, John did not take advantage of that.)

Further still, with regard to the second paper, I did allow a few students to rewrite their paper correcting their grammar and punctuation (but not changing the content at all); they could then resubmit it for a slight increase in the grade (for example, a C+ might turn into a B-). John was one of these few students, but he did not bother to correct and resubmit his paper.

3. With regard to John's class participation mark, those marks were based not only on quantity, but also on quality, of contribution. As for quantity, attendance was also taken into account: John missed four three-hour classes, which I consider substantial in a course totalling a mere twelve classes. As for quality, John's contributions were very poor. For example, in a discussion about whether one is morally 'allowed' (the weak version) or morally 'obligated' (the strong version) to reveal that someone is HIV positive, John's contribution was something like 'And what about at places like Casino Rama where they have a separate trash can for needles in the washrooms?' Such a comment is indicative of John's persistent (that discussion occurred during the last class) inability to understand and follow the arguments we covered throughout the course—and that, not my unfairness, explains his failing grade.

It is certainly quite possible that I used different assessment standards than John is used to: ethics is quite a different course than, say, marketing or accounting. However, I believe I used standards appropriate for the course, and they are, thus, not unfair. And I have used the same standards for John as I have used for the other students in that course—

which is to say, again, that I have not been unfair. (Of course, much depends on one's definition of 'fair'—as this was a topic we explored at some length in the course, it's disappointing, but not surprising, to see John using the term with such imprecision.)

The course after that one did not go well either.

Another student went to the Dean to complain. Apparently she had offended him, shown a lack of respect, when she pressed him for reasons in support of his opinion and then had, heaven forbid, pointed out the inadequacy of his reasons.

As was your job. In a critical thinking course.

Others followed. They couldn't get past 'Everyone's entitled to their own opinion.' She agreed that everyone *was* entitled to their own opinion, but added that unless said opinion was well-supported, no one should be expected to agree with it.

At the end of the first term, almost half of her class was failing.

She reassessed her curriculum, her lesson plans, her assignments, her tests, her grading, and as far as she was concerned, all was well. She had carefully designed preparatory exercises ("Hi, my name is A, and I believe X is right/wrong because Y"); she had presented the content visually for the visual learners and orally for the aural learners; she consolidated each step with an overhead quiz followed by immediate feedback; she had prepared study questions to guide their reading of the essays in the text; she had the students identify their work by number only in order to reduce bias when she marked their papers; she had prepared model answers to every question on the mid-term. In short, she knew how to teach.

So, she concluded, it wasn't her. Or more precisely, it wasn't her teaching.

It was the students. They didn't do the homework, they didn't spend enough time and energy on the assignments, they didn't prepare for the tests. Hell, many of them didn't even attend class on a regular basis. (They wanted marks for simply attending.) (Which she refused to give.)

The course was mandatory and they resented that.

It was a Humanities course and so not worth their time and energy.

It was a Philosophy course and therefore a 'bird' course; they refused to see that thinking critically about ethics was actually quite demanding—being able to discern relevance, being able to follow an argument …

It was taught in a portable, not in one of the auditoriums, and so it had low status.

It was taught by a sessional, not a tenured professor, another indication of low status.

And it as taught by a woman. Authority is not female. Her students would not, could not, listen to or learn from her.

Male students simply refused to accord her the respect they accorded male professors, despite her similar, and sometimes even greater, competence. How did she know this? She was asked once to present a guest lecture in an economics class, and as she waited outside the open door, having arrived, of course, a few minutes early, she was absolutely amazed at the deference, the politeness—students waited to be called upon! And not once did she hear any of them tell the prof he was full of shit.

Men feel entitled to deference from women, she'd tried to explain to the Dean, and they get really upset when they don't get it. My male students are no exception, she'd said.

If she hadn't had that chance to compare … And of course men have a vested interest in *not* making such comparison possible, because if women continue to take their failures personally, they, men, can continue to take their successes personally.

She invited one of the Faculty of Education professors to sit in on one of her classes, take a look at her course outline, her materials, her grading, and provide an assessment. He agreed to do so. And gave her a glowing evaluation.

Didn't matter. The customer is always right.

At the end of the year, she carefully read the summaries of her students' evaluations, hoping for some insight …

She received a score of 3.39 (on a scale of 5) on Tests. She was at a loss. There had been only one test: students had to identify and explain the logical fallacy present in three of five given items; they had the entire class (eighty minutes) in which to do this. Did they think that was unfair? They had been focusing on that particular task all week. Surely eighty minutes was enough time.

She received a 3.12 on Course Content/Value. Well, that's a sad comment on our society, isn't it. The ability to make ethical decisions, the ability to negotiate one's way through the grey of right and wrong, isn't very important.

A 3.0 on Course Content/Difficulty. Of course, they found it too difficult. They had trouble with the newspaper articles she used. Which were written at a grade eight reading level. They couldn't say what the author's point was, let alone what reasons were offered in support of that point. A colleague had told her that the Nelson-Denny results at the university at which he'd previously taught indicated that an alarming number of students were reading at a grade four level. And these are the people who, apparently, determine whether or not I kept my job, she thought.

She received a 3.56 on Course Objectives/Clear. She had articulated them orally and had written them on the board four times throughout the year; she'd also included them in the course outline she handed out on the first day, which she went through with the students on that first day.

She received a 3.33 on Organized/Well-planned. A mystery. She was compulsively organized.

When she got to the 3.2 on Labs, she stopped reading. The course didn't have any labs.

Apparently an average score of 3.5 was required. The university-wide average was 4.0. She was amazed: most of her colleagues simply stood at the front of the room and lectured for an hour. (Then again, most of her colleagues were male.)

Consequently, the following year, she wasn't asked to teach any courses.

It was all so very painful. Especially given the teaching experience she'd had in Toronto. She couldn't bear to think she'd never have that again. But she had to admit that part way through the year, she'd started bracing herself for the hostility before she even entered the classroom. They'd broken her.

"[The Dean] could have been prepared with statements of full support for her, were students to bring complaints to him," Valian would write. About another professor. Who had, apparently, had a similar experience.

That sentence would have made her weep.

"He could have suggested that, to solidify her authority, she schedule several moderately rigorous quizzes early in the semester."

That one would have made her laugh.

But it wouldn't've mattered. None of it would've mattered.

Because just as her newspaper-reading colleague at the mental health home turned the page, their supervisor entered the office. And she never found out about the remedial English position.

23

Which is too bad, because it turned out she *couldn't* keep reading, writing, and thinking about the issues that intrigued her without a university affiliation. Or, rather, she could—she just couldn't get what she wrote published.

Encouraged by the papers she'd had published while she was in the M.A. program, she tried. She became a community member of the university library, but that entitled her only to the stacks. She could make interlibrary loan requests for other material, specifically books the library didn't have and articles from journals the library didn't subscribe to, but it cost $26 per request.

One referee was particularly harsh in accusing her of not having bothered to read anything published in the last five years.

She also suspected the consideration of her submissions was affected by their dot-matrix printing; there was no way she could afford a laser printer.

But she found out about another position several months later. The local women's group had gotten funding from the government for a study about women and the environment, and they were looking for a researcher. Just two days a week, fifteen hours, but at $25/hr, that meant $1,500/month. Her mortgage was $400, heat, hydro, house insurance, car insurance, property taxes, gas and food, each at $100/month give or take—she'd have $500 extra. Each month!

Even so, she kept the relief position. You never knew what could happen.

So finally, in her early forties, she was able to order out for pizza. Just because she wanted to. And hire someone to fix the roof that leaked every time there was a heavy rain. It had taken her that long to not be poor, to not have every dollar, literally every dollar, 'marked' for something more important—

A chainsaw started up. Damn. She was down at the dock and had just started the next journal. Some people bought whole logs, instead of pre-cut firewood, to save money. Never mind that it was others who paid a price for their savings. She'd hoped that it wouldn't start until October, but apparently— She marked her place and went back up to the cottage for her earplugs, headphones, and her beloved CD player.

Although she had stopped playing years ago, shortly after she obtained her Associate, in fact, and even though she had also stopped composing, music continued to mesmerize her. She found the beauty of certain pieces so mesmerizing, she would listen to them over and over and over and over. For hours. Literally. She loved the repeat function on turntables, though that worked with single songs only if they were on 45s. Later, she made dozens of 'singles' cassettes, the same song recorded over and over on a cassette for the whole side. And then CD technology—with the single repeat function, she could repeat a single song indefinitely. Any song. She bought a carousel CD player that held 300 CDs, and then another—and still didn't have room for all of the music she wanted to have at her fingertips …

It seemed to her that certain harmonic progressions resonated with the human brain. Perhaps they were sonic equivalents of fractals and the Fibonacci sequence. Perhaps that explained the attraction of Pachelbel's *Canon*. Certainly the four-three suspension had a physiological effect on her. She could *feel* the resolution; it *must* effect a chemical change.

A great number of pop and rock songs attracted, addicted, her—those with a certain emotional quality and passion in the voice, but also with a certain quality of composition and beauty of instrumentation— Judas' vocal from *Jesus Christ Superstar*, Alison Moyet's "Winter Kills," Alannah Myles' "Song instead of a Kiss," ELP's "C'est La Vie," the vocal section from Vangelis' *Heaven and Hell,* and from Pink Floyd's *Dark Side of the Moon,* Shakespeare's Sister's "Stay," Damien Rice's "The Blower's Daughter" … They all captivated her. Absolutely.

For others, it was the endlessness—"L'été indien," Leonard Cohen's "Closing Time," Nyman's "The Heart asks Pleasure First," much of Philip Glass, and of course, Pachelbel's *Canon* … They were moebius strips in sound.

And some pieces were simply, completely, pure. Bach's *Air on a G String.*

And then there were some pieces, like Barber's *Adagio*, that were too sad to listen to for anything but the end. The piece moved her so deeply, she was sure the first notes alone changed her biochemistry.

She selected Nyman, then went back down to the dock and re-opened the journal.

> Rebecca Goldstein is partnered with Steven Pinker. But maybe she got into that social circle on her own and then just met him.
>
> Anderson's big breakthrough came not when she married Reed, but when "O Superman" topped the mainstream charts in the UK.
>
> But how did that come about?
>
> And/So was that my mistake? Sending my stuff only to the US and Canadian stations? Where art, innovation, intellect isn't appreciated?

So all that effort, all that knocking on doors, had served only to exhaust her, impoverish her, demoralize her. You have to be called. There's no point in being active. Things happen to those who don't do anything to make things happen.

> Reading of Philippe Leduc who invested hundreds of hours and paid 160 musicians for the production of 4 CDs.
>
> Where did he get the money? How did I get to be so poor?
>
> He went to university, got a degree in music, and then what? Why did my world stop there? How did my life diverge, what path didn't I take that I should have?
>
> He's a composer with more than 1,000 radio and tv themes to his credit. Okay, so that's where his money came from. But how did he get a thousand chances— What job ad in the paper did he see and apply for? Did he see a notice on a bulletin board somewhere? Did he send a cassette to the NFB, like me, and his got chosen?
>
> Apart from that's, like, one a week for twenty years. I guess if you don't have anything else you have to do, like go to work— Well, that *was* going to work.

Janice said Greg, now a Sociology prof, wouldn't do any of it if he weren't getting paid. That stopped me. The books he writes, it's *part of his job*.

What men do at work gets presented as—*achievements*.

That's why there are no famous female whatevers! They don't have *jobs* doing whatever. They don't have careers doing whatever. Nobel Prizes are won by people just doing their jobs. Not by people following their passion on their own time, their own dime. On spec. Outside.

And women don't get the jobs. Not the Nobel-prize-work kinds of jobs.

She turned the page.

"It was kind of a personal story that made me write a huge piece. Because I just needed to kind of get rid of some things. It was meant probably just for me, but by chance it went to Milan Slavický, who later became my teacher, and it was he who told me I should enter the Academy of Arts and study composing. And I said 'No, that's not possible, I'm not really prepared for that.' And he actually made me take the entrance exam. Then I failed, and he made me do it a second time. So it's his doing, actually."

She kept coming across stuff like this, and it continued to make her so angry. To have had such support, such encouragement. Someone who didn't even really want to do it. *Gets to do it.*

'By chance'? How does that kind of chance happen?

Women never got that kind of chance. Even if they were prepared for it. Even if they passed the exam the first time. With flying colours.

If a man had submitted what I've submitted over the last twenty years, he'd be published and performed, and reviewed and purchased, by now. And if it wasn't good enough right away, he would have had the way paved for him to get better.

...

I just want to smack Solomon. He's just had a novel published, by St. Martins, through an agent. I ask how did he get his agent? And he glibly says something like oh, he just sent his manuscript around. Me too, I respond, trying to keep a lid on the simmering— Well, he smiles, keep at it.

I've been writing since I was thirteen. That's almost thirty years. And my publishing record—

Of course he doesn't know any of this. But he assumed—what? That I'm just some housewife writing in her spare time? How insulting.

I want to ask how often *he's* been published in magazines and journals, whether *his* stuff has appeared in any anthologies, whether *he's* received any grants, whether *he's* been read on CBC …

I want to scream at him that I've been writing longer than he's been alive.

So don't you *dare* tell me to 'keep at it'.

She hated people who said that if you want it bad enough and work hard enough at it, your dream will come true. Bullshit.

Don't give up, people say, some authors had five, fifty, a hundred rejections before they were published! Five? Fifty? A hundred? How about a thousand? How about 5,000? According to my records, I have made *over 5,000* submissions to magazines, journals, agents, publishers, theatres, directors, record companies, musicians, performance venues, and concert series.

The people who say that are successful people. People whose dreams *have* come true. People who have mistaken necessary conditions for sufficient conditions.

They don't want to admit that there are thousands just as good, just as hard-working, who didn't get lucky.

No one has the time or the inclination to do a world-wide, or even a city-wide, search every time they need someone, and then choose the best. A meritocracy is unlikely purely for logistical reasons.

So success is always a fluke. It's always a matter of being in the right place at the right time. Maybe with the right material.

And since you're nowhere, here in your cabin on a lake in a forest …

The cream does not rise to the top. It sits at the bottom and curdles.

Janis Ian has yet to make money for her music. Janis Ian!! "In 37 years as a recording artist," she says, "I've created 25+ albums for major labels, and I've never once received a royalty check that didn't show I owed them money." What? *What??*

Doris Lessing wrote two novels using a pseudonym. They were rejected by her own publisher, and when they were eventually published, under that pseudonym, by another publisher presumably, they received "lukewarm reviews" and "paltry sales".

Something is very wrong with our system.

…

People with far less ambition, and effort, and publishing success, are asked to do readings. Not only have I never been asked, when I have asked, when I submitted proposals to all the reading venues in Toronto I could find (after sending several query letters to the Canada Council, The Writer's League, and a few others to obtain a list), my proposals weren't even been acknowledged. Let alone rejected.

And so I had to send each and every one of them a follow-up query letter.

It shouldn't be this hard.

…

But you've been trying to make it happen instead of just going to where it might happen.

No, I did that too. I lived in Vancouver, Toronto, Montreal.

Yeah, in a basement apartment somewhere. You didn't mingle with people who might make it happen, you didn't tell them your name, give them your phone number …

Right. You know what they would have used your phone number for.

But then it *did* happen. Her soliloquies were discovered and performed by a feminist theatre in New York. She drove down to see the premiere and was interviewed after the show by the journalist covering the arts scene.

"So in this post-feminist world, what motivated you to write these soliloquies?"

"Oh, well, since we still very much need feminism, I don't think we're in a post-feminist world," she replied, but then continued, answering her question, "Shakespeare 220. I wrote the first one twenty-five years ago, when I was an undergrad and—"

The look on her face. The journalist was horrified.

"What have you been doing in the meantime?" she stuttered. Kris' answer had obviously derailed the story line she'd been preparing, new young feminist playwright—though, of course, her appearance, her apparent age must have already derailed that …

"What have I been doing in the meantime?" Kris looked at the woman with an odd look on her face. "Writing everything else I've written that's not going to get discovered, produced, performed, or published."

Because of course no one in New York knew she existed. Not even the agents to whom she'd been sending her material for twenty-five years. Certainly not a feminist theatre company *she* didn't know existed.

She looked up at the sun. By mid-afternoon, the weekenders would start to arrive, though fortunately there would be fewer of them, now that it was late September— Late September. She had only a week left. One week.

• • •

She walked for miles, deep into the forest, all the way to the maple trees which were, yes, ablaze! The reds, oranges, scarlets, tangerines, burgundies, golds—all so vibrant! She sat there for over an hour. Trying not to cry.

• • •

Her parents showed up one day. Unannounced. Certainly uninvited. It was a surprise visit.

It was an ambush.

She was gracious, and kind. She wanted them to see that she was happy and healthy, she wanted to give them that peace of mind before they died. As they had said, by way of explanation for their sudden appearance, they were 'getting on'.

She gave them a tour of the cabin. She thought they'd like that, and it was the sort of thing one did. As they passed through her study, she took a copy of *Satellites* out of the box on the floor and presented it to them. A gift. Her father riffled the pages start to finish, then held it up, that stupid grin on his face, and dangled it dangerously by its cover. "*How* many pages?" he asked, mocking its thickness. She rescued it, saying nothing. But she wanted to tell him to get the hell out of her house.

> It's such a taboo to say your parents weren't good parents, to realize they were just ordinary schmucks. But people don't suddenly turn into saints when they get pregnant or get someone pregnant. They remain the ordinary schmucks they were to begin with.

She also gave them one of her cassettes. They looked at it oddly. "That's me," she said, "my pieces." She found it later, after they'd left, lying on the desk.

> All these years, I thought they were somehow, nevertheless, proud of my achievements. But they aren't, really. They're too stupid to be proud of a daughter who is a writer, a composer, a philosopher. The only thing that would make them proud is if I'd gotten married and had kids.
>
> …
>
> And not only not proud of my achievements, but resentful. The better I became, the more they thought I was showing them up, they with just

their high school diplomas.

Her father in particular seemed to resent her achievements.

Of course. You were a woman, besting a man.

She pointed out the photograph on her wall of the road through the bush to the family cottage. Not only had she run it often, with such pleasure, she had always been so happy when they drove in. It was a good memento.

They didn't recognize it. When she identified it for them, neither of them was very interested.

And that's when it hit her. The cottage, the piano lessons, the dance lessons—they were all just what middle-class people did. They were status-markers. Her parents didn't really love the lake or the arts. *That's* why she didn't get any support. For her dream of living in a cabin on a lake in a forest, for her aspirations to become a composer, a choreographer. She wasn't supposed to take those things seriously, for their intrinsic value. They certainly didn't. That she did was a sort of backfire on them. A calling their bluff. No wonder they responded the way they did.

> They didn't ooh and ahh when I took them down to the water to see the view, the little cove. That surprised me. Confused me. I thought—

> All this time I thought it was me.

> I didn't understand. Why provide piano lessons and then not want to hear me play? And then sell my piano like it was a piece of furniture? Because it was. To them.

> Why buy the cottage and then later sell it like it was just a piece of real estate? Because it was. To them.

> It had nothing to do with me.

Yes. Their decisions had nothing to do with you. And that was exactly the problem.

> Even taking me to the library—was that just because that's what good

parents do? I wasn't supposed to fall in love with books, I wasn't supposed to ever want to write one.

My god— Everything. Were there *no* genuine values in their lives? They protested when I accused them of being Catholic, of believing that some man in Italy had an inside line to God, of believing that contraception was morally wrong. They were so hurt, so confused by that. Now I understand. They didn't really believe those things. Again, I'd called their bluff. They went to church on Sundays because that's what good people did and by god, they were (to be seen as) good people. And I, naïvely, called them on it. No wonder they hated me so.

When they sat down—she'd offered tea—her mother said she hoped they could "go forward from here". Well, isn't that convenient, she'd thought. No need to apologize. No need to take responsibility for what one says or doesn't say, what one does or doesn't do.

It wasn't until after they'd left that she realized her mother had thought that *she* was the one who'd needed to apologize. For what? Not feeling any love or affection? One can't apologize for that.

And anyway, whose fault was that? She'd never felt any love or affection from *them*, so how, why, did they expect *her* to feel any in return?

Duty. That was all she'd felt. Her mother was nothing if not dutiful.

And if they had come asking for money to move into a nursing home, she supposed she would've found a way to provide it. It was what a dutiful daughter would do. She owed them that much. They'd supported her for fifteen years. It was her turn.

But they didn't ask.

When she inquired about their health, her mother told her about the aneurysm her father had had; he'd suddenly stiffened and lapsed into unconsciousness. She'd been understandably terrified, but he'd shrugged it off. "It was nothing," he said, and she thought for the hundredth time how right her decision had been. If she'd had to be so close to such a thick layer of stupidity or denial, she'd've *had* to try to rip it off. And it would've taken forever. Her lifetime, at least. And for what? It's not like what she'd finally uncover would be beautiful. Or useful. It would, quite probably, be nothing.

> My brother's making $80,000. Of course. The C student with just a B.B.A.

> But he's a man, a husband, a father.

> And still, my parents give him money, they say he needs it, he's had bad luck. We're probably talking thousands.

> Not that I would have accepted anything from them. I left. I'm not entitled. I understand that. I accept that.

> The point remains.

When they got up to leave, her father gave her twenty bucks—"Go buy yourself a pizza," he said. Oh so generously.

> I get twenty bucks for a pizza. As if I'm still eighteen. Despite them being *in my house*. Who did they think bought it?

> You *seem* eighteen. To him. To them. No husband, no kids, and you still dress 'like a teenager'—in jeans, a sweatshirt, and track shoes.

Never mind that so many teenage girls wear make-up, heels, blah, blah.

> On top of all that, besides all that, women are forever children. We can never grow up, we can never achieve adult status. Hell, look how long it took to get the vote.

At one point during the visit, her mother insisted that she *was* proud of her.

And she suddenly realized that her approval didn't matter anymore. Because it couldn't possibly be real; her mother could never really *understand* what she had achieved.

The visit was, in retrospect, a release. It was clear that she would never please them. They would never approve of her, her life, her choices, her achievements.

I even regret inviting them in. Their presence has now contaminated my home, my cabin on a lake in a forest, my refuge.

Despite her honesty about not rejoining the family, coming down for Christmas, etc., etc., they sent a letter, a week later, suggesting another visit. She said no, let's leave it as is. Next time she might not be so gracious, so kind. And she saw no value in brutal honesty at that point.

A week after that, a parcel arrived, with strict orders not to return it. It was her bronzed baby shoes.

Guess she's finally accepted the divorce.

A picture from her high school graduation was also enclosed. She remembered her mother taking it; she'd posed under duress. In fact, she'd gone to her graduation under duress. The ritual didn't interest her at all, graduating didn't matter at all, it was the journey, not the arbitrary end, that was so valuable. But her mother seemed *so* upset that she finally relented and went. For her.

"Weak minds are always fond of resting in the ceremonials of duty." Wollstonecraft

"It's my favourite," the enclosed note said.

She looked nothing like herself in that picture. In fact, she barely recognized herself. Hair nicely combed, in a dress her mother had picked out, a pretty smile pasted on her face. Sterile, conventional, and oh-so-appropriate.

That's what she sees when she looks at me. No wonder she still loves me. Thinks she still loves me.

She's like an anorexic looking in the mirror and seeing a fat body.

She realized then that she was fixed in time for them. She was so right to leave. They would *never* have taken her seriously; they would never have treated her like an adult.

They wanted a dishonest relationship, she thought. A relationship with someone who was not her.

And yet her mother had kept insisting she knew her. *That's* what had hurt her the most, she realized then: the possibility that she might not know her own daughter. It was all about her, the visit. It was an attempt at vindication. See, she *did* know her daughter.

Never mind that the hug had to be asked for. And was as fake as can be.

> And she's still so hurt, so angry, that I don't love her. But I don't. I just don't. And I can't force myself to. The best I can do is stay away, so she doesn't see every day that I don't.
>
> …
>
> I was right to leave. And stay away. They haven't changed. Yes, she wrote, "We're truly sorry." But—three words? After twenty years?
>
> And then she spent a whole page "setting the record straight" about how it was *her* idea that I get the large oak table from the attic to use as a desk, oh what a nice and thoughtful person she is, and see she *does* know me.
>
> …
>
> How does forgiveness fit with justice? When you forgive, aren't you absolving someone of blame? Casting justice aside?
>
> So the question becomes when do you cast justice aside? Because if it's all or nothing, then to forgive is to become amoral. Psychopathic.
>
> Or is forgiveness simply saying it's okay that you do blameworthy shit. But why, when, would it ever be okay?

She closed the journal. Then made a fire, turned out the light, and listened to Kourosh Dini's *Calm.* And the loons, through the open window.

24

Next day. Only half a dozen journals to go. She settled on the deck, since it was the weekend, and stared down the hill for a while through the trees to the gently undulating, brushed silver, water.

For the longest time, she'd felt that if Craig were to pull into her driveway one day, they could pick up where they'd left off. With the good parts, the fun parts. It was that way for a lot of stuff. She felt like she could just walk into drop-in, or her grade thirteen English class, the one she taught in Toronto with all those gifted students, and carry on as if—

As if she was still twenty-five. She'd still *felt* twenty-five. She certainly hadn't felt forty-five. After all, she'd still been doing, and wanting to do, pretty the much the same things. Reading, writing, thinking, listening to music, not composing, okay, and not playing the piano, but it was right there, she *could* just sit down and play, she could even start composing again, and she wasn't running much anymore, her left iliotibial band flared with pain every time she did more than a mile or two, but she could, and did, walk for five or ten miles without pain, and the long paddles had the same long-distance feel.

Nothing had really changed since she was twenty-five. All the external changes that marked the passage of time for others—kids growing up, promotions, jobs turning into careers—hadn't happened for her.

But she couldn't go back and carry on as if. She couldn't go back. Ever. To any of it.

One night, overwhelmed by such a strong longing for her past—for selected parts of her past—she'd sat on the deck stairs and listened to Janis Ian's *Aftertones* and Dan Hill's *Hold On* (they most of all had become associated with the passions of her university years) as she stared out at the moonlight on the water and wondered where the last twenty-some years had gone.

To here, she'd realized. With immense satisfaction. They'd gone … to get here. Alone in my cabin on a lake in a forest, madly in love with being … here. And with being alone, she'd realized.

Unfortunately, the lake started to become more populated. What she had thought was crown land was not. Even what she had thought were large lots were actually small developed lots beside small undeveloped lots. On some of the undeveloped lots, people built cottages and became just weekenders. On others, they built homes, typically retirement homes, and became permanent residents.

> The guy down the lane always moves with such fatigue, as if he's had a hard day's work, something conferring virtue, instead of a long day in his lazyboy. Or as if he's so old, which presumably confers wisdom. Or as if to remind everyone of his football injury, as if it were sustained performing an act of heroism, and not an act of stupidity.

Even so, even with more people moving into the neighbourhood, friendships with women continued to elude her; they were all married with kids, and even if the kids were grown up, she'd have to listen to them talk about them all the time. Fair enough, she supposed, since that was what their lives were all about, but she wasn't interested.

And friendships with men, regardless of their marital and parental status, seemed impossible.

Where were the unmarried women? Or at least the women without kids?

> I am such an anomaly: an unmarried straight woman without kids.

> Why? Why is that so rare? It feels ordinary to me. Normal. Unremarkable.

> I have never wanted to be a wife. The very word defines you. Totally. It wipes out everything else you might be or might become. You are 'the wife'. End of story.

Being a mother would do the same thing, it would make me nothing more than that.

And it would not have been enough. Oh god, not nearly enough. To spend one's whole life, all of one's time and energy, nurturing another human being?

It's not me, but the girlfriends and wives, the moms, who are unfulfilled, having had to spend so much time and energy on someone else, hardly ever enough time on themselves. No dreams, no passions, except biological self-replication and then lifelong addiction to their kids, to a few other human beings. Talk about dreaming small.

To people who asked why she hadn't gotten married, she asked why they had.

Later, she'd simply respond by saying that she preferred the purity and focus of a solo.

Either way, they wouldn't understand.

People accused her of being selfish, when they found out she didn't have any kids. What? She didn't think she was selfish. She took only what she needed. So there would be some left for others.

It's they *who are selfish; people who replicate themselves are, thereby, taking* more *than their share.*

It didn't occur to her to give what she had. That's what people who have more than enough do. And she never had more than enough.

Of anything.

I've paid my own way through life. And yet, I don't feel particularly *entitled*—to anything. I considered myself lucky, not entitled, to get even a part-time job in my chosen field.

Rita, on the other hand, a kept woman, feels enormous entitlement to her huge and beautiful house, her shiny new minivan, her stylish clothes. How can she do that?

...

I think I have underestimated how much men *like* their wives to be dependent on them. I have always considered dependency to be a burden, a responsibility. To have to support someone else—you accepted it because that's life: you get a woman pregnant, you man up and support her and the kid.

But I'm beginning to see not the responsibility, but the power: when someone is dependent on you, you have a lot of power over them. *That's* why men's masculinity is measured in terms of dependents.

It didn't help that whenever someone said something, she usually responded by describing something similar that had happened to her (because invariably what people said was simply a description of something that had happened to them). But she did that as a way to express empathy, not to change the focus to her or to minimize what had happened to them.

She didn't know what else to say, how else to respond. A vacuous 'I understand' or 'And how did that make you feel?' seemed so … inane.

And she'd learned, she'd definitely learned, that voicing any socio-political critique was even more alienating.

She turned a few pages.

They accuse, everything's about sex with you.

Of course everything's about sex. We call each other Mr. and Ms.—Male and Female. As a matter of routine. As a matter of etiquette.

...

They also say I 'have issues'. What the hell does that mean? I recognize that there *are* issues. I'm conscious, after all. Important issues. Controversial issues. Matters of importance about which people disagree.

...

"I am exhausted by the reverberations after even the simplest conversation." May Sarton, *Journal of a Solitude*

Yes. And not only exhausted after, but distracted during. Compelled to respond, comment, enlighten, to reveal the reverberations, the implications, the assumptions.

Most people don't think enough. They can't. They don't have time. Between their nine to five and then their kids. No wonder they have unsupported opinions. No wonder they rely on tradition and convention. They live such unexamined lives.

So what are my options here? Either I alienate them or I ignore them. Either way …

At some point she realized that when her eyes glazed over, people thought it was because what they were saying was over her head. She was aghast. Her eyes glazed over because what they were saying was so basic, she understood perfectly well what they were taking great pains to explain to her, but she couldn't interrupt them, they would not be interrupted, so she—zoned out a bit. It was either that or walk away.

No wonder she stopped talking to people.

She had worked so hard not to be friendless. And yet she was.

Other people didn't seem to have to work that hard.

Yes, I am intense. Yes, I am driven. (Or was.)

But how often have *men* been shunned for that reason?

Maybe her social ineptitude was due to an inherent inability to read people. Truthfully, thought, she thought she *could* read people most of the time. She knew what they were thinking and feeling. She just didn't care.

Or maybe her social ineptness was the result of having been surrounded all her life by people with whom she had nothing in common. If she'd had a chance to be with people like her, her shyness, no, her awkwardness, might have slipped off like an unzipped straitjacket.

Or maybe it was all due to the singlism in our society. Being solo made her stand out, it made people look at her, and then not include her. Once, when a new couple moved in down the lane, within weeks they were invited to dinner by the Wagners. She'd been there for almost ten years, and had yet to be invited to dinner by the Wagners. They were on friendly terms, chatting when they passed each other on the lane, but apparently that was all she was entitled to. Time and time again, that sort of thing had happened.

> Being single—Erica Jong said it—has "the unquestioned status of a social pariah."

> This obsessive pairing off, everyone twisted into twos …

> Yes, well, you don't have to face yourself when you're facing someone else.

> People who commit themselves to another person aren't committed to themselves. They can't be.

> …

> Okay, so, I never invited anyone to dinner either, but nor did the new people. They did *after*, to reciprocate.

> …

> Not only is the unmarried woman an outcast, she's an irritant. A provocation. What was it Robin Lakoff said? The reason everyone's uncomfortable with single women is "the absence of male control over her".

No wonder men were so hostile to her. She challenged the system that gave them power. Simply by existing.

In any case, all of the above was exacerbated by sexism, its expectation that women, more than men, *should* read people, *should* care about them, *should* be attached to someone.

One day, one of her neighbours, the lazyboy football one, told her she needed a partner.

"What do you mean?" I ask. I knew exactly what he meant.

"You need a man!"

How insulting.

I respond, smiling (damn it), "What would a man do that I can't?" The guy who came to fix the water situation didn't solve the problem. For three years I've had to dive down and adjust the valve. The guy who installed the ceiling fan didn't do it right. It wobbles. It's not a man I need, but tools and skills.

His comment is particularly sad, and frustrating, after all I've done on my own: I took out a wall, put up the insulation, and built the lean-to; I split my own wood; I shovel my own driveway. And still he says I need a man.

So if the facts contradict the belief, deny the facts.

He tells me about another lady who lived here alone, she went crazy, gave away all her money, then hooked up with a guy who had cancer. What? First, I'm not a lady. Second, not all women who live alone are the same. Third, what part of that is the crazy part?

And Bruce—he sees me kayak every day for hours then says he didn't think I could have been the one to drag the fallen trees across the path (to deter the dirt bikes) because some of them are pretty heavy.

. . .

I am once more appalled to recall, to imagine, what perverted mental structure caused my father to believe that my brother's academic achievements were greater than mine. I got the straight As, I got the scholarship, I got the honours 4-year degree—but somehow his C average in a 3-year B.B.A. program counted more.

It was impossible for them to conceive of the possibility that she might have been competent. In any way. Let alone *more* competent. Than them.

I introduce myself to my neighbours and invariably every one of the men turns 'Kris' into 'Krissie'.

Straight women didn't accept her because she didn't do the feminine thing and she didn't have a husband or kids. Lesbians didn't accept her because she wasn't sexually oriented toward women. Straight men didn't accept her because she wasn't interested in being their mother or the mother of their kids or their girlfriend or their sexual partner. Or their subordinate. And gay men didn't accept her because she was female.

Well, fuck 'em, she thought. Fuck 'em all.

The problem with scar tissue is that it's less sensitive.

The truth of it is she really wasn't interested in other people, in the minutiae of other people's lives. Perhaps because she subjected the detritus of her own life to such thorough analysis. Perhaps the only people who *are* interested in others are those who are superficial about their own lives.

Or maybe such people aren't really interested in other people's lives either, maybe they just pretend. Why would they do that, she wondered. To have friends? But surely a friendship based on pretence isn't a friendship worth having. Maybe their need for friendship was greater than hers, such that even those friendships *were* worth having.

She was, however, immensely interested in ideas. So maybe she just never found the right people. Those who talked about whether abortion was morally acceptable, about whether economics was gendered, about whether suicide could be rational. Not about the weather.

She finished her cup of tea, then, since the weekenders would more likely be on ATVs than on jetskis or even in fishing boats, she headed out onto the lake.

• • •

As she paddled along the shoreline, her eye was caught by a movement—and a little mink stared at her for a second before it disappeared into an eroded bit of the bank. No doubt, its cozy home.

A little further on, she saw it again, swimming across the marshy part. No, she realized, it was a squirrel she was seeing. It was smaller and not diving at all. She watched, as if to make sure it made it all the way across. She hadn't known squirrels could swim that far.

Once she got to the end, she drifted for a while. The sun shimmering on the water, the trees so vibrant, the silence so … alive.

Even though the evenings were getting colder, she decided to stay out for the sunset. She might have only a few more chances to do that.

Once the colours had faded to black, she paddled back in the lovely, dark moonlight, hearing the loons call out on her way.

• • •

Another slice of cold pizza, another cup of tea, another fire.

> The Scarborough Board of Ed has a course called "Environmental Action" now. Seven years ago, when I drafted all those courses and sent them around, trying to become a freelance teacher in the continuing education circuit, environmental something-or-other was one of them. They weren't interested. So how is it they have a course in it now? And how is it they didn't call me?

Oh please. Do you really think they kept your application on file? Under 'E' for 'Environmental Courses', maybe? Someone else just suggested the same thing, but to a different person. And, obviously, at a different time.

> And now prayer in the schools is *illegal*. I lost a job because I refused to stand for it. And now it's illegal?!

> "All progress is initiated by challenging current conceptions." G. B. Shaw

But all challenges of current conceptions do not lead to progress.

She turned a few pages.

> The premise of Alexander Irvine's *Buyout*—those in prison for life

without parole can buy out: if they agree to be euthanized, they get paid 5 million dollars which they can donate to whoever, whatever. It's an intriguing premise: that one can make more of a difference by dying than by living. Not to mention by committing a crime first.

...

Of course it's ridiculous to be a writer when I don't tell stories well, when I don't even *like* telling stories. Beginning, middle, and end doesn't interest me. Describing what people are wearing doesn't interest me. I like the ideas. So I'm just not a *literary* writer. I'm a *philosophical* writer. But I don't enjoy writing philosophy essays, that stiff, dry, academic style. So ...

To be still searching for my genre, in my forties—it's pathetic really.

No, that's not quite true. I've tried, written in, several different genres. It's just that none seemed to be successful. In terms of getting published.

Yes, she *did* like the ideas. Which is why one day, thinking she should write a letter to the editor about some current, and disturbing, event, but then thinking why bother, it occurred to her to start writing—well, they were longer than letters to the editor, but they weren't quite op-eds because they weren't exactly about current events—she didn't know quite what to call them. But she did know they were a lot more fun to write than academic papers because they could have 'attitude'. They were also a lot more fun to write than stories because she could get straight to the point. And, she hoped they were a lot more likely to be published. And, therefore, read.

Many were ethics pieces, and some were social philosophy pieces, but most were in a category as yet unnamed. They were philosophical investigations of ordinary things. Casual day at the office, the expectation that women wear make-up, tax exemptions for churches, the prohibition of drugs in sports, the emphasis on militarism in high school history curricula ...

What if living, rather than dying, required that we do something very intentional, something not instinctive or with built-in gratification (like eating)? Would more people die because at some point they just couldn't be bothered?

...

Nothing good can come of a world in which half of its most intelligent species is raised to be insensitive. Especially if that's the half that's in power.

She became excited about her pieces, thinking the whole literary thing, focusing on prose and poetry, had been a wrong turn. Hadn't they said her stories were too didactic? Her pieces part essay? Okay, then. She wanted to say something, she wanted to make a point. Maybe she should have been trying to be not a Margaret Atwood, but a Michelle Landsberg.

Philosophers are ill-suited for fiction, for which the rule is 'Show, don't tell.' We are not mimes. We do nothing but tell. We speak, we explain, we argue, we object, we refute. We conclude.

Besides, that rule has always seemed to me to insist on a reversion, to something primitive, like pictograms. If you need pictures, go to Lascaux.

She started submitting her work to various newspapers and magazines. When she had half a dozen good, and published, pieces, she sent them around, proposing a weekly column. "Thinking about it" was the title she suggested.

Nothing.

She didn't realize that becoming a columnist was a promotion, granted after years of being a staff reporter. (Unless you were Thomas Hurka, apparently, a philosophy professor who somehow got an ethics column in *The Globe and Mail*.)

He probably submitted his proposal on university letterhead.

So again, she couldn't get there from here.

She found Katha Pollitt's bio, but it didn't really tell her how she became a columnist. It told her, instead, that she first married Randy Cohen, a *New York Times* columnist, and then she married Steven Lukes, a political theorist.

So maybe it did *tell you how she became a columnist.*

And when she saw *Marley and Me*, in which the main character, a man, of course, gets a job as a columnist without even trying, without even wanting it, she just wanted to scream. Because it wasn't, apparently, just fiction.

> "After I was San Francisco Poetry Slam co-champ, I got offered a columnist job, which led to another and another and another."

> What? How does being a poet lead to being a columnist? And 'got offered'?

> I submitted my resume, which listed degrees in Literature and Philosophy and a long list of published papers and op-ed pieces, to dozens of papers *asking to be* a columnist. Nothing.

Then one day a philosophy magazine in Europe responded to her query. Until then, she hadn't known there were such things. Philosophy magazines. They liked her stuff. A lot. In Europe, philosophy was taught at the high school level. Had been for quite some time. And the magazine wasn't an elite academic thing. So they liked that her material had an 'accessible tone' and, at the same time, philosophical rigour. They were willing to pay.

It was too good to be true.

What really happened was that the editor of the magazine wrote her a letter, thanking her for her submission, but explaining that they already had a feminist philosophy column. (She hadn't identified her proposed column as feminist.) (Yes, it was informed by an understanding of sexism, but …)

She wrote back to tell him that his response indicated that they needed more than one.

They probably had more than one masculist philosophy column.

He'd also called her pieces rants.

If you'd been a man, he would've called them impassioned arguments.

But, so, maybe she just had the misfortune to be an artist and an intellect in a country that didn't think much of either. And she didn't know, or couldn't afford, to move to a different country.

Well, show me the country in which women's *artistic and intellectual capacities* are valued.

> Okay so I'm not Bill Maher, or even a Michelle Landsberg, so no one will publish my short little bits. And no one publishes short story collections. So write a novel. Another novel. Put all your short bits into a novel.
>
> One problem. In a novel, stuff happens. There's a story.
>
> Can't you just have an interesting conversation with someone? Do they have to be telling you a story in order for you to stay interested?
>
> More than that, there's a plot. Stuff happens in order. So you're always wondering what happens next. That's supposed to make you want to turn the page. Things are supposed to eventually reach a climax.
>
> But this isn't sex. This isn't sex as experienced by males.
>
> Why can't one just live in the present? Without being relentlessly focused on what happens *next*?
>
> Because everything in our society discourages it. Stores advertise their summer clothes in February. TV stations are now putting animated shit on the bottom telling you what's on next. Distracting you from enjoying what's on now.

It made sense really, the obsession with linear development. It was so male.

When she and Craig had gone on a canoe trip together, he was *so* focussed on getting from point A to point B that he refused to stop along the way even when the lightning started. She still remembered screaming at him, how dare he put her life at risk like that!

And the standard career path— Ah. No wonder she didn't have a career.

And if most publishing decisions are made by men …. And they're incapable of experiencing the joy, the intrigue, of the journey …

Men want action. They want resolution. Like her father, they want to know what happens, where, when, and how. They're not too interested in why.

They mistake movement for progress.

No wonder women's writing isn't published unless it's 'women's fiction'.

And not only was she plot-challenged, she was, of course, character-challenged.

> They all want the character to grow. And they want the character to be one they can identify with.

> Well, make up your mind.

In another rejection letter, perhaps concerning one of her revised fairy tales, the editor had complained "Your main character is so unlikeable."

> So?

> "People don't want to read about people they don't like."

> Wait just a minute. Most of the stuff on tv and in movies—*I* don't like the main character. It's almost always some man who thinks he's so frickin' important. Surrounded by one or more vacuous women.

Men *need to like the character.*

> I could write an anti-novel.

> No, that won't work. It would be innovative.

She stared into the fire and grimaced.

> It wouldn't fit into any established genre. And that was exactly why my hybrid essay-story-monologues were rejected.

> Okay, so I could write a non-novel. Something with just theme and style. And dialogue. Lots of dialogue. What do we call that?

> A journal.

She sighed. She knew no one would publish the journals of an ordinary person. Because they wanted a fascinating life *story*.

Right. Like the lives of the rich and famous are necessarily fascinating.

Okay, she eventually thought, if not a column, then maybe just a published collection. She selected and polished a hundred of her short pieces, arranged them into some sort of order, gave the collection a snappy title, then started sending it around.

One editor rejected it, saying it was "too all over the place"—but she was sure she'd seen similar non-thematic collections.

All of the others didn't even acknowledge receipt.

Then she discovered that publishers were publishing anthologies of what they were calling 'popular philosophy'—*Seinfeld and Philosophy*, for example. She sent a query, suggesting *The Ethical Issues of ER*, but by then, she was told by the editor, the fad was passing and they didn't think they'd be publishing many more volumes in the series.

He lied. It's still *going strong.*

But (and because?) even the one about *Buffy the Vampire Slayer* was edited by a man. And most of the articles were written by men.

> How often do we have to do those studies in which identical resumes bring the man, but not the woman, a job offer? A job offer with a higher rank and salary?

> "Men's achievements buy them more than women's achievements buy them." Where had she read that?

> Walter Carlos became Wendy Carlos then dropped off face of the earth.

Another editor, to whom she'd suggested a volume of environmental ethics pieces pitched for non-philosophers, said that he was confident she could edit a volume as well as anyone else, but sales would be higher if they went with a big name.

She stopped sending out queries.

25

Next morning, happy to see that it was going to be a warm, sunny day, she took her tea and the next journal down to the dock. For a while, she just watched the rippling water and listened to the squirrels she couldn't see, who were no doubt starting to stash for the winter, then opened her journal and started turning the pages.

> Reading about two people in love, exchanging a secret smile. Part of me longs to have experienced that sort of thing, and part of me is bothered by the secrecy. Is my inability to be in a relationship due to my sense of justice, that everyone should have an equal chance, equal status? My relentless democracy, my anti-elitism, my intense dislike of tribalism in any form? A couple is just a tribe at its smallest unit. Then family, then peer group, various other groups, nation …

But surely she was wrong to see couples that way, as exclusionary. And yet— they are.

> But is exclusion *necessarily* wrong? Is it always wrong to have favourites?

> Is it because I've been excluded—marginalized, ignored, rejected—all my life that I so intensely object to it? And yet, it's because I so intensely object to it, that I've been excluded all my life. My belief has prohibited me, prevented me, from becoming part of, included in, a group, however small.

> Is it just the exclusion thing or is it also the equality thing? Because I don't think anymore that everyone's equal.

She flipped through a few more pages.

I have a hard time imagining that being in a couple would bring out the best in me, would improve me. Relationships have always diminished me, lessened me, reduced me, narrowed me, constrained me. Brought out the worst in me.

Well, you might say, that's just because you haven't met the right person. Okay. And I'm unlikely to. The odds are against. Let's do a Drake thing here. The number of men times those with IQs over, say, 120, times those who are unmarried, times those my age give or take 10 years, times those with at least some artsy interest, times those with at least some athletic inclination, times those who don't want to get married, times those who don't want to have kids, times those whose path I'm likely to cross. I suppose I could be happy with someone without the artsy interest or athletic inclination, but the rest are deal-breakers. So how many did we come up with? What are the odds?

…

No, I am complete on my own.

Still, the ostracization hurt. And it had taken its toll.

In my interactions with other people, I've *always* had to sequester part of my self, lest I alienate the other with my intelligence or my critical observations. People don't like people who are smarter than them. And they certainly don't like people who object in any way to their beliefs or opinions.

I've become, in real life, a sort of avatar: superficial, with smoothed over features, and incomplete, with stiff movements.

But the self-censorship had taken an ever greater toll.

I'm so used to handicapping myself, I've forgotten how to go all-out.

She should have stopped writing for the masses sooner.

I cut my own legs out from under me and then wondered why everyone was treating me like I was crippled. And why I didn't make it to the finish line.

But her sense of ethics, of justice, of personal responsibility to make the world a better place hadn't allowed her to do so.

She turned the page.

> Judith Stacey's *And Jill Came Tumbling After*, Joyce Nelson's *The Perfect Machine*, Roethke, Proust, *Women on War*, Naomi Wolf's *The Beauty Myth*, *The Marriage Premise*, Ruth Herschberger's *Adam's Rib*, Daniel Dennett, Fritjof Capra's *The Tao of Physics, Beyond Biofeedback*

She'd always managed to read one or two books a week, but now, since she was no longer a composer *or* a writer, she started plowing through the list she'd started way back in university, books she'd always wanted to read but never had the time.

She didn't have access to the *New York Times Review* or anything similar, so her list was rather idiosyncratic. Her fiction list contained mostly just names she'd heard of, who knows how, when, or where. Her nonfiction list was a result of cruising the bibliographies, from one book to another. Certainly her research for *Satellites* generated her feminist list, fiction *and* nonfiction. But her curiosity led to the books on neurochemistry, for example. She'd occasionally do specific searches in the subject card catalogues, and her year in Montreal had provided her first experience of computerized library databases and a great number of additions to her list.

> "Whenever one of the women asked him a question, he would direct his answer to the woman's keeper." Eva Heller

> "A society that glorifies war, deifies sports, and trivializes intellectual achievement ..." article in *Humanist in Canada*

> "Despite what seemed like a life-time of effort on her part, there was still a host of male scientists who only talked to each other, insisted on interrupting her, and ignored, when they could, what she had to say." Carl Sagan, *Contact*

She flipped through a few more pages.

At some point, she realized that she'd become invisible. She wasn't coming across as a sexual being anymore, and so as far as men were concerned, she didn't exist.

They weren't interested. In *anything* she might do. At first she thought that this was something new, something that happened when women became middle-aged, but then it occurred to her that it had probably always been that way. She had *always* been invisible except for her sexuality. Outside of that, she was nothing to them. They had *never* been really interested in anything she might do.

It is devastating to realize in your forties that no one *ever* really took you seriously.

She looked up from her journal and stared across the cove. That realization had changed—everything. Her achievements, her failures—they were *all* due, one way or another, first to her sexuality, then to the absence thereof.

Sharon Drury was, or could've been, every bit as good as Hennie Bekker if she'd had access to the same resources. So why did Bekker make it and Drury not?

Her picture shows a middle-aged woman. No glamour. No heat.

But Bekker isn't much to look at either.

Doesn't matter in his case. He's a man.

She suddenly realized why married women 'disappeared'. (She had tried, over the years, to find Jen, Diane, Susan, and a few others. Unsuccessfully.) It's not, or not just, because they change their surnames or even because they spend their energies being a wife and perhaps also a mother instead of something that would make them visible. It's because becoming married takes them off men's radar. Since they're no longer sexually unavailable (they're already taken), they're exempt from men's attention. And since men's attention is required for things like book contracts and concert performances, and university appointments and council positions ...

She sometimes thought she should have identified full out as a female composer, a female writer. But her sex just seemed so irrelevant. In theory.

In practice, well, given that the mainstream is so bloody male, it had clearly been a waste of her time, and energy, to try to make it in that world. She should have run to the feminist— What? She *did* eventually submit to the feminist magazines and publishers, the few of them there were ... What else was there to have done?

"When women go off together, we call it separatism. When men go off together, we call it Congress." Kate Clinton

She should have joined women's groups. Made connections there.

But how? She had lived pre-internet. And mostly non-urban.

She turned another page.

Matthew has a Ph.D. and is an electrical engineer at Honeywell. Russell Grantler has his Ph.D. and is now a professor of philosophy.

Never a good thing, to read the Alumni Notes.

Craig, of course, has his Ph.D. and is a practising psychotherapist.

That continues to be a laugh and a half.

Walter Loumis is a speech-writer, and Harold Evstone has his own recording studio and is providing music for video artists.

Even the B students had eclipsed her.

The B male *students.*

And Ivan, she'd noted with mounting despair, who had one-tenth the initiative and one-tenth the ideas—there he was, off to New York as a sound assistant for some famous theatre group. And he wasn't even likeable, he had long greasy hair, he was insufferably slow at everything, and he ate with his mouth open.

It was depressing.

It was humiliating.

No doubt they all had wives, and kids, in addition to that career. They had it all.

Wait a minute. '*Providing* music.' What does that mean? He's not *composing* music? He's just—what? Obviously, whatever it is, it's *a* business. *That's* the key.

Even Andrew has his own studio now; he's hired a few other teachers, they're offering music and dance, he's getting commissions to write video soundtracks … He was four years old when I started teaching him. And *I* was the one who got him started on composition: unlike my own teachers, I encouraged it, I still remember the scary story he told as he provided sound effects on the piano …

So even my students are ahead of me.

How? How did *he* manage to turn teaching a few students in his parents' basement into a 'real' Music Studio? She didn't know. And she didn't know how to find out. She assumed you'd have to rent a building, or space in a building, and she couldn't afford that. End of story.

How would she have known about business loans? In any case, she would have considered it too risky: if the business failed, she'd—what? The bank would repossess everything she had. Or something.

As for how he'd gotten commissions to compose soundtracks for videos, she'd asked him once, and he'd said he'd approached student videographers, offered his work for free, and it just happened from there.

But she'd done that! When she was in Toronto, she'd went to every single indie film co-op and put up a notice on the bulletin board. And nothing happened. From there.

She read about a company that provided music for dance performances. A company, but essentially just four composers available to write music for dance groups. She'd wasted so much time taking courses at the Conservatory, getting her ARCT in Composition. She should have just joined, or formed, a company.

But of course she had no idea how. To do either.

She noticed they were all men.

Men overstate their experience, their qualifications. Women understate. Who was that journalist who said that whenever she called a man for an interview, he agreed, whether he was an expert on the matter or not; women often declined, on that basis.

It occurred to her that she hadn't even put the graduate symposium on her cv. It was no big deal. But she'd organized it, during her year in Montreal. And a man would've said so. Pretentiously.

> When Benjamin Whorf was appointed to teach a term at Yale, he wrote to someone to ask for help preparing materials. How the hell do these unqualified people get hired? How is it that someone who needs to ask someone else for help to do the job they've been hired for gets hired? At *Yale*? Is that the norm?

> Do men apply for jobs they *want* to do, not ones they *can* do, and then they just ask others for help?

> The nerve! To ask someone else for help to do your job! Did Whorf intend to pay that other person?

She'd never even *applied* for a job she didn't know how to do. She assumed she wouldn't get hired. Because she wasn't qualified.

And she was right.

> "In the experiment conducted at the University of Michigan, college students completed a paragraph which began, 'After one semester, John finds himself at the top of his medical school class.' Another group completed the paragraph with the name 'Anne' substituted for John. Students wrote that John had a wonderful personality, an active love life, and an outstanding academic and professional career. But both male and female students described Anne as 'neurotic,' 'lonely' and 'a grind.' They assumed she was dateless and despised. That she could be both successful in medical school and a normal female was inconceivable. … [A] social studies teacher in Oakland, California tried it in her high school class. In one class, two boys working independently wrote that Anne happily left the classroom where the grades were posted, walked out into the street and was run over and killed by a truck."

She couldn't make up stuff better than that.

• • •

She headed into the forest. It was a perfect day for a run, not windy, not humid. She'd stopped running altogether several years ago , knowing her knees wouldn't last forever, but, well, they didn't need to, did they? She broke into a trot every now and then. It felt so good, to be bounding over the rocks and roots once more …

Out on the water—she'd decided to make time for both—the lake was like a mirror and as she paddled, she stared into it, at the slightly disjointed planes of wavering reflection …

• • •

When she returned, she continued through the journal, stopping here and there to read the wandering entries.

> I don't look into anyone's eyes anymore, not wanting to see the lack of understanding, the complete lack interest, the rejection.
>
> And not wanting them to see the same things in my eyes.
>
> …
>
> Now that I'm no longer interested in men, at all, I realize that the men who seem to value women the least are the ones who spend the most time trying to impress them.
>
> …
>
> Marriage for men means getting a cheerleader, maid, cook, and administrative assistant. Marriage for women means *being* a cheerleader, maid, cook, and administrative assistant. I had my hands full being my own cheerleader, maid, cook, and administrative assistant.
>
> …
>
> It's hard to tell what a person's like when you see them in isolation. I mean if they were laughing and having a good time, you'd think they were crazy. Even smiling might be suspect. And people's resting expression depends more on simple physiology than personality.

How many fun-loving people are never seen to crack a smile or burst into laughter simply because they were never seen in the company of people with whom they could do that?

I miss having fun. I haven't had fun with anyone since … drop-in.

…

Owen Flanagan's *Consciousness Reconsidered*, Hofstadter's *Gödel, Escher, and Bach*, Huxley's *The Art of Seeing*, Bacon's *Atlantis*, Ouspensky's *The Fourth Way*, Marshall McLuhan, Lewis Carroll, Alison Lurie, Diane Schomperlen, Alice Walker, Suzette Haden Elgin

…

"All premeds drop her Life class. … For Politics, take Hamilton. He's magnificent…" Joan Slonczewski, *The Highest Frontier*

It sounds so unremarkable. But I never heard that sort of insider talk. It's like I've gone through my whole life both deaf and blind.

…

"Peter Gzowski probably being one of the people who have got to finish sentences all their lives will probably not even have noticed that sentence finishing is a privilege accorded to only a few." Helen Potrebenko, *Hey Waitress*

…

"Women regard phones as instruments of convenience and communication. Men see them as power sticks. He is mortally offended if he is put on hold. Women, who have been on hold for centuries … Watch a man when he is on hold. He seethes, taps his fingers, grinds his teeth, rolls his eyes …" Florence King, *He: An Irreverent Look at the American Male*

She stared out at the water for a long time, just watching the sparkles run around the surface. A pair of ducks appeared—not mallards, but the ones who always looked like they were having a bad hair day—and started swimming around the perimeter of the cove.

She had this nagging suspicion that she had given up too early. Crichton wrote *State of Fear* at sixty-four.

Yes, but after The Adromeda Strain *and* Jurassic Park *and some dozen novels in between. That is to say,* after *he had a readership. It would be something completely different to still be writing 'on spec' at sixty-four.*

She should have joined a writers' group. Learned the craft.

> If I'd figured out that I needed to learn the *craft* of writing—if I'd realized that the *art* wasn't enough—

> I could be writing a *State of Fear* now, by now, if I'd taken a different road to here, if I'd found my genre. Feminist sf, say.

> But *Fugue* and *Satellites*—weren't they—they weren't—

> By the time I figure it out, I'll be sixty.

> It's like I've been a writer all my life, yes, but I've been pouring it out onto the ground instead of into bottles. Instead of into something that can then be published, and then, and so, read by others.

> It's the making of the bottle that has so eluded me. The *appropriate* bottle. Too prosaic for poetry. Too didactic for stories. Too plot-challenged for novels. Too short for nonfiction. Too not-current-events for op-ed pieces and columns.

> Why is the *form* so goddamned important though? Can't people simply engage with the *content*?

> ...

> Sometimes I think I backed the wrong horse. When I kept writing and stopped composing. But it wasn't a choice of one or the other. It just—I just—had so much to *say*.

Well, there's still time. Isn't there? Can't one make a career in ten years?

Sure—if one knows how to make a career.

Besides it's all digital now. I'd have to start over.

Well, just with the tools of the trade. Music is still music. Beauty is still beauty.

…

Can't I make a lateral jump to Crichton? Do I have to go back and start over?

And then there's the matter of *for what*? Three years on a Crichton novel to have it sit in my desk drawer? Because that's what would happen. I still wouldn't be able to get an agent or a publisher.

And even if I figured out how to publish my books online or as ebooks, what reason do I have to think that would have any different result than my earlier self-publishing efforts?

She stared out at the water again.

Which is worse, to have tried your hardest and failed or never to have tried?

In her twenties, she would've said the latter. Now she wasn't so sure.

I used to have a hundred ideas for plays, stories, poems, pieces, albums, and dozens of works-in-progress, but now so few ideas seems significant enough to warrant my time and energy.

That's when she realized it wasn't about having enough time. It was about having enough passion.

That's why people don't create masterpieces after forty.

But why *don't* people have enough passion after forty? Is it just that they don't have the energy?

Passion requires a strong sense of ego, a belief that the self matters.

The explanation made perfect sense.

She found it hard to settle for anonymity, for not being known as a composer, or as a writer, or as a philosopher, no matter how minor. No doubt the difficulty was exacerbated because she had no friends, no one who even knew her name.

'Have you seen the moon?' 'Yes. Yes, I have.'

How did I let him run through my fingers?

'I need me, you need you, we want … us.'

How did we get from quoting that to each other to

'What am I to you?' 'Absolutely nothing.'

What did I do?

Nothing. It wasn't about you.

And maybe *that's* the appeal of marriage, she thought. It guarantees someone knows your name.

And part of her felt guilty for giving up, for choosing personal pleasures—reading, thinking, listening to music, walking, paddling—over fulfilling her potential. But so what if she didn't fulfill her potential as a composer or a writer or a philosopher? Especially if it gave her greater pleasure to listen than to compose, to read than to write? Hedonism isn't necessarily selfish. It can be merely self-interested.

But her writing, and even her music, at least the social commentary collage pieces, was intended to change the world. So in giving up, she was giving up social activism, social *responsibility*.

"No matter what the initial characteristics (or gifts) of the individuals, unless there is a long and intensive process of encouragement … the individuals will not attain extreme levels of capability in their particular fields." Benjamin Bloom, *Developing Talent in Young People*

So true.

So … give it up. It's not gonna happen. No matter what you do. Now.

Still, she had a hard time giving up the desire, the obligation, to do something significant with her life.

But then she thought it's all premised on 'should'—I *should* fulfill my potential, I *should* try to make the world a better place. Why *should* she?

What would happen if she turned her back on what she *should* do?

What do I actually *want* to do?

Ah. A different question from what do I want to *be*.

I want to be a composer, but it seems I no longer want to compose. I just want to listen.

I want to be an Atwood. Or a Plath. Or a Crichton. But I don't want to leave my cabin to do book tours, nor do I want to do all the other stuff that's required to be an Atwood or a Crichton. And you can't be a Plath anymore. You can't just write and send it out.

Well, I'd be content with a place several tiers down. I'd be happy if my books sold a couple hundred a year. Not a million. But not fourteen.

No, maybe more than a couple hundred. I'd be content if my writing provided enough to live on comfortably. Enough to buy not just day-old stuff at the grocery store, enough to turn up the thermostat when I'm cold, enough not to worry about the next car repair.

And what do I want to *do*?

On any given day, I want to wake up whenever, have a good cup of tea, and some tiropita from my favourite bakery in the city, write for a couple hours (and know that someone somewhere sometime is going to read what I'm writing), then go for a long walk, or a long paddle, on a beautiful, beautiful day, a quiet day, a warm day, a sun sparkly day, I want to see chipmunks, rabbits, deer, beaver, otters, I want to watch the sunset, then have a bite to eat, a slice of cold pizza would be perfect, watch a bit of tv, then read a good book and listen to some good music, then go to bed and hear the loons.

Is that too much to ask for?

Maybe, she thought, thinking of all the horrible lives being lived.

And yet, she had it. Most of it. Much of it. Some of it. She wasn't a composer, she wasn't a writer, she wasn't a philosopher, she wasn't a teacher, she wasn't a choreographer, she wasn't even a runner anymore, but she had her cabin. Her beloved cabin on a lake in a forest.

You've had sixteen years of sheer joy here at your cabin on a lake in a forest. And a fair amount of time to do whatever you wanted—read, write, think, run, paddle, listen to music …

As for all the things she wasn't, she'd had the chance. She'd done what she'd wanted to do. It just didn't turn out the way she'd hoped.

Okay, so I didn't become a composer and a writer. Well, I did—and I have a couple archive boxes to show for it, one full of my compositions, the other full of my journals and manuscripts—pathetic, really, but— But apparently no one knows. That I am, that I was, a composer and a writer.

If a tree falls in the forest.

So, she thought, why *not* just live the rest of her life in pursuit of happiness? Instead of social change? The route to hedonism is simple: a recognition of the futility of individual acts and the fickleness of collective acts, with regard to achieving their ends.

Such a route is understandably more often discovered by women whose individual acts are acutely more impotent than those of men, given the existing power structures, and whose collective acts are acutely more restricted, given the existing social structures.

Still, she struggled to give in to a purely hedonistic life.

Well, 'purely' except for having to scramble for work. Again. Her relief shifts at the mental health home had disappeared some time ago, and now the funding for the research position wasn't renewed. So she was out of a job.

If it had been a full-time job, there would have been more … something. But since it was just a part-time job, she wasn't even given two weeks' notice. It was as if they'd assumed she didn't really need the job, that losing it would be no big deal.

On the contrary, since it *was* just a part-time job, it was even *more* necessary than a full-time one, since it meant she didn't have, couldn't've had, that much set aside. She had enough to see her through the next six months. That's it. So losing it was a very big deal.

People weren't giving their kids piano lessons anymore. Someone else had started offering dance classes in the area. Supply teaching was out—recertification would have been necessary. Ditto night school and summer school. She called the Boards to ask about tutoring, and they did add her name to the list, but they weren't very encouraging. Apparently it was a long list.

She looked in the paper. Nothing really.

It's not like think tanks list their openings in the classifieds.

Nor are think tanks what you think they are. Not that it would have mattered.

She kept an eye open for notices in shop windows. She went into the post office, the local car dealership, the lumber mill, asking if they needed … what? Office help?

She realized that choosing part-time work in order to have the time and energy to write had been a serious wrong turn. Not only because the sacrifice was made for nothing, given the lack of a writing career, but because the sacrifices had been more than she'd anticipated. She'd thought, reasonably enough, less money in return for more time and energy.

Part of the problem was that she had been thinking of a full-time *teaching* job, in which case, since you had prep and marking to do—at least with a full-time English teaching job—Math teachers had it so much easier, she thought—her evenings *as well as* her days would have been lost. But most jobs were literally nine to five, Monday to Friday. So she would have had evenings, and weekends. To do more than just watch tv, if it wasn't a soul-sucking job like that camp job.

She also would've had sick days. With a part-time job, when you're sick and can't make it in, you lose your shift: you lose pay.

And holidays. Paid holidays. With a part-time job, all your 'holidays' are unpaid.

And health benefits. She'd had to pay for her dentist appointments, for her optometrist appointments, as well as for her glasses.

And she would've been eligible for Unemployment Benefits. (She hadn't realized that you had to work a minimum number of hours *at the same place* for UI to kick in.) (And yet, each place deducted UI.) As it was, whenever she lost one of her jobs, she had to make up the difference from her savings until she found a replacement.

In fact, not only do full-time employees get more benefits than do part-time employees, the *kids* of full-time employees get more benefits than part-time employees. They get access to the employee's health benefits—*they* get dentist appointments, *they* get new glasses. That is to say, people who don't contribute at all to the company get more than people who do. How unfair is that?

It's all about the man, she realized once more. The world is built by men for men. (That women were now full-time employees getting benefits for their kids was probably just an unintended, and unwelcome, byproduct. That would likely be corrected somehow.)

And, with a full-time job, she would have had connections—at least if it had been a full-time position in academia.

Then there was all that time she spent looking for jobs, because as soon as one of her dance classes got cancelled or three piano students decided not to return after the summer, she had to make up the difference.

And the time spent juggling everything so she *could* have enough dance classes and enough piano students and enough relief shifts.

On top of all that, there was the difference in basic pay. Hour for hour, part-time work paid less than full-time work even if it meant doing the same thing. Full-time workers in the mental health residential program got around $15/hr, whereas the part-timers on relief were paid around $10/hr. The difference between full- and part-time teachers was even worse: six courses as a full-time teacher earned you $30,000, which worked out to $5,000 per course; night school and summer school courses, despite being the same 110 classroom hours per, paid only $1,500 per course, which worked out to, for the same six course load, a measly $9,000.

It had left its toll. The stress of not knowing from one month, from one week, hell, from one *day* to the next, if she'd get enough work that month to pay the mortgage, to buy milk for her oatmeal. (Brown sugar was too much to hope for.) The stress, and the anger, when she didn't. (She had three frickin' degrees!)

But perhaps what took the greatest toll over the years was the difference in perceived value. She'd discovered that if you're part-time, you don't get taken seriously. Your input is less often solicited, whether regarding shift schedules or company policy. Your work is thought to be less important, no matter what you're doing. Your paycheque is thought to be less important as well, so you often have to wait longer for it. You're automatically considered a beginner who needs more supervision, who's expected to prove herself. Over and over. And over. She was so very tired of proving herself. And she was tired of working twice as hard for half as much.

It did not escape her attention that an overwhelming majority of part-timers were women. Was part-time work devalued because women did it or were women put in part-time positions because such positions were devalued?

And whose *idea was it to make such a big distinction based on* how much?

> And okay, it was my choice not to live in a city. The job opportunities here are few and far between. But since there are four high schools within driving distance, I thought supply teaching would be reasonably lucrative. In addition to whatever music and dance students I could get, I thought surely I'd have enough.

But, after sixteen years, she didn't.

Eventually, she drove to the Employment Office in North Bay. The woman to whom she was assigned took one look at her resume and said she couldn't believe she couldn't find a job.

"Well, I can't," Kris had said. Bluntly. "Can you? Find a job? For me?"

An hour later, the answer was, essentially, no. Not unless she relocated.

> If Murphy Brown got fired, in which of the following positions would she be happiest?
>
> > a. her replacement's secretary
> >
> > b. Corky's researcher
> >
> > c. a Vegomatic demonstrator in a shopping mall
>
> Hah. She wouldn't get hired for any of them.

The woman suggested that she go to the local office temp company.

So she did. What choice did she have? She was willing to do anything to keep her cabin on a lake in a forest.

But they wanted proficiency with Word. She was proficient in WordPerfect.

So she developed proficiency in Word. Along with her typing speed, she thought maybe …

But the placement officer still looked … discouraging. Yes, her age could be a factor, but there was also the matter of her attire.

So she went to a thrift shop, bought a pair of black cotton pants and—all of the tops in the women's section were clingy or prissy or— She picked out a couple men's dress shirts. No, she thought a moment later, they'd want her to tuck them in. She went back to the women's section and found a couple loose-fitting knit tops, half-sweater, half-sweatshirt. One had beads sewn around the collar. So maybe they won't insist I wear jewellery, she thought. Another had an appliqué of little kittens near the shoulder. She sighed as she added it to her selection.

They didn't have one with a snarling Doberman.

As she was checking out, she realized her track shoes would have to go.

No doubt they would have decreased your typing speed.

But no way was she buying a pair of heels. She found an old pair of penny loafers. They'd do.

> Standing there, between the men's and women's clothing sections, it suddenly dawned on me. All this time, people have thought I was a lesbian. It would explain so much. It wasn't because I was smart or shy or clueless or female. 'It' being, in general, exclusion, dismissal …

> I didn't wear make-up (hated the way it made my skin feel), or perfume (gave me a headache), or dresses (hated having my legs on display), or high heels (couldn't run in them) … I guess I looked butch. I fit the lesbian stereotype. Short hair, motorcycle, my god, even the jeans and flannel shirt (warm and comfy).

> But eschewing the feminine doesn't mean you're lesbian.

It does if men only have two categories for women: hot or dyke.

It was discouraging to be, again, at that point, an office temp.

But at least she had her cabin on a lake in a forest.

26

And then she lost even that.

She took a long swallow of her tea, staring out at the water which seemed to shimmy in place. Like an unsuccessful re-set.

Maybe it was because the highway from Toronto had become four-laned, maybe it was because Muskoka had become full, maybe it was because more people had more credit, maybe it was because more people made more people, but every spring, every summer, every fall became filled with the noise of excavators, construction tools, renovation tools … It will stop some day, she told herself; there is only so much land that can be developed. In the meantime, she retreated into the forest or up the river, into quiet, into beauty.

She could have dealt with that loss of paradise, using earplugs and going further into the forest, further up the river, but what happened was that, because of all the 'improvements', she supposed, property taxes skyrocketed, doubling each year for three years in a row. Over the sixteen years since she'd bought her little cabin, they'd gone from $400 a year to $4,000 a year. She had to start paying in monthly installments, and her monthly property tax payment was now as much as her monthly mortgage payment. The price of everything else also increased as local business owners took advantage of the presence of rich people from the city: wood to heat the cabin cost more, gas at the pumps cost more, even more than it did in the city, even the local grocery story jacked up its prices …

She'd managed to do some renovating herself over the years—she'd replaced the original windows with thermal double-paned ones, she'd added more insulation, she'd even had a well installed—but she wished now that she'd funnelled that money into additional mortgage payments instead. She could have had an extra year. Almost.

Between the few office temp gigs she was getting and the even fewer relief shifts at the mental health home (they'd started calling her again), it wasn't enough to break even. She had to start dipping into her meagre savings to pay the bills.

She got lucky when the reporter at the local newspaper was injured, and they wanted a replacement. For two months, she made a solid $500 per week. But then the regular reporter returned.

Two months later, and down to her last thousand, the local library advertised for a part-time librarian. She applied. Immediately. Oh god, how she hoped—

But no, the position went to someone else.

"Her husband recently passed," the head librarian explained.

So?

Then she understood.

Wait a minute, she wanted to scream, I've *never* had a husband, let alone one until just recently. Which means *I've* had to support myself—which I gather is your point—for the past twenty-seven years!

"If I'd known you were deciding on the basis of need," she said, curtly, "I would've submitted last year's income tax return instead of my cv." The woman just looked at her.

She didn't even get an interview for the part-time literacy assistant position at the elementary school.

> What's a 47-year-old woman with three degrees supposed to do? Seriously, if you have an answer, call me.

At twenty, as drop-in supervisor, she'd been responsible for an entire program and a small staff.

What the hell had happened?

She kept cutting back until she could cut back no further. The phone alone, kept in case she ever had to call 911, cost $50 month. Her trips into town became biweekly, then monthly.

She continued to live within her means and accumulated no debt: she knew how to live on ten dollars of food a week, books from the library were free, she had hundreds of CDs, she had a kayak, she had hiking shoes—

She sold her piano. It bought her almost five more months.

> I played my "Op.1 No.1" yesterday and almost wept. If that's what I was writing when I was fifteen, I *could* have become a George Winston or an André Gagnon by now. Maybe even a Philip Glass.

Then, to erase the pain, she'd played Bach's *Prelude I*. For half an hour straight.

And then she carefully lay the felt along the keys, gently closed the fallboard, and locked it.

She sold her studio equipment as well, but everything had become digital, so it didn't bring much. She kept her Sennheiser headphones, which she'd long ago started using with her portable CD player, and the razor blade she'd used for splicing tape. It could be a reminder.

Then winter came and it was a cold one and by mid-February, she'd used up all the wood in her lean-to. She put up a tarp and a blanket to wall off the studio part of the cabin which she wasn't using anyway. She set the thermostat for her baseboard heaters to sixty. Then fifty-five. Then fifty. The water pipes wouldn't freeze until forty, so she still had a way to go. But even if she didn't use *any* electricity, the monthly bill was $75—it was that much just to have the service.

She started using one of those oil radiators with the fins, dragging it behind her from room to room like an IV cart.

Could you go on welfare when you own property? She didn't know. She suspected that if part-time work at minimum wage wasn't enough to keep her cabin, welfare benefits wouldn't be either.

She was right.

She wasn't disabled, the government assistance officer pointed out. She hadn't been abused. She didn't have kids. She wasn't a senior citizen. And since she was a first-time applicant, there was a five-week waiting period.

Then one day, the letters started coming. From the township, from the bank, from the lawyers.

Oh god, but she cried. She couldn't bear to leave.

And she couldn't stay.

27

Long story short, she ended up with $50,000. Instead of her cabin. It wasn't enough to buy another cabin. Not even a start-over one. She even investigated lots on which she might put a trailer. But the problem was that everything *started* at $75,000 and no bank would give her a mortgage. Not now.

She found an 'owner take-back mortgage' possibility, but it wasn't on a year-round road and it had no hydro hook-up. She considered making do with wood and propane, and seeing if she could park her car where the plow stopped, but more to the point, it was nowhere near any employment opportunities. If she made the down payment of $25,000, then lived on $10,000/year, she'd run out in just two and a half years. Then what?

She thought of just moving into town, but then realized she could go anywhere. Since it wasn't a matter of affording a cabin on a lake in a forest somewhere, she could move to, well, New York. Or Boston or Princeton or … California?!

She'd liked living in Vancouver, Toronto, Montreal … She could go to a park or a café, and the person who would sit down beside her would be someone worth meeting …

In New York, that someone could be, or know, an agent or a publisher.

But no, when she'd lived in Vancouver, Toronto, Montreal, she hadn't met anyone.

Besides, how could she pay rent in Princeton or New York? It would be three, four times rent in town.

Well, she could get a job. A full-time job. One commensurate with her abilities.

That possibility intrigued her. After all, she wasn't doing anything else. Now. It would be too risky to move first. If she couldn't find a job wherever, she'd end up a bag lady. So she decided to move if, when, and to wherever she could find a job.

In the meantime, she rented a room in town. The room above the hairdresser's beside the railway tracks. There hadn't been much to choose from. The presence of people ever near bothered her, as did the frickin' billboard out her window, but what could she do?

There wasn't enough space for her oak table. Or for all of her books and records. Over the years, she'd replaced much of the latter with used CDs, so it didn't hurt as much to sell those. The loss was more symbolic than anything. The books on the wall, the record albums, they were like photographs, mementos of her life. Of her self, of what she was when she'd acquired them.

Back when, she wished she'd been able to keep her motorcycle, but she couldn't afford it *and* a car.

She deeply regretted not taking her kayak with her. But there would have been nowhere to put it.

She drove up to the Employment Office again.

"Relocation is now an option," she told the woman.

She started to apply for jobs … everywhere.

They tried the universities first, but there was a long line of fresh Ph.D.s ahead of her. Then they tried Boards of Education. Same problem, basically. Publishing companies? She could be an editor, a copyeditor, a proofreader. No. Nothing. Then they tried the government. Again, nothing. Film, tv, music, dance, recreation … her broad experience counted for nothing; status is gained by specialization.

"Your return address may be a problem," the woman confessed. 'R. R. #2, Powassan' said 'country hick'.

So again she considered moving first, *then* finding a job. Because what would she do in *Powassan* once her money ran out? Was it better to be a bag lady in Toronto than in Powassan? Well, she thought, better to be a bag lady in sunny California …

Once they'd exhausted the jobs commensurate with her abilities, they started on the rest.

But no one wanted to hire someone pushing fifty.

No wonder people are obsessed with youthfulness. Your life is expected to stop at thirty.

In the meantime, she hired herself out as a cleaning lady. Mostly in the affluent part of town. The part where all the teachers lived.

She thought that maybe somehow with that, and the office temp thing, and the relief shifts— She thought if she could put aside a couple thousand a year, in ten years, she'd have $70,000 instead of $50,000. Probably still not enough for another cabin on a lake in a forest, but …

She tried to keep her head, her spirit, above water by driving to the forest a couple times a week. Not *her* forest, partly because the township had put up a 'No Parking' sign at the logging road entrance, but mostly because it hurt too much to be that close to her cabin and not be able to—

She also bought a cheap kayak when Canadian Tire had a sale. It wasn't nearly as nice as hers, but it would do. Though the lakes that had public access were few and far between. And not nearly as beautiful.

Didn't matter once the kayak was stolen. She'd had to leave it on top of her car.

But her $50,000 dwindled, rather than grew. One year it'd be a car repair, new glasses, and a dentist appointment. Another year it would be a few rent payments when she lost a few cleaning clients or didn't get enough office temp gigs.

She was back to where she had been in her early thirties, scraping by.

She was back to oatmeal for breakfast. No milk. Certainly no brown sugar.

She closed the journal, stared out across the cove for a while, then decided that since it was a windy day, she'd go for a walk in the forest instead of a paddle on the lake. She put her windbreaker on, over her sweatshirt, and headed out.

• • •

She stopped at the little creek on the way in, just to sit and listen to the murmuring flow. Then continued on as far as the maple trees, the leaves so bright, so alive as they quivered, dying.

• • •

When she returned, she headed down to the dock again with a fresh cup of tea and one of her chocolate bars. She noted that it would be a while before the magic began, so she opened the journal to where she'd left off.

> Okay it was my choice not to get a full-time job. I needed, I wanted, the time and energy to be a composer, to be a writer. But I forfeited money, career, pension, benefits—for nothing.
>
> Oh, stop your whining. You're healthy, you've experienced nothing traumatic, you didn't have to claw your way out of a war zone, you haven't had to kill—
>
> Maybe the subtle, ordinary tragedies are worse. Especially if they're common to a full half of humanity.
>
> Still, such a whiner.

No. That's just another way to silence women. When men complain about injustice, it's justified indignation.

> I ache for those days, living in my cabin on a lake in a forest, each second a drop of gold. I can't bear to live not ever feeling that again, that beauty, that peace, that exhilaration—the sun, the water, the forest—
>
> …
>
> It's the death of the delusions of grandeur, it's the acceptance of

mediocrity and the probability of failure, that changes you. I no longer imagine myself a Chopin or Scriabin, or Vangelis, or Roger Waters, or George Winston— Or Atwood, or Plath, or Nancy Kress— Or Katha Pollitt—

How can I recapture those visions of splendour, those vistas of potential?

She read a lot, in her room above the hairdresser's. She had little else to do with her time.

"As a woman, as a nonacademic, with none of the respectability and certification even a bush league college lends its faculty, some years she applied for 30 grants and got none." Marge Piercy, *Summer People*

"So often then the pieces would be performed exactly once for an audience of 3 hostile critics, 14 superior academics who thought you ought to be writing in their particular mode, a handful of musicians ..." Marge Piercy, *Summer People*

So the grass *isn't* greener ...

. . .

"She's had her life. Why give her yours too?" Marge Piercy, *Braided Lives*

Exactly.

. . .

"A man proud of discovering he could actually get up in the morning by himself, make his own breakfast. She could not imagine a woman living who would think such a thing worth reporting." Marge Piercy, *Vida*

"Vida learned how ineffective she was in meetings, how often she missed the real portent of what was happening and charged off a cliff expecting agreement. She had come to know well that dreadful sense of space yawning under her after she had spoken. She had not the skill or patience to manipulate consensus beforehand. She relied heavily on being right." Marge Piercy, *Vida*

That's how it's done? By manipulating consensus before hand?

All this time, she'd simply given the reasons for her requests. At first, she figured that was because she was a philosopher: philosophers are all about having reasons, evidence, support for one's claims. But she also understood, eventually, that that was the way of someone who didn't feel entitled. To anything asked for.

Women asked. Explained. Men ordered. Expected.

She also realized that giving reasons made it less likely to get what she wanted. People didn't want to hear the details. The complexity apparently overwhelmed, and angered, them, put them on the defensive. Especially if she were talking to a man.

Being reasonable, being so focused on sound arguments and evidence, being a philosopher, being a *female* philosopher—it had made her completely unable to succeed. In a patriarchy.

> "He displays an impressive command of the languages of music, genetics, computer science, and neurology, but more exciting is his willingness to engage in abstract thought, to argue and persevere, to carry arguments through the rooms of logic …." Richard Powers, *The Gold Bug Variations*

And if he were a woman, he'd be criticized, not praised, for that. It would read something like this:

> "She flaunts her knowledge of the languages of music, genetics, computer science, and neurology, and persists in engaging in abstract thought, arguing and persevering …."

> …

> Hofstadter says he didn't introduce a female character because he didn't want to introduce sexual politics. Jesus. Our very presence can be seen only in terms of sex. Even by men as 'advanced' as Hofstadter.

> …

> "Most marriages depend on a dull association of material and social

interests held together by ignorance on the one side and hypocrisy on the other." Edith Wharton, *The Age of Innocence*

When the sun started to descend behind the trees, she marked her spot, closed the journal, and waited. This might be the last time— There. Now. The sun reached just the right angle, and— My god, it was *such* a vibrant green. She watched as the light slowly panned from left to right, she could almost feel the tingle as it spread, as it touched each branch … And then up, to the tops of the trees, and then— It was over.

Once the dock was in shade, it was noticeably cooler, so she put on her extra sweatshirt, then continued through the journal.

> "One Sunday morning, frustrated and in a playful mood, she had tried to initiate sex. Evan sprang from the bed as though she had proposed sodomy … 'You can't turn me off and on like an electric light switch,' he objected." Doris Anderson, *Two Women*

Maybe that's what it was. It wasn't that he found me unappealing. He rejected my advances because *he* wanted to be the one to control.

Jesus.

…

In one of J. D. Robb's novels, Roarke says to Eve, "I know what you need." He's talking about bringing fresh clothes and her weapon harness. But the simplicity of it. The immense love of it.

She wished she had had someone who knew what she needed.

To take the time, the energy, to pay attention, and think about what one has observed, to figure out what the other needs, in order to be happy, fulfilled …

She'd done that for Marilyn. Bought her that easel desk that could be angled at will when she saw that she was working awkwardly on a horizontal surface. Asked if she wanted to talk about Roy leaving her for Vicki, and was genuinely prepared to listen right then and there for however long it took.

She'd done that for Craig too. Bought him a camera case when she saw the makeshift bag he used whenever he went out to the conservation area. Kept her distance when he was stressed, didn't make any more demands.

Yeah, but apparently that wasn't *what he needed. He should have said.*

Why can't people just tell you what they need? Because they don't know themselves? Am I that rare?

…

Reading about the father who, after seeing some tragedy on the news involving a little girl, gets into bed beside his sleeping daughter and just holds her tight all night.

My father never held me tight.

Actually, no one ever did.

…

Oh stop feeling sorry for yourself. You did well to leave Craig and Peter. And none of the others would've been any better.

There isn't one person you genuinely regret leaving, regret letting slip away.

Except Marilyn.

But even then, if she was getting all grandmothery, if she was becoming 'spiritual' …

…

It's been kinda nice, though, to have lived without expectations. Without others expecting anything of you. The upside of not having any friends or family or colleagues. And of being female.

I've pursued only what I really want to pursue.

Those less driven might have languished into nullity.

Then again, that's not quite true, since I pursued what I really wanted *out of the options I was aware of.*

Still, no peer pressure to muddy the waters.

But also, no help to calm, or advice to clarify, the waters: since I wasn't expected to do anything, it wasn't required; since I wasn't expected to achieve anything, it wasn't warranted.

…

"… adopting a jocular tone, as though he couldn't quite take her seriously." Doris Anderson, *Two Women*

Yes. That's it exactly, she thought. The tone her father had always had when she'd tried to discuss something with him, it was as if to say 'Here we go again, psychoanalyzing, getting all philosophical'— Had she ever mocked his life's passion?

He didn't have any passion, remember?

And why are men so resistant to any self-knowledge?

Is it that or are they just resistant to discussing *anything* with a woman. A woman who might actually know more than them.

"[At Yale] There was a girl [sic] who studied even while walking between classes; when it rained, she covered her books in large plastic baggies so she could continue despite. When at graduation she was awarded the Warren Prize for the highest scholastic standing and it was announced she had gotten thirty-six As over the years, she was booed." Christopher Buckley, *Wry Martinis*

…

Women who have worked hard to get to where they are often accused of just being lucky. But the two are not mutually exclusive. You're lucky if you're been rewarded for your hard work. Especially if you're a woman.

...

"A potential difficulty for our species has always been implicit in the close linkage between the behavioural expression of aggression/predation and sexual reproduction in the male. This close linkage involves (a) many of the same neuromuscular pathways which are utilized both in predatory and sexual pursuit, grasping, mounting, etc., and (b) similar states of adrenergic arousal which are activated in both. The same linkage is seen in the males of many other species; in some, the expression of aggression and copulation alternate or even coexist, an all-too-familiar example being the common house cat. Males of many species bite, claw, bruise, tread, or otherwise assault receptive females during the act of intercourse … In many if not all species it is the aggressive behaviour which appears first, and then changes to copulatory behaviour when the appropriate signal is presented. … Lacking the inhibiting signal, the male's fighting response continues and the female is attacked or driven off." James Tiptree, Jr. (Alice B. Sheldon), "The Screwfly Solution"

That would explain so much. Their general attitude of aggressive hostility toward me now. Because I don't give the signal that would otherwise inhibit the aggression. Because I'm not interested in them sexually anymore.

She'd thought that maybe it was because before males become sexual, the only touch that was permissible was aggressive touch. Eleven-year-old boys can't walk arm in arm like girls can. So boys, when it becomes permissible to touch, to touch women, touch them the only way they've been allowed to touch to that point. Aggressively.

And make-up! I've always scorned women for that. For making themselves look young and for making themselves bait *as a matter of routine*. And in the process equating 'young' with 'sex'. But if it's just a *ritualized* signal, of sexual availability, of sexual readiness, to keep the men in sexual advance mode instead of aggressive mode—

But god damn it, men, can you not put a third option in your repertoire?

"We know the men do better with a female along, not only for physiological needs but for a low-status non-competitive servant and rudimentary mother figure." James Tiptree Jr., "With Delicate Mad Hands"

Again, an explanation. I refuse low status, I compete, inadvertently, and I was not mother figure. So men do *not* do better with me along, with me around.

...

"Swallow's entire adult life was a series of crusades to prevail against the obstacles put in her way by MIT, first to matriculate in the chemistry department, then to be admitted to the Ph.D. program, and finally to be given a tenured faculty position." H. Patricia Hynes, *The Recurring Silent Spring*

What a waste. What a shame.

We spend all our energy battling obstacles put in our way, we have nothing left to *do t*hat way. And the thing is, I'll never know which of my difficulties were such obstacles *put in my way.*

...

Susan Eng (lawyer and head of the Metro Police Commission or something) graduated from high school, from grade thirteen, with a 97.5 average, and when she didn't get a scholarship she was advised to become a secretary.

So it really wasn't just me. God, that's so depressing.

She also watched more television than she used to. There in her room. Above the hairdresser's.

She'd stopped watching the news long ago. Nothing but men looking serious and, thus, important.

As they talked about other men looking serious and, thus, important.

In fact, she'd pretty much stopped watching tv period. Nothing but.

Hockey scores were presented right after the news of Chernobyl. That's how it'll be. Right up to the end.

But every now and then there'd been a series she'd enjoy. *This is Wonderland* had been one of her favourites. And occasionally, a movie would interest her.

Watched the movie *Precious*—

Where was the principal knocking at *my* door saying 'Hey, you've got Harvard material here, don't let your daughter waste away at some no-name university getting a teaching degree …'?

My sister resists, procrastinates, complains 'Teacher wants us to read and write every day in our books, how are we supposed to do that?' and she's the one who gets the attention.

I complied with that teacher's request. Enthusiastically. I take to writing like a fish to water. But no one notices. No one helps. Because I don't need help.

YES I DO! YES I DID!

I needed help to get from 'okay' to 'great'.

Because 'okay' is not enough. Not by a long shot.

Where was the person calling my parents to tell them that I should have a better music teacher, that the woman down the street would cripple me, would certainly not teach me how to compose, how to become a great composer.

Where was the person calling my parents to tell them I should be a legal philosopher, that's the kind of brilliant my mind was.

We ignore the good students. And so they never become great.

No wonder there's so little greatness in the world.

We don't care about great. We resent ambition; we resent effort. It makes the rest of us look bad. If the cream doesn't rise to the top, so what? And we don't really care about excellence. We're a democracy; we value, to the point of being ruled by, the lowest common denominator.

> Instead, we root for the underdog. We cheer when 'Precious' becomes literate. *Literate.*

> We applaud when the moron becomes marginally average.

She knew she was being vicious. Still.

> Guess I'm at a disadvantage because my father didn't rape me. My mother wasn't a drunk, and I didn't become an addict.

At least she wasn't black. She understood white privilege. She'd had it all her life.

Or not. Feminist presses were enlightened enough to have programs that privileged those of colour. Ditto many funding agencies. Leaving white women—where?

But she also understood, as did John Lennon, or more correctly, more probably, Yoko Ono—the song was written by the two of them—that sex trumps color: "Woman is the nigger of the world."

She looked from the journal out at the sky. There were clouds on the horizon. She'd finish the journal, then paddle out onto the lake for what could be a fantastic sunset.

> "What father didn't even read his own son's book?" the guy in another movie asks with disbelief.

> Mine.

> And worse than not reading it was my lack of expectation that he, and she, do so.

> Worse still was my acceptance, my understanding, that they wouldn't, didn't. They weren't interested in the subject so why should they read it? I got that.

What I didn't get, what I didn't even consider, was the whole parent thing. I didn't consider the possibility, the likelihood, that if I had a daughter and she wrote a book, *of course* I'd want to read it, it wouldn't matter what it was about. The thought that they would read it simply because it was written by me, their daughter, didn't occur to me. And, apparently, rightly so.

Why didn't that occur to me way back then? I would've been appalled and angry. Instead of hurt.

Well, because that would have been favouritism. And I didn't expect favouritism. And that's the problem. You *should* expect favouritism. From your parents. You're supposed to be special to them. Everything you do is supposed to be special to them.

But then you would have dismissed their applause as biased.

Yes but their interest could have been, should have been, genuine.

And then when I responded in kind, not treating *them* like anyone special, thinking simply (well, not 'simply') that since I didn't like them it would be stupid to stay in a relationship with them, they were so hurt.

"But they're your parents!"

Yeah, well, *I'm their daughter!*

...

After all I've done, after all the people I've met— My parents, brother, and sister are still so bloody *influential*, are still what I'm reacting against, raging at.

I moved out, left them all behind, thirty years ago! Thirty adult years without them compared to seven adult years with them. Why do they have so much power over me??

Will I *never* recover from my childhood?

• • •

She paddled out into the middle of the lake and drifted, watching as the colours slowly intensified, then just as slowly evaporated away until there was just darkness. Lovely darkness. Through which the loon's call flowed like amber honey.

• • •

When she returned, she had a bite to eat, then made a fire. She had only two more evenings. There would be only two more chances to stare into the flames …

She considered her CDs. She'd gone through twenty-six of her top thirty … Eno?

No, Albinoni. As she watched the flames, orange and red, appearing and then just … disappearing, she listened to the stately, and sad, beauty of the *Adagio*.

28

She did try, once more. To create a new life. To pick herself up once more from having slammed into a brick wall. Maybe she could become a housesitter. Live in nice houses here and there, look after people's dogs and cats and plants while they were away, see a bit of the world finally.

Her car had become unreliable—she'd often have to walk to the houses she had to clean—fortunately the deal was she'd use *their* cleaning stuff—but she figured she could take a train or bus to the housesit locations.

The problem was she didn't know how to find people who needed housesitters. She called the university—maybe faculty members looked for housesitters when they went somewhere during the summer or while on sabbatical. The young woman she spoke to said she didn't know. Could you ask around? Maybe put me in touch with someone who does know? Please? She left her number.

A week later, the woman called back. There were, in fact, a couple housesitters' associations she could join. The membership fee was $40, but then you got a newsletter twice a month listing all the housesits available, in Canada and the States.

It was tricky, arranging a schedule without gaps, but otherwise, she'd have to keep paying rent and phone. Once she had the next eight months lined up, and confirmed, she gave notice to her landlord, packed up all her stuff, and drove away.

At her first housesit, when the owner returned she happened to have playing, on his CD player, her sax pieces—the set of three, one a solo with rain in the background, one a duet with wolves, the third a duet with loons.

"Who's that?" he asked, cocking his head toward the stereo.

"Me," she said. "Well, I composed the pieces. I had three different guys perform them."

"Really?" he replied. "You composed that?"

She ignored the disbelief heavy in his voice.

They talked for a bit, and he suggested she make videos for each piece and post them on YouTube.

"Yeah, I don't know how to do that," she said. And truthfully, she was too tired to learn. In addition to obtaining three degrees (Literature, Education, Philosophy), three diplomas (Piano, Composition, Dance), and ESL certification, she'd learned how to be her own recording engineer, and publisher, and distributor, and publicist—did she have to learn how to be a videographer too?

Then she added, overcoming a lifetime habit, "Do you?"

"Yeah."

"Oh." She smiled. Broadly. Then asked, "How much do you charge?"

They agreed on a price.

Within a week of posting the videos, a sax player contacted her, asking if he could buy the scores, asking if she had more pieces for sax, he'd like to do a whole album of her work. He already had a contract with a studio and could commission new pieces—*he could pay her.*

Or, the young woman at the university didn't write down her phone number. She had her hands full, too full, with inquiries from students.

She sighed. It had been merely the most recent in a long line, a very long line, of dead-ends. Legitimate or constructed. Because she couldn't help wondering whether, if she'd been a man, the young woman *would've* had time to attend to her request.

She held her cup of tea, wrapping her hands around its warmth. It was getting colder. It was the end of September. It was the end of the month.

She looked out across the water, to the trees edging the cove. Still, forever, beautiful. So beautiful.

A long while later, she continued through her journal.

> "There was one editor who believed in me, and when I was very hard up would always buy something to keep me going." Marion Zimmer Bradley

> How did he know she was hard up? I would never say I need this, the money, the publication—it's irrelevant.

> So they decide what to publish based on need? Not merit, not quality?

> And they would *pay* for her stories? Must only be fantasy and sci-fi magazines that pay.

Even the university literary journals hadn't paid for her work.

> "His pre-emptive tone indicating the right to speak for them all ..." Joyce Rebeta-Burditt, *Triplets*

> I used to think men were so manipulative, so strategic, using that voice, knowing that people would listen to them, obey them, that doors would open for them when they spoke with such serious, low-pitched, pause-filled voices, but now I realize I've given them way too much credit. They're nowhere near that conscious. Of themselves. And what they do. It's just that they've been taught since birth that that's the way men talk. Actually, it's not even been *that* conscious. It's just something they've picked up by osmosis.

> And after a point, they've been doing it like that for so long, speaking with authority, talking as if they know what they're talking about, they've come to believe their own bullshit. And then it's no longer even an act, however unconscious.

> ...

We're way too serious about being serious. Because we think it's connected to being important.

That's why women are encouraged to smile.

She stared out at the water, unsmiling.

I read today about how someone finally got a piece in *The New York Times* after three years of aggressive networking.

She hadn't stood a chance, she realized now, mailing her work from R. R. #2, Powassan. All those submissions and queries … She should've rented a box in Toronto and arranged forwarding. But again, she hadn't taken into account, or would not contribute to, and so insisted on challenging, people's propensity to stereotype.

She also hadn't stood a chance in the world of relationships or the world of work either. Either she didn't know the norms, or she did and refused to endorse irrational and/or manipulative standards.

"I'm not as stupid as when I was younger, when I could never even ask for what I wanted, but always had to wait suffering and in silence for it to offer itself to me." Marge Piercy, *The High Cost of Living*

Yes. That's a perfect description.

Her middle class manners had kept interfering. Both the upper and lower class 'can' just 'take' what they want. She was supposed to be polite. And wait for it to be offered.

But it wasn't just a class thing.

Women's problem is that they never speak up. They never ask for what they want. If you don't tell people what you want, how do you expect to get it? Are they supposed to read your mind? You'll spend your whole life waiting for someone to offer you, to invite you to, whatever it is. I know.

But men don't tell people what they want either. They simply expect others to give it to them. And … the self-fulfilling prophecy.

Even if I had asked for directions through life, well, whenever a woman asks a man, anything, if he doesn't know, he'll pretend to know and tell you anything—so that's not helpful. And if he *does* know, he'll tell you anything *else*—because otherwise you'll succeed, you'll become better than him, you'll have the upper hand; knowledge is power to men—they keep it to themselves.

And there were simply no, or too few, women to ask.

I didn't understand what 'opportunity' meant. When someone said 'This is such an opportunity,' I thought they were referring to just the thing in front of me. I didn't get the whole stepping-stone thing. Because that required buying into the 'what other people say matters' thing. Otherwise how could one thing *be* a stepping stone to another thing? The person 'in charge' of the *next* thing would have to accept, be influenced by, what the person of the *first* thing said.

And who cared what other people said? I never considered that those other people might be genuine authorities, experts, people whose opinions are justifiably listened to. Most of the people I'd met to that point who had something to say about me *weren't* genuine authorities, experts, people whose opinions are justifiably listened to. And/or I always thought people could, or should, form their own opinions.

Or did you not care what other people said because you've never been able to handle negative criticism?

No, she thought to herself, it was more that she didn't know whose criticism to listen to. She'd received so much.

Women get criticized so much more than men. If we listened to all of it, we'd go insane, because of course it's contradictory.

In any case, Valian would show that "Women generally benefit less from their positive achievements than men do."

So much for the stepping-stone thing.

I stopped entering competitions because my experience of competition, which was limited at that point to high school and small town, was that winning *didn't* go anywhere. I never expected it to. You entered a competition and if you won, you could say you were better than someone else. Whippee-doo. I didn't realize that for some competitions, winning, or even placing, meant that doors opened for you, meant that people would actually seek you out. That had certainly never happened to me.

Like that young woman who dropped out of *So You Think You Can Dance* because it was bad timing in terms of her med school acceptance or something. Such a shame. She probably had bad advice. Or no advice. Like me. Probably no one explained to her that what she thought about competitions was wrong in this case—maybe right for her experience up to that point, but wrong for *SYTYCD*. That she was committing dance suicide just by dropping out. I wouldn't've thought that at her age. I would've been as naïve as she seemed to be about the way things worked. How would I have known? How *could* I have known? No one told me. It wasn't my experience. *Unlike* that kid who said he lives "on a frickin' farm"— *he* knew, *he* realized, that this was the thing that could change his life. He understood. How is it he did and she didn't?

And, by the way, where is So You Think You Can *Think?*

She read about someone who submitted only to the upper tier magazines and journals, and that's how he'd become so famous. She didn't even know which ones were the upper tier. Her parents didn't know. Her high school teachers didn't know. And that exhausted who she could go to for information. She didn't ask her university professors, because by then she was already convinced she was odd, strange, doing something weird, this whole being a writer thing. Amazing, when you think about it. Wanting to be a writer would have been perfectly normal for someone in a Literature degree program. That she didn't see that is a measure of just how heavy the 'You're weird' vibes were from her family. Or how heavy the weight of her family was. Given her nonexistent friends.

And since she had no sense of the different levels of prestige among journals and magazines, she listed them all on her previous publications list. Thus displaying, apparently, either desperation or a lack of discrimination.

The truth was she was simply clueless as to status. And ideologically uninterested. And genuinely unimpressed with it, believing it to be, in most cases, undeserved, unreal, just a lot of hype.

'Status' was, for her, from the beginning associated with 'status *symbol*'— something someone wanted so they could look rich or important. So they could *look* rich or important. Not so they could *be* rich or important. Status was fake.

Similarly, she'd never thought that 'reputation' could be legitimate, like character. Perhaps because the first time she heard the word, it was in the context of caution not to flirt because then you'd get a reputation for being a slut. So like status, reputation was linked to perception. Not reality.

So why would she distinguish between magazines and journals, or universities, on the basis of status or reputation? She didn't realize that some journals had a legitimate record of publishing good stuff, and some had a record of publishing whatever was submitted. She saw only the issue in which her own material appeared. Because she certainly couldn't afford a subscription to any of them. Which was why she got so angry whenever the rejection letters were accompanied with suggestions to read a copy of their magazine before submitting. How could she possibly afford to do that? She was submitting to poetry journals, short story journals, feminist magazines, sf magazines, and philosophy journals. Even if she were to purchase just one issue from five of each, that would've been two or three hundred dollars. Half her year's food budget. Besides which, you couldn't generalize from one issue. Insufficient sample.

And to judge by its cover, by its appearance, to assume that a glossy, four-colour, perfect-bound magazine contained better poetry than a mimeographed, black-and-white, stapled sheaf of pages—also flawed reasoning.

After all, *her* poem was in there. And it was a good poem.

She stared out at the water again. There were so many important things she hadn't known. Really important things.

She didn't know that ninety percent of all non-fiction books are sold on the basis of a proposal. You're not expected to have written the book before you query agents and publishers. She could've done so much more if she hadn't spent all that time completing all those fiction manuscripts—if, instead, she'd spent her time writing non-fiction proposals about all the issues she wanted to write about.

And since there was so much she hadn't known, she had wasted so much time. So much energy.

And so here she was, at fifty, with not much left of either.

Hope is based on the future. And the future, *my* future, is here. It's now.

And so bereft of hope as well.

• • •

Out on the water, she focused on the distant treeline and marvelled, once again, at the masterpiece before her: a relatively steady descent was broken by a lone spire, then two clusters, the second taller but less dense, then two single trees; toward the end, toward the point where the shoreline curved away, the mass lost its coherence, its integrity, and disintegrated into individuals, until there were only three singles and a bunch of bushes left.

She headed up the little creek and parked at the rapids. This time of year, they were weak, but the sound was still pretty. She could still lose herself in it for an hour or two.

After that hour or two, she paddled back out, then rounded the corner into the marshy area, and made a sudden stop. A moose was browsing. Just twenty or thirty feet ahead of her. And it was huge. Solid muscle covered in dark brown fur. She held her kayak still and just watched. It moved so majestically. And rightly so.

It reminded her of another time, when she'd seen a moose and its mooseling swim across the river. She'd kept her distance, but had been close enough to hear the little one bleating as it swam.

She resumed paddling, all the way to the end, basking in … everything. All the way to the end.

On the way back, on her slow way back, as the sun lowered toward the horizon, she watched the reflection of the moving water ripple through the trees.

• • •

She docked the kayak, made another cup of tea, and picked up the journal again.

> I am not who or what I have thought I was.
>
> Which is disconcerting.
>
> Only disconcerting?
>
> Well, no, if I am less than I thought I was, it's also disappointing. And a little embarrassing.
>
> And if I'm different, it's a shame. The waste.
>
> …
>
> Turns out how I saw myself was quite different from how others saw me.
>
> I took myself seriously. No one else ever did.
>
> I considered myself near the front and center. Everyone else considered me marginal. At best.
>
> I considered myself strong, I considered myself competent—
>
> How is it I've managed to be so clueless about this—this disjunct—all of my life?
>
> I thought I'd be judged by my accomplishments. And I tried so hard to be good enough.

It's not about being good enough. Remember?

She looked out at the water.

> "Examination results lead us to believe that female students write more

and that what they write is better. But when such good women students enter the world of work … Women have never been more than 20% of the published writers … [and] less than 6% of column inches of review space was directed to women's books." Dale Spender, *For the Record*

No surprise there.

And I'll bet we're over 80% of the English and MFA degrees! I remember one, ONE, male student in the program at WLU.

And I'll bet he's published.

Jennifer Colt has written three books in a series, one of which is in the top ten on Amazon. And she can't find an agent or publisher for the fourth one.

Susan Juby did not win the Leacock.

…

"She appeared to want knowledge for itself and not because it could lead to a career." Robertson Davies, *Rebel Angels*

Yes! Who would have thought knowledge would lead to a career?

Though maybe that was a class thing. I always thought in terms of jobs, not careers.

Then again, show me that career. Show me a career to which knowledge, knowledge in any of the humanities, leads. Other than university professor. And then tell me again how many Philosophy professors are women.

…

A doctor applying to Greenpeace for the position as the ship's doctor sat in teahouse with friend who said a friend of hers was on a ship … "I had been wanting to do that for years, but enquiries to Greenpeace had gone unanswered," he said. The friend got in touch with her friend …

She had to accept that all her letters—query letters, application letters, letters to the editor—had been completely useless. It was a hard lesson for a writer to learn, for someone who takes words so very seriously.

Lorrie Moore's MFA instructor put her in touch with her agent.

I should have gone for coffee with Alexina Louie, Wes Wraggett, my thesis advisor— Instead, I kept it all professional.

The professional is personal. The personal is professional.

I need to start over.

But I can't.

Even if I could.

I'm not that smart.

…

Lola's son—The University of Waterloo didn't even grant him an interview, but Johns Hopkins—*Johns Hopkins!*—offered a scholarship—*a scholarship!*—based on the same thesis.

She had drawn so many incorrect conclusions.

Keith's play was workshopped at the Factory Lab, performed at Magnum, and then he was commissioned to write another play for them, and he's received a Canada Council grant, and he's been here, in Canada, only since 1982, and he has a full-time job teaching English and Society, Challenge, and Change at an alternative school. *That should be me! How is that him and not me?*

It's not fair! I deserved it!

And yet, Timothy Findley had to write advertising copy for a country and western radio station even after he had two novels published.

It was increasingly clear to her that success is a complete accident.

We as a species must have survived only through dumb luck.

…

"When he was writing his book, his publishers [it was already accepted? before he'd written it?] would call every day to ask if he'd written something and to send it."

Someone that *not* driven, that *not* hard-working, someone who requires that much wheedling, that much hand-holding, *that's who gets published?*

He'd send it and it'd go to his editor who'd return it and it would be unrecognizable. *His editor rewrote it that much? It was that bad? And still it's published? And still he (not the editor) is called a writer?*

WHAT   THE   FUCK.

…

"You believe all that nonsense, you think if you work hard and jump all those academic hurdles, they'll reward you just as if you were a man and give you a job and let you in their club!" Marge Piercy, *The High Cost of Living*

The high cost indeed.

So the answer to 'How did I get here—from there?' is 'You couldn't've gotten anywhere else. From there.'

For a dozen reasons.

It had clouded over, so there would be no magic and no sunset. Perhaps tomorrow. She had one more day, one more evening, one more night.

• • •

As she walked through the forest, she realized that her whole life in public as a woman had been a compromise, no, a repression of her interests and abilities. No wonder she was so reluctant to compromise on the little things, the daily things. No wonder she liked living alone.

And yet, and yet, here she was, at fifty, so very alone.

No, not just alone, she thought. But lonely. For so long.

It takes a great deal of courage to live without having anyone you can call and say 'Hi, it's me.' With having to leave 'In case of accident, call __________' blank.

And she was running low on courage.

No one had ever said "I love you" to her.

Then again, since "I love you" is a surrender, a threat, a plea, or a justification, perhaps you haven't missed anything.

She walked on.

I am unloved though, that's the truth of it. No one will miss me. There is no one to come to a funeral. Literally. No one. How pathetic is that?

And yet she had loved—so many things so very much.

Which is better, to have loved or to have been loved?

It was starting to get dark by the time she turned around and headed back. Some people would have thought she was foolish to be in the forest at night, but she wasn't afraid. In fact, she found the moonlit forest positively enchanting.

• • •

When she got back, she stood on the dock and scanned the lake, hoping to see, to hear, the loons once more—it had been a couple days—but they must have left already. She may have already heard them for the last time.

Sadly, she went back up and inside, ate the second last slice of pizza, then made a fire.

More and more, she was overwhelmed by the loss, the permanent loss, the knowledge that she could never go back. To drop-in, to shooting pool in the student lounge, to how she felt listening to Dan Hill, and riding her motorcycle, and running for miles and miles, to teaching those brilliant students in Toronto who thought she was so cool, to her cabin on a lake in a forest—

Everything was potential, everything was possible, she was becoming—then suddenly she was. There was no *is*. She hadn't *become*—anything. Either that or what she had become wasn't at all what she'd expected, what she'd hoped for.

It was all ahead of her and then in a blink of an eye it was all behind her.

> this is the season.
> i go out
> stumbling through gardens gray
>   dusty gossamer
>   barnacled birdnests
> flowers ghosting on the fringe.
>
> once
> striding through forests fey
> i felt gilded treebark and
> chipmunks giggling and
>
> a falling leaf touched my hair.

She'd written that at twenty-four.

And had had no idea what she was talking about.

No idea.

She listened to Pachelbel again that night. And Bach's *Prelude I*. Her sax pieces. And "lament". All the while, just staring into the fire.

And then Barber's *Adagio*.

29

She'd lost herself. The person sitting in the room above the hairdresser's wasn't anything like the young woman cruising into the parking lot at drop-in on her motorcycle or the teacher surrounded by gifted students sitting on the grass discussing Camus. Or even the person who years later had run a marathon on dirt roads from one lake to another, so strong and sure …

> For some of us, the costume and make-up come early. For the rest of us, the mask comes later and oh so gradually until one day we catch a glimpse of ourselves in the mirror and suddenly understand why everyone's been treating you like a sour-faced middle-aged woman.

> It's hard, living when you look like someone else. Ask that *Black Like Me* guy.

She'd spent the first half of her life working through, against, being defined by her sex. Was she to spend the second half working through, against, being defined by her age?

Yes, she'd become a middle-aged woman. (Somehow it wasn't what she thought she'd grow up to be.)

So when people looked at her, they saw a middle-aged woman.

But, worse, they saw a *conservative* middle-aged woman. (For weren't all middle-aged women conservative?)

They didn't know about her *Art of Juxtaposition* or *ProVocative* albums. They didn't know about her *Satellites* collection or her *Particivision* stories. And they certainly didn't know about her motorcycle.

And unless you're with people who knew you when, it's just too exhausting to describe who and what you are. It would take a lifetime. So I don't bother. But that just makes it worse.

That's why people stay married, she suddenly realized. To have close to you someone who knew you when, who still sees you, still *reflects* you, as the person you were at twenty, the person you will always be, really, inside, while your outside gets further and further from the truth.

She had no one to reflect her as she was. That's what made it so hard to hang on. To what she was.

She wished she had somehow kept in touch with some of the drop-ins or some of those students. They saw the real her. Interesting, creative, radical, feminist, atheist. Offbeat, funny, smart …

The sky had cleared overnight and it was, happily, a bright, sunny day. She watched the sparkles as she held her cup of tea, her journal, the last one, open on her lap.

Maybe her whole life had just been a tragedy of bad timing.

But no, she *was* in the right place at the right time. She was right there! For feminist poetry, she'd been right behind Adrienne Rich, Anne Sexton, et al, and for feminist fairy tale revision, right before Atwood, et al. For speculative fiction, she'd been contemporary with Robert J. Sawyer, Nancy Kress, Sheri Tepper, et al. For new age music, she was composing at the same time as David Darling, David Lanz, et al. For social commentary audio collage, she was right behind Laurie Anderson. For environmental ethics, she was there before it was even named. It was *all born* in the 70s when she came of age. Why hadn't she managed to ride any of those waves into the 80s?

When what she submitted was on the crest of the wave, cutting edge, it was rejected because it didn't fit the box. But once the boxes were recognized, established, she was told they were already full, thank you. She couldn't win.

She rebelled against prayer in the schools and was fired. Now it's the law. She went to teachers' college to teach philosophy in the high schools and was ignored. Now it's on the curriculum.

It made perfect sense to give up. She had been just spinning her wheels all this time. Furiously spinning her wheels. And staying in one spot. Just getting deeper and deeper into—failure.

But why had she so consistently failed?

Because I wasn't good enough.

It was staring her right in the face. Had been for years.

But all those reviews in the indie magazines and all those comments in the rejection letters …

Suddenly she didn't trust them. If quality wasn't part of anyone's evaluation—

Suddenly she didn't trust even her own judgement. Yes, she was still certain that some of her pieces, a very few, and some of her poems, again, a very few, were good. But that was it.

Maybe she *was* just a hobbyist.

She stared out at the water, desperation creeping, seeping, through her veins as she raised the cup to her lips.

If she *had* been good enough, people *would* have called her, *would* have presented her with all those opportunities she so doggedly sought.

Her whole life had been a delusion. She wasn't a composer. Never had been. She wasn't a writer. Never had been. She wasn't a philosopher. Never had been.

And never would be. Any of them.

She'd spent an impassioned life driven to achieve—mediocrity.

No, that's not true!

She couldn't bear that to be true.

But what evidence did she have to the contrary? A stack of unpublished work about which people had said kind things when they'd said no.

No, Narada *contacted* you! The Art of Juxtaposition *made it into the top ten of the year! The OAC grants! All those publications in journals and magazines!*

Even if it wasn't true, even if she *was* good enough, she would never be able to be a composer, or a writer, or a philosopher. Not then. Not now.

Which was worse? That she *wasn't* good enough or that she *was*?

Or, door number three, that being good enough was irrelevant.

But then Narada—   And those grants—

Stop it. Just stop it, she told herself. Enough.

"Is there no way out of the mind?" Sylvia Plath

She went up to the cottage and made another cup of tea. Then she carried it and her last slice of pizza back down the dock.

I want a do-over.

Oh god, how she wanted a do-over.

It's not that she regretted doing what she did, but of course she wondered, now, if she'd done it differently— If she knew then what she knew now—

But what did she know now? That would have made any difference?

I have a feeling I missed a really important turn.

You weren't even facing the right direction most of the time.

Well, there was still time— There was still time to be, to become, good. Even great.

Douglas Adams' fame was built on just three books.

Maybe I can write three more books.

That no agent or publisher will accept. Because you don't have 'a platform'. Or don't know the right people.

And even if she *did* have enough time and energy for a do-over—Ruth Hermence Green wrote *The Skeptic's Guide to the Bible* at sixty-four—again, what would she do differently?

She stared out at the water, the sparkles dancing over the surface in stark contrast to the inky blackness spreading across her mind.

It's sad to think it's only me.

And unfathomable to realize it's not.

How many others had lived lives like hers? Lives like raisins— She saw mounds, huge piles of dreams being pushed by idiots in business suits riding bulldozers ... Dreams not just deferred, but being torn, crushed, buried to rot.

Every single high school must have had one of her in every single graduating class. How much intelligence, how much sensitivity, how much passion had been wasted, *allowed* to waste away?

The world was seriously fucked up, she concluded. Not for the first time.

How was it we couldn't figure out how to— *Was* capitalism the problem? Because it paved the way for those business suits, for those interested primarily in profit? And squeezed out everyone else, relegated them to the sidelines, the trash cans?

But that's nuts. How can there not be enough room for all the ability there is in the world? What kind of society doesn't *make* room for all the ability there is?

This society. Which is set up as a star system. There's room at the top for only a precious few. It's a pyramid, an iceberg, instead of—

Doesn't make room for all the *artistic* ability. Or *cognitive* ability.

Especially when it's in a female body.

It's a star system set up by men (because they're addicted to hierarchy) for men—and a few exceptional women, who are exceptions because, and only as long as, they're hot.

She sighed.

She'd been passionate—*passionate*—about thinking, writing, music, running, dance. She'd known what she wanted to do at thirteen. She wrote her first poem at ten, published at fourteen, got a degree in English Literature. Another in Philosophy. Had piano lessons from eight, composed her first piano solo at fifteen, obtained an Associate diploma in Piano, and then another in Composition. She'd started running at thirteen, and would eventually be running over forty miles a week. Had jazz lessons from six, added modern, and a bit of ballet, studied and passed the Associate exam, started choreographing. She'd sent, in total, over 5,000 queries to journals and magazines and agents and publishers and record companies and musicians and concert producers and figure skaters …

All to end up sitting in a room above the hairdresser's beside the railway tracks.

> Am I bitter? Of course I am. And angry! On behalf of everyone who ever had the desire and the ability to make it, to make something meaningful, something important, something beautiful, and who worked hard and relentlessly to achieve that, and—

She had nothing.

And no one.

She was, had been, an outsider. In everything she attempted.

> still winter
> shroudy skies
> in the mourning
>
> still mourning
> dawn dribbles through curtained pain
> seeps into puddle on sill
> evaporating

> still evaporating
> crusts upon my bed
> i'm holding on to mould
> and whimpers of immortality
> i twitch
>
> still twitching
> i crawl around the wasteland of my life
> around the wasteland
> around the waste

She'd written that at twenty-four too.

Her life wasn't going to get any better. At this point, if it hadn't already happened, it wasn't going to. The concert performance that would put her on the map, the publishing contract, the great job just around the corner …

She would live out the rest of her life in a room above the hairdresser's by the railway tracks.

It was too much.

It was not enough. Not nearly enough.

She'd given it three years. And every day, of every one of those years—

Her cabin had been the only thing keeping her from complete despair. She could deal with not making it as a composer or a writer or a philosopher, and having a shitty job, and not having any friends, if at least she could come home at the end of the day and go out onto the lake or into the forest. Or even just sit and stare. Out at, across, the cove. But to lose even that—

She had come to need the solitude.

And the beauty. It was like oxygen to her. The water, sparkling, twinkling, shimmering, gleaming, glittering—it was like a perpetuum mobile, the visual equivalent of Glass, Nyman, Pachelbel. And the trees, in all their—

So she'd come back, here to her beloved cabin—

Yes, dear reader, this cottage that sleeps ten is my beloved cabin on a lake in a forest.

—for one last month.

Cleaning ladies working at minimum wage can't afford to rent a cottage for a whole month, even when that month is off-season September. She'd used what was left of her savings. You see where this is going.

She wanted to go back, with every fibre in her being she wanted to go back to eighteen, to her first year— She wanted to start over, or even just do it all again.

But she couldn't go back.

Nor could she see a way to go forward.

She'd considered moving. But there wasn't much else available in Powassan. And if she moved to another town, still close enough to forest and water, it would be a longer drive to the houses she cleaned. And what would she do if she didn't clean houses?

Her car needed a new battery or an alternator or something, and she had no money for it. One of these days it wouldn't start for good, and then what?

Welfare might, or might not, cover her living expenses. And it would be fifteen years before she could collect Canada Pension. Possibly more, since they kept changing the age of eligibility. In any case, it probably wouldn't change in her standard of living by very much. Her contributions, given her employment history, would have been pretty minimal.

Rent, heat, and food would continue to increase more quickly than her income, so she would just get colder and hungrier. Though as for the latter ... she had so little appetite these days.

Her eyes would grow older, and she wouldn't be able to afford a new pair of glasses. The pleasure of reading would diminish.

The pleasure of listening to music might continue, since her hearing was still good. Too good, in fact, because she could hear every shred of conversation from the hairdresser's below, and it was so bloody annoying— Not to mention the train every time it passed. Even with earplugs in and headphones on.

Oh god, she looked out across the cove, it made her weep to remember the years she'd had here.

Every day, every day for the last three years, she'd missed it. Her life here. The simple but absolutely life-giving pleasures of the sun on the water, the quiet of the forest, the rise and fall of her paddle, even the snowfall against the trees.

She had stayed in a shitty relationship with Craig for eight years because she didn't know any better.

Now she does.

She had soared, absolutely soared, on passion and promise, for almost twenty years. When that passed, she was content, perfectly content, to simply live in her cabin on a lake in a forest. To just sit down at the water, perhaps reading, or listening to music …

To live the rest of her life in a small room, to wake up every day and see a fricking billboard out her window, to hear the train plow through her brain again and again—

Yes, yes, she didn't have cancer, there weren't landmines all over the place, she had access to unpolluted water—

But it was all relative, wasn't it.

Quality is more important than quantity, she thought. Her decision to be here was proof of that.

She'd given notice to her landlord, and to all the people whose houses she'd been cleaning. All of her stuff, such as it was now, was in her car, parked in the driveway behind the cottage. The cabin. Her cabin.

She looked out across the water, read the last entry in her journal, then closed it.

She'd considered taking her journals with her and tossing them overboard as she went, like ashes from an urn. But she didn't know if she could. She didn't think she could bear to see her words blur, become illegible, as they drifted down, sunk ... *Never* to be read.

She was afraid she'd dive in after them, unwilling to let go of her life.

Then it isn't time yet!

But it was. It was way too early, but it was time.

> "There comes a time when you get tired in a way that's final." Ayn Rand, *The Fountainhead*

So instead, she just left them—behind. Sitting on the dock. Beside her empty cup. She had what she needed, the memento from her studio tucked in her pocket.

• • •

She stared at the cottages and houses as she paddled past. All of them were unoccupied. Too bad she couldn't live in one of them, rent-free. In return for mere occupancy and upkeep. They're not in use anyway, it was such a shame. Could she convince any of the owners they needed a housesitter? To deter vandals? She should have thought of this before. Last weekend. She could have gone around and asked.

The thought of just breaking into one occurred to her. She could occupy it unofficially. If she was gone by spring, they wouldn't even know. Or at least they wouldn't know who it had been. It would have to have a woodstove, she thought, scanning the shore line for a tell-tale stovepipe. And enough wood to last the winter.

But what would she do next summer?

She passed the stream and the marshy part, then paddled along the stretch of crown land.

Well, she still had her tent. She could live in the forest. She knew places ... She could hide her kayak near the shore. She could get safe drinking water from the spring. But what would she do for food?

But of course all of that was the least of it.

She couldn't bear to go on, a failure.

She who had thought she was so smart had been so incredibly stupid.

And naïve. So unbelievably naïve.

In short, she had been, she was, a fool.

Her ignorance was so immense, if anyone on the inside knew how little she knew, and yet had persisted, for so long, so completely clueless, they'd laugh at her. No, they'd pity her. Her pathetic, lifelong delusions.

She simply couldn't bear the humiliation.

And now that she'd had her month, now that she'd had her cabin on a lake in a forest again, she couldn't, just couldn't go back to—

But she'd had her month. And it had been just as breathtaking as— She'd had seventeen years here. So all in all, she felt—fortunate. She'd been far more fortunate than most, she knew that.

But she also felt—done.

I can't do it anymore. I can't keep clawing my way back from despair.

I did it after Craig. I did it after Peter. And I did it after I lost Marilyn, the only friend I ever really had. I did it when I lost all hope of teaching. I did it after the music died. I did it after the nth rejection of my literary writing and again when my philosophical writing was virtually unacknowledged.

She passed the next cove, then paddled around the last curve and into the most beautiful part.

All the arguments for talking someone out of it didn't apply. It'll get better, it'll get easier, your whole life is ahead of you, think of the people you'll leave behind—

9 781926 891743

It wouldn't get better. It wouldn't get easier. Her whole life was behind her. And there was no one.

She was tired of dreaming of kaleidoscopes.

Bits of bark hung from the birch trees like a leper's bandages.

She felt relief. And sadness. Deep sadness. And helplessness.

Once past the little island, she settled back into the seat, rested her paddle across her lap, and just drifted.

She had to be out by Friday, tomorrow, at three. So she had this last afternoon, one more evening, one more night, then one more morning—

Maybe she should pick a time when it wouldn't hurt as much to leave it all. By tomorrow afternoon, she'd be hearing ATVs and dirt bikes …

No, she wanted a perfect moment. Just one more perfect moment when the sun was sparkling on the water, and it was quiet, so quiet, except for the loons calling, their beautiful—

Like now.